King's Envoy

To Ava,

Best wishes

Cas Peace

13. 11. 2012

Rhemalda Publishing
Rhemalda Publishing, Inc. (USA)
P.O. Box 2912, Wenatchee, WA 98807, USA
www.rhemalda.com

First American Paperback Edition

Copyright ©2011 by Caroline Peace
Editing by Kara Klotz
Text design by Rhemalda Publishing
Cover art by Eve Ventrue www.eve-ventrue.darkfolio.com
Author photo by Martin Saban-Smith www.saban.co.uk

ISBN-13: 978-1-936850-13-6
ePUB ISBN: 978-1-936850-14-3
ePDF ISBN: 978-1-936850-15-0
Library of Congress Control Number: 2011920941

Printed in the United States of America
10 9 8 7 6 5 4 3 2 1

The paper used in this publication meets the minimum requirements of the
American National Standards of Information Services - Permanence of Paper
for Printed Library Materials, ASNI Z39.48-1992.

Visit Caroline Peace at her author Web site www.caspeace.com

Dedication

This novel is dedicated to my true and loyal friend, "Bobbie." (Karen J. Faulkner, 8/11/56—27/05/97)

She would have loved this and would have been a great source of early encouragement when my self-confidence was low. I just wish she was here to read it.

Sleep well, Bobbie, until we meet again.

Namarië!

Acknowledgements

I must thank my husband, Dave, for his love, belief, encouragement, incredulity, support and constructive suggestions.

Also my parents, Barbara and Dennis for ... well, everything, really.

Heartfelt thanks are due also to my many long-suffering proofreaders; to Jan Church for her enthusiasm and the A++; to Erin Peace, Sallie Jones, and my brother Dave Snell.

Special thanks must go to Barry Tighe, Gerry Dailey, Gordon Long and Judy Sutherland for all their hard work and constructive comments.

Also to the hundreds of readers on Authonomy who helped me polish and hone this book.

Special thanks also for unasked and unknowing help during the writing of this novel must go to AH*NEE*MAH for "Spirit of the Canyon." For me, the hauntingly beautiful "Light from the East" will always be Sullyan's theme.

Central Albia

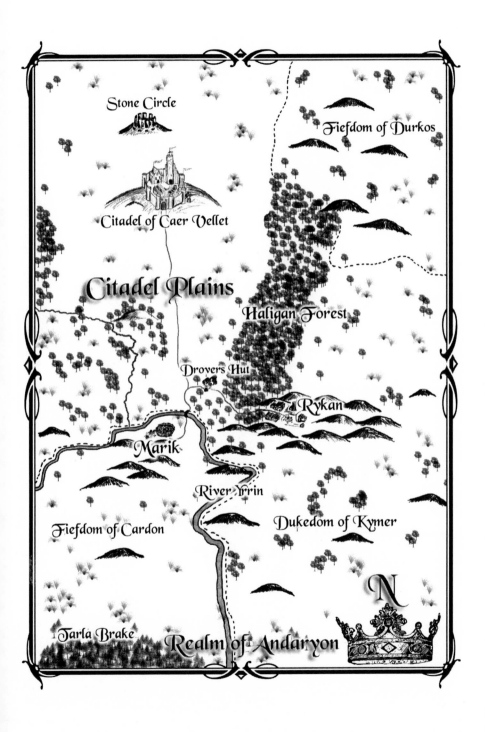

King's Envoy
Artesans of Albia

Book One

Cas Peace

Rhemalda Publishing

Chapter One

Albia, the Fourth Realm
Hyecombe village in Loxton Province

"Are you quite sure about this, Taran?"

Cal's voice echoed in the gloom as Taran Elijah closed the cellar door behind them. He raised the lantern and sharp-edged shadows fled up the walls.

Taran glanced at his Apprentice standing three steps below him and ran a hand through his short brown hair. It came away clammy and he wiped it on his shirt.

"I have to go, Cal. It's my last chance."

Cal frowned, taking in Taran's tall but sturdy frame, clad in leather pants and boots, the sword belted at his side and the pack of supplies slung over his shoulder. He met Taran's hazel eyes. "What if there's something we haven't thought of ?"

Trying to keep his voice level, Taran said, "I've tried every way I can think of to find another teacher. My father was right, there simply aren't any Artesans left in Loxton Province. Maybe even in the whole of Albia. Entering the Fifth Realm might be dangerous, but it's the only place I'm going to find other members of our craft."

The words sounded sharper than he'd intended. As Cal turned

to descend the steps, Taran saw him shrug. He followed, his heart pounding.

When Cal reached the bottom, he crossed the floor to the only items the cellar contained—a bedroll and a night pot. Taran watched the younger man drop a small pack of food on the floor and turn to face his Master.

Taran halted opposite Cal and gave him what he hoped was a reassuring smile. He shrugged out of his pack and laid it down. He was beginning to tremble, although it was more from tension than excitement.

Where's your courage, man, he berated himself. *You're twenty-eight years old and a Journeyman. It's not as if you haven't created a portway before.*

Ah yes, came a sly thought, *but not without your father watching your every move, making sure you got the sequences right.*

Taran took a deep breath, filling his lungs with cool, chalky air. He shoved away his misgivings. His father had died two years ago—he'd have to do this by himself. He was perfectly capable. Journeyman was the third of the eight Artesan ranks and he had mastered the primary element of Earth. He could also influence the secondary, Water, and was well on the way to becoming an Adept. All he needed was a bit more instruction and what he had planned for today would, with just a little luck, be the means of obtaining it.

He set the lantern on its shelf and cast his gaze to the cellar's rocky floor. It was formed like a shallow bowl and would help shape the Earth force he intended to call. Across the space, he caught the diamond glitter of Cal's eyes.

"Ready?"

Cal shrugged again. "I'm ready. It's not as if I'm doing anything."

"You'll be guarding the portway, Cal. Without you, I wouldn't be doing this in the first place."

And probably shouldn't be doing it now, he thought, unable to quell his doubts. Once he had formed the portway, he intended to leave it active. This was a huge risk, he knew—a breach of every rule he'd been taught.

Never, ever leave a portway open, son. You don't know what might make use of it ...

His father's disapproving tone resounded in Taran's mind, yet he was determined to ignore it. He was terrified of becoming stranded in the Fifth Realm and, even if all went according to plan, creating a new portway when he needed to return would cost him too much time and energy. The skills of a Journeyman weren't sufficient to determine where such portals would open, so he could end up many miles from his village when he came back.

Asking Cal to maintain and guard it was the best solution Taran could think of. He intended to weave his young Apprentice's strength into the structure as he formed it so all Cal had to do was stay in the cellar. He had his bedroll, supplies and the lantern. He'd be alright.

Everything would be alright. It had to be.

Catching Cal's nod of acceptance, Taran took a slow breath, closed his eyes and gave himself a moment to settle into the cellar's thick silence. He turned his gaze inward and sought his psyche, the unique pattern through which an Artesan channeled his power.

The whorls and spirals materialized in his mind. Soft with pearly colors, the pattern's familiarity soothed Taran's nerves. Gathering his strength, he called on the power every Artesan possessed—metaforce—and it rose, suffusing his soul. His heart exulted as the power grew and his body sang with potential.

Taran reveled in its glory. This was as much a part of him as his arms or legs, yet he could never have used the wondrous gift without his father's years of instruction. Metaforce was present in everyone, though only Artesans could learn its control. Taran's lessons with his Adept-elite father might not have been pleasant— Amanus was neither a natural nor a sympathetic teacher—but his yearning to expand his knowledge was overwhelming. The same need was driving him to attempt this risky trip.

Once his entire body was attuned to the power, Taran turned his attention to Cal. The young man was inexperienced; he was only just starting to learn about metaforce and could only influence Earth. He was strong, though; Taran could sense his fledgling power rushing through his veins.

Reaching out with his psyche, Taran melded it to Cal's, feeling his Apprentice surrender control. He raised his arms, palms downward, and sent his metasenses deep into the rock, searching for the Earth's elemental signature.

Within minutes, a familiar, thrilling tingle shot through Taran as the primal element responded. Slow, majestic, immeasurably powerful, the energy of Earth rose at his call, filling the bowl at his feet.

He glanced at Cal but the Apprentice's eyes were fixed on the ground. Cal was mesmerized and Taran understood why. Like a creeping mist, the Earth force lapped about their feet, rising at Taran's command.

Beads of sweat rose on his forehead and his breathing deepened. Journeyman he might be, but this still wasn't easy. He had to maintain a steady pull or his efforts would be wasted.

When he sensed he'd reached his limit, Taran turned his attention to shaping. With Cal's energy boosting his own, he molded the Earth force until the characteristic spherical shape of a portway began to form. It rose until it was floating, a ball of Earth force just larger than a man, shimmering with opalescent beauty. When it was complete, Taran anchored it, fixing it within the Veils, the substance that separated each of the five Realms.

All it needed to become a gateway through the Veils was the force of an Artesan's will. One simple command and it would open, allowing Taran access to the Fifth Realm.

A small sigh of relief escaped him. This time, after months of frustrating failures, his Artesan powers hadn't let him down. He released his hold on the element of Earth and let the power drain from his psyche back into the rock beneath his feet.

Glancing at Cal, he grinned. "This is it."

Cal didn't return the grin. Instead, he once more eyed the sword at Taran's waist. "Even with me guarding the portway, this is going to be dangerous. What if you don't win the challenge? What if you're wounded?"

Irritation rose, yet Taran knew Cal's concerns were real. Ever since he'd found the passage in his father's notes that had spawned this plan, Cal had been against it. Artesans might be mistrusted in Albia—to the point that the craft was dying—but they were revered in Andaryon, the Fifth Realm. Andaryans were known for their love of dueling, yet, despite their warlike nature and distressing habit of raiding vulnerable Albian villages, they had strict codes governing such duels. The notes had suggested that if Taran challenged an Andaryan Artesan and won, or even forced a draw, he could name any prize he chose. Knowledge would be Taran's choice and once the possibility of achieving his dream had arisen, he simply couldn't ignore it.

Still, the risks were real.

"It's a chance I'll have to take. Stop worrying. I have faith in my skills, even if you don't."

Cal's face fell and Taran immediately regretted his words.

"Besides, Rienne will patch me up if I'm careless enough to get wounded."

He'd intended to reassure, but mentioning Cal's lover only seemed to make things worse. The Apprentice frowned and glanced up at the ceiling.

"Do you think she'll be alright on her own?"

Taran smiled. "Of course she will. Why shouldn't she be?"

"But what if one of the villagers calls? What if someone wants you?"

"I think that's highly unlikely, Cal. They try to keep out of

my way as much as I try to keep out of theirs. I've no desire to
be thrown out of the village for practicing 'unnatural acts'. And
since you brought it up, make sure you don't make any noise
down here. You know how suspicious they are … "

"What if one of them falls sick? They might come looking for
medicine..."

That was a real possibility, thought Taran. He blessed the day
a year ago when Rienne came to the village, a traveling healer
dispensing cures. Her extraordinary skills had made her instantly
popular and when she'd fallen for Cal's dark good looks and
decided to stay, she'd brought the respectability that Taran had
never enjoyed. He and his father had only ever been tolerated
in Hyecombe, but with Rienne in the house, his neighbors were
forced to be at least civil. They might avoid speaking to him and
Cal, but they braved his door for Rienne.

"She knows what to do," he said. "And if any of them get
curious, she can tell them we've got the flux. That'll silence their
questions."

He gave his Apprentice another smile. "I won't be gone long.
This is only the bargaining stage, so I'll be back before you've
had time to miss me. Just stay alert. The portway's my lifeline and
I'm relying on you to keep it safe."

Turning away from Cal's doubts, Taran faced the portway.
It was the smallest, tightest structure he could form and it was
firmly anchored. There was nothing else to wait for.

He picked up his pack, checking he had everything. He wasn't
taking much. The blade his father had given him, some food,
and his bedroll. They should be enough to see him through this
enterprise, along with the skills of his arm. And they should be
more than adequate, for every Albian male learned how to use a
sword. Taran was no exception and he was more than competent.
It was time to put his training to use.

He nodded to Cal and drew a deep breath.

Stepping into the portway, he left the cellar behind.

Chapter Two

The deep bass drone of Earth power clung to Taran like a cloak as he pushed his way through the portway. His ears were ringing by the time he emerged, stepping abruptly into the blinding light of a small white sun.

He squinted against the glare and gasped. The air was uncomfortably hot. The five realms might exist within the bounds of the same world but each was completely separate. While it was midday in the Fourth Realm, Albia, and early autumn, here it was nearer to evening and clearly still summer hot.

Taran turned, checking the portway was still stable. It looked vague, faded by the sun's glare. He could feel Cal's power within the structure, though, and was reassured. His Apprentice was in control.

Taran turned his back on it and gazed around.

A wide landscape shrouded in heat haze confronted him and he swore. The Andaryan end of the portway had opened into a range of hills rather than cultivated lands, and he cursed his bad luck. If only he had the ability to control the portway's opening. Although, if he had possessed such skill, he reflected, he wouldn't have needed to risk this venture. And anyway, he had no detailed knowledge of the Fifth Realm, no idea where its people might be found.

The harsh, low scrub covering the hills was baked brittle and there was little shade. Taran gathered his thoughts, wondering which direction to take.

Everything he knew of the Fifth Realm had come from his father's notes. Amanus hadn't thought much of his son's talents and had never brought him to this warlike realm. Any direction was a gamble and Taran supposed that was appropriate. After all, this whole plan was a gamble.

Choosing a westerly direction, he moved away from the portway. As he walked, he carefully committed his route to memory. His metasenses would guide him back but it always helped to have landmarks. This was his final chance, the last thing he could think of. Either he made the best of it or resigned himself to never increasing his knowledge.

He shuddered; the thought was too dreadful.

As he trudged through the hills, both the heat and his frustration made him sweat. There wasn't a single sign of habitation. Not a footprint, nor a wreath of smoke, nor a sound to lead him to people. He began to pant as he struggled up yet another low hill, shading his eyes against the rapidly setting sun. Again he cursed—all he could see was heat haze.

He closed his eyes, feeling a stray wisp of evening breeze touch the damp hair on his neck. Turning to face it, he welcomed its coolness. When he opened his eyes again he stared at a dark line stretching to his left that could only be trees. He considered it before making up his mind. Even if the forest was as empty as the hills, at least it promised shelter from tomorrow's heat.

Hitching his pack higher and gritting his teeth, Taran made for the trees.

By the time he emerged from the hills, it was nearly dark. The forest had lured him and he had hoped to reach it before nightfall. Now he saw that although the hills ended sooner than he had thought, the distance had been deceptive, for the trees were actually farther away than they seemed. It would be folly to go on in darkness. Much safer to camp in this shrubby little copse, he thought, and make for the forest in daylight.

Weary, he dropped his pack to the ground. He lit a fire but the surrounding scrub was tinder-dry, so he shielded the meager flame well. Once he had eaten, he stamped it out; he had his blanket and wouldn't risk a brush fire. Warmly wrapped against the night chill he could already feel, he stretched out on the ground. As he closed his eyes, he accessed his psyche, surrounding himself with power. Bringing Cal's pattern to mind, he sent his Apprentice a call.

Cal answered immediately, reassuring Taran with his watchfulness. Not that Taran distrusted him, but the younger man was far less experienced than even Taran, and his strength was being drained by the effort of maintaining the portway.

Once Taran was satisfied that Cal was in control, he broke the link. Before settling to sleep, he drew power through his psyche once more. Attuning it to the element of Earth, he cast tendrils of power into the ground, trusting them to wake him should he be approached in the night.

As weariness claimed him, despondency rose. He had the most depressing feeling that this venture was doomed to failure, just like all the rest.

✤ ✤ ✤ ✤ ✤

Andaryon, the Fifth Realm
The dungeons of Duke Rykan's palace in Kymer Province

The cell door crashed against the wall as Sonten flung it open. His nephew jumped and let out a curse. Sonten grinned. The boy should have been expecting him; he'd have to control his reactions better than this. After all, Jaskin would have far worse than his uncle's wrath to face if their plan failed.

Impatiently, he waited while Jaskin calmed. The boy's hands were resting on a strange metal object lying on the table before him. The sight of it made Sonten's obese frame quiver with tension. His fat fingers gripped the door jamb and his voice rasped in the chilly gloom.

"Well, boy, have you finally done it? Can you use the damned thing?"

It galled Sonten that his Artesan powers were so feeble. He hated needing Jaskin's greater skills to make his plan work. Even this step had taken many secret days to achieve. Thank the gods the boy was still young enough to be manipulated.

His nephew raised his head and regarded his uncle with an Andaryan's characteristically pale, slit-pupiled eyes. They gleamed like a cat's in moonlight.

"Of course I can. Didn't I tell you all I needed was privacy and time?"

His condescending tone irritated Sonten, though he ignored it.

Yes, you enjoy your little triumphs, he thought, *secure in the knowledge that I need you. One day, my boy, when you least expect it, you'll pay for your arrogance.*

Sonten approached the table, intent on the innocent-looking artifact. Known as the Staff, it belonged to their overlord, Duke Rykan. A slim rod the length of a man's forearm, its ceramic sheathing glittered metallic green. Or was it blue? The changing hues flickered across it, rippling over its etched surface.

Beautiful but deadly, thought Sonten, suppressing a shiver. Despite his fear, it fascinated him.

"Will he notice?" he demanded. "Will he sense what you've done?"

He met Jaskin's gaze, knowing the boy understood his fear. They were treading a dangerous path and everything was at risk. Should the Duke realize they'd taken the Staff, or—gods forbid—learn they were plotting to overthrow him, their deaths would be lingeringly brutal. Rykan had a fearsome reputation; neither of them wanted to incur such powerful wrath.

Jaskin leaned back in his chair. "No Uncle, I've told you before. I've only used my knowledge of his Grace's psyche. I've influenced the Staff, not taken control. I doubt I could do that anyway, my powers aren't as strong as the Duke's. But I've left no imprint, no clue that I've touched it."

"What's next?" asked Sonten, greedily eyeing the Staff.

Jaskin ran a hand through sweaty hair. "I don't know about you, but I need a bath."

Sonten glared at him; that wasn't what he'd meant.

Jaskin rose and picked up the Staff. It flared as he touched it and Sonten flinched. Seeing his nephew grin, he scowled. The Staff was a dangerous instrument and he couldn't help fearing it. Among other things, it was capable of stealing whatever power its Artesan victim possessed. While Sonten might not have much in the way of power, he did not relish the thought of it being sucked forcibly out of him.

Carefully, Jaskin placed the Staff in its padded iron chest, which was kept locked in this unused part of the dungeons. Despite his subjects' fear of him, the Duke wasn't taking any chances that someone might steal it. The irony of this wasn't lost on Sonten. The Staff was invaluable—irreplaceable—and like Jaskin, the Duke had labored through many sweaty hours to imbue it with his power. He was waiting for the right time to use it and hadn't been down here for days. In his position as senior general, Sonten often had legitimate reason to visit the dungeons. Still, he couldn't help fearing the Duke might suspect what they were up to. So he locked the chest and the door to the cell as usual, placing the keys in the pouch at his waist.

"I need to conduct an experiment," said Jaskin, his voice echoing in from the dank corridor outside the cell. "I need to test my control."

"His Grace has … "

"I can't use one of the Duke's wretched prisoners, Uncle. What if it went wrong? How would we explain ourselves?"

"But … "

"Besides, I need someone unsuspecting, someone stronger than those useless peasants. Not one of them is higher than Apprentice and if our plan is to succeed, I need to be sure the Staff can do what his Grace has been told."

Sonten stayed silent, watching his nephew think.

"What we need is a brief trip back to your mansion in Durkos. That would give us time to search out someone suitable."

"But that would be even riskier than this," objected Sonten. "The Albian raids are due to start soon and his Grace wants me to oversee them. How would we explain our absence?"

Jaskin shrugged. "That's up to you. Can't you invent something, some emergency in Durkos needing your personal attention?"

"It's too dangerous."

"I know it's dangerous, Uncle, but what choice do we have? Once the raids start, it'll be too late."

Sonten narrowed his eyes. "They're a waste of time and men, these raids. I can't see why his Grace is so keen to capture the human witch. Surely we have far more important concerns."

"She's not a witch, Uncle. She's reputed to be a powerful Artesan. If his Grace can absorb her powers, it'll help in his bid for the throne. And it wasn't his idea, remember? It was that Albian Baron's."

Sonten scowled. The Duke's alliance with the Baron was a sore point and Sonten definitely didn't approve. Not that the Duke took any notice of Sonten's opinions.

"If it makes you feel any better," said Jaskin, "I think his Grace is using the Baron. Once he's served his purpose, he'll be disposed of."

"And then he'll move on the throne," gloated Sonten.

Jaskin smiled. "But before that happens, I need to test the Staff. Once I'm sure I can take the Duke, we can choose our time."

Sonten nodded, triumphant greed warming the dark corners of his heart.

Suddenly, Jaskin froze; his eyes wide with fear. "Was that a horn?"

Sonten felt the blood leave his face and his knees turned weak. "He can't be back already, surely?"

But Jaskin wasn't listening. He had bolted for the stairs. As Sonten forced his bulk into motion, he heard his nephew racing upward.

Chapter Three

Deep in thought, chin-rolls resting on his chest, Sonten fretted as he rode through the early sunlight. He had only managed to get the Duke's permission to visit Durkos with Jaskin for two days, supposedly to deal with a peasant uprising. It was the best fabrication he could come up with on such short notice and it was a measure of the Duke's preoccupation that he had fallen for it. Even so, Sonten was under strict instructions to return as soon as possible. The raids ordered by the Duke's ally, the Baron, were imminent, and the Duke wanted his General to oversee them.

Sonten scowled. Overseeing the raids was a waste of his time. All his commanders had been thoroughly briefed; they all knew exactly what was required. Still, if his Grace wanted Sonten there, Sonten had to obey. It galled him that his own rise in power was so dependent on the Duke's patronage, but if his plans succeeded, he would do far more than merely share his overlord's success.

As he accompanied Jaskin toward the forests bordering Durkos, Sonten hugged those plans close to his heart.

He and his nephew were escorted by eight huntsmen from Sonten's personal retinue. They were hand-picked, trusted men, and they were well aware how vital it was that the Duke didn't learn of this excursion. Sonten had also brought two of his favorite tangwyrs. The monstrous raptors were hooded and lashed by stout jesses to their wooden perches, which were being carried by horses trained not to spook at their smell.

Fondly, he watched them. In appearance, they could have been the offspring of a vulture and a giant bat. Their lanceolate beaks and vicious, saw-edged talons were driven by sail-like feathered and leathery wings. They were ferocious predators and efficient scavengers. In the wild, they rode the thermals high over the Andaryan plains and their unnerving red eyes could spot prey on the ground from miles above. In captivity—you could never call them tame—they were useful for intimidating or punishing rebellious peasants.

Jaskin had objected to Sonten bringing the monsters—he needed his victims alive and preferably unhurt, not lacerated by the claws of a tangwyr. Sonten had assured his nephew they were for show only. He knew how important this venture was.

The party rode through the hills toward the forest villages where Sonten hoped to find some peasant Artesan, some low-born talent who would never rise above the status fate had dealt him. Sonten's province had many of these, as he wasn't given to elevating lowborns, especially not those whose powers were stronger than his.

The day threatened to be hot; fierce summer temperatures often persisted long into autumn. The horses kicked up dust scorched by the summer sun. As the party descended the final hill and approached a shadowed copse not yet warmed by the early light, the lead huntsman, who had been scouting, rode back to them.

"There's a camp ahead, my Lords. One man only, still sleeping. He's an outlander and by his gear, I'd say he's Albian."

Jaskin shot Sonten a glance. "Did you hear that, Uncle? An Albian trespassing on your land. You know what that means, don't you?"

Sonten grinned. Only Artesans possessed the power to travel between the realms and outlanders—especially Albians—were fair game.

"Looks like luck's on our side," he said as he nudged his horse closer. "But how will you know what rank he is? What if he's more powerful than you?"

Jaskin snorted. "Don't worry, I'm not about to wade in without some assurance of safety. I want the first one to be unprepared. Until I know exactly how the Staff works, I don't want to face a shielded man. Wait here while I see what we've got."

Jaskin dismounted, removed his green-edged black cloak and followed the scout. Sonten waited impatiently. Within a few moments, the younger man was back, a satisfied grin on his face.

"Well?"

"He's about my age, possibly a year or two older. And he's either an experienced Apprentice-elite or a very inexperienced Journeyman."

"How can you be so sure?" demanded Sonten.

"He's laid a mesh of metaforce. Don't ask me to go into detail. But I was able to approach without waking him, so it's not very strong. The point is, either rank is perfect."

Sonten dismounted and the huntsmen did the same. "So what do you intend?"

"I'll challenge him to a duel. I'm quite within my rights, he's trespassing after all. I want you to stay back while I do this, Uncle, stay out of his sight if you can. It's highly unlikely he'll beat me, but if it looks as though he might, I'll use the Staff. I want the Staff kept out of sight until I need it. He won't know what it is, but he's an Artesan, so he might sense its power. You'll have to hold it until I'm ready to use it."

Sonten paled. The thought of holding the thing, with its strangely shimmering colors and mind-stealing potential, terrified him.

His obvious distaste made Jaskin grin. "It can't hurt you, Uncle, I've told you before. It needs to be activated by an Artesan with stronger powers than yours. Don't worry, you're perfectly safe."

Gods, but you'll pay for your smugness, boy, thought Sonten, stung by this reference to his handicap. But as Jaskin held out the Staff, he passed his reins to a huntsman and accepted the dreadful thing. He concealed it beneath the ample folds of his cloak and hung back among his escort.

They followed as Jaskin walked toward the copse.

✦ ✦ ✦ ✦ ✦

Taran's metasenses pricked him and he instantly woke, leaping to his feet and snatching his sword. He stopped short, biting back a curse, as he registered the confident stance of the young man standing before him. And he had every reason to be confident, Taran realized, with armed hunters at his back. His failure to sense them sooner made Taran scowl. Apprehensively, he waited for the man to speak.

"You're trespassing, Albian."

The man's arrogant manner and rich clothing confirmed Taran's immediate suspicions—he was an Andaryan noble. Taran's sleep-muddled mind struggled to frame a reply but he wasn't given the leisure.

"The penalty for trespass is death."

Taran stared, knowing he was trapped. The huntsmen stood with bows unnocked but he knew how swiftly they could draw and shoot should he make a threatening move. And though the ugly giant birds they had were hooded and leashed, they could be loosed in an instant if he tried to run. His only chance lay in the bargain he hoped to make.

He opened his mouth to answer but was again interrupted.

"However, I came out this day for sport. What do you say to a duel, Albian, to determine your fate? If you win, you're free to leave. If you lose, you submit to my will."

The noble's pale, slit-pupiled eyes were avid and he fingered the hilt of his sword as he spoke. The motion drew Taran's gaze. Events were moving a little fast for him despite this seemingly favorable turn. He had not expected things to work out like this—according to his father's notes, he should be the one making the challenge—but in the end, did it matter? And what choice did he have? The noble had him at a severe disadvantage and would be within his rights should he decide to kill Taran out of hand. Even if he wasn't, there was nothing Taran could do about it. No one would protect him if he could not protect himself.

He gathered his courage and faced the noble. He looked a little younger than Taran's twenty-eight years but Taran had faith in his own skills. He was taller than the noble and he was agile and fit, there was no reason to believe he would not win. And the noble was an Artesan, Taran could sense it. He didn't know what rank but that wasn't immediately important. His father's notes indicated that Taran only had to force a draw to win the right to the noble's aid. If he turned out to be incapable of teaching Taran himself, his duty would require him to find someone who could.

"I accept," he said, trying to keep the nervousness from his voice. The younger man grinned and Taran frowned. Those slit-pupiled eyes, unique to the Andaryan race, made his facial expressions unfamiliar. Taran would have to be very careful when reading his moves in the duel.

✣ ✣ ✣ ✣ ✣

As he watched this exchange surrounded by his escort, Sonten's heart filled with contempt. That the Albian was alone was foolish enough, why was he accepting challenges as if he had a choice? Where was his second to agree the rules of combat? Didn't he know that without witnesses, such agreements were void?

His derision grew when he realized the Albian wasn't even going to bargain terms with Jaskin. The Andaryans' love of dueling and the complicated haggling that preceded such bouts was well known throughout the five realms. This outlander must be naïve indeed if he thought Jaskin's honor would constrain him to the codes. The General huffed. Honor was not involved when fighting outlanders.

He began to relax. His nephew's plan had worried him because it carried an unnecessary measure of risk. But if Jaskin's opponent was so ignorant of the codes, then he wouldn't be much of a threat. Sonten could enjoy the duel and their first experimental use of the Staff would bring them another step closer to success.

He elbowed the nearest huntsman. The man moved out of his line of sight and spread his cloak over the General's head, shielding him from the strengthening sun. Sonten saw Jaskin's glance and acknowledged the gesture, patting the weapon that rested against his thigh.

He crossed his arms over his ample chest and watched as the duel commenced.

✣ ✣ ✣ ✣ ✣

Ϩaran followed the noble as he moved away from the huntsmen, seeking room to maneuver. Suddenly he stopped and turned, staring into Taran's eyes. Taran studied him without locking gazes. It was tempting to stare back but he resisted the impulse, knowing it would be a mistake. He needed to focus his attention on the noble's body; if he turned out to be the experienced swordsman he seemed, his eyes would give away nothing.

Taran raised his sword to the salute. With no warning, his opponent lunged at him, blade aimed directly at Taran's chest.

Despite the distance between them, Taran was caught off guard. Wrong-footed, he parried awkwardly, only just managing to slide away.

He tried to protest but his opponent didn't give him time, immediately lunging into another strike that clashed on Taran's hastily raised blade. The contemptuous look in his cat-like eyes told its own story and Taran realized protest was futile. The noble was after sport and Taran was his prey; there would be no quarter given and no respect paid to the rules.

Dismayed by this flagrant disregard for the codes, Taran struggled to force his mind back to sword play. He must not let his fear and outrage interfere with his skill. Those opening strikes, treacherous though they were, had alerted him to the talent and lack of moral code he was facing. The noble wouldn't be an easy conquest. He was fighting on his own soil and by his own terms. Taran was the usurper, the outlander, and he was alone.

For the first time since conceiving the plan, Taran acknowledged this flaw. But it was too late now, he was locked into this fate. He threw himself into the combat, determined not to lose.

He cut and blocked, grateful that his skill had saved him from injury during those first deceitful moves. His pulse raced. His opponent was coming at him again, striking at his unprotected left, causing Taran to veer sharply aside. He swept his blade around, hoping to catch the noble off balance, but he had already danced out of the way.

Taran circled the noble warily, searching for weak points. The sun's heat was increasing, he was sweating profusely. He lunged at the noble, forcing him back across the dusty ground, but the man disengaged and came at Taran again, giving him no time to draw breath. *We're too evenly matched,* thought Taran, *there's no advantage.* Sunlight struck blindingly from steel as his blade clashed and rang on the noble's, labored breaths grunting through his throat.

They struggled back and forth for half an hour or so. Taran was bleeding from many superficial cuts; he was bruised and sore, but so was his opponent. Neither, it seemed, could gain the upper hand. Now that Taran's early anger had been forgotten in his struggle for survival, he began to despair. A strange heaviness was weighing his arm and he was having trouble holding his own. He was dismayed; his stamina was usually greater than this. But his concentration was centered on his opponent's latest flurry of vicious cuts and it took him a while to figure out what was happening.

He couldn't understand it. What he suspected should not be possible. He and the noble hadn't learned each other's pattern of psyche, there was no way the other man could be affecting Taran's life force. But it was undeniable. Insidiously, and contrary to all the rules and codes, the noble was draining Taran's metaforce and using it to empower himself.

Outraged and confused, Taran's mind shut down like a steel trap, cutting off the other's leaching force. In panic, he accessed his psyche, using his own Artesan skills to bolster his flagging strength.

"Foul," yelled his opponent. "The use of metaforce is forbidden by the codes."

Taran saw the watching huntsmen stir at this cry. Infuriated by its hypocrisy, he realized he had walked straight into a trap. He couldn't impeach the noble though, it was too late. And anyway, there was no one to believe him.

As he automatically blocked a low swipe to his leg, Taran recalled a glance exchanged between the noble and someone among the huntsmen. Coupled with the strange eager light in his opponent's eyes, these signs should have warned Taran that something was amiss. Yet it had passed him by and this new failure only increased his frustration.

Enraged by the deception, Taran attacked with a burst of vicious strokes. The noble gave way before him but there was a knowing look in his eye. Now Taran understood that he had planned this all along. He had never intended to honor the contract. With no witnesses to speak for him, Taran was totally unprotected. He would have cursed himself savagely if only he'd had the strength.

He heard a strident call as someone among the huntsmen yelled, "Use your own powers. He's broken the rules, after all."

Alone and without an ally, Taran went cold, realizing the full extent of his peril. A surge of righteous rage flooded his soul. He might have been careless and foolish in allowing his opponent to accuse him, but he wasn't the one who had broken the codes.

The noble's treachery meant Taran was free to use his powers. He did so and soon his opponent, in response to the call, formed a ball of Earth element, which he flung at Taran's feet. Too slow to counter it, Taran stumbled. Now they were fighting on two levels. This was highly dangerous as it was impossible to concentrate on sword play while using an Artesan's skills.

Icy fear made Taran shiver. This bout would end in his death unless he could defeat the noble.

Exhausted though he was, he redoubled his efforts.

✠ ✠ ✠ ✠ ✠

Sonten moved stealthily, hoping neither fighter would notice his approach. He'd felt relief on sensing Jaskin's drain of his opponent's strength but it turned to rage when the Albian failed to succumb. Fearful for his nephew's safety, the General needed Jaskin to end this duel. He watched closely and eventually saw his chance. As Jaskin drove his Albian opponent backwards with a succession of powerful lunges, Sonten cried, "Use the Staff, boy."

He tossed the weapon across the beaten earth.

✠ ✠ ✠ ✠ ✠

Taran was distracted as the Staff skidded to his opponent's feet. The noble snatched it up and it flared blindingly, blue and green light rippling down its length. He drove at Taran with his sword but even as he parried the blows, Taran felt his opponent calling up power. He stared in shock—the Staff's flickering tip was pointing at his heaving chest.

A killing bolt of pure elemental energy flashed from the Staff. With a wide-eyed look of horror, totally unnerved by this unforeseen event, Taran only just managed to twist sideways. He was showered with dirt as a sizzling bolt of Earth power pulverized a rock behind him.

Fear and anger goaded Taran and he leaped at his opponent, lunging into broadsword strokes he had learned from an itinerant swordmaster years ago. The noble had obviously expected Taran to be stunned into inaction. Taran rained blows onto his blade, striking viciously, trying to keep him off balance. There was a discordant clang and Taran's sword arm went numb. The noble roared a curse as his sword was sent spinning from his hand.

"Yield," panted Taran but his opponent didn't falter. Raising the Staff, he attacked Taran with renewed ferocity. Huge bolts of Earth energy shot from its tip, forcing the exhausted Journeyman to deflect them.

Taran's powers were stretched far beyond their straining limits. Terrified, he only had one choice and he grabbed it, throwing all his remaining metaforce into one vast Earth shift. The ground bucked beneath his opponent's feet, nearly toppling him, and Taran rushed him. Ignoring the Staff's awful power, he brought his sword around in a powerful backhanded sweep. The noble's head suddenly dangled from a half-severed neck.

The body collapsed, spraying blood, and the deadly Staff fell at Taran's feet. Spattered with red, still gripped by terror, he stood panting heavily. Trembling, he leaned on his sword.

There was shocked silence.

There was a roar—"Treachery!"—from the huntsmen and they leaped into action, rushing toward Taran, baying for his blood.

Trapped, exhausted and facing certain death, Taran panicked. Sheathing his sword, he snatched the Staff and channeled his own power through it. Unthinking, he called up his reserves and threw the largest barrier of Earth element he could manage against the rushing men. The effort of using the alien weapon burned his brain and the pain was excruciating. Yet the yelling huntsmen were flung back, momentarily stunned. Taran used the respite to take another gamble.

He called a feeble Earth ball and lobbed it behind the huntsmen's horses, even that small power causing him incredible pain. This time luck was on his side and the horses stampeded toward him. Gasping, half-blinded by pain, Taran managed to grab the reins of a passing horse and wrench it to a halt. Agony shot through his arm as it nearly popped out of its socket. The horse curvetted wildly and Taran had to scramble into the saddle, still holding the Staff tightly. Before he'd even found his balance, he was kicking the horse toward the hills. Hopefully he could shake his pursuers and relocate the portway.

For a while, he thought he might succeed. He turned the horse, racing through the maze of hills, trying to hide his tracks. Fear gave him strength but he knew it wouldn't last. As he crested a rise, he risked a glance over his shoulder, his laboring heart lifted by the absence of pursuit. His lungs heaving, he sent the horse pounding down the far side of the hill.

His relief was short-lived. Inevitably, he heard racing hoofbeats; some of the hunters had regained control of their mounts. The portway was still some way off and he risked another backward glance.

A desperate denial escaped his lips. The huntsmen had brought a tangwyr with them. The creature's hood had been removed and that could only mean one thing.

They intended to fly it at him.

The tangwyr's ferocity was legendary, even in Albia. Without a bow, Taran stood little chance of protecting himself as it was trained to bring down men. As a Journeyman, he had mastery over Earth and could influence Water, but these elements wouldn't help him here. Neither could he dismount and use his sword. If he did, the huntsmen would be on him.

His breath sobbing painfully, he kicked the horse once more.

He heard a raucous cry and gasped in terror; the hideous creature was free. Another glance behind him revealed that the riders had slowed, evidently expecting the tangwyr to do their work for them. Despite his straits, Taran felt satisfaction—his use of power had taught them some respect, at least.

Respect, however, had no value in the talons of a tangwyr.

As he cursed himself for a fool and for allowing himself to be trapped—how many times had he tried to drum caution into Cal's head?—he glanced up. Horror overtook him, turning his muscles to water. The awful spectre of a swooping tangwyr filled his vision.

He threw himself off the horse, landing heavily. The Staff dug into his ribs and he felt the rake of talons on his shoulder. As he struggled to his feet, the downdraft of powerful wings nearly knocked him back down. He heard the creature swoop away up the hillside, wings booming as it beat for height. Panicking, coughing, Taran fled, praying the portway was nearby.

He was sure the hill looked familiar and the thought galvanized him. He could sense the portway but his endurance was fading fast. His throat was raw, his chest tightening painfully as he pushed himself past his limits. His muscles were burning and losing their strength. He was weakening rapidly.

The ominous beat of giant wings grew louder behind him.

Wildly, he looked around, knowing the portway was near. Suddenly, his vision cleared, showing him what he'd been praying for—an opalescent shimmer hanging in the air. He gathered his will and sent a panicked command through the Veils to Cal. Relief flooded him as his Apprentice responded and he saw the portway ripple, a sign that Cal was alert.

He sprinted toward it but was brought up short by a harsh scream from above.

Horrified, he looked up and stared directly into the mad red eyes of the tangwyr. It plummeted, its sinewy neck twisting toward him, serrated talons aimed at his heart. He had nowhere to go and no room to dodge, but he couldn't risk leaping into the portway in case he took the thing with him.

Unthinkingly desperate, he raised the Staff. He grabbed for Cal's strength and felt his friend's compliance. Empowered, Taran took an almighty risk with both their lives and channeled their joint metaforce through the alien weapon.

It glowed incandescent and bucked in his hands. Taran screamed with the pain of controlling it. He forced his will on it, his lungs still gulping air, and directed its tip at the tangwyr's breast.

Deadly energy roared out, causing the plummeting monster to twist aside. It was too slow. Raw power caught the leading edge of one vast sail-like wing, charring the feathered membrane to a crisp. With a piercing shriek, the creature curled around itself, cartwheeling toward the ground.

Taran didn't wait to see it hit. Near to fainting with pain and exhaustion, he cast himself into the portway, blindly trusting Cal to bring him safely through.

Chapter Four

Sonten was cursing as his horse pounded after the huntsmen. He kicked it up the next rise, hoping to see the kill. Roaring instructions his men couldn't hear, Sonten saw the tangwyr's swoop. He watched in speechless fury as the Albian Artesan, Jaskin's intended victim, used the Duke's priceless Staff to escape the monstrous bird.

But it wasn't until the dying raptor's shrieks had faded that he realized the irreplaceable Staff had vanished as well.

This shock, coming on top of his nephew's brutal murder, made Sonten's stomach heave. Awkwardly, he slid from his lathered horse and fell to his knees. Already tasting the Duke's wrath and feeling the sword twisting through his guts, Sonten retched helplessly while his men rode to him.

He was on his feet by the time they reached him. His face was an unpleasant shade of purple, his body quivering with rage. The huntsmen dismounted while he strode up and down before them, their heads hanging in shame.

His voice tinged with panic, Sonten harangued them.

"You lost him. You bloody lost him, you useless rabble. Why did you let him get away? He murdered my nephew, the Albian bastard, he deserves to die. And he's taken that damned Staff too! What am I going to say to the Duke? How do I explain that one? Well? Does anyone have anything to say?"

They were silent.

Sonten glared in fury. His plans were ruined and his shocked brain was working feverishly. He was going to be in fatal trouble unless he could come up with a suitable story. In the meantime, his rage demanded a scapegoat.

"Well?" he roared.

The men flinched and their leader stepped forward. "My Lord, he was too quick. We couldn't reach him in time. He was out of bowshot, so I thought the tangwyr was our best chance. I never thought he'd ... "

"You never thought?" raged Sonten. "That's about right, Perik! Thinking was never your strong suit. Well, you've made your last mistake. This is a disaster and someone has to pay for it. Guess who it'll be?"

He stared menacingly, knowing he was being unfair. Perik had done his best. His frustration at the man's escape was deepened by the knowledge that he had used the Staff instinctively, whereas it had taken Jaskin many sweaty days to learn how to influence the thing.

The thought of his nephew's body lying on the blood-soaked ground made Sonten seethe. All that risk and effort wasted, all their plans thrown away. And now his own position—indeed his very life—would be forfeit when the Duke discovered the Staff's disappearance.

Terrible fear swamped Sonten. He trusted these men, they had been picked for their loyalty, but if one of them should mention …

Panic overrode reason and his sword whipped from its sheath. Fat he undoubtedly was and not as skilled as some, but Perik never saw the steel that punched through his ribs and heart. He was dead before his reproachful eyes fastened on Sonten's face. His dying gaze was ignored, his limp body allowed to slump to the ground.

Sonten turned his back on the dead man and stared at the rest.

"Let that be a lesson to you. If even one of you breathes so much as a word of this … I won't tolerate fools and I won't stand for failure. Do you understand?"

They shuffled uneasily, murmuring assent.

"You all know what that murdering bastard looks like. He's trespassed on my lands once, he may do so again. You're all charged with watching for him. Constantly, do you hear? I want no slacking, no matter how exhausted you get. I want to know instantly of any Albians in my province and I want them detained alive.

"Galet, you're now leading huntsman. Think carefully about Perik's fate and make damned sure you don't suffer the same. Am I clear? Good. Now pick that up, get back to my nephew's body and follow me back to the mansion. I have to speak with Commander Heron before I return to his Grace, and on top of everything else I now have a bloody damned funeral to arrange."

Still swearing, Sonten clambered onto his mount. Viciously, he kicked its stocky sides. The beast flung up its head and grunted. Lumbering into a canter, it bore its angry rider back to his estate.

✢ ✢ ✢ ✢ ✢

"Feverbalm, boneknit, willow. Oh yes, and serraflower. Hmm, those are looking a bit old now, I could do with a fresh supply."

Sitting at the wooden table in the small cottage kitchen, Rienne regarded the packet of dried flower heads she'd taken from her medicine bag. Bright cerise pink and heavily scented when fresh, they had faded to a ruddy brown, their aroma all but gone. Frowning, she picked one up and gently rubbed it under her nose.

"Definitely past their best," she murmured, replacing the tattered flower head among its fellows. She reached into the bag beside her but stopped as a strange noise reached her ears.

Was that a scream?

Instantly, she was on her feet and turning toward the kitchen door. Her hand closed on the latch but again she froze.

"Rienne. Rienne!"

No, it hadn't come from outside. It had come from the cellar. Her blood chilled and her heart thumped as she recognized Cal's voice. He sounded strained—frightened—and fear sped her steps as she raced toward the cellar.

She wrenched the door open and a draught of dank air hit her face.

"Rienne!"

"Alright, alright, I'm coming."

As swiftly as she could, trying not to twist her ankle on the barely illuminated stone steps, Rienne hurried down. When she reached the bottom, she rushed to Cal's side.

"What is it? What's wrong? Oh, good gods …"

She fell to her knees, staring at the tall, slim body writhing in Cal's arms. Weirdly flickering light from the ball of Earth force threw Taran's sweat-soaked face into harsh relief. His short brown hair was plastered to his head and he was moaning and twitching. He was also unconscious; Rienne could tell that much, even if she couldn't yet see why.

"See to him, Rienne. I have to shut this thing down."

Cal leaped to his feet and Rienne took his place, wrapping her arms around Taran. As soon as she touched him, she could feel the intense heat radiating from the trembling Journeyman. There was blood on his clothes, some on his skin, yet the only wounds she could see were superficial. Had he been poisoned? Was it some kind of fever? If so, it had taken hold swiftly; he'd been gone less than a day.

"Gods damn it!"

Cal's expletive drew her attention away from the man in her arms. Raising her eyes, she saw him staring at the portway in anger.

"What is it?" Her voice betrayed her fear. Rienne was no Artesan; she didn't understand the power the two men possessed.

"It's resisting. I used the right sequence but it won't close."

"Perhaps you forgot something … ?"

"No. There's something wrong."

Rienne was about to speak again when Taran's body suddenly bucked. She gave a shocked gasp and clutched at his arms. "Cal … !"

"Sod it. Maybe I'm being too subtle. He's always telling me I'm being too subtle … "

"Will you hurry up? I can't hold him much longer."

Taran's moans were increasing in pitch and Rienne suddenly remembered their neighbors. She'd left the cellar door open; what if one of them heard something and came to investigate …

"Cover your ears, Rienne. This might make a bit of noise."

"No, Cal. Remember what Taran said … " But she was too late. Too late even to cover her ears. She didn't see what Cal did but there was a grating squeal and suddenly pressure was building in her head, wind rushing across her face. The pressure became unbearable and she opened her mouth to scream.

Then the portway vanished and the cellar was clear.

She sagged with relief and Cal sank to the floor. There was a moment of blessed silence before a rasping groan dragged their attention back to Taran.

"What's wrong with him?" asked Cal, his dark gaze traveling over Taran's many wounds.

Rienne didn't bother speculating, her priorities lay elsewhere. "Help me get him upstairs. I can't do anything for him down here."

Cal took Taran's shoulders and Rienne grabbed his feet. Together they just managed to lift the Journeyman's dead weight. As his body came up, there was a metallic clang and Rienne saw a glittering rod roll across the floor. The sound made her jump and Cal frowned at the thing, clearly not liking the look of it.

"What in the Void is that?"

"I don't know and I don't care," she gasped. "Get up those stairs Cal, before my strength gives out."

They struggled up the narrow stairs, barely managing to carry Taran to his bed in the little front room. The Journeyman's body was jerking, he was radiating heat and his skin was sheened in sweat.

They laid him down and Cal stood helplessly, staring at his Master's writhing body. "Don't stand there," snapped Rienne. "Get me some hot water and my medicine bag."

By the time Cal returned, she'd removed Taran's filthy, blood-stained clothing. It was as she'd thought; his wounds were not life-threatening. The convulsions, however, alarmed her because she could see no reason for them.

Grabbing her bag, she fumbled through it and emptied the contents of a herb pouch into the hot water Cal had brought. Then she used the infusion to sponge Taran's body. He still showed no signs of waking and his moans were growing louder. Cal stared at her in confusion.

A louder groan escaped Taran and Cal gasped.

"What's happening? Why won't he wake?"

Despite her experience and talents, Rienne could only shake her head.

Suddenly, Taran's body thrashed, nearly casting him to the floor. Cal threw his arms across his Master's body, desperately trying to pin him to the bed.

"Help me, Rienne," he urged. He failed to subdue the frantic movements. Taran's violent lunging dislodged Cal's hold and he had to grapple for the cartwheeling arms. "Please, Rienne, do something."

Although she was nowhere near as strong as her lover, Rienne had dealt with delirious patients before. Swiftly gathering the folds of the rumpled coverlet, she threw it over Taran's body. Together, she and Cal just managed to secure his jerking arms within its clinging folds. They wrapped him, kneeling on either side, securing the coverlet tightly.

Another raw groan escaped Taran's throat. It was a dreadful sound filled with deep distress, and it tore at Rienne's heart.

Cal gave a whimper of fear. "You must have some idea of what's happening to him. Isn't there anything you can do?"

Rienne stared at her lover, gray eyes wide. "I don't think this has a physical cause, Cal. I only deal with the body, not the mind. Isn't that your territory? Can't you … get inside him somehow, see what he's seeing?"

Cal shook his head. "I'm only an Apprentice, Rienne, I'm not that skilled. I can hear him if he speaks to me, but I can't reach out to him. Gods, I feel so useless!"

They both watched with growing fear as perspiration continued to drench Taran's body. Without releasing the coverlet, Rienne used the herb water to cool his face but nothing she did calmed the thrashing. His wounds were being aggravated by the jerking but there was nothing she could do about it.

She frowned. Taran's breathing was becoming ragged and his skin had turned gray. Cal had also noticed and he stared at her. She met his anguished eyes, seeing the blood drain from his face.

"What's happening? He's getting worse. Is he going to … ?"

Suddenly, Taran screamed. The raw sound echoed about the chamber and Rienne's blood froze. Tension abruptly dropped from Taran's muscles and his body collapsed as if boneless.

Cal leaped to his feet, his eyes wild. "What the … ? Why has it stopped? Rienne, is he alright? He isn't moving. Rienne!"

"Shut up, Cal, let me concentrate."

Carefully, aware that her hands were trembling, she placed two fingers on the artery in Taran's neck. Relief washed through her when she felt a faint and frenetic pulse. Nodding to reassure Cal, she took up the herb-infused cloth, sincerely hoping the pungent smell would revive the stricken man.

The silence was loud in the small chamber and Rienne prayed none of their neighbors had heard Taran's cries. She was well aware of the villagers' suspicions and knew that arousing their anger could have serious consequences.

Cal was hovering in concern and she glanced up at him. "It's alright, Cal. His heartbeat's beginning to slow. I think he's coming out of it."

Cal's breath hissed through clenched teeth. He slumped to the bed and passed a hand across his brow, brushing lank hair from his eyes. Rienne saw he had been sweating almost as much as the Journeyman. Anxiously, they both watched Taran's face as their friend struggled slowly back to consciousness.

✢ ✢ ✢ ✢ ✢

Saner images began to displace the madness in Taran's mind. He had remembered red eyes boring into his and a numbing heat pervaded his every sense, as if his body had been scorched. The fire threatened to overwhelm him again, tip him back into the nightmare of his desperate escape. Then coolness touched his brow, soothing his aching mind, and relief washed through him.

He could feel smooth sheets beneath him and thought he was in his own bed. He forced his sore eyes open. The room was dimly lit but familiar. He was in his own house, in his own bed, and he could even tell that his wounds had been tended.

A figure was stooping over him, holding a damp cloth. Taran saw it was Cal, and his dark-skinned Apprentice's face was lined with worry.

Taran tried his voice. "Cal?"

It came out more like a croak than a name. He tried to moisten his lips with no success.

"Taran?" said Cal. "Oh, thank the gods. We thought we'd lost you. Do you want some water?"

Without waiting for an answer, he slipped an arm beneath Taran's shoulders and raised him just enough to sip at the cool water in the cup he held. It was steeped in herbs and Taran really hoped that some of them would dull the dreadful throbbing in his head. He drank gratefully and Cal gently laid him down. Then he strode to the door and Taran heard him calling for Rienne.

The healer entered through a glimpse of firelight, dark hair falling about her shoulders. She bent forward and placed a cool hand on Taran's brow, smoothing back his hair.

"Are you feeling better now? We've been so frantic for you. What on earth happened?"

Taran felt weak, quite unequal to the task of explaining himself, but they deserved no less. They had both tried to dissuade him from going into Andaryon, and now they had probably saved his life.

That thought brought horrific memories flooding back and he turned his eyes to the ceiling, his face burning with shame.

"Gods, but I'm a fool," he groaned. Cal snorted and Taran glanced at him. "I wish I'd taken your advice. I never should have gone."

Cal frowned and Taran paused before adding, "Cal, I killed someone."

He heard Rienne gasp. Cal's dark eyes widened and he slumped to the bed, staring in disbelief.

"How the hell did that happen?"

Taran saw Rienne retreat to the foot of the bed. The healer looked anxious. She might be confident and knowledgeable when dealing with medical matters, but she was shy and uncomfortable when out of her depth.

He tried to reassure her with a smile but her expression didn't lighten. As he pushed himself higher on his pillows, Taran took a steadying breath, trying to force down the humiliation he felt. So much for reversing his run of bad luck, he thought. Now he was a killer as well as a failure.

He forced himself to tell his tale, beginning from when he

had found himself alone among the parched Andaryan hills. Cal and Rienne listened, sympathy and horror in their eyes, not even interrupting when he described the noble's killing. But when he related the tangwyr's attack and his desperate use of the Staff, Cal gasped in understanding.

"So that's why I have the ancestor of all headaches. I thought it couldn't just be the effort of bringing you through the Veils."

Panic engulfed Taran. "You did remember how to close the portway, didn't you?"

Cal nodded. "Of course I did, I followed the procedure you showed me. But … it didn't work quite right. There was … resistance."

"Resistance?" Taran felt himself go cold. What lengths might the noble's companions have gone to in order to find him?

"Don't worry, I handled it," said Cal. Taran shot him a look and he added, "No, it's alright. Really. I dealt with it. But … there might be a problem."

"What problem?"

"Well … you brought something back with you."

Taran groaned, guessing what it was. "Oh gods, it's the Staff. Where is it?"

"Still in the cellar. I didn't like the look of it but we had our hands full trying to stop you battering yourself to death. It was all we could do to get you up the stairs, so we left it. Why did you bring it back?"

Taran flushed, shamed by the terror he had inflicted on his friends. His many previous incompetent attempts at furthering his knowledge were humiliating enough, but none was as destructive as this.

He tried to force down a tide of self-blame but couldn't escape the fact that he had killed an Andaryan noble. No doubt the man's retinue would call it murder, and they would seek vengeance. That, coupled with Taran's theft—however unintentional—of a weapon the Andaryans would surely want back, meant this situation was far from resolved.

In his fear, he ignored Cal's perfectly reasonable question.

"Did you lock the cellar door?"

Cal nodded. "I never leave it, you know that."

There was nothing Taran could do right now. He was weak, he was sore. "I'm not up to dealing with it now," he sighed, "I need to sleep. Maybe I'll feel stronger when I wake. We'll open a new portway, send the thing back. I don't want it here any longer than necessary."

✣ ✣ ✣ ✣ ✣

Rienne watched Taran close his eyes and sink back onto the pillows. Glancing at Cal, she left him sitting on the edge of the bed.

She left the sleeping room, moving through the cottage until she reached the cellar door. There was more to this than Taran had said, she was sure. Something in his eyes … It was fear, she realized, and felt herself go cold.

Standing in front of the cellar's wooden door, she regarded the lock as if it might undo itself. She trusted Cal, yet couldn't resist giving the lock a tug. It was firmly secured, as he had said.

Reassured by that if by nothing else, she returned to the warmth of the living room fire and sat staring into the flames.

Chapter Five

When Taran next awoke, it was daylight. Tentatively, he moved his limbs, relieved to discover only the soreness of his wounds and the aches to be expected after the previous day's exertions. This was a good sign, so he decided to try his powers by reaching out to Cal. Gently, he gathered his will and released a quiet call.

Instantly, he wished he hadn't. White-hot slivers of fire licked his brain and he gasped in shock. Had the Staff done permanent damage?

However, the experiment was obviously successful because he could hear someone thundering down the stairs. Cal burst into the room and, despite his pain, Taran couldn't help but smile. Cal had dashed from his bed, totally naked.

"Taran, what is it? You sounded like you were in pain … ?"

Taran hastened to reassure his Apprentice even though he felt far from happy about his condition.

"Sorry Cal, I didn't mean to startle you. I was testing myself, but I'm obviously not recovered yet. Sorry."

He was sorrier still when a sleepy Rienne came into the room, a blanket clutched around her body against the early chill. Her soft gray eyes were full of anxiety, but when she realized it was a false alarm, she gave Taran a reproachful look and dragged Cal back to bed. Taran sighed and lay back, wondering how long it would be before his mind recovered. He didn't dare think it might not.

Such depressing thoughts eventually forced him to rise. He couldn't go back to sleep and tossing in his bed did him no good. He dressed, his muscles stiff and sore, and left his room. As he crossed the living space, he lit a taper from the banked fire. He approached the cellar door, seeing with satisfaction that it was securely locked. Taking the key from around his neck, he unlocked the door and descended the steps. A musty smell hit his nostrils. He touched the taper to a lamp resting on a nearby shelf and held it up, illuminating the center of the floor.

There lay the abandoned Staff. Setting the lamp down, Taran crouched to examine it.

Even in the warm lamp light there was something cold and vicious about it. His skin crept as he remembered the deadly energy that had flashed from its tip. Memories of blue-green light flared before his eyes and gooseflesh rose on his skin. How had it been made, he wondered? More importantly, why? He felt sure the noble's challenge had something to do this terrible object, yet what he had hoped to accomplish, Taran had no idea. He knew that the Staff was a metaphysical instrument, some kind of amplifier of metaforce, but whether it had uses beyond the offensive, he couldn't tell. He had never heard or read of anything like it before.

He stared—had light just rippled down its surface? Or had his hand trembled, causing the lamp to flare? Suddenly, he didn't want to be here, squatting next to this deadly weapon. He straightened and extinguished the lamp. As he climbed the stairs, he resisted the impulse to run.

✢ ✢ ✢ ✢ ✢

Nearly a week passed before Taran felt strong enough to attempt the Staff's return, despite his growing sense of urgency. Badly frightened by his first painful attempt to use power, he waited two days before accessing his metaforce again. To his great relief, the pain was significantly less. Even so, he waited another day before believing his sore brain had returned to normal. His confidence was only restored after two more days of careful experimentation.

He knew Cal was relieved to see he'd recovered; his Apprentice had been hovering around him even more than Rienne did. Now the two of them stood side-by-side in the cellar, preparing to open another portway.

Despite the risks of opening a breach in the Veils in a populated area, Taran felt safe building the portway in the cellar. He was hidden from prying eyes and the cellar's thick stone walls and deliberately concave floor helped contain the small leakage of Earth element he wasn't yet strong enough to control.

The Staff still lay in the center of the floor. Taran didn't want to touch it again and he had forbidden Cal to do so. His intention was to raise Earth force directly under the Staff and form the portway with the weapon already inside. Once the Veils were breached, he would use his metaforce to push it through to Andaryon. He did worry that it might damage whoever picked it up, but he forced himself to ignore his conscience. He had to get rid of the Staff.

Now the two men stood side-by-side, eyes closed and arms outstretched, palms facing downward to direct the flow of metaforce into the rock of the floor. Quieting his mind, Taran felt deep within until he could access his psyche. Its familiarity surrounded him, flooding him with metaforce.

Turning his attention to Cal, Taran could feel him doing the same. Cal was slower, less confident, but his strength was growing. Soon he was ready and Taran felt him give control of his power to his mentor.

Linked to Cal, Taran isolated the areas of their psyches that were attuned to the element of Earth. His senses sank into the rock beneath his feet, calling to the forces buried there. With a thrill that never failed to move him, he felt the weighty rise as the primal element responded to his call. Trying not to lose concentration, he drew it into the shallow depression in the floor.

Slowly, as he called for more power, sluggish tendrils of Earth force began to lick at his feet.

Opening his eyes, he nodded to Cal. It was his Apprentice's task to mold this energy into a spherical portway, but it had to be done slowly and carefully so no gaps appeared in the construction.

When Cal had completed the portway, he opened his eyes, looking to Taran for approval. Forming portways was his latest achievement and he was proud of his new ability.

Taran smiled. "Well done, Cal."

He anchored the structure within the substance of the Veils so it would remain firm. Pushing aside the slight headache he always felt when expending power, he drew a breath and prepared to activate the portway.

The Staff still lay quiescent; it hadn't reacted to the primal element. But when Taran's metaforce touched the portway, there was a subtle change. Frowning, he glanced at Cal, but his Apprentice hadn't noticed. When he looked back at the portway, his skin began to crawl.

Slowly, ominously, its color was changing. Usually portways were translucent, an opalescent mist shot through with the odd spark of silver or gold, occasionally red. This one, however, was beginning to take on a greenish tinge, much like the color of the Staff. Taran didn't like it one bit.

Either Cal sensed Taran's unease or he finally noticed what was happening. He shot Taran a look. "Why's it doing that?"

Taran bristled at the question. "How should I know? Maybe it's something to do with the Staff. It's an Andaryan artifact, who knows what effect it might have? Let's get this over with, Cal. The sooner that thing's back where it belongs, the happier I'll be."

Cal raised no argument and Taran turned back to the portway. Exerting his will, he drew power to activate it. The shimmer grew hazier, as it should, but the strange color intensified. Taran felt prickling down his spine and tried to ignore it. Gently, he put pressure on the portway. His usual method was to push with his metaforce, sending his power slowly through the Veils until they were breached.

This time however, it didn't work. The surface tension of the portway refused to give. He tried twice before withdrawing, frowning in puzzlement.

"What's wrong with it?" said Cal.

Taran shook his head. "There's resistance. Didn't you say there was resistance when you tried to close the last one?"

"Yes, but it was nothing like this. It didn't turn that weird color, either."

"Alright, here's what we'll do. I'm going to try once more, but if that doesn't work, I'm going to make a sudden thrust and break a hole just large enough to push the weapon through. Then we'll back out and shut the portway. Ready?"

Cal shrugged and nodded.

Taran gathered his strength and pushed down on the portway. It refused to budge. With a swift warning to his Apprentice, he drove a needle of force at one spot in the center of the portway, directly over the Staff.

There was a soundless detonation. Brilliant green light flooded the cellar and Taran and Cal were hurled violently against the walls. They struck forcefully and slumped to the ground, stunned.

Taran was first to gather his wits. Alarmed, he saw the portway was swelling, glowing brighter, building toward an overload. He sprang to his feet in panic: if he lost control of it, the uncontained metaforce could kill them.

"Quickly, Cal," he yelled, dragging at his Apprentice, "help me shut it down!"

Using all of Cal's strength as well as his own, Taran tried to unravel the structure. It resisted him, the green glow deepening every second. "I'm going to break it," he snapped. "Watch yourself."

His heart pounding, he aimed a bolt of their combined power against the portway. With a hideous shriek, it shattered, releasing uncontrolled energy that rebounded around the cellar. Taran and Cal dove to the floor, crouching as low as possible.

When it finally dissipated, they struggled to their feet, the aftershock ringing in their aching ears.

Cal stared around the cellar. "Bloody hell."

Plaster had been ripped from the walls and parts of the ceiling. The depression in the floor was much larger than before, and it was smoking.

The Staff still lay in its place, completely untouched.

Cal glanced at Taran, his dark eyes huge. As the dust of the explosion began to settle on them, Taran shook his head. This was beyond his experience and he spread his hands in hopelessness.

"I think we should leave it, go back upstairs and padlock the door," said Cal. "We need to think this through."

Taran could only agree.

✦ ✦ ✦ ✦ ✦

Heading for her last patient of the day, Rienne walked through the peaceful village. The pale autumn sunlight felt good on her back. She walked easily, her medicine bag light on her shoulder. Its lack of weight reminded her that she was getting low on supplies and she knew she ought to visit the herb seller in Shenton. However, she didn't relish the exhausting ride on the elderly, badly sprung mail coach. Then she smiled, thinking perhaps she could get Cal to go for her.

As she flipped the braid of her long dark hair over her shoulder, she considered how lucky she was. A responsible trained healer of twenty-five, she had found her vocation as well as her true love. Growing into a slim, attractive young woman out of an awkward childhood—she was the youngest child with four demanding older brothers—gray-eyed Rienne had eventually discovered a talent for healing. Once the long years of study and training were behind her, she had searched for a town or village lacking a local healer. Luck had brought her to Hyecombe, where she had met Cal. Just over a year later, she felt settled. She and Cal intended to marry one day, Taran had offered them a home, and Rienne was firmly established as Hyecombe's healer.

Life was looking good.

She passed the bakery and emerged onto her own street. A small hamlet, Hyecombe only had two streets, but it did boast a tavern. Rienne made her way inside, pausing on the cool flagged floor to let her eyes adjust to the gloom.

The main room was warm and smelled of smoke from the huge fireplace. Rienne threaded her way through the empty tables, making for the bar. As she passed the door to the little private room she saw a group of men inside, talking in low tones over jugs of malty ale. Clad in combat leathers with swords by their sides, they were obviously Kingsmen.

She frowned, wondering what they were doing here. The military didn't often visit Hyecombe. Before the civil war nine years ago, each local lord had responsibility for his own demesne and small villages like Hyecombe were protected by their own farmhands and laborers. However, once Prince Elias Rovannon quelled the uprising and killed those responsible for murdering his father, King Kandaran, he'd been determined not to suffer the same fate. So he changed the old order, and Lordsmen became Kingsmen. Garrisons were established throughout every province and trained swordsmen loyal to the Crown relieved farmhands and laborers of their protection duties.

Now, each village had an appointed elder initially responsible for keeping order. Any issues too weighty for the elder to deal with were referred to the local garrison, but Rienne knew there had been no incidents in Hyecombe. So why had the Kingsmen come?

Remembering why she was there, she put them out of her mind. "Paulus?" she called, slipping her bag from her shoulder.

"In here, Rienne," came the muffled reply.

She walked through the door at the side of the bar into the storeroom behind. She smiled a greeting. "Evening, Paulus."

The storeroom smelled thickly of hops and malt, ale and old wood. The tavern-keeper, a balding man in his middle fifties with missing front teeth and work-roughened hands, looked up from the barrel he was scrubbing. His dour expression lightened as he saw her.

"And a good evening to you, Rienne. How are you today?"

He straightened, trying to suppress a grunt, but there was no fooling Rienne. She set her bag on the floor.

"I'm fine, Paulus, which is more than can be said for you. That back looks bad. It's been painful again, hasn't it? You haven't been following my advice."

He looked sheepish. "How do you do that? Been taking lessons from that young man of yours?"

She wasn't to be sidetracked. "Never mind Cal, where's that assistant I told you to get?"

Paulus ducked his head. "I've not found one yet. I can't really afford to pay one, not on the amount of customers I get. Mind you, if I had more like that lot out there, it might be a different story."

Rienne's skilful fingers explored the sore muscles in Paulus' back. His hard-faced wife had left him over a year ago and he had been running the tavern alone ever since. Her acid comments and sour face were missed by no one—least of all her husband—but her strong arms and capable hands had at least relieved some of the burden.

She stopped probing and turned to rummage in her bag. "What are they doing here?"

He grimaced, massaging the small of his back. "There's been some trouble farther south apparently and they've been sorting it out. Gods, but they can drink."

Rienne frowned, a packet of herbs in her hand. "What sort of trouble?" She hoped they weren't going to be overrun by brigands. The High King's forces were generally quite successful at keeping order but there were always bands of brigands around and they favored remote hamlets like Hyecombe.

Paulus shook his head. "From what I've overheard, it sounds like outlanders." Beckoning Rienne closer, he lowered his voice, confiding, "They've been talking about them being from beyond … you know … the Veils."

Rienne smiled. Despite Albia's history of occasional attacks by raiders from other realms, most people refused to believe such beings existed. If they were talked about at all it was in whispers, as if speaking of them might make them more real.

Rienne had no time for ignorance or prejudice. Knowing how interested Taran would be, she tried to find out more. "Have they said what type of outlanders?"

Paulus grimaced. Gossip was his trade as much as ale; customers who kept their voices low and their business close to their chests did him no favors no matter how much they spent.

"I only heard snippets as I served their ale. But one of 'em mentioned demons, I'm sure of it."

Rienne stared at him. Andaryans were indistinguishable from Albians except by their eyes. Their alien, cat-like pupils, almost colorless irises, and warlike ways caused most folk to refer to them as demons.

"Andaryans? Are you certain?" She knew that at one time Andaryans had raided freely through the Veils. Soon after her arrival in Hyecombe, Taran had told her that around twenty years ago, a bargain had been struck with them and their raiding had greatly decreased.

"That's what I heard," insisted the barkeep, warming to his tale. "Sounds like they were pretty vicious, too. That's why these lads were sent to sort it out. They're a crack unit from that garrison up near the Downs." He caught her eye, looking at her strangely.

"You know, Rienne, I've heard it said there's a witch in command up there."

She laughed in his face. Paulus might be a tavern-keeper and peddler of gossip, but he was also Hyecombe's elder and respected as such. His status as the area's largest business owner lent him a certain authority, which he cultivated. He was not usually given to such fanciful statements.

"Oh really, Paulus. Come on, you know who I live with. I don't fall for stories like that."

But Paulus remained serious and the odd look never left his eye. "I mean it, Rienne. If you have to fight demons, you want to follow someone who knows their ways."

Rienne was prepared to grant that point, she supposed it made sense. However, she knew from Taran's desperate searches that there were few, if any, Artesans left now, besides him and Cal. He would certainly know of any who were so close by. She presumed that was what Paulus meant—the terms "witch" and "Artesan" were interchangeable in most people's minds.

She dismissed the barkeep's gossip. She couldn't imagine that a company of Kingsmen, hard-bitten, rough and uncompromising as they usually were, would be willing to follow an officer who possessed the generally despised Artesan gift. It was far more likely that their commander was simply an experienced and effective leader.

"Well," she said, "whoever they've been fighting, I hope they got rid of them. I have enough to do around here without treating people wounded by raiders. Now Paulus, I want you to take these herbs. Infuse two pinches in warm water and drink the infusion twice a day, morning and evening. And find yourself an assistant, even if it's only a boy who can mop floors and scrub barrels. Otherwise, your back will seize up completely, and then where will you be?"

Smiling nervously, he took the packet of herbs. If her prediction came true, he would be in danger of losing his livelihood. He passed her a few coins.

"Thank you Rienne, I'll see what I can do. Will you be in tonight?"

She tucked the coins into her bag. "Probably," she said. "The boys usually like a drink at the end of a long week."

✦ ✦ ✦ ✦ ✦

Taran heard the cottage door open. Cal jumped up from his seat by the fire to relieve Rienne of her bag. While she went upstairs to change, Taran made fellan, a dark, aromatic and bitter drink brewed from the seeds of the fellan plant. He handed her a cup when she returned and she sat down next to Cal.

"Well?" she said. "Did you have any success returning that weapon?"

"We tried," said Cal, "but it didn't go as we planned. Something went wrong with the portway and it blew up in our faces."

"Blew up?" echoed Rienne. "What does that mean exactly?"

"It means don't go down the cellar," said Taran. "A lot of plaster's come down and it's a real mess."

"You mean it literally blew up? Were you hurt?" She looked them over, relieved to find no sign of injury.

"Not physically, just a bit of backlash," said Taran. "Nasty headache, that sort of thing."

"I've got willow extract, if you need some," she offered.

"Thanks Rienne, but it's nearly gone now, which is more than I can say for the Staff."

Watching the sombre expression darken Taran's face, Rienne remained silent. She was out of her depth. They weren't injured, so she had nothing to offer.

Cal seemed to sense Rienne's unease. "Are you any closer to deciding what we should do?" he asked Taran, even though they had puzzled it through while waiting for Rienne. "I don't fancy building another portway around it, that's for sure. What about moving it, building one and then carrying it through?"

"If you're volunteering, be my guest," snorted Taran. "The last thing I want to do is touch the thing again. Something about it seems to be making the Veils react, but I have no idea what it is. I don't know what to suggest. My father has nothing in his notes to cover situations like this. As far as I can tell, he never came across such a thing. And there's no one else we can ask."

He sat with his eyes downcast. As if trying to lighten the tension, Rienne said, "I saw Paulus earlier. He's got a company of Kingsmen at the tavern, on their way back from dealing with some outlander raiding somewhere farther south. He said he'd heard them mention demons."

Far from relieving the tension, her words made Taran stiffen.

"What? Andaryans raiding through the Veils again? But what about the Pact?"

Although he'd known little enough, Taran's father had told his son about the agreement brokered to stop Andaryans raiding wholesale into Albia. Apparently, some twenty years ago, a Senior Master—the highest of the eight Artesan ranks—had somehow managed to convince Andaryan nobles to curb their aggression. Raiding still went on, but it was mainly perpetrated by slavers from Relkor, the Third Realm. Rienne's news was bad indeed if Andaryan raids were starting again.

Taran felt a peculiar cold sensation run the length of his spine.

"I don't know anything for sure," said Rienne hurriedly. "All I know is that Paulus overheard the swordsmen talking and thought they had mentioned demons."

"Dear gods, I hope not," said Taran.

His heart suddenly turned over and he swore. "Cal, what if they're looking for the Staff?"

Cal's dark eyes went wide with fear.

A note of dread in his voice, Taran said, "I need to talk to Paulus, see if he overheard anything else."

Chapter Six

The early dark of an autumn evening covered the fields. It was broken briefly by an eerie shimmer appearing over newly turned earth. There were no eyes abroad to see it or the band of riders emerging with cautious stealth from its depths. Illuminated by the swirling light, their horses' breath stirred the chilled air. Then the controlling mind released the structure and the shimmer vanished.

"Right, lads," came the husky voice of their commander, "you heard what his Grace said—maximum chaos. Hit 'em hard, keep 'em guessing. Kill any who get in your way but don't hang around. And don't forget, lose touch with either Race or me and you won't get back. His Grace won't wait for you to catch up. Let's go."

The thirty-strong band followed its commander toward the edge of the field, tracing the line of its boundary hedge. Lights shone from the houses in the distance and the horses strained at their bits as they caught their riders' tension. Well trained and obedient—it didn't do to cross Commander Verris—the men curbed their restive mounts, waiting for the order to charge.

Soon they reached the outskirts of the hamlet, still unseen. Slit-pupiled eyes scanned the gloom; teeth gleamed in the lamp light as lips parted in predatory smiles. Verris took them as close as he dared before forming them into prearranged groups. He intended to cause as much panic and confusion as possible; if some of the villagers were killed, that would only add to the havoc.

He checked his men—they were ready. He took a small flint from his pouch and dismounted, then kindled a small flame in the earthenware bowl he had brought. He passed it around to the men and they each dipped a tarred branch into the bowl. Once the torches were lit, Verris tossed the bowl aside and remounted. He grinned in anticipation as he raised his arm, gave a cry, and released his eager band.

With whoops and yells, making as much noise as possible, the raiders set heels to their horses and raced into the hamlet, tossing firebrands into thatch, barns and vegetable gardens. The noise and the torches brought the villagers pouring from their homes, desperate to douse the flames. Any villager unfortunate enough to stumble into the path of a raider was cut down, but, obedient to their orders, the invaders didn't actively seek victims. Chaos was their goal and chaos they caused.

Unfortunately, the raid didn't go as smoothly as planned. Alerted by other attacks in the province, the local garrison had sent patrols to watch. Normally, they wouldn't have stood a chance of countering such a random raid, but as fortune would have it—or misfortune—a small unit of Kingsmen had been offered billeting by the hamlet's elder. Aroused by the noise and trained to react swiftly, they raced for their horses and prepared to repel the outlanders.

From his vantage of safety, Verris yelled for a retreat. Not all his men heard the call and he sacrificed them to the swordsmen. *Serves them right*, he thought as he galloped away, the rest hot on his heels. Their deaths might teach the others to pay closer heed.

As he yelled at his men to close up, Verris raced for the open fields where they could lose their pursuers in the dark.

✣ ✣ ✣ ✣ ✣

After supper, Taran, Cal and Rienne walked to the inn. It had no name as it was the only tavern in the area, drawing its clientele from the surrounding farmlands and the village. Because of this, it was only full at the end of the week, and this was when Taran felt most comfortable. Folks from the outlying farmsteads were not as familiar with his nature as the villagers, and he and Cal could relax with their ale.

Paulus, who had been a good friend of Taran's father and knew very well what they were, had a philosophical outlook. He took their custom happily, knowing their coin was as real as anyone else's. He also often accepted Taran's help behind the bar and the wage he paid supplemented the small amount of gold Taran had inherited from his father. Taran's strength also helped relieve Paulus' back.

They entered the large, smoky common room with its warming smells of food, and found a vacant table by the wall. The barkeep came over as soon as he saw them; it was early yet and he still had time to chat. He brought their drinks with him—mugs of dark, mellow ale for Taran and Cal and mulled wine for Rienne. They smiled appreciatively as he set the tray on the table and sat down.

Taran opened the conversation.

"Rienne said you had a company of Kingsmen here, Paulus. Are they still around?"

"No," he said, "they moved out earlier. Got word by messenger of more trouble, they said, though I don't know where."

"And you don't know any more about them other than where they came from?"

Paulus flicked a glance at Rienne. "No, I don't. What's your interest in them?"

Taran hesitated. He knew Paulus well—the man seemed more like an uncle than a friend—and he'd often listened to Taran's tales of woe when some experiment or other went wrong. But this latest problem was more serious and the Journeyman didn't want the details spread around the village. He knew about Paulus' love of gossip and if his neighbors learned that he had an Andaryan weapon concealed in his house and that its rightful owners just might come looking for it, he and his friends would be forced to leave quickly. However, if he wanted more information, he was going to have to tell Paulus something. He made a decision.

"Would you mind if we waited behind tonight? There's something I'd like to tell you but it had better be in private."

"If you're prepared to buy beer all night, I'll listen to anything," said Paulus.

"I'll help behind the bar, if you like."

Paulus grinned. "Well, I'll not turn down the offer. Just don't scare away any customers."

Taran made a face. "I'll be over when I've finished my ale."

He was as good as his word and worked hard behind the bar. The tavern grew crowded as many people seemed to have seen or heard of the Kingsmen passing through and wanted to compare theories with their neighbors. Taran heard all sorts of speculation, but no one knew anything for certain.

The talk had long since turned to other topics, the rumors too insubstantial to hold the drinkers' attention for long, when a sudden commotion turned all heads. The door was thrown wide with a crash and two men staggered in, one supporting the other. Both were obviously down to the dregs of their strength.

"Raiders. We've seen raiders!" rasped one of them, his words shocking the crowd into momentary silence.

It didn't last long. Chairs scraped back as people surged to their feet, some running to help the two men, others bolting out the door.

"It's Jaspen and Dyler," exclaimed Paulus. Taran only vaguely recognized them; they were from one of the remoter farmsteads.

Those who had run outside returned, confirming there was no immediate sign of raiders. The two men had been helped into chairs by the fire and Rienne's competent tones cut through the villagers' urgent questions.

"Be quiet, give them some space. Paulus, can you bring some brandy?"

When Paulus produced a bottle of brandy, Rienne made each man take a healthy swallow.

"Leave them be," she snapped as the crowd once more clamored for answers. Used to obeying her commands, they subsided but stayed close, forming a loose ring about the two men.

Once the brandy had taken effect, Rienne asked, "Do you feel up to talking now?"

One of them, a thin, lined man with faded blue eyes and calloused, work-worn hands, glanced fearfully up at her.

"We was attacked."

"What, raiders attacked your farm?" demanded Paulus. "Are Tula and the girls alright?"

The man shook his head.

"No, they wasn't after the farm. They wasn't even on our land." His voice was hoarse with exhaustion and he took another swallow of brandy. "They was bein' chased by a group of Kingsmen. Me and Jas was goin' home through the fields when we heard 'em comin' from over Brookbarn way. There was about twenty of 'em, all ridin' hell for leather, and the Kingsmen was comin' up behind 'em. We dodged for some trees quick as we could but the demons"—there was a sharp intake of breath from the rapt crowd—"they had seen the trees, too, and they headed straight for us. The Kingsmen, they chased in after 'em and caught up to some of the stragglers. There was a lot of screamin' and clashin' of swords, and some of the demons got cut down. Jas, here, he got caught in the thick of it and one of the dead demons crashed right on top of him. He was pretty well stunned and I 'ad to push the brute off 'im before we could get away."

"What happened to the raiders?" asked Taran. "Where did they go?"

Dyler shot him a look. "How should I know? We didn't wait to see. I hope our lads massacred the lot of 'em."

On hearing he'd been stunned, Rienne took a closer look at the silent Jaspen. A worried look in her eye, she asked Paulus to give the two men beds for the night.

"You can't expect them to make their way home after this," she said. "Come on, someone help me get them upstairs. They need peace and quiet, not all these questions. And bring that brandy bottle."

A couple of villagers came forward to help the two men stand. Taran would have helped, too, but Rienne flashed him a deterring glance.

He and Cal went back to their table. The evening had been drawing to a close before the two farmers burst in. Now Paulus shooed the rest of his customers out. Once they had gone, he sat down next to Taran and took a healthy swallow of his own brandy.

"That's a bit close for my liking," he said. "We'll have to start sleeping with scythes by our beds if this carries on. Kingsmen won't always be there to chase the demons off."

When neither Cal nor Taran commented, he shot them a narrow-eyed look. "Please tell me this has nothing to do with what you wanted to talk to me about."

Rienne came back down the stairs and Taran glanced at her questioningly. "They're both sleeping," she said. "They should be alright by morning."

He turned back to the barkeep. "I don't know for sure, Paulus, but it's a very strong coincidence if not."

He told his tale and Paulus listened quietly, sipping his brandy until Taran had finished. Then he shook his head.

"I really don't like the sound of this. I never heard the like from your father, that's for sure. A dead noble, a dangerous weapon you can't return, and now these raids? This is serious stuff, my boy. If you're prepared to admit you're out of your depth, then you need help."

"Well, yes, I know that," agreed Taran, "but where can I go? You know the trouble my father and I had trying to find other

Artesans. There aren't any, at least not in Loxton province. Who could I turn to about something as serious as this?"

Paulus hesitated before replying and eyed Taran oddly. "I told Rienne today that I'd heard rumors about a witch being in command of the garrison near the Downs."

"And I told you what we think of tales like that," snorted Rienne.

"But what if it's true?" Before any of them could respond, he stared pointedly at Taran. "What if it's someone like you?"

Taran shook his head. "It can't be. After all these years of searching, don't you think I'd know if there were other Artesans nearby? And even if I'd failed to find them, my father would have known. He'd have told me."

Paulus wagged a finger. "Amanus didn't know everything, my boy. Too many swordsmen have come through here saying the same thing for me to discount it completely. But even if it's not true, isn't this Staff a military matter? If the demons are looking for it, there are likely to be more raids. The garrison ought to know."

"I suppose so," said Taran. "But even if you're right, we can hardly go marching up to a garrison of Kingsmen and say, 'Hey, does anyone here know anything about Andaryan weapons?' You know what they're like, they would laugh in our faces. We'd either be locked up as troublemakers or thrown out before we got a chance to explain."

"Well, now," said Paulus, "I just might be able to help you there. I've never told you this because I was asked to keep it quiet, but I happen to know a young chap in that garrison. His name's Captain Tamsen. From what he told me, his commanding officer is quite interested in outlanders. Since you've asked me, my advice is to go there and ask to see Major Sullyan. Tell them I sent you; that should get you in. After that, it's up to you."

Taran held Paulus' gaze. He felt sure the barkeep was holding something back, but he couldn't think what or why. After a short pause, and because he lacked any other plan, he said, "Where is this garrison?"

"Only a couple of days' ride away," said Paulus. "Take the north road to Canstown then the Tolk turning. Someone up there can tell you exactly where it is, I'm told it's well known."

Thanking Paulus, they left and hurried home. The news of a raid so close to Hyecombe had made them all nervous and Taran bolted the door securely. He was feeling confused and uncomfortable and wanted to think through Paulus' advice. Leaving Cal and Rienne to their fellan, he went to bed.

✛ ✛ ✛ ✛ ✛

Early the next morning, Taran was joined in the cellar by Cal. Together, they stared at the damage to the walls and ceiling. The Staff still lay innocently on the floor, gleaming in the light of the lamp.

"Have you thought any more about what Paulus said?" asked Cal.

"Of course," snorted Taran. "Haven't you?"

"If we go to the garrison, we'll have to take Rienne with us. I'm not leaving her here with the Staff."

"Would you leave her if we took it with us?"

"Perhaps. Do you think we can?"

Taran shrugged. "I suppose we'll have to try. I can't say I'm keen to handle it, but maybe we can rig up some kind of pack to carry it and use the wash tongs to lift it. That might work."

"Have you made up your mind to go?"

Taran glanced at him. "Yes, I suppose I have. It can't do any harm and last night's shock has made it more urgent than ever. Has Rienne left on her rounds yet?"

"She went about ten minutes ago. She'll be out 'til noon, I think. She asked me to go to Shenton for some medical supplies. The mail coach should be here in an hour."

"We'd better get on with it, then."

It was Cal's suggestion to fetch the wash tongs from the scullery before finding a pack to hold the Staff. As he sensibly pointed out, if the thing resisted being moved, they would be wasting their time on a pack. Taran took a thick pair of leather gloves with the tongs.

"Do you really think you'll need those?" Cal asked.

"How should I know? I just remember what it felt like to hold the Staff the first time and I don't want to take any chances."

After locking the cottage door against casual visitors, they went back into the cellar. Not that visitors were likely, but Rienne might return early and Taran didn't want her around while they experimented with the Staff.

He positioned himself at the side of the depression in the floor. Once he had donned the leather gloves, he took the tongs from Cal. They looked not half long enough. He decided to poke the Staff with them first to test for a reaction. He glanced up at his Apprentice, who was watching from the opposite wall.

"I think we'd better be shielded," he said.

Cal nodded and Taran sensed him reaching for his psyche, calling a protective flow of metaforce around him. Taran did the same.

"I'm ready," said Cal.

Taking a deep breath, Taran leaned carefully over the pit, tongs extended.

As the tongs neared the Staff, it began to glow. Taran frowned; he hadn't expected it to react. Tentatively, he extended his arm and the closer he got to the Staff, the brighter it glowed.

Suddenly, he lost his nerve and withdrew his arm. The glow faded.

"That didn't look promising," said Cal.

His pessimism goaded Taran. He decided to take a chance and just pick the thing up. Maybe it was meant to glow? The memories of his ordeal in Andaryon were hazy at best and he couldn't remember if the Staff had been glowing the first time he'd held it.

"I'm going to pick it up," he said, reaching out again. Swiftly he rolled the Staff into the tong's wooden jaws and picked it up.

✠ ✠ ✠ ✠ ✠

When the lurching, spinning darkness began to lift, Taran's first impression was that he was too close to the fire. His skin was burning and he tried to move away from the heat. He felt hands on him, holding him down, and he struggled, because he really was too close to that fire.

Abruptly, he heard loud voices. Someone was yelling in his ear. He tried to shout, "Shut up," but his throat wouldn't open. Dispassionately, he thought he sounded like a strangled pig.

Then a large quantity of icy water dumped over him and the shock made him yell. He opened his eyes and found both Rienne and Cal staring down at him, she with an empty bucket in her hands.

"That's better," he heard Cal say. "I think he's coming back."

Rienne said, "Thank the gods. I really didn't know what else to do."

The words had no impact on Taran. His head was ringing and his ears were full of water. He tried to rise and felt Rienne holding him up.

"Taran, can you hear me?" he heard her ask. He considered that, not really sure what it meant.

"He's not fully conscious," she said, her voice sounding oddly muffled. "Get him into bed, Cal, and get these wet things off him. I'll give him something to help him sleep and perhaps he'll be better when he wakes."

Taran was aware of being carried to his room and couldn't help wondering why Cal had turned white. His skin, hair, clothes, even his eyelashes were white. Considering how dark the young man's skin usually was, this struck Taran as irresistibly funny. He tried to laugh, the strangled pig sounding even worse. But the effort was too much and he slipped into darkness.

✤ ✤ ✤ ✤ ✤

Cal helped Rienne strip Taran's clothing. The healer wrapped Taran in the coverlet and gathered his sodden clothes, which were as smothered in white plaster dust as Cal was.

"Here," she said, wrinkling her nose, "take these to the scullery."

Cal took the sopping bundle and walked unsteadily out of the room. Rienne stayed a moment, looking down at Taran. She was genuinely fond of him and hated seeing him like this.

Sighing, she left him and made her way to the scullery. The last thing she wanted to do today was wash a load of chalky clothes, but it seemed she had little choice. On the way, she passed the door to the collapsed and ruined cellar where Cal and Taran had been trapped for two hours. Her lips pursed as she thought how fortunate the two men had been in their escape.

When she entered the tiny scullery, she saw Cal slumped in a heap on the floor, tears welling from his eyes.

"Oh, Cal." She flew to his side, holding him quietly until the tears subsided. She took his face in her hands and made him look at her.

"This has gone far enough, do you hear? If the Hodgekisses next door hadn't heard that ceiling come down, I don't know what might have happened to you. Paulus had to break the door down. The cellar's a ruin and the floor up here's none too safe, either. What on earth did you think you were doing?"

"Trying to move the Staff," mumbled Cal. "We were going to take it to the garrison."

"Oh, you're going then, are you? Well, for one thing, that damned Staff isn't going anywhere, it's totally buried. And for another, the two of you are going nowhere without me. Not that either of you is fit to travel at the moment. Look at you, you're covered in plaster dust. I'd better heat some water for a bath."

She bustled off, leaving Cal in a heap. How, she wondered in exasperation, had they gotten themselves into this?

Chapter Seven

Later that evening, Taran woke from his drugged sleep. As he came to, it struck him that these disasters were happening far too frequently. Enveloped in shame, he decided enough was enough.

Tears formed in his eyes—he had put his friends in terrible danger. Before, he'd been a fool and failure. Now he was also a murderer, and his remorse over the noble's killing was becoming inextricably linked to how he felt about his powers. It seemed that every time he tried to increase his knowledge, he made more disastrous mistakes. Break his heart though it might, those around him would be better off if he renounced his Artesan powers altogether.

And there was still the frightening and very real possibility that he was personally responsible for the resurgence of outlander raids, whether in retaliation for the noble's death or in response to the theft of the Staff. Probably both. Taran's heart raced in fear as images of dreadful repercussions crashed around his aching skull.

He was still wallowing in the depths of self-pity when Rienne came softly into the room, carrying a bowl of something hot and savory. She saw the look in his eyes and gave a low cry.

"Oh, Taran, are you in pain?"

"It's only my pride that hurts," he muttered, his voice still scratchy with dust. He coughed and she brought the bowl of soup to him. She helped him sit up and passed him the bowl and spoon.

Cal followed her in and sat with him while he ate. "We've got to go to the military now, Taran."

The Journeyman nodded, although he had no hope of finding help.

"I'm sorry I got you both into this," he said. "I wouldn't blame you if you wanted nothing more to do with me after that last little fiasco."

"Little?" snorted Rienne. "You call a collapsed cellar little?"

Taran stared at her. "Collapsed? What, completely? What about the Staff?"

"Buried under feet of rubble," said Cal. "It took me ages to dig you out and then we were trapped until Rienne came home and let the ladder down. The stairs are gone."

Taran groaned—it was getting worse. "I'm so sorry," he said again, a catch in his voice. "What a mess."

Rienne chose to take him literally. "Nothing a bolted cellar door and a good broom won't take care of. But that'll have to wait 'til morning. You never got my supplies either, did you Cal?"

In spite of himself, Taran chuckled. "Oh, Rienne, I can see why he loves you so much."

She blushed. "Get away with you." She removed the empty soup bowl. "I'll get you some drinks."

They spent the rest of the evening discussing their next move. Taran decided the cellar should be made as safe as possible and left locked up. It wasn't as if the Staff was going anywhere, buried under all that rubble, and he was fairly sure the Andaryans couldn't know exactly where it was. If he was right, the village was as safe as anywhere else at the moment.

Rienne adamantly refused to stay behind and Taran's suggestion that she move in with a neighbor was met with a sour response.

She said she would make arrangements for her patients to see one of the healers in Shenton; she had no cases that needed continuous attention.

"Besides," she added darkly, "the way you two have been behaving lately, you'll need me."

Taran couldn't dispute it and Cal's relief was obvious.

He decided they would leave the day after next, as horses had to be purchased for Cal and Rienne. Taran had his father's gelding stabled at the livery and it was a good beast, but it couldn't carry all three of them. Rienne still wanted to make the trip to Shenton, both to restock her supplies and also to arrange medical coverage for the village. Cal elected to go with her, leaving Taran to organize supplies.

The Journeyman felt so much better for making a positive decision. That had always been his father's domain and Taran missed his confident, commanding ways. Amanus hadn't thought much of his son's abilities—and had pointedly said so on many occasions—but he had always been there. Taran had been deeply affected by the recent disastrous events, and the mere thought of finding someone to advise him lightened his mood.

He was still apprehensive about the garrison's reaction to his tale, but he wouldn't look that far ahead just yet.

✤ ✤ ✤ ✤ ✤

Despite his unease, Taran felt a certain excitement the following day. He hadn't traveled since he met Cal a year and a half ago.

He spent the morning at the livery looking at the mounts for sale. He finally selected two that looked sturdy and biddable. Rienne was a fair rider but Cal was nervous of horses and would need a steady mount.

Using some of his small store of gold, he paid for the animals and their gear. He arranged for them to be ready, along with his own bay gelding, by mid-morning the following day. Then he strolled over to have a bite of lunch with Paulus while he waited for the mail coach's return. As he had hoped, Paulus agreed to keep an eye on the cottage while they were gone. In return, Taran helped behind the bar.

Paulus expressed his concern over the incident with the cellar and offered to get some men together to clear it out while Taran was away.

"I don't think that's a good idea," said Taran hastily. "Thanks for the offer, Paulus, I really appreciate it, but apart from the trouble you'd have convincing anyone to go in there with you, the Staff's still buried under the rubble. I'd rather it remained undisturbed until we get back."

"Not dangerous, is it?" asked Paulus.

"Not in itself, no," said Taran, knowing this was probably a lie, "but it's something that needs … careful handling by the right people, if you know what I mean."

"Probably not, but I'll take your word for it. Alright, I'll see that no one disturbs anything while you're away."

"Thanks, Paulus. You're a good friend and I won't forget it."

The mail coach passed through the village around mid-afternoon. Taran met Rienne and Cal as they jumped down from the elderly carriage and waved to the coachman. They were loaded down with bags and supplies and at Taran's dubious look, Rienne said, "This is only essential stuff, Taran. You don't think I'd let us go on a trip with only the clothes on our backs, do you?"

"No, of course not," said Taran. He relieved her of a couple of bags and rolled his eyes at Cal, who grinned.

Back at the house, Rienne distributed what she had purchased. She'd bought spacious saddlebags for each of them and a spare to hold food. Taran was amazed how much she managed to fit into each bag, folding and stowing everything neatly. He and Cal let her be, as she seemed plenty competent with the piles of clothes, food and medical supplies.

Cal helped Taran prepare a meal while Rienne completed the packing. Once they had eaten, they gathered around the fire with fellan. The day had been warm and pleasant but the evenings were growing chilly. Rienne made them go over what they were each taking one last time until even she could think of nothing else they might need.

"Just as well," commented Cal, "or the poor horses will hardly be able to move."

"Don't exaggerate," said Rienne. "You'll be glad for what we're taking at some point, you'll see."

They speculated about what might happen when they reached the garrison, but as they only had Paulus' mysterious hints to guide them, it was pointless. Taran was glad to abandon the topic as thinking about the Staff only raised anxieties and bad memories. The prospect of travel had helped keep them at bay and he was relieved when Rienne suggested they retire.

✦ ✦ ✦ ✦ ✦

The next morning was bright and chilly. Taran took a last look at the bolted and padlocked cellar door, collected his gear, and followed his friends into the street. He closed the hastily repaired cottage door and turned the key in the lock. The drapes had been drawn to keep out prying eyes. Paulus met them outside the tavern and accepted the key from Taran.

"Best of luck," he said. "Don't forget, ask for Major Sullyan. If that doesn't get you in, ask to see Captain Tamsen. He ought to remember me. And don't worry about the house, I'll see it's alright."

"Thanks, Paulus. I'll owe you a good few nights behind the bar for this," said Taran. He was desperately hoping the village would be safe from raiders while he was gone.

"Don't think I won't collect," laughed the barkeep. "Go on, be off with you."

Taran led the way to the livery where their mounts were waiting. Stablelads helped arrange the saddlebags and held the horses' heads while they mounted.

Cal eyed his piebald cob suspiciously. "I hope this thing's reliable."

"Quiet as a lamb, sir," said one of the boys, grinning as he held the bridle. "Usually ridden by an old lady to visit her daughter in Shenton."

"I've heard that one before," muttered Cal, taking the reins. The stocky little cob did seem very steady and gradually Cal relaxed.

Taran set a gentle pace, following the high road north toward Canstown. It was a major route and well traveled, so the road was in good repair. There were other travelers on the road and once, in the distance, they even saw a Roamerling camp.

'Roamerling' was a derogatory Albian term for the nomadic people of the First Realm, Endomir. To escape their homeland's ferociously icy winters, these dark-skinned wanderers haunted the other realms during the cold months. Traveling in their close-knit family groups, they peddled herbs and cures, and the favors of their sloe-eyed girls. They were shunned and treated with scorn by Albians during daylight hours and trusted by no one. Under the anonymity of night, however, villagers would often visit the noisy circle of wagons and firelight to part with their gold and indulge in furtive pleasures.

Taran saw Cal watching the nomads with a wistful eye. "Do you miss the time you spent with the Roamerlings before I met you, Cal?"

Cal smiled briefly, his teeth very white against his dark skin. "Not really. I'm still grateful they took me in after my family threw me out, but I knew I couldn't stay with them forever. I did learn some interesting skills from them, though."

Taran grinned back. "Which skills are you talking about? Pick-pocketing or playing the whistle?"

Cal patted the silver longwhistle in his pocket. It never left him and the haunting tunes he produced often entertained his friends. "One resulted in the other," he laughed. "Thank goodness you found me that night, Taran. You saved me from a life of petty crime."

They rode on, leaving the Roamerling camp behind. At midday, they stopped for a snack, and then continued on for the better part of the afternoon until reaching the major crossroads that would take them to Tolk. This was a much larger city, laying far to the west. As usual, at a crossing of the ways like this, people were camped: traders and travelers like themselves, all taking the opportunity to hear other wayfarers' gossip.

"I think we'll stop for a breather, too," said Taran. "You never know, we might hear something interesting."

They dismounted and tied the horses to a railing. They joined the cluster of people sitting or standing under a copse of trees. Judging by the trampled ground, this was a popular rest site.

Their fellow travelers hailed them, eager for news. Taran and his friends traded inconsequential village gossip, careful not to mention their real business. Most of what they heard concerned the raids; everyone was talking about the unrest. One man even knew of a pitched battle that had occurred recently near his village. More importantly, he also knew the raiders were definitely Andaryans.

"Crack fighting unit they sent to sort it out," he said, relishing the tale. "From that garrison to the northwest, they were. Fighting was very fierce, by all accounts, and I heard the demons were unusually savage. Managed to wound one of the garrison's senior officers and kill a few of his lads, although eventually our boys ran off the demons. Thank the gods."

"How long ago was this?" asked Taran, as the flesh of his arms tingled ominously.

"A few days," replied the man. "Been any fighting over your way?"

Once all the stories had been told, Taran thought to ask whether there were any inns on the road. Only one, he was told, about two hours farther. He drew the others away, hoping to reach the inn before nightfall. It was growing colder as the afternoon wore on and he felt the need for a warm fire and supper. The news he had heard had unsettled him badly and he rode in troubled silence.

When they finally reached the inn, it was very unlike their tavern at home. Obviously a major stopping point for wayfarers, it was much larger than they were used to, having two or three common rooms and a couple of small private rooms. It also had plenty of rooms to rent and horse stables. They gave their horses to a couple of young stablehands and followed the aging landlord, who introduced himself as Milo, to the rooms they had rented for the night. After dumping their bags, they freshened up and trooped down to the commons for some roasted meat stew and some ale. Once replete and feeling nicely drowsy, they lounged by the huge fire, listening to the other guests.

The inn wasn't crowded as the traveling season was nearly over. Soon the roads would become increasingly wet and muddy, and only those with the most pressing business would be on them. The trickle of information that night was disappointingly light. There were two merchants on their way back from a trade fair, a family returning from visiting relatives in Tolk and interestingly enough, two Kingsmen who stayed in a corner and appeared to be watching the other guests as closely as Taran was.

The murmur of conversation was too low for the Journeyman to catch, but from what he could see, the merchants were busy counting their profits and discussing the new clients they had made at the fair. The family was obviously tired from its long trek from Tolk and retired early. The two swordsmen, both hard-faced young men wearing combat leathers with no rank insignia, sat drinking ale in silence.

Taran, Cal and Rienne decided to retire. As he passed the bar, Taran caught the landlord's eye. "We're planning to call in at the garrison tomorrow," he said. "Could you give us directions?"

The landlord raised his brows. "I can, aye," he said. "What do you want at the Manor? Not many people go knocking on their door and if you don't mind me saying, you're all a little too old to enlist. No offense."

Taran ignored the man's jocular tone, he didn't want to be drawn into giving too much away. "We have some information that might be helpful to them, that's all. I didn't know it was called 'the Manor,' it sounds like a strange name for a garrison."

"Not really," smiled the landlord. "Local people call it that because it was originally Lord Blaine's manor. When King Kandaran was killed during the civil war, Mathias Blaine came out in support of his son, Prince Elias. It was Blaine's men and military expertise that allowed the Prince to regain the crown. In recognition of his support, Elias made Blaine General-in-Command. Since then, he's been turning his manor and lands into a garrison of some prestige." He pointed to the swordsmen, adding, "Those are two of his lads. Maybe they could help you?"

"Thanks, but I think we need to speak with someone higher up the chain of command," said Taran. "If you could just give us directions?"

"As you wish," shrugged the man and told Taran the way to the Manor.

As he turned to leave, the innkeeper added, "You'll be lucky to talk to anyone more senior than the gate guard, you know. The place is pretty empty at the moment, what with all these raids going on. It's a bad business if all that's going to start up again. There can only be a couple of companies at the most left at the Manor right now, and one has only been back a short while. Brought in quite a few wounded, by all accounts."

Taran nodded. "Yes, we heard. Thanks for the directions. Can the horses be ready straight after breakfast?"

"Of course. Have a pleasant night."

✣ ✣ ✣ ✣ ✣

The following morning, stiff from riding and strange beds, the three travelers gathered their bags, paid for their rooms, and rode on. It was a glorious autumn morning with warm, bright sunshine, cool wind, and trees in the full glory of their changing colors. There was no one else on the road but the local farmers were out in their fields, gathering the last of the harvest. One or two waved as the little party rode by but most were too involved in their work and didn't even glance up.

At noon, Taran called a brief lunch stop, and shortly afterward they came across the final turn that would lead them to the Manor.

The countryside became increasingly wooded; gone were the fields and farmhouses. The track they followed wound between forested slopes and marshy stands of alder and birch. The autumn sun didn't reach far between the trees and the air grew colder and slightly damp. They began to shiver and hoped they were nearing the end of their journey.

After a few miles of riding through the quiet woods, during which they frequently caught sight of an impressively tall and well maintained stone boundary wall, the trees drew back from the road. Soon a gap in the wall came into sight, protected by tall and heavy wooden double gates. In one gate there was a smaller sally port that opened to reveal a sentry carrying a crossbow. He had clearly been alerted by the sound of their horses' hooves and he watched them warily.

Taran halted his horse and handed the reins to Cal. He dismounted and approached the guard, who continued watching in silence, his weapon loaded but pointed away from Taran. The Journeyman smiled, trying to ignore his misgivings. He failed.

Ever since taking that last turn through the woods, he had been feeling increasingly uneasy. His mind kept replaying what Paulus had told him and the more he thought about it, the more uncomfortable he became. He now wished he had asked Paulus to explain himself fully before committing to this trip, but it was too late now to turn back or get answers to the questions crowding his mind.

How had Paulus known the young man he had mentioned,

Captain Tamsen? Why had he been asked to keep it quiet? If there were people within the High King's forces who were interested in outlanders, why not tell Taran sooner? Had his father known? Paulus' enigmatic comment that Amanus hadn't known everything pricked at Taran's mind. His father had known everything—at least as far as Artesans were concerned—or so he had always told his son. Despite his father's low opinion of Taran's talents, Taran knew Amanus would never have kept something this important from him.

These doubts, coupled with Taran's sense of shame, flooded the Journeyman's mind, clouding his judgment and troubling his heart. He was more and more convinced he would find no help here. He was fully prepared to be rebuffed and was unsure what manner to adopt. But the sentry was waiting and so were Cal and Rienne. He squared his shoulders and took a breath.

"Afternoon," he said. The sentry merely nodded, which did nothing to settle Taran's nerves. He decided on the direct approach. "We'd like to see Major Sullyan, please."

The man's flat expression never changed. "What's your business?"

Taran hesitated. "We have … information that may be useful to him."

Amused scorn flickered briefly in the sentry's eyes. "And what information would that be?"

His condescending attitude raised nervous irritation in Taran.

"It concerns the outlander raids in the south," he said. "More than that I'm not prepared to impart to"—he scanned the man's rank insignia—"a corporal."

The sentry's eyes narrowed sharply. "Major Sullyan has better things to do than gossip with civilians," he snapped, "especially those not willing to state their business when asked."

He was obviously off to a bad start, so Taran pushed down his nervous annoyance, took another deep breath, and changed tack.

"Alright," he said, "we were recommended to come here by our village elder. He knows someone stationed here and thought our information would be of interest to the Major. If we can't see him, can we at least see Captain Tamsen? Maybe he can decide whether our news is important enough to tell Major Sullyan."

The sentry looked Taran over in silence. Then he said, "Wait here."

He went back through the sally port and Taran saw him talking to a companion, a lean youngster, also dressed in combat leathers. He couldn't hear the whole conversation but as the sentry turned back, Taran heard him say, " … and be quick about it."

The youth flipped a salute, leaped into the saddle of a tall, thin horse, and set off up the track at a mud-spattering gallop.

The sentry sauntered back to Taran.

"I've sent a runner to the Captain. If he thinks it's worth it, he'll come speak with you. If not, you'll have to be on your way. You can bring your party inside while you wait."

Chapter Eight

The sentry opened one of the large gates and let them through. After showing them where to tie their horses, he ushered them into a squat wooden building to one side of the track. It seemed to be a guard house, offering protection from the weather but not much more. He invited them to sit and then went back outside to resume his post.

While he waited, Taran tried to decide what he should say, but the more he ran it through his mind, the more nervous he became. Despite what Paulus had said, he knew no one here would understand the reasons behind his actions. He concocted various explanations but, although all were true, none sounded less than fantastic. Some were even downright implausible. And although the sentry's dismissive reaction had met Taran's expectations, he still felt flustered, embarrassed and out of place. He was going to make a thorough fool of himself but it was too late to back out now.

Before long, he heard galloping hooves. As the runner's horse slid to a spectacular stop outside, Taran saw it was carrying two men. The one sitting behind the saddle slid stylishly down and slapped the beast's rump.

He was a tall, young man with a handsome, fresh face, indigo eyes and a crop of dark, curly hair. He was lithe and muscular and Taran estimated his age at twenty-five or so. He wore the usual combat leathers and a captain's insignia—a single gold thunderflash—glinted on his jacket.

He came smiling into the room and, despite his nerves, Taran instantly felt a strong liking for him. As he grasped the hand the Captain held out, Taran noticed a fleeting look in the young man's eyes that he didn't quite understand.

"I'm Captain Tamsen," the young man said, in a light, pleasant voice. "I believe you've been asking to see Major Sullyan?"

"That's correct," replied Taran. He introduced himself and his friends.

The Captain's dark blue eyes evaluated them. "What can we do for you? I'm afraid the Major's unlikely to see you right now, our company's not long back from the field."

"Yes, we heard," said Taran, "but it's in connection with the raids that we want to see him. A friend told us to come. He said the Major might be able to help with a certain matter that could be affecting the situation."

The Captain's eyes narrowed and Taran thought he caught a hint of amusement in them. His heart fell.

"You'll have to give me more than that," the young officer said. "Who is this friend of yours?"

"His name's Paulus and he's both an elder and the keeper of our tavern. We live in a village down near Shenton," said Taran.

A mixture of comprehension and wariness came into the Captain's eyes. "Ah yes," he said, "I remember Paulus. So he sent you? What did he tell you, exactly?"

"Not much," admitted Taran. "Just your names and that the Major might find our information interesting."

The young man considered this for a moment. "Very well," he said, "maybe we should hear what you have to say, but I can't guarantee you an interview with the Major. Come on, I'll take you up to the Manor. I expect you could all do with some fellan."

He smiled, his eyes lingering longest on Rienne, who colored slightly. He led them outside and left instructions with the corporal to have someone care for their horses and bring up their saddlebags.

"We'll be in the Major's office," he called over his shoulder as they began walking up the track. Taran heard the corporal detail the runner to fetch stable boys and then the athletic horse and its young rider tore past them up the track, skidding around the corners and scattering mud everywhere.

"Mad fool," said the Captain, smiling indulgently.

Rienne spoke, surprising Taran, as she was generally shy. "Were you out fighting the raiders with the Major's company, Captain?"

He turned his dark-blue gaze on her. "Yes, ma'am. We've only been back a few days."

"You weren't wounded? We heard the officer in charge was injured."

His expression clouded. "No, I was lucky enough not to be among the casualties this time. Others, though, weren't so fortunate."

Rienne colored, obviously embarrassed, and Taran thought he must have had friends among the dead and wounded.

The track they followed led through extensive grounds that were part wood, part pasture. As they turned a final corner, the Manor came into sight. Taran realized they must have entered the grounds from the rear; he could see an impressive driveway curving away from the porticoed main doors. If the grandeur of the building was anything to go by, it must have seen much pomp and ceremony when it was a private residence.

The Manor was huge and imposing. Constructed of the local sandy-gray stone, the house was three stories high. Built in a style that was a good two hundred years old, it was essentially square-fronted with wings on either side. Originally, it would have stood alone, but many modern buildings had sprung up around it and

Taran supposed they were barracks and workshops that had been added as need arose.

They were led to a side door, where another corporal was on guard. He saluted smartly as the Captain passed him. Taran was asked to give him their names and this he duly did.

"Someone will bring their bags up later, Wil," said the Captain. "Have them sent to Sullyan's office."

"Yes, sir."

The Captain led them deeper into the building through an echoing maze of stone-flagged halls and corridors studded with doors. Some of the doors were open, giving glimpses of offices and lecture rooms; some were closed, murmuring voices behind them. They passed few other people on their way and Taran remembered what the innkeeper had said about the place being nearly empty.

He found the Manor's interior surprising. Its impressive external façade, suggestive of wealth and opulence, had led him to expect lavish ornamentation. Instead, there was a utilitarian air to the place, almost a coldness, as if its former life had been stripped away. The bare bones of the place were all that remained.

Eventually, after climbing an impressive flight of marble stairs and traversing a carpeted corridor, the Captain halted outside a solid wooden door. It was identical to all the others and Taran thought it must take weeks to learn which door was which.

The Captain opened the door and ushered them inside. He invited them to sit.

"I can't promise the Major will see you," he said, "but if you'll wait here, I'll find out. Someone will bring you refreshments." He left, closing the door behind him.

Taran glanced around the room as Cal and Rienne took chairs in front of a heavy wooden table. The lack of personal items or military paraphernalia puzzled the Journeyman: if the room was an office, as the Captain had implied, then surely it was seldom used. All it contained was a heavy, dark wooden table, a few chairs, and rush matting on the floor. There was another door behind the table opposite the one they had entered, but it was firmly closed.

The austerity of his surroundings bothered Taran. He felt uneasy, almost abandoned, and the feeling heightened his anxiety over how his story would be received. He was suddenly convinced that coming here wasn't such a good idea.

However, he couldn't leave now. Resigned to the wait, he sank into a large, comfortable chair and tried to control his nerves.

The wait was interminable and Taran's patience was quickly exhausted. The Captain had obviously forgotten them, even the promised refreshments hadn't arrived. On the verge of anger, Taran was about to look for someone to complain to when the door finally opened.

A slender young woman entered the room and Taran glared at her, seeing a chance to vent his frustration. She was in her late teens or early twenties and was dressed in a loose-fitting white shirt and dark green breeches. There was no rank insignia that Taran could see; she was obviously some kind of secretary or aide. Well, he thought, at least they might now get the promised fellan.

The woman didn't speak as she slowly crossed the room and Taran frowned. How small she was, he thought, the top of her head would only just have reached his shoulder. Her delicately featured face was drawn and pale, and suddenly he noticed that she walked with a slight limp. The more he watched her, the more he revised his initial dismissive impression because despite her pallor and frailty, she was beautiful. A magnificent wealth of shining tawny hair rippled over her shoulders and back. This was eye-catching and unusual enough, but it was her eyes that captivated Taran. Set in her small, fine-featured face, they were huge and golden: very striking. He couldn't recall ever seeing eyes quite like them.

As she reached the heavy table, she steadied herself with one hand and turned to face them. "I am sorry you have had such a long wait."

Her voice was soft and low with a musical lilt, the likes of which Taran had never heard. She spoke gently, deliberately, without blurring her words together as most people did. Lovely as her voice was, however, Taran's concern for his village and fear of embarrassment got the better of him. He was in no mood to wait any longer.

"We came here with potentially important information," he said. "Is Major Sullyan going to see us or not? I appreciate he might be busy, but we've been on the road for two days. I'd rather not waste any more time."

Her huge eyes fastened on him and a peculiar shiver ran the length of his spine. Before she could answer, however, the door burst open and a huge man, well over six feet tall, solidly muscled and florid of face, strode forcefully into the room.

At last, thought Taran, as the man he had been expecting finally appeared. The newcomer's imposing presence and well worn combat leathers gave him a distinct aura of authority even though Taran couldn't see any rank insignia. He stared at the man, expecting to be noticed, but the newcomer didn't even glance at him.

"There you are," the big man snapped, his deep bass voice filling the room. "I've been looking all over for you since Hanan told me you'd left the infirmary. What on earth did you think you were doing, walking out like that? How the Void do you expect us to cope if we don't know where you are? You know it's far too soon to be resuming your duties."

The woman turned her golden eyes on him. "Bull," she said flatly.

Taran frowned; was the word a profanity? No, he realized, it had sounded more like a name.

Whichever it was, it was spoken with profound weariness. The young woman was now leaning against the edge of the table.

The big man ignored this and plowed on, his commanding voice indignant.

"Look at you, for the Void's sake! You can hardly stand, let alone resume your duties. Be reasonable, Sully, even you must realize you're not well enough yet. You're drained and exhausted. Hanan says you should still be resting."

The woman held up a hand and a glinting stone set within a gold ring on her middle finger spat fire. "Bull," she repeated, a little louder.

Taran could hear a warning in her tone but the huge man chose to ignore it. Mistake, he thought.

The blustering tirade continued, the man's military bearing and deep commanding voice used to full effect. Eventually, the woman held up both hands as if to ward him off and her captivating eyes snapped sparks. With an effort they could all see, she pushed herself from the table, drawing her slight body up to full height.

"BULLDOG!"

The word held real power and its echo caught the edges of Taran's mind, causing him to shift uncomfortably. She gestured toward him and the large man's head turned sharply, only now, it seemed, registering the presence of strangers.

His florid face went quite pale. He took a step closer to the woman, holding out a hand in apology.

"Sully, I'm sorry. I didn't mean … "

She leaned against the desk again and waved a slender hand. "Oh Bulldog. If you want to be forgiven, bring us some fellan. Make it strong. And send Robin along, will you?"

"Yes, yes, of course." The big man hastily quit the room, casting a shame-faced glance over his shoulder.

The young woman walked unsteadily around the table and sank into the chair behind it, facing her guests. Cal and Rienne glanced at Taran in bemusement but the Journeyman thought he understood. He caught the woman's gaze.

"That man, Bulldog," he said, "he called you Sully. You're Major Sullyan, aren't you?"

A wry smile came to her lips. "I am. Are you disappointed?"

"I don't know yet." He frowned. "You're certainly not what I expected."

"No," she replied, still smiling. "Bulldog was."

Her perception made Taran blush but he was spared the embarrassment of admitting she was right because Captain Tamsen entered the room. He crossed to the table and perched on the edge, swinging one long leg. He gave Taran a brief glance before bending his head to the Major's.

"Whatever did you say to Bull?" Taran heard him murmur. "He seems flustered."

Her lilting voice sounded weary. "He overstepped the mark, Robin, and I will not nursemaid his sensibilities. He ought to know better. He of all people should know to trust my judgment."

The Captain smiled. "I'm sure he'll get over it. He's on his way with the fellan." He raised his head, looking inquiringly at Taran. "Now then, what was this information you wanted the Major to hear?"

Taran was feeling increasingly unsettled. He'd screwed himself up to admit his mistakes to a scornful senior officer; the last thing he'd expected was to be faced with a woman. He hadn't known there were any serving in the High King's forces. This shock only underlined his certainty that he shouldn't be here. The Captain's casual manner was one frustration too many and suddenly, Taran didn't want him to hear what he'd come to say.

Directing his reply to the Major, he said, "I'd rather talk privately, if that's possible."

She gave a small sigh. "Robin is the captain of my company and Bull is my aide. Both would be involved if a response to your information was necessary, so you may speak freely in their presence."

The door was pushed open once more as the big man, Bull, returned. He placed a tray of steaming cups on the table, giving the

Major a shame-faced grin as he did so. She smiled back wearily. Her Captain reached for a cup and passed it to her, pursing his lips as she accepted it with trembling hands.

The big man then served Taran and his friends and there was silence while they all savored the hot, strong fellan. Taran frowned as Bull seated himself across the room from the Major, but he made no comment. His erroneous initial impressions had rattled him badly and he was feeling more uncomfortable by the minute.

"So," repeated Robin eventually, "what did you wish to discuss?"

Taran glanced at Major Sullyan, but she seemed lost in her fellan, her eyes closed. He sighed; if he had to parade his shame he might at least be granted the Major's attention.

A prickling sensation shot through his body and he glanced back at her face. Her eyes had opened and she was studying him closely. He frowned, surprised he should feel her gaze so strongly. He was sure there was a hint of amusement in her eyes.

The young Captain was waiting for a response. Taking a deep breath, Taran tried to control his nerves. He had not counted on having to explain himself to three people—one of them an extremely beautiful young woman—but as he let his breath out, he began his tale, addressing the Major.

"My name is Taran Elijah and my friend here is Cal Tyler. This is his partner, Rienne Arlen. She's a healer." Taran thought he heard a sharp breath from the Major as he mentioned his name, but she didn't speak. "A friend of ours recommended we come to you."

Interrupting him, Robin spoke casually to the Major. "The village elder, Paulus. Near Shenton."

Sullyan made no reply, her eyes soft and unfocused. Taran was irritated by the interruption but took hold of his temper; he didn't want to antagonize anyone.

He continued, "I've known Paulus all my life and have often

confided in him when no one else would listen. Normally, listening is all he does, but this time his advice was to come to you, Major. He felt you might have some interest in the problem."

Robin interrupted again. "Paulus knows a little of what we do here. He knows not to bother the Major with trivia so he must think your problem worthy of her attention. You'd better get to the point."

Already uncomfortable, Taran was growing increasingly irritated by the Captain's high-handed manner. He'd given the Journeyman an initially favorable impression. Since then, his attitude seemed to have changed.

To steady his nerves, Taran took a mouthful of fellan. The hot liquid ran through him, reminding him of the awful heat as he'd fled the Andaryan huntsmen. Once again, he realized that Major Sullyan was watching him, her startling eyes hooded and unreadable. At that moment, Taran decided to keep some parts of his humiliating tale—including its fatal outcome—to himself, at least until he knew a bit more about these people. He could always add it later.

He placed his empty cup on the tray and glanced at Robin. The younger man was still perched on the edge of the desk, hovering protectively by the Major's side. There was a plainly fake expression of polite interest on his face and Taran felt a sudden urge to replace it with respect.

"I am an Artesan," he stated abruptly. "I hold the rank of Journeyman."

He watched for a reaction but was disappointed. The polite interest didn't waver and the young man didn't speak.

Annoyed, Taran proceeded.

"I was taught by my father, who reached the level of Adept-elite before his death two years ago."

There was a moment of silence. Then:

"Your father was Amanus Elijah."

The soft voice was Major Sullyan's and Taran gaped at her. Her gaze had sharpened and her eyes were now huge and golden and, he thought, faintly sad.

"How do you know that?" he gasped. "Did you know my father?"

To his astonishment she dropped her eyes. "I met with him once. He is dead? I am sorry. He was a good man and a capable Adept."

Despite his shock, Taran bridled. Her casually dismissive assessment of his father's talents caused him to miss the obvious. "Capable? He was highly skilled," he snapped.

Out of the corner of his eye, he saw the Captain smile faintly, but Sullyan didn't comment.

Stung by their less-than-respectful attitudes, Taran blundered on. "There are very few people left now who possess his level of knowledge. He might even have been the last Adept-elite."

He saw Robin open his mouth and even heard Bull stirring.

"Be still."

The command, though softly spoken, was instantly obeyed by the two military men. The Major raised her eyes to Taran's. "You did not come here to discuss your father, I think, and we are all now aware of your status. To the point?"

Taran had the distinct impression his outburst had done him no favors. Mention of his father—whom he'd adored but could never please—always put him on edge.

With an effort, he thrust his indignation aside, deciding to gloss over his many failed experiments. They would never understand, so what was the point in relating them?

"Since his death," he continued, "I have been trying to raise my rank to Adept. I knew I'd never find another tutor in Loxton, so eventually I decided my only option was to cross the Veils into Andaryon, the Fifth Realm. I knew from my father that Artesans were plentiful there and the notes he left suggested there was a way of persuading one of them to teach me."

Glancing at Robin, Taran saw the polite interest replaced by a frown. Of course, he thought, they don't understand what I'm talking about. He only had Paulus' word that they might help him, although the Major's astonishing revelation about his father seemed to bear that out. However, given most people's fear and mistrust of Artesans—and the military's understandable attitude toward raiding Andaryans—he knew his fears were correct. He should explain and leaned forward in his chair, readying what Cal called his 'lecture voice'.

"Those of us born with the Artesan gift can learn to control our personal power, known as metaforce. We can use this to influence and even master the four elements," he said. "We raise ourselves through several levels of competence by study and experiment, mostly learning from those of higher rank. That's why I needed to find another teacher. There are hardly any Artesans left in Albia now, and my father was probably the most experienced of his kind."

"Enough."

The abruptly spoken word startled Taran. The young Captain rose from the desk, turned to face Major Sullyan, and snapped, "Major, these people have no idea who you are. I can't just sit here and let him preach like this."

"Peace, Robin. You cannot blame them for their ignorance."

Sullyan's lilting voice contained a note of exhaustion that countered Robin's annoyance. Concern flooding his handsome face, he bent to her. The big man, Bull, also came to his feet, the three guests obviously forgotten.

Robin spoke softly. "You ought to rest."

Sullyan waved him away. "Leave be, Robin. I am well enough."

As he watched her, Taran suddenly noticed that Sullyan's startling eyes were no longer golden. They had turned black, the pupils so dilated that no sign of the iris could be seen. This was so strange that his fascination momentarily eclipsed his discomfort.

He saw the young Captain place a hand on her shoulder.

"Sullyan," he repeated, "go rest. I insist."

Taran imagined that such an order would provoke the same reaction that had upset Bull earlier. Yet where the big man's bluster had earned him a power-filled reprimand, Robin's gentle insistence brought compliance.

Slowly, Major Sullyan stood. She turned to Taran.

"Taran Elijah, I ask your pardon. Robin is right, I need more rest. If you will, remain and discuss your business with him and Bull. I shall hope to speak with you later."

She turned toward the door behind the desk and Robin opened it for her. Taran caught a momentary glimpse of a comfortable apartment beyond with all the personal touches that were absent from the office.

The Captain turned to face him before following the Major through.

"I won't be long," he said. "While I'm gone, Bull will explain the situation. There are things you should know before we hear the rest of your tale."

Then he was gone, closing the door behind him with a definite thud. Taran heard the gentle murmur of voices for a moment, then all was quiet.

Chapter Nine

A new sound caught Taran's attention. It was the big man, Bulldog, chuckling.

He came around Taran to take the seat vacated by the Major.

"I'm afraid you'll have to excuse Robin," he rumbled. "He's very young and takes his duties extremely seriously."

"He seems very protective of the Major," said Rienne. Taran glanced at her, once again surprised that she had spoken.

The big man smiled. "Yes he is, and with very good reason. You see, Robin's in love."

Rienne flushed crimson. "Oh."

"Don't worry, dear heart," he soothed, "we're all in love with Sullyan. You would be too, if you spent any time with her."

Taran knew he'd caught the slightly indignant expression on Cal's face, for he turned to him and laughed. "Oh yes, young man, even you."

Cal bridled. "I have a love of my own," he stated, and took Rienne's hand. She blushed again.

The huge man grinned. "So I see. Nevertheless, we all fall in love with her one way or the other. You'll see."

"Well she can't love you very much or she wouldn't have yelled at you earlier."

Taran glared at Cal for this show of bad manners but Bull's good humor was undented.

"Young man, that just shows how little you understand us. I had better do as Robin suggested and explain the situation."

He looked back at Taran. "I'm afraid I have some bad news for you, my friend. Your little lecture just now was quite wasted. You see, Major Sullyan is also an Artesan, and a powerful one. She holds the rank of Master-elite."

Taran's eyes widened in horror as this incredible news sunk in. His blood froze; he had actually had the temerity to lecture a Master on the rudiments of the Artesan craft. He couldn't believe he had failed to recognize the aura of her power. Now that he knew the truth, he understood Robin's outburst.

The memory of what he had said, plus a growing suspicion, completely drained his face of color. He felt so stupid.

"Oh, gods," he groaned. He forced himself to ask the next question, although he didn't really want the answer. "And the Captain? I suppose he's an Artesan too?"

The huge man nodded. "Adept-elite."

Taran blinked. Faintly, he asked, "And yourself?"

"Also Adept-elite. I'm retired, though."

Cal spoke up. "Retired? How can you retire from being an Artesan?"

Taran heard the disbelief in Cal's voice and would have smiled if he wasn't feeling so dreadful. He knew that if Cal ever reached the illustrious rank of Adept-elite, he wouldn't be able to imagine ever giving it up.

Bull smiled. "Only in a military sense. The Manor is one of the High King's largest garrisons but it's also a training center. Old soldiers, and especially old Artesans, never die, but sometimes they have to retire."

"Major Sullyan might be a powerful Artesan," said Rienne, "but she's not in the best of health. What's wrong with her?"

The big man shook his head. "She's not ill, dear heart, just exhausted. She was recently wounded—quite badly—and has drained herself trying to recover."

He looked across at Taran, who could feel his face still flaming in an agony of deep embarrassment. "As a Journeyman, I presume you know what it's like to overexpend your power?"

Taran nodded, thinking of his own pain-filled recovery after his terrible experience with the Staff.

"That's why we were so worried about her, and why Robin went with her just now." He cocked his head at Taran. "He stands for her."

Taran regarded him blankly and Bull raised his brows, pointing at Cal and Rienne. "I presume one of these stands for you?"

Taran was bemused. "Stands for me? I don't understand."

The big man's geniality disappeared. "Don't tell me you have no one to stand for you? What are you thinking of, man? One of the first lessons you learn as an Artesan is never to use power without having someone to stand for you."

Taran's incomprehension continued and Bull snapped, "Surely your father taught you that? As Adept-elite, he must have passed that on?"

Taran shook his head, frowning at the criticism.

"Who trained Amanus?" demanded Bull.

"I don't know," said Taran. "My father never spoke of it. Training wasn't something he enjoyed."

"Well that's obvious. He certainly didn't do a great job with you."

Taran stared in dismay, not wanting to argue with an Adept-elite, two full levels above his own rank. His heavy heart sank even farther. His every concern about his reception was being fulfilled, in an even worse way than he had imagined.

Bull pointed a large finger at Cal. "I can sense this one has some latent power. Are you training him?"

"Yes, he's my Apprentice," replied Taran, expecting more censure. His answer however, seemed to pacify Bull.

"Well then, he's the one who should stand for you. Whenever you expend power, you have him by your side to provide reserves in case you overtax your strength."

"Like when I pulled you out of the portway?" said Cal.

Taran flashed him an irritated glance. Cal was only trying to help, but now that Taran knew how skilled these people were, his dread of explaining himself was growing. They were bound to condemn what he'd done.

Apprehension suddenly shot through Taran. "If the three of you here are all Artesans," he said, "then is everyone … ?"

The man barked a harsh laugh. Quickly he sobered, casting a guilty glance at the inner door.

"No, my friend. That really would be too much for you, wouldn't it? No, there are only a few of us here. At present."

That enigmatic statement hung in the air as Robin re-entered the room. Soundlessly, he closed the apartment door, walked around Bull and resumed his seat on the edge of the desk. His handsome face was paler than before.

Replying to the look Bull gave him, he said, "She's sleeping. I've done what I can, I hope it's enough. She really could do without this fool's problems on top of Blaine's demands."

"Captain," said Bull warningly, "don't overstep yourself."

The young man accepted the reprimand calmly. "I'm sorry," he said, turning to Taran. "I didn't mean to be rude. We nearly lost her this time and I'm still worried about her. Has Bull explained things to you? Do you understand why I got so upset at your little speech earlier?"

"Yes, of course," sighed Taran. "I just wish Paulus had been a bit more explicit, he could have saved me a lot of embarrassment."

Robin's chuckle lightened the mood. "Elder Paulus was told only as much as was good for him and not enough to have warned you." Taran frowned but Robin didn't explain. "Bull, will you make us more fellan? Then we can hear what these people want to tell us."

Bull rose, removing the used cups. As he left to refresh them, Taran asked the Captain, "You mentioned Blaine just now. Did you mean Lord Blaine?"

Robin's face darkened and his voice was full of disdain. "He's General Blaine now. Our illustrious leader. He's in overall command of the High King's forces and this garrison is his home."

Taran gathered there was no love lost there and thought he understood why. "Do I take it that General Blaine's not an Artesan?"

Robin shook his head. "No. He is."

Taran went cold. "But … does that mean the General is a Senior Master?" He was aghast; surely two Artesans of such high rank couldn't live so close to his home? Surely his father would have known … ?

"No," said Robin curtly. "Blaine's only a Master."

Only, thought Taran. "But that means the Major outranks him by far. How does that work?"

Robin snorted. "High King Elias Rovannon's military forces are promoted solely based on achievement in the field. Artesan rank counts for nothing, Blaine sees to that. Gods, he doesn't even use his own talents. He's too afraid of censorship, of upsetting Elias' nobles, of … "

He pulled himself up, cutting off what threatened to become a rant. "As you can see, Journeyman, I don't like the situation. But the Major accepts it, so I would be obliged if you kept this to yourself. Military politics are a complicated and a very dirty pond. I don't recommend you step in it."

Closing his mouth, he stared defiantly at the three of them.

Bull returned with fresh, steaming fellan. As he passed around the cups, he threw an exasperated look at the Captain. "Got it off your chest now, lad? Feel up to listening to someone else's problems?"

Robin grinned. "Sit down, you big ox, and shut up." He curled his hands around his cup. "Now then, Journeyman, you have our full attention."

✠ ✠ ✠ ✠ ✠

Taran relayed his story, or at least as much as he felt able to reveal. He didn't mention the fatal outcome of the duel. He still felt acutely embarrassed that he'd been trapped that way and was aware that had he taken Cal to stand for him, as Bull put it, he would have had a witness. The noble couldn't have tricked him then.

The two military men listened without interrupting. They seemed to accept what he told them without suspecting the bits he skipped. Even Cal grasped what Taran was doing and didn't betray him with some ill-timed reaction.

When the Journeyman related the parts concerning the Staff, Robin's expression intensified.

"I've never heard of such a thing," he said. "What did it feel like to use it?"

Taran shuddered. "It felt like I was cooking my own mind. It felt like I was boiling my eyes. It felt like my skin was crawling with every parasite you can think of and some you couldn't imagine. It felt like I was dying slowly and painfully and forever. It felt like hell."

Robin grimaced and Bull blew out his lips. "Don't spare us the details, will you?" he said.

Robin chuckled. "I wish I'd never asked. So what possessed you to use it in the first place? Why didn't you just hit the tangwyr with an Earth ball? You have mastery over Earth, after all."

Taran was too shamed to admit he'd not even thought of it. "I was terrified and exhausted. I wasn't thinking straight. The huntsmen were right behind me and the portway was too close to endanger. I suppose I reacted instinctively, using the greatest power source I could find."

Robin's eyes darted to Cal. "You do realize you could have killed yourself and your Apprentice? The two of you were linked and you were meddling with powers you didn't understand."

Rienne glared at Taran. "You never told us that!"

Taran sighed. "As nothing came of it, I didn't see the need." He tried to sound final but Rienne wasn't finished.

"Cal and I didn't agree to stay with you so we could have our lives put at risk. I trusted you when you said you were training him and helping him control his power. I'm not sure it's worth it now. What did you get us into?"

"Steady, Rienne," soothed Cal. "Nothing came of it, like he said, so there's no harm done."

Rienne quieted but Taran could see she was still angry. He could hardly blame her.

Turning back to Robin, he asked, "So what do you think? Are the raids connected to what I did, are the Andaryans looking for the Staff? Why couldn't I return it? If I was doing something wrong, I'll go back and try again, although it wasn't an experience I want to repeat. Both of you are more powerful than me, so perhaps one of you could do it … ?"

Robin glanced at his companion. "What do you think, Bull? Does this warrant the Major's attention? Neither of us can leave the Manor at the moment, not with things as they are."

The big man was silent before replying and then he looked squarely at Taran, his honest brown eyes regarding the embarrassed Journeyman with uncomfortable clarity.

"The raiding issue is one thing and needs some careful thought," he said. "As for the Staff, if our friend here has told us the full story then I'd say he simply didn't have the strength to return it. The procedure's simple enough, although I've never come across a weapon like he's described. However, that elder had a reason for sending him here and I don't believe we've heard it yet."

The big man's perception made Taran go cold. He still said nothing, using all his training to keep his secret hidden.

Robin broke the silence. "Well, whatever we decide, it's too late for today. I won't disturb the Major now that she's sleeping. We need time to think it through and consider our next move. I'll speak with Sullyan in the morning." He turned to Taran. "Do you have somewhere to stay?"

"We didn't have time to arrange lodgings," Taran replied. "Is there a tavern nearby?"

Bull shook his head. "There are no taverns nearer than Milo's, which is two hours' ride if you don't know the shortcut. It's growing too late for that. I've got space in my rooms, if you don't mind sharing."

Taran raised his brows. "Is that permitted? This being a garrison, I mean."

Bull's eyes twinkled. "The Manor doesn't always conform to military regulations."

Robin grinned. "If that's settled, I'll see you in the commons later. Perhaps we can get to know each other better under more comfortable circumstances." He stood and the others followed his lead. "I'll bid you farewell for now."

To Taran's surprise, he turned and opened the door to the Major's apartment. Once it closed softly behind him, Taran looked inquiringly at Bull. The big man ignored him. Gathering the spent fellan cups, he invited them to follow him.

As they left the office, they collected their bags, which had been deposited outside. Bull led them down several identical hallways, passing a few people on the way, most of whom greeted him with a nod. Turning a corner, Taran saw the corridor stretching before them was carpeted, giving the place a more homely feel.

"These are our personal quarters," the big man explained, "those of us with sufficient rank, that is." A knowing look entered his eye as he glanced at Taran and pointed. "Those are Robin's rooms over there, and these are mine."

He pushed open the heavy door with his foot and led them into a spacious, comfortable suite. Once he had shown them where they could sleep, he said, "I have a few duties to attend to, so feel free to rest and refresh yourselves. There's plenty of hot water for washing"—he indicated the hearth, smiling at Rienne—"and when I return I'll take you to the commons for supper."

He left them, pulling the door gently shut.

✤ ✤ ✤ ✤ ✤

After a couple of hours, Bull returned. His guests had bathed and changed into more comfortable clothing and Rienne had even washed the fellan cups he'd left in the small cooking room, as well as some other dirty plates that clearly indicated Bull's bachelor status.

They were lounging comfortably around the room's stone fireplace, Taran watching Cal consume some fiery liquor he had daringly liberated from a bottle on a low table against one wall. Taran had refused the drink, feeling he ought to keep a clear head, but Rienne had accepted some. She sipped hers cautiously.

Taran raised his head as the door opened. Bull entered, followed by Robin. He, too, had changed and was now dressed casually in loose shirt and breeches. He looked much younger out of combat leathers. He nodded at Taran and chuckled when he saw what Cal was drinking.

"You're in trouble, big man," he said to Bull. "Here's another connoisseur of fine liquor. By the looks of things, you'd better hide that bottle."

Cal colored. "Sorry, should I not have touched this? You did say to help ourselves."

Bull laughed. "No friend, you're welcome, if you've the taste for it. Not many do." He smiled at Rienne. "I have to say I'm surprised your lady likes it."

She blushed and put her glass down.

"Don't mind me, dear heart," he chuckled. "I'll go and change and then we can eat."

He disappeared through the door to his sleeping room and Taran heard the sounds of drawers opening and water splashing. He turned to Robin, who was lounging against the wall.

"How's the Major?"

Robin's dark eyes lost their focus and there was a momentary silence before he replied.

"She's still sleeping."

Taran stared in open admiration. "You can link that easily?"

"Of course," said the Captain, "I'm an Adept-elite after all. You're a Journeyman, surely you can, too?"

Taran looked away. "Not like that."

There was a small silence.

"Forgive me," said Robin gently. "I find it too easy to forget that others are not as fortunate as we are. It must have been hard for you without a mentor. If you were going to be here long enough, I'd speak to Sullyan about training. One of us could surely spare you a few hours."

This casually worded statement set Taran's whole body trembling. It was his deepest desire and he simply couldn't help himself. His aura must have been all too easy for an Adept-elite to read because Robin's voice was full of sympathy.

"Has it been that hard for you?"

Taran flushed. "You have no idea," he said hoarsely. Gaining enough knowledge to raise his rank was what he'd been dreaming of for years, even before losing his father. He was incredibly jealous that Robin had a Master-elite to learn from.

Fortunately, he was spared further embarrassment by Bull, who emerged from his chamber wearing similar clothes to Robin. Even off duty, Taran observed, the military couldn't help but wear uniform.

The big man smiled. "Who's ready for supper? I could eat a horse."

"If Goran's cooking, you might have to," commented Robin.

Bull laughed and led them back into the corridor.

The commons was large and airy. Two vast stone hearths cast firelight into the room, which was mellow with the hum of voices, and a rather delicious meaty smell came from a door in one corner that led, Taran supposed, to the kitchens.

As they entered, Rienne glanced at him, murmuring, "Not horse tonight, I think."

Her comment made Bull roar with laughter, which drew amused glances from many in the room. Despite her flaming face, he threw his arm around her shoulders. "I like your little lovely, Cal, my boy. You watch out, you might have competition for her affections."

Cal scowled and Rienne cringed but Bull didn't seem to notice.

He guided them to a free table not too close to the fire and called across the room. "Goran! Five more hungry mouths over here."

A couple of younger men seated at the next table sniggered. "Good job we were in here early tonight, lads. Looks like Bull has an appetite."

There was general laughter and other, more ribald comments about Bull's appetites that had Rienne blushing furiously.

"Now, now, boys," reproved Bull loudly, "where are your manners? There's a lady present tonight, so mind your language."

A quiet voice that dripped menace said, "A lady? That'll be a change."

Robin, seated next to Taran, reacted viciously, startling the Journeyman.

"That's enough, Parren. I wouldn't annoy me tonight if I were you."

Taran stared around, searching for the source of the comment. His gaze lit on a sallow-faced, lean young man seated across the room. His pale eyes were disturbingly empty and his cruel, thin lips formed a nasty smile.

"Annoy you, Tamsen? I wouldn't dream of it. Come on, lads, let's find somewhere more comfortable."

He stood, his two companions rising with him, and left the room. A few men saluted as he passed but the sallow young man ignored them.

Robin stared after him, his dark eyes hooded.

"Forget him, Robin," said Bull, "remember what she's told you. Don't let him rile you, he's just itching to provoke a response. I thought you'd learned not to react like a cadet?"

Robin dragged his attention back to his friend. "I have," he said. "Mark my words, Bull. One day I'm going to make him pay for his spite."

Bull sighed theatrically, slapping a hand over his heart. "Oh, to be young!"

He received a companionable punch on the arm and their attention was diverted from the unpleasant incident by the arrival of young lads carrying steaming plates of food.

The rest of the evening passed in a pleasant haze of jovial conversation and good food. The crowd in the commons slowly dwindled to just a few latecomers lingering over their meals. Taran was feeling drowsy and contemplating retiring for the night when he saw the commons door open.

An imposing man strode into the room. Tall and muscular, his angular face bore a stern expression. He wore casually smart clothing with an impressive array of rank insignia gleaming over his breast. He halted inside the doorway and every man in the room rose, saluting.

Casually returning the homage, the man glanced around the room until his eyes found Robin. He strode over, casting his gaze around the Captain's companions, noting the unfamiliar faces. Dismissing them, he addressed Robin.

"Where is she? I hear she's left the infirmary."

Robin saluted again before replying. "In her rooms, sir, still very weak. She needs more rest."

His tone was neutral but the older man's eyes narrowed. "Are you implying some criticism, Captain?"

Robin stood his ground. "Not at all, sir. I believe she intends to see you first thing in the morning."

"You'd better be right," the tall man retorted. "First thing, understood?"

He turned on his heel and strode from the room. As the door swung shut behind him, Robin hissed out his breath and sank to his chair.

Bull rolled his eyes and Taran broke the silence.

"I take it that was General Blaine?" he asked.

Bull nodded.

"Our illustrious leader," spat Robin, echoing his earlier statement. "Gods, why can't he leave her alone?"

"Robin," warned Bull, shooting a glance at the others. "Come on," he said suddenly. "It's late and we're all tired. I think a good night's sleep is what we need. We can start fresh tomorrow."

He led the way out of the commons and back to his apartment. Outside the door, he laid a hand on Robin's shoulder. "Get some sleep, lad," he advised kindly. "She won't need you before morning."

Robin's glance was weary. "I expect you're right. Good night to you all, I hope Bull's snoring doesn't keep you awake."

He crossed the corridor and disappeared into his room. Taran saw Bull smile and shake his head as he ushered his guests through the door.

Chapter Ten

The corridor's deep carpeting muffled Sonten's footsteps as he strode toward his chamber. It was late and he was tired, having spent many hours communing via his messenger with the commanders of the Duke's raiding forces.

It galled Sonten that his weak Artesan powers forced him to use an intermediary to communicate his orders. His messenger, however, a youth named Imris who had joined the Duke's household earlier that year, was far too timid to question Sonten's lack of power.

Unlike some, he thought sourly.

Heron, the commander of Sonten's personal bodyguard, never voiced personal opinions. Sonten was under no illusions about Verris, though. He often caught a gleam of contempt in the man's eyes and was well aware that Verris maligned him behind his back. If not for the fact that Verris was the Duke's man, Sonten would have been rid of him long ago.

Unfortunately, his Grace paid far too close attention to what occurred among his forces for Sonten to fabricate a serious misdemeanor. No, for the moment Verris was safe and the ambitious commander knew it.

"My Lord?"

Lost in thought, Sonten jumped and swore, feeling sweat prickle him before he'd identified the speaker. He cursed his lack of control and for maybe the hundredth time since returning to the palace deplored his damnable misfortune. If only his Artesan gift was stronger, he could have concealed his terror. But of course, if it was, he wouldn't be in this dreadful position, forced to constantly fear for his life.

For seven nightmarish days, since watching his precious dreams burn on his nephew's pyre, Sonten had dreaded this summons. Seven days of jumping at shadows, of sudden cold sweats, of erratic heartbeats whenever he heard the Duke's voice rise above its normal, silken tones.

But no summons came. Incredible as it seemed, his Grace hadn't discovered the theft of the Staff. Sonten had fully expected to return to a palace in uproar, turned upside down in the hunt for the thief. He'd fully expected to be accused of the crime, to be seized, chained and thrown into the cells, there to await his Grace's brutal pleasure.

Instead, the Duke had received the news of Jaskin's death with gratifying sympathy. He'd even offered to help Sonten punish his murderers.

The rebelling peasants—Sonten's excuse for the two-day trip to Durkos and on whom he'd conveniently blamed Jaskin's death—would have been slaughtered by his Grace if not for the Albian raids and the unalterable timing of his schedule. Sonten would have found the whole situation amusing if not for his precarious circumstances.

The reminder of those circumstances made Sonten speak viciously to the hapless servant who'd hailed him.

"What the hell do you think you're doing? How dare you creep up on me like that? You imbecile! You might have given me heart failure."

The servant cringed. "Forgive me, my Lord," he whispered, "I meant no harm. The Duke sent me to find you. He wants to see you urgently."

Sonten turned cold. The moment he'd been dreading had come.

His Grace had discovered the Staff was missing and now Sonten's life was forfeit. He swayed with shock, steadying himself against the wall.

"My Lord? Are you well?"

He fixed the terrified man with a bloodshot eye. "Of course I'm not bloody well," he spat. "But you'll keep it to yourself or suffer a beating. Now be off with you, I can find his Grace without your help."

The servant bowed and scuttled away. Sonten knew they all feared him. It wasn't unusual for him to have a servant flogged in order to relieve the tension of a difficult day.

However, it would take more than a pleasurable flogging to help him now. He must face his fate, meet death as bravely as he could. He drew a breath and pushed away from the wall. Wiping sweat from his face, he made his way to the ducal chambers.

✢ ✢ ✢ ✢ ✢

"Ah, Sonten, there you are. Come in and close the door, we have arrangements to discuss."

Taken aback, Sonten stared at the darkly regal figure seated by the fire. Pale yellow eyes glared impatiently while he hesitated. "A ... arrangements, your Grace?"

"Yes, Sonten, arrangements. What's the matter with you, man? You look like you've seen a ghost. For the Void's sake, shut the damned door."

Stung by the Duke's irritation, Sonten obeyed and approached his overlord, feeling confused by his lack of rage and air of tense anticipation. He didn't dare believe his luck had held once more.

"I've just had a message from Verris," the Duke said. "I take it you've heard how successful the raids have been?"

Sonten had to swallow his anger. Verris had deliberately flouted his commands in reporting directly to the Duke. "Yes, your Grace, I spoke to Commander Heron not an hour ago. It seems the men are doing everything you asked."

"They know damn well what will happen if they don't." The Duke's deep voice was full of menace. "In the light of this, Sonten, I think it's time to leave for Cardon. I want everything ready tomorrow. Contact Heron, tell him to intensify the action. I want them hit at dawn and hit hard. Tell them to concentrate on destroying the buildings, causing as much damage as possible. They're not to get sidetracked into hand-to-hand fighting, their original orders stand. I'll need every available man when the real offensive begins, despite those extra levies. Verris knows my intentions, make damned sure Heron does, too."

Indignantly, Sonten said, "Heron is a good man, your Grace, and an able commander. He knows his orders just as well as Commander Verris. I'd even say he's less likely to allow his men to stray. Verris has his eye on plunder, unless I miss my guess."

The Duke tilted his aristocratic face up to Sonten's and there was a sardonic gleam in his eye. "You don't like Verris, do you, Sonten?"

The General bridled. "My personal feelings don't come into it, your Grace. I'm only concerned for how well the man carries out his duties."

The Duke's predatory smile widened. "Of course you are, Sonten. Rest assured Verris will carry out his duties to the letter. He knows what will happen if he doesn't. I trust you've already given orders to ready the carriages?"

"I have," replied Sonten, offended by the implied slur. His irritation, added to his relief at not facing imminent death, made him bold. "Your Grace, are you sure this is wise? You're courting unnecessary danger by making this trip to Cardon. Can't you rely on the Count to follow your instructions? Surely this whole plan of the Baron's carries more risk than the rewards can possibly justify?"

The Duke's saturnine face darkened. Fluidly, he rose from his chair, deliberately towering over the shorter man. The anger in his eyes shot straight to Sonten's heart and the General cursed his own brazen criticism.

"Are you questioning my judgment, Sonten?" The Duke's deep voice dripped menace. "I didn't summon you here to voice your opinions. I haven't supported your ailing province all these years so you could parade your craven reservations. What do you know of the rewards I shall reap, what do you know of the risks involved? You have no idea.

"You're impotent, Sonten, a metaphysical eunuch. Concentrate on my battle plans, prick those Albians 'til they bleed. Leave the power and the politics to those who know what they're doing."

Sonten tried not to cower but the Duke's anger was flaring. The man was charismatic and powerful, capricious and brutal; it was hard not to be intimidated when he could take your life without a thought. He had seen the Duke's killing rages before.

"My apologies, your Grace, I meant no criticism. I am merely concerned for your safety, as is my duty."

The Duke stared balefully, as if weighing Sonten's sincerity. Or maybe his usefulness. Whichever it was, he obviously decided it was worth more than the brief gratification he would get from killing Sonten. He turned away, missing Sonten's slump of relief.

Casually, he said, "My alliance with the Baron is none of your concern, Sonten. If he perceives my actions as being beneficial to his plans, then well and good. By the time he realizes his mistake, he'll be powerless to influence my hand. I will have won my desire. And those who help me win it, Sonten, by loyal and unstinting service, will not be forgotten. Bear that in mind next time you think to question me.

"Now, go rouse your messenger and contact Commander Heron. I want to leave at first light with a full honor guard and the retainers I've already selected. You'd better come, too, I might need you while we're there."

Summarily dismissed, Sonten left the room, his thoughts frantic. If the Duke hadn't yet discovered the shocking theft of the Staff, then the success of this venture would mean he soon would. Perhaps the length of time since its actual removal would put Sonten in the clear, a fact he hadn't even considered. He'd already supplied his overlord with a perfectly good reason for Jaskin's death, so why should his Grace suspect him? Providing he kept a cool head and betrayed no guilty thoughts, he should be safe.

He might not have much power but one thing he did know, having heard Jaskin say it many times. Weak Artesans, in common with the ungifted, still had strong natural shields, strong enough to protect their thoughts from casual probing. So if Sonten didn't give himself away, he should have nothing more to fear.

Smiling nastily and feeling better than he had since his nephew's death, Sonten strode toward the servants' quarters. He would send someone to rouse Imris, who had been released to his rest.

Yet even as he framed the orders he would give Heron, realization slammed into Sonten's mind. Abruptly, he stopped, all thought arrested. Disbelief flooded his heart; how could he have been so blind? Why had he let his fears override his natural cunning? Why hadn't he seen the obvious, dangling right before his eyes?

Shaking his head at his laughable stupidity, Sonten resurrected his plans. He didn't need Jaskin, with his youth, his contempt and his condescending comments. What he needed was an Artesan who owed him allegiance. What he needed was a man who'd already been bought.

Grinning maliciously and lighter of step than he'd been for days, Sonten roared for his Artesan messenger.

✣ ✣ ✣ ✣ ✣

The sun rose in a pale pink haze. Low rays slanted through swirling mist, catching in the horses' eyes. Hooves stamped and harness jingled as maned heads tossed and jaws champed the bit. Breath from many nostrils plumed into the frosty air and swords were eased in their sheaths.

Battle fervor gleamed in slit-pupiled eyes.

Both commanders watched their men. This was the last effort, the final feint before the main offensive, and they were determined to do their best. Much was at stake, not least the Duke's favor. Rewards awaited those who did well. The threat of death loomed for those who did not.

The two leaders eyed each other, rivals on the same side. Verris smiled slyly and Heron turned away. Verris knew what the other man thought of his far-reaching ambitions; the self-righteous Heron would never let personal gain deflect him from his duty. Well, let him dance attendance on his fat general, thought Verris. As if that would get him anywhere. Verris didn't intend to be merely a commander for long.

He saw Heron give a casual nod and move out his men. Verris snorted and did the same. The two companies took opposite directions, the horses curvetting and straining to be off. It had been a cold night and their muscles were stiff; the short ride would warm them and prepare them for the assault.

Verris cast a scornful look over his shoulder. Heron thought he was superior because his Artesan rank was one level higher than Verris,' but Verris intended to show him that metaphysical prowess was not the only route to success. He was one of the Duke's personal retainers and he intended to catch the great man's eye, one way or another. Once he had sufficiently impressed the Duke, promotion into his elite guard would follow. That would be one in the eye for the haughty Heron.

Full of his plans, Verris urged his men to greater speed.

Their orders were to create panic among the Albians by catching them off guard before they were awake. There were three towns to the north and west of their starting position, with villages and hamlets between. Verris and Heron would aim for the smaller settlements first, crush them under their horses' hooves and send the peasants running for the towns. Then they would sack the towns too, set fire to the houses and destroy what they could.

Let the Albians run, gloated Verris. Let them empty the towns and run for their lives. There would be enough booty left for him and his men, even after the lords had taken their cut. Verris intended to have his pick of what was left. At least his boys knew better than to keep gold for themselves.

Heron was far too soft with his lot. Whoever heard of letting them keep what they found? That was no way to get rich and Verris intended to be very rich one day.

His men let out a cry, telling him they had sighted a village. Yelling them on, he reined back his snorting warhorse and watched the mayhem his lads inflicted. Very soon, clouds of sooty smoke billowed up, cries of wounded and terrified Albians singing in Verris' ears.

He took a moment to scan the horizon, scowling as he saw other signs of burning. Heron, it seemed, was busy, too. Roaring at his eager men, Verris ordered them to break off the attack and pushed them on to their next target. He left the screaming survivors huddling in their burning homes or fleeing for the nearest town.

Laughing loudly, he galloped after his men.

✣ ✣ ✣ ✣ ✣

Taran, Cal and Rienne woke after a comfortable night, undisturbed by any snoring from Bull's room. They breakfasted simply in the apartment and the big man excused himself shortly after, saying he had duties to attend to. He told them they were free to wander the Manor grounds and left them instructions on how to reach the commons again.

"You won't see the Major until at least this afternoon," he said. "And then only if what she hears from Robin interests her. Her time is heavily committed and she'll let Robin deal with anything that doesn't warrant her personal attention. If I were you, I'd spend the morning reviewing what you told us yesterday. See if there's anything more you can add."

He stared meaningfully at Taran and the Journeyman knew he had guessed some things had been left unsaid.

"Either Robin or I will meet you in the commons at noon. Feel free to use my rooms until then."

"Thank you for your hospitality," said Taran. "We'll do as you suggest."

Bull nodded and left.

Despite the big man's advice and his fear of the Staff, all Taran could think about was the possibility of training. He knew there wasn't the slightest chance of learning from Sullyan, but Robin's casual mention had suggested to Taran that he might be willing to give some guidance. Taran's estimation of the Captain had increased immeasurably on learning his Artesan rank and he was eager to learn anything he could, even from someone three years younger.

At midday, he led Cal and Rienne to the commons, getting lost only once. An amused cadet put him right when he strayed into a lecture room by mistake. Guided by the smell of food, he finally opened the right door. He was a little dismayed to find no familiar faces in the half-packed commons, but no one seemed to mind when he took a free table.

The light meal was over and the room beginning to empty when Robin finally appeared. Dressed in combat leathers, he looked much more poised than he had the previous night. He greeted them gravely and smiled when Rienne inquired after the Major.

"She's much improved today," he said, "although a morning spent with General Blaine might change that." He turned to Taran. "She wants to speak to you later but she's given me some instructions to carry out before then. Will you come with me?"

Puzzled, Taran stood, the others following as Robin left the room. Hurrying to keep up with the long-striding Captain, Taran said, "Am I permitted to ask what the instructions are?"

"You'll soon find out," said Robin obliquely.

He led them outside, leaving behind the buildings as they walked down a wooded track in the autumn sunshine. Eventually, it opened into a wide circular arena of short-cropped grass, bordered by wooden benches. It was deserted, silent except for bird song.

Taran gazed around, sensing an air of combat about the place.

"What's going on?" he demanded.

The Captain waved Rienne and Cal to the benches. He guided Taran to the center of the arena and faced him squarely.

"In the light of what you told us yesterday, and especially in view of your training, the Major has asked me to assess your level of competence."

Offended, Taran bridled. "My father trained me well. I can assure you I earned my rank."

Robin smiled. "I don't doubt it. Nevertheless, that's what I've been asked to do. Do you agree to the test? If your abilities are what you say, you have nothing to fear. I intend you no harm, I only want to familiarize myself with your psyche and techniques."

Taran hesitated, but in reality he had little choice. He also realized he might learn something new. He made up his mind to embrace the chance to surprise Robin into a measure of respect.

"Very well," he said.

Robin smiled again and Taran realized the Captain had sensed his resolve. "Observation number one," said Robin. "Conceal your emotions from your opponent."

He held out his hand for Taran to clasp. The Journeyman took it, physical contact being essential for the two men to learn each other's unique pattern of psyche. It took Taran a few minutes to commit Robin's incredibly complex pattern to memory and he was impressed anew when Robin took less than seconds to memorize his own.

They stepped apart and the Captain led Taran through the various disciplines of the Journeyman rank, from communication to control; from wielding power to portway-building. They meshed psyches in order to communicate and this highlighted the differences in their rank. Taran was overwhelmed by the depth of the Captain's pattern compared to his own. Despite feeling overawed and awkward, he did his best to impress.

He heard Cal give the occasional grunt of admiration as they worked and knew even he could tell that Robin had by far the superior power. As Adept-elite, two levels higher than Journeyman, Robin not only had mastery over the elements of Earth and Water, but could also influence the tertiary element, Fire. Yet despite these obvious differences, Taran thought he'd acquitted himself well.

Bull appeared halfway through the session and sat by Cal. Taran saw his Apprentice put an arm around Rienne's shoulders, drawing her away from the big man. He didn't think Cal noticed Bull's smile.

Taran finished the final test. As Robin nodded approval, he released the Earth power he had called in order to form the largest portway he could make and the element drained from his psyche. Taran nearly sagged; the effort had left him perspiring.

He heard Bull say, "Well done, lads," but his attention wasn't on the big man.

The look in Robin's eyes told Taran someone was standing behind him.

Chapter Eleven

$\mathcal{T}$aran turned around to see that Major Sullyan had entered the arena. His heart lurched at the sight of her.

The afternoon sun in her glorious hair had transformed her from the frail-looking creature of the day before. Pristine combat leathers accentuated her slender neatness, and a steel blade was belted at her right hip. Her double-thunderflash rank insignia and battle honors gleamed above her left breast. Her golden eyes shone with health and her smooth skin radiated a faint amber bloom.

Taran stared in stunned admiration, the rapid thump of his heart unconnected to his earlier exertions. He knew with a certainty rooted deep in his soul that he had never seen anyone so beautiful in his life.

Gracefully, she moved toward Robin, showing no trace of a limp. Placing her hand on the Captain's arm, she smiled up at him.

"That was well done, Robin. Now tell me what you learned."

The Captain turned to face Taran. "He's been well trained but there are gaps in his knowledge, as you thought," he said. "He builds a strong portway but his psyche is weak in places and his control is not absolute, as it should be. He also suppresses his emotions instead of using them."

This casual assessment irritated Taran but he couldn't deny that while he felt exhausted, Robin showed no sign of physical effort.

The Major was regarding him. "And his offensive skills?"

"We haven't got to combat yet," said Robin, "I thought he'd appreciate a rest first. We can begin now, if you like."

"No," she said, still gazing at Taran, "permit me."

"Major," the Captain protested, "there's no need to exert yourself. That's what I'm here for."

"Peace, Robin. It has been a while since I had to exercise such control. It will be good for me. Besides, I am curious."

Unbuckling her sword belt, she laid the weapon on a bench before inviting Taran to precede her into the center of the arena. "Are you ready, Journeyman? I promise not to overtax you. I am not at full strength yet."

Taran nodded, although he felt apprehensive. He moved to the center of the grassy space and turned to face the Major. He raised his mental shield.

With a light laugh, she said, "Start with offense, Journeyman. Cast me an Earth ball and do not withhold your strength. You will not harm me."

Stung by this casual dismissal of his powers, his face reddened. But she didn't comment, merely watched as he shaped a powerful ball of Earth force. He did his best, and when it was formed he threw it at her with no warning. Had it reached her, it could have knocked her from her feet, but she batted it almost playfully away and watched it dissolve.

"That was clumsy, Journeyman," she said, smiling slightly. "I am sure you can do better."

He tried again and so began one of the most exhausting afternoons of his life.

The Major put him through every one of his small store of offensive maneuvers, effortlessly countering each one. She showed him how to improve some of his weaker attempts and then had him try again. She warned him to raise his shield and, despite her promise not to overtax him, the effort of defending himself from her attacks soon drove him to his knees. He heard Cal give a cry of protest. He kneeled, panting on the grass as Sullyan approached him.

"Enough," she said gently. She helped him rise and guided him back to the benches, where he sat with his chest heaving and his head hammering, feeling like he had been run over by a coach and six.

To his amazement she said, "You have much talent and strength for a Journeyman, but you need more training. Robin was right, you have far too tight a rein on your emotions."

He looked at her in puzzlement and she smiled.

"You must accept them and use them, Taran Elijah, not seek to override them. You cannot grow and develop until you realize the power of your passions. You have much potential, for you are a very passionate man. But you have been fortunate to survive the Veils by yourself, my friend. I would advise you not to brave them again without further instruction."

He sat in silence, trying process the Major's words. With the cloth Rienne gave him, he mopped his streaming face. Slowly, his breathing calmed.

He realized that Robin was standing with his arms folded, a stern look on his handsome face. However, it seemed that Taran was not the object of the Captain's disapproval.

"Why did you do that?" he said, glaring at Sullyan. "I am perfectly capable."

She shot him a look of warning but he ignored her.

"It was a waste of your strength," he added. "Why overtax yourself unnecessarily?"

She reacted archly. "Are you questioning my judgment, Captain?"

Taran frowned; it seemed that Robin was deliberately goading her.

"I just don't think it was wise after what happened last week, that's all. You did say you weren't at full strength."

Taran could see the Major's startling eyes had narrowed, and he could feel irritation emanating from her. He could feel something else, too, and suddenly wondered why Bull was watching them so intently.

"Very well, Captain," said Sullyan. "Shall we see if my strength has returned?"

She moved back out into the arena and Taran just caught the fleeting smile on Robin's face. The Captain's eyes were fixed on Sullyan as he said, "Are you sure, Major? I don't want to tire you."

Taran heard a faint chuckle beside him and he raised his brows at Bull.

"Now you'll see something," murmured the big man. "Just watch."

Taran turned his attention back to the arena just in time to see the Major throw a Fireball at Robin's head. He gasped. The young man barely dodged it and the Fireball hit the grass, sparks flying into the air.

Taran stared in admiration. As a Journeyman, he couldn't even influence Fire yet, let alone manipulate it. Neither had he sensed Sullyan form the Fireball, which was controlled so exquisitely the sparks didn't even scorch the grass.

"Not good enough, Captain," she called, "I believe I taught you better than that. Remember, evasion will not suffice for the test."

She tossed him another, which he managed to counter by channeling the crackling energy through his psyche. He retaliated with a powerful Earth ball, immediately following it with a barrage of pelting hail.

Suddenly they were dueling in earnest and Taran watched spellbound, envious of their casual control over power he could scarcely dream of. His admiration increased as he saw a demonstration of skills he had only read about in his father's notes. Fascinating as it was, he felt some satisfaction when Robin, by now perspiring freely, panted, "Major, enough."

She didn't heed him. Staring at him, her own eyes huge and black, Sullyan warned, "Robin, I am not playing now."

"Watch out," said Bull urgently to Taran, "you'd better shield yourselves. I'll take care of Rienne."

Taran felt the big man throwing a shield of metaforce around Rienne, but he and Cal were left to their own precautions. Swiftly, they raised their inner shields and just as well, for what followed was the most vicious sally of offensive moves Taran had ever seen.

Sullyan moved about the arena with cat-like grace, catching Robin off guard on more than one occasion. Her attacks used the full powers of Earth, Water and Fire and soon the young man was in trouble. He was perspiring heavily from the sustained effort of defending from her attacks while still trying to launch his own. Eventually, he staggered, cried out, and went down.

Immediately, Sullyan abandoned her attack. "Robin!" she exclaimed, running to him and crouching by his side.

The young man leaped abruptly to his feet, surprising the Major. Taran gasped as a glowing network of fiery lines appeared around Sullyan. Crackling and snapping with power, the glowing net formed a cage, surrounding her completely. Robin stood off, panting for breath. One hand was clenched to his chest but a smile of triumph lit his eyes.

Bull slapped his knees and cried, "Well done, lad."

Taran's eyes were popping with amazement; he had never seen or heard of anything like this before. "What on earth is it?" he asked Bull.

"Firefield," said Bull as he dropped the shield he'd been holding over Rienne. "He's been waiting months for a chance to use it."

Sullyan stood within the fiery cage. Her face was unreadable, her pupils huge. Slowly, she stretched out one hand, only to snatch it back when the glittering lines of power sparked in reaction. She put her hands on her hips, her enormous eyes fixed on Robin.

"So," came her lilting voice, "playing with Fire now, are we? What a nasty little trick that is, Robin, using my love for you against me."

"Maybe," panted Robin, "but who taught me?"

"Did I?" she said, turning within the cage to inspect its construction. "Then you learned the lesson well. Your power and control are growing."

The Captain smiled.

"But Robin, did I also teach you this?"

Fast as a striking snake, she threw back her head and flung her arms out with a snapping gesture. The cage shattered into tiny glittering pieces that hissed and dissolved on the grass.

The violent disruption of the Firefield and the resulting jolt to Robin's already depleted metaforce caused the Captain to give a small cry of pain. He sank to one knee. Free now, the Major approached him and kneeled beside him. Laying her hand on his hair, she stroked it lightly.

"You have done well today, Robin, very well indeed. I am proud of you. Let me help you regain your breath."

"I'm fine, Major," protested Robin but Sullyan insisted.

An amber glow appeared briefly in the air between them. Taran saw Rienne lean forward. He frowned, realizing she had recognized the healing it contained. He noticed Sullyan was watching her also, her dilated eyes narrowing speculatively. The aura faded and Sullyan helped Robin up.

His face had lost its ashy paleness and expression of pain, but his breath was still ragged. The Major regarded him a moment, her hand on his arm.

"Did you see how I broke the Firefield?" she asked. Robin nodded, too out of breath to speak. "Then let this be your final test of Fire. Learn the technique and you will be confirmed a Master."

She stepped away, collected her sword and left the arena, moving effortlessly as if she hadn't just exhausted two men with her power. Robin stared after her and Taran was astounded to see that his dark-blue eyes were filled with tears.

Bull stood and pounced on him, enveloping him in a crushing bear hug. Coughing, Robin pushed the big man away.

"Get off me, you ox," he gasped. "I can't breathe."

He collapsed onto the bench next to Taran, fighting to control his breathing while struggling with his emotions.

Bull was grinning foolishly. "I told you all that extra coaching and practice would pay off, didn't I? That was very clever of you, making her angry like that. She'd never have fallen for it otherwise." He slapped the Captain's back. "I'm so proud of you, lad."

Robin shook his head, bemused. "I still can't believe it's going to happen. Mind you, it'll take me months to learn that snapping trick. I can see the mechanics of it but channeling the power won't be easy."

"You'll get it," said Bull and Robin shot him a smile.

They rested in the sun while Taran eagerly questioned Robin about the Firefield. A movement across the arena caught their attention and a young cadet ran toward them. He stopped in front of Robin and saluted.

"Major Sullyan sent me to find you, sir," he said. "She wants you in her office. All of you."

Robin frowned at Bull, who shrugged. "Better go," he said, waving at Taran. "Come on."

They trooped out of the arena and headed back to the Major's office. They heard murmuring voices inside and before Robin could knock, the door opened. General Blaine strode out.

Robin and Bull snapped a salute. The General returned their homage before continuing down the hallway, but he ignored

Taran and his friends. As he entered the room behind Robin and Bull, Taran saw Sullyan poring over a stack of parchments. She glanced at him briefly before addressing Robin and Bull.

"General Blaine has received some disturbing reports, gentlemen. It seems a sizeable party of raiding Andaryans has crossed the Veils and is terrorizing the southern part of Loxton Province. Two towns have already been evacuated and three villages have been burned to the ground."

Bull swore. Taran turned deathly pale.

"This is getting out of hand," said Robin with a frown. "What on earth's going on?"

"I intend to find that out, Captain. I want you to detail scouts to investigate."

"Yes, Major. Dexter in command?"

"You agree he is ready?"

"He's ready. He won't let you down."

She nodded. "Give him orders but allow him to select the rest of the men himself. Report to me later."

She turned to Taran.

"Journeyman, I must ask you to forgive my lack of attention to the matter that brought you here, but as you can see, events have overtaken us. However, if you can spare us one more night, I should have time to speak with you this evening. Will that suit?"

"Of course, Major. We'd be glad to stay. Is it alright with Bull?"

The big man indicated his acceptance. Sullyan nodded to him and he ushered everyone out of the office. As he led the way back along the corridor, he gave Taran a pointed stare before turning to Robin.

"This situation with the raids sounds pretty serious."

"It certainly sounds odd," agreed the Captain. "Why would the Andaryans suddenly break a Pact they've held for more than twenty years? The scale of it just doesn't make sense."

"You know what demons are like," said Bull. "Revenge is as

good an excuse as any."

Robin shook his head. "Surely this can't just be over the theft of a weapon. There must be some other reason, something extra. Burning villages? Driving townspeople from their homes? That's not just raiding, Bull, that's war."

Bull grunted and shot Taran another glance. The Journeyman went cold; he was sure he knew the reason for these terrible attacks but had kept quiet too long to simply blurt it out.

They were nearly at Bull's rooms. Suddenly Taran realized that the man coming toward them was the sour young captain from the commons last night. He was flanked by the two men who'd been sitting with him.

Robin scowled. "Damn it, it's Parren. Just what I don't need."

Taran saw the warning glance Bull threw Robin but the sour man was too close for any cautionary words.

Parren halted before them, pointedly eyeing Robin's sweat-stained clothing. His own leathers were immaculate.

With a sneer, he said, "You look a little disheveled, Tamsen, if you don't mind me saying."

"I do mind, Parren. You'd look disheveled if you'd just gone three rounds with Major Sullyan. Not that you'd last that long."

Parren's flat eyes narrowed. "And how is the Queen of Darkness today, still suffering nobly? Surely a fine young man like you could think of a way to take her mind off it? No? Then perhaps I should give you a few tips. Or maybe they would be wasted. Word is, you're just not up to it."

His two companions sniggered.

Robin went white. Unobtrusively, Taran gestured for Rienne and Cal to step away.

"You keep your filthy comments to yourself," the Captain snarled. "How dare you talk about the Major like that? You wouldn't have the courage to say it to her face, you treacherous snake."

"Calm down, Robin," hissed Bull, but he was too late.

"Did you just call me a coward, Tamsen?" drawled Parren. "I'd say that was slandering an officer's character. That's a calling-out offense."

"Come on, Parren, you're going too far," said Bull, moving between the furious Robin and the arrogantly smiling Parren. "You goaded him."

"Keep out of this, old man," spat one of Parren's men. Taran noticed his corporal's insignia. "You might get called out, too."

"You wouldn't dare," snapped Bull. The threat in his eyes quelled the corporal but Parren wasn't done.

"What's the matter, Tamsen? Sending your lap dog to fight your battles for you? Not so cocky, are you, when you've no skirts to hide behind?"

Taran saw Parren's other companion, a sergeant, make an obscene gesture, implying Robin's lack of manhood. His mate sniggered again.

Two spots of color flamed dangerously in Robin's cheeks. "I'm not afraid of you, Parren, I never have been. If you want to settle this, I'm perfectly willing."

"Heard and witnessed," said the corporal.

Bull groaned and shook his head. "Oh, you young idiot. You had to let him get to you, didn't you? All that control gone to waste."

"He's had it coming, Bull, and I've had enough of his foul remarks." Robin glared at Parren. "Name your time."

The sallow man glanced out the window, a smirk on his lips.

"Two hours, Tamsen," he drawled. "I'll give you that much time to rest. Wouldn't want to take unfair advantage after you've been, ah … sparring … with a woman."

He sauntered off, his two men swaggering behind. The corporal turned and leered at Rienne while the sergeant made another obscene gesture. Its import was unmistakable and Rienne shuddered. Taran drew her away.

The silence was strained by the time they reached Robin's rooms.

"I must freshen up before I give Dexter his orders," he said. "Can't go like this." He cast a glance at Bull, who was glowering. "Well? Are you going to second me this afternoon or not?"

"Yes of course I am," said Bull. "Someone has to sweep up the bits when you are done with them. Just make sure the Major doesn't hear of this. She'd slice off your nuts and feed 'em to the rats if she knew."

"If Parren doesn't do it first," said Robin. He disappeared into his room.

Bull led the way into his suite. Shutting the door firmly, he leaned against it and stared at Taran. The Journeyman thought he knew what was coming, and he was right.

"You know more than you've let on about why there are suddenly Andaryan raiders overrunning the southlands," growled Bull. "Use the washroom, freshen up and change your clothes. Then I want some answers and I warn you, Journeyman, I'm in no mood for evasions. I've just seen enough of that to last me a lifetime. Now go wash and think very carefully before you come out."

Dismissed like a naughty child, Taran did as he was told. He was perfectly ready to tell the whole story. The entire affair felt like it was quite out of hand and he needed to know that someone in authority—someone with the power to act—knew all the facts. He wasn't going to enjoy the experience, though.

When he emerged wearing a clean shirt and breeches, he saw that Bull, Cal and Rienne were all seated around the fire. His two friends had closed expressions on their faces and Taran regretted leaving them alone with the implacable Bulldog.

The big man hooked a chair over with his foot and imperiously waved Taran into it.

"Sit," he ordered, "and talk."

✦ ✦ ✦ ✦ ✦

Twenty minutes later, he was outraged.

"You killed him?" he roared, leaning forward. "You actually killed an Andaryan noble? Oh, you bloody fool, what on earth did you do that for? Who was he? Tell me his name."

Taran flushed. "I don't know," he said, "we weren't introduced. It happened so fast. I was trapped into accepting the challenge, Bull. I had no intention of killing him or desire to, but he was obviously bent on destroying me and they weren't going to honor the contract. What choice did I have?"

"What choice? What choice? You bloody idiot, if you'd followed the correct procedure, taken a second as witness, and put all the proper restraints on them, they would have had to honor the contract. You're supposed to be a Journeyman, don't you know anything?"

Suddenly overwhelmed by guilt, fear and embarrassment, Taran snapped. Years of struggling to teach himself, years of pain and frustration, failure and danger, boiled to the surface. He jumped to his feet, startling Bull, and his eyes blazed as power surged within him.

"It's all very well for you sit in judgment," he yelled, "you've had it easy. All this experience and guidance around you. All the support you could possibly want. You have no idea what it's been like for me. No idea how hard I've had to struggle to gain the least bit of knowledge, squeezed by dint of my own sweat and hardship year after year. I should be Adept at least by now, if not Adept-elite, but what chance do I have? How can I possibly achieve my potential? How can I satisfy this thirst for knowledge and control?"

Fatigue washed over him and he sat heavily. With his arms resting on his knees, he hung his head.

"I know I've been foolish. I wish to heaven I could undo it. I'm sure it's because of me that those poor people in the south have lost their homes and maybe their lives. But done is done and can't be undone. I have to live with that."

Hearing Bull shift, he raised his head. The big man was giving him an evaluating look.

"Yes," he said, "we all will. Let's just hope we can."

He rose and crossed to the table, where the bottle of fiery liquor sat. He poured a shot into a glass and passed it to Taran.

"I'm sorry, Journeyman. Perhaps I shouldn't have been so harsh with you. You're right, it is easy to forget how fortunate we are and I sympathize with anyone who has talent but no way of refining it. If it's any consolation, I can tell you that you've impressed the Major. Knowing her, she'll be keen to see you advance."

Taran was astonished. "The Major is impressed with me?"

Bull smiled. "Oh, yes. That little episode in the arena earlier proved it. She hasn't tested anyone but Robin for a long while now and that alone speaks volumes for her interest. I don't know what it is about you, but mark my words. She'll not see talent like yours go to waste."

Before Taran could take this in or reply, Bull glanced out the window.

"We'll have to leave it there for now, I have this ridiculous duel to witness. You'll get the chance to go over it again tonight when we meet in the Major's rooms."

He paused, including Cal and Rienne in his gaze.

"I'll warn you now to be on your best behavior. This is a very rare occurrence and you're all very privileged. The Major guards her free time jealously, but she obviously thinks a lot of you. Just mind your manners.

"Now, I really must go and make sure our idiot Captain comes out of this with all his bits intact."

A thought seemed to strike him. "It might be wise of me to arrange independent witnesses to this. I've known Parren a long while and I don't trust him. I wouldn't put it past him to try something underhanded. If I showed you where to wait, would you be willing to watch for us in case it goes amiss? I can hardly claim impartiality if it goes to a martial court."

Taran glanced at the others. "Of course we will. You don't really think it'll go that far, do you?"

"It could. Who knows with that reptile Parren? We'd better get going or I'll be late and that won't improve Robin's chances. I just hope to the gods the Major doesn't get wind of this or she'll have his balls. Oh, pardon me," he said, glancing at Rienne.

She smiled. "Don't mind me, I'm a healer, remember? I've probably seen more balls than you've had hot baths."

He snorted. "Yes, you probably have. I just hope we don't need your skills before the day is out. Let's get you hidden and then I can go and support Robin."

Chapter Twelve

Bull led them up a trail through the woods. It wound for some way before he slowed. The afternoon sun was beginning to lose its warmth and the light was dimming as he showed them a stand of shrubs where they could hide. Judging by the footprints on the ground, they weren't the first to use this vantage.

"Don't reveal yourselves while Parren and his second are here, no matter what happens," Bull warned them. "Once it's over and they're gone, I'll call you and we can all go back together. Hopefully, Robin will beat him quickly, but if it looks like there might be trouble, let us handle it. Your impartiality will be compromised if you try to help."

He left them and they made themselves as comfortable as they could in the fading light. Soon Taran heard voices and then Captain Parren and his two men came into sight.

He saw Bull step forward. "What's this, Parren? Only one second is permitted, you know the rules."

"Yes, but we're not exactly conducting this under military law, are we, old man? If you want to complain to Blaine, go right ahead."

Bull snorted and Taran knew there was nothing he could do.

"So where's our young witch-lover?" purred Parren. "Not lost his nerve, I trust?"

Bull balled his fists but answered calmly. "Turn around, Parren."

Obviously expecting deceit, the sallow Captain swung around. Robin was standing behind him, having come soundlessly—and more to the point, solitarily—up the track.

Taran smiled, thinking, Score one to our side.

Parren however, was not impressed. "Hah. Trying to sneak up like a thief, were we?"

"If I had been, do you think Bull would have alerted you?" said Robin lazily. "I could have run you through already."

"You don't have the nerve," spat Parren.

"I don't have the need," said Robin.

Taran was pleased to see the young man had himself fully under control and admired the relaxed way he leaned on the pommel of his sword. He looked down as Rienne anxiously nudged him; she had seen the gleam of steel. She had probably been hoping they would use blunted dueling foils, he thought, but it seemed they both meant real business.

He watched as Parren's corporal stepped forward and handed the thin Captain his weapon. Parren hefted it, testing its balance. He made a few fancy passes in the air, a show obviously meant to unsettle his opponent. Robin, Taran was pleased to see, ignored him.

Bull stepped up to the corporal to formalize the rules but Parren interrupted.

"There's no need for that. I propose we fight until one of us yields. Far more satisfying, don't you agree, Tamsen? Or are you afraid you can't outlast me?"

"Don't agree to that," said Bull.

Robin looked Parren over, as if measuring his strength and skill. "Oh, I don't think I have anything to worry about. This scrawny little weasel has no muscle except where his brains should be. He won't give me any trouble."

Bull rolled his eyes but Parren's corporal said, "Heard and witnessed," and that settled it.

Taran glanced over to where Parren's sergeant was lounging against a tree. His casual posture bothered the Journeyman for some reason but he couldn't put his finger on it. The man was doing nothing overtly suspicious.

Robin and Parren faced each other and Taran switched his attention back. Bull and the corporal stepped away to give the combatants space. Robin looked relaxed and under control but Parren was like a coiled spring, his thin frame tense and alert.

Robin began the salute but Parren immediately seized the advantage by lunging at Robin's breast. Taran gasped. The noble he'd killed had used exactly the same treacherous tactic.

"Foul!" roared Bull as Robin barely brought his weapon around in time to parry the stroke. Parren took no notice and Robin, realizing his opponent wasn't going to play by any rules except his own, threw himself into the fight.

It was immediately clear to Taran that both men were highly skilled. Despite their ferocity, their deadly moves looked like a dance as they countered and attacked each other with consummate ease. Two or three times they came together with locked wrist guards, but always sprang apart again to renew the attack. Taran, trained in swordplay, could follow the moves and appreciate the skill involved, but he heard Rienne gasp at every stroke. She was watching from a healer's viewpoint, he supposed, seeing each contact as a wound.

Despite the fading light, the combatants were soon sweating and panting. They were so evenly matched that it would likely come down to physical endurance, unless one of them made a mistake.

Taran felt Cal nudge his arm. Following his Apprentice's nod, he looked at Parren's sergeant, immediately seeing the man's furtive behavior. Instead of following the fight as the corporal was doing, this man kept throwing glances over his shoulder, as if waiting for something. His gaze seemed centered on the area behind Bull and in another moment, Taran saw why.

He drew in a shocked breath; a third man was creeping through the trees toward Bull. There was a knife in his hand and Taran stared at Bull, desperately hoping the big man would realize he was being ambushed. But Bull's attention was fully occupied, trying to watch both Parren and his two seconds at the same time. Clearly, the possibility of a third man hadn't occurred to him.

Taran stood rooted to the spot, unable to alert Bull.

Parren and Robin had moved farther across the clearing and Taran could see Parren deliberately trying to keep Robin from spotting the man creeping closer to Bull. He held his breath as the man pricked Bull's back with the knife. The big man stiffened and Taran heard Rienne gasp. Bull backed out of the clearing at knifepoint and both men disappeared into the trees. The sergeant followed.

Dismayed, Taran glanced at his friends. He knew that Robin and Parren were tiring; it was obvious, despite the fading light. Neither had suffered serious damage yet, but it could only be a matter of time. As he watched in an agony of indecision, he saw Parren maneuver Robin around until his back was to the corporal. Suddenly, Parren gave ground, appearing to stumble.

Seeing his chance, Robin made a lunge that should have sent Parren's blade flying from his hand. Quick as a flash, however, the corporal sprang forward, giving Robin's back a hefty shove. Robin was unbalanced and went down with a cry. Parren leaped for him like a striking snake, pressing his sword to the hollow of Robin's heaving throat.

Taran could stay quiet no longer. With Bull somewhere in the woods and maybe even dead for all he knew, he had to act. Followed by Cal and Rienne, he rushed out of concealment only to be met by the corporal, who snatched Robin's sword and barred his way.

"Oh, no," he purred, "I don't think we should disturb Captain

Parren just now, do you?"

He menaced them with Robin's weapon and Cal moved in front of Rienne to protect her. The corporal smiled nastily.

"You can't let him do this," protested Taran, indicating the fighters.

"Oh, can't I? You just watch me. Now, move back to where you were and keep quiet. No one will get hurt. No one here, that is. Move."

His attention riveted on the two combatants, neither of whom had reacted, Taran allowed the corporal to herd them farther away. Robin, he saw, still lay on the ground, his chest heaving raggedly. Parren, equally out of breath, held his blade at Robin's throat, clearly savoring the moment.

"So," he gloated, his voice just reaching Taran, "that's a win to me, yes?"

If Robin replied, Taran didn't hear it. Parren's blade had already drawn blood; one tiny thrust, thought Taran, and it would all be over.

"What," said the sallow man, "no protestations, no pleading? No begging for mercy? Well, that's a shame, Tamsen. I would like to hear a little begging."

Unaccountably, Taran saw the thin man stiffen. His face paled and no wonder, thought the Journeyman, for a few inches of bright steel suddenly emerged from high between Parren's parted legs.

"Begging?" said an ominous voice from behind the Captain. "Yes, a little begging is definitely in order. But you can drop your sword first."

The weapon fell from Parren's hand and Robin rolled to his feet. With astonishment, Taran saw Major Sullyan standing behind Parren, her blade pressing high between his legs. Parren had to hold himself awkwardly erect to avoid being cut.

"Robin," said Sullyan flatly, "liberate our friends and retrieve your weapon from Corporal Rusch."

Robin hurried to obey while Parren stood straining upward, sweating far more profusely than he had been before. Robin snatched his sword from the corporal's hand, much to Taran's relief.

"Where's Bull?" he demanded.

The man nodded in the direction the sergeant had taken, and Robin slipped cautiously between the trees. Taran could hear him calling Bull's name. Soon, they reappeared, and Taran felt Rienne sag with relief.

They came over to where Taran and his friends waited, and all of them turned back to where Sullyan still held Parren motionless.

Seeing them safe, she regarded her captive. Taran watched, almost mesmerized, as she held the edge of her sword between Parren's legs, allowing him no room to move. He noted with interest that she held the weapon in her left hand.

The thin man's complexion, sallow at best, had turned waxy. His wild eyes were bloodshot. Considering the amount of moisture on his face and staining his shirt, his mouth was obviously lacking because he kept licking his lips.

Eventually, Sullyan removed her blade from between his trembling legs and ran its tip over his body, moving around him as she did so. Facing him, she stopped, her blade resting against his chest. He was shaking violently. Taran could appreciate how the proximity of such a razor-sharp weapon near the vitals could cause such fright.

"What were you thinking of, Captain?" said Sullyan flatly. "You are in no shape to indulge in such physical activity if a short bout of fencing leaves you so breathless. Do you need further instruction, is that it? Would you care to go a few rounds with me?"

Parren's eyes bulged.

"I asked you a question, Captain Parren."

He tried to reply but no words came. Sullyan stared at him and even from where he stood, Taran felt her patience snap.

"Dueling while on duty," she stated, prodding his chest with the tip of her sword. "That is a chargeable offense, Captain, as you well know. You will pay the penalty. But treachery and trickery—your favorite weapons—the military has no laws to deal with those, does it?"

Parren watched her, his expression sullen.

"My own laws will have to suffice, then, as I have warned you before."

She slid the tip of her weapon caressingly across his cheek. He flinched but her sudden strike was too swift. She laid his face open and he gasped, crumpling with the pain. Staring down at him dispassionately, she wiped her blade on his back.

"Stand up, man."

He struggled to his feet, hands clasped to his bleeding face.

"At attention."

He obeyed, trembling with pain and shock.

"Report to Sergeant-Major Harker and tell him that I order you confined to the cells until dawn. That applies to Sergeant Morin and Corporal Rusch as well. They are to be stripped of their rank and transferred to another garrison. Your fate I leave to your commanding officer; he will receive a full report of your conduct today. Now get out of my sight and get that cut dressed before it festers."

Parren saluted, his flat eyes full of hatred and fear. He stalked away, his hand clasped to his face. The corporal dashed after him.

Sullyan stood leaning on her sword, staring at the ground. Taran waited for the storm to break but it didn't come. As she raised her glorious eyes to Robin's, he saw they were damp with tears.

"Are you hurt?" she asked softly.

Robin shook his head.

"Bulldog?"

The big man spread his hands. "No, Major. No harm done."

Suddenly, her golden eyes were full of fire. "No harm?" She whirled on Robin, leveling the point of her sword at his chest. Despite her obvious fury, it betrayed not a tremor. "Get cleaned up, Captain. I want to see you and Bull in my office in one hour. Understood?"

They sprang to attention, their faces pale. "Yes, Major."

She turned on her heel, sheathed the weapon with a curt snick, and strode off.

"Bugger," said Bull. "Now we're in for it."

✣ ✣ ✣ ✣ ✣

They made their way through the gloom back to the Manor. As they walked its corridors it became apparent to Taran that news of the afternoon's events had preceded them. Many of the men they passed had a congratulatory word for Robin, and a few even slapped him on the back.

"Well done, Captain," said one hard-faced young man. "He's had that coming for years. Shame you couldn't have finished him off, you'll have to watch your back even more now."

"Thanks, Baily," said Robin.

By the time they reached their private quarters, the Captain was in better spirits. "How bad can it be, Bull? A good dressing-down and a bit of contrition and it'll be over."

Clearly, Bull wasn't so sure, but seemed reluctant to pour cold water on Robin's good mood. "Go freshen up," he advised. "We'll wait here for you."

Robin disappeared into his rooms and the others followed Bull into his.

"How do you think the Major found out about the duel?" asked Taran.

"I've no idea," sighed Bull, "although not much escapes her notice. And it's a good thing, too, or our young friend over there would have been skewered by now."

Rienne looked appalled. "Parren wouldn't really have killed him, would he? Surely that sort of thing is forbidden?"

Bull snorted. "Of course it is. All sorts of things are forbidden, but as you've just seen, that doesn't stop them happening."

Seeing Rienne's expression, he softened. "In a confined community like ours, dear heart, it's inevitable that factions arise and offenses get taken. Blaine's very strict about these things but they still occur. Usually, the senior officers get wind of anything really serious and disputes are either settled by organized competition, a spell in the cells or, in the worst cases, a martial court."

Ruefully, he shook his head. "Parren's different, though. He might be a troublemaker, but he's also smart, he's never the one to start anything. Robin's been warned about him before, so he really ought to know better. He allowed Parren to trap him into a situation he couldn't control and I fear he'll pay for it."

"I know how that feels," said Taran.

Bull shot him a look. "I guess you do. Perhaps we've all been a bit judgmental in our dealings with you, Journeyman. Let's hope this incident doesn't affect the Major's reactions when you have to confess tonight."

✣ ✣ ✣ ✣ ✣

The hour before Bull and Robin were due to report to the Major was spent in a discussion of the finer points of swordplay, Bull intrigued to learn how knowledgeable Taran and Cal were. Dissecting the duel move by move, they agreed that in skill, elegance, effectiveness and control, Robin had won hands down.

Just before the hour was up, Bull changed into his dress uniform, telling Rienne it was a buffer against Sullyan's anger, which, he added, was legendary. When Robin appeared a few minutes later, they saw he had the same idea.

"My word," exclaimed Rienne, "don't you both look handsome?"

They beamed at her and even Cal found a smile. Right now, even in the light of Rienne's admiration, he didn't envy either man. They left to keep their appointment, Robin looking resigned but not overly worried, Bull appearing anxious. Taran could feel waves of nervousness coming from the big man and wondered what could possibly cause such deep concern.

It wasn't long before he found out. He, Cal and Rienne had made themselves comfortable around the hearth, the Journeyman trying to decide the best way to approach his interview with the Major. He had nearly gotten it straight in his head when the sound of heavy footsteps in the corridor brought him back to the present.

The footsteps stopped and the door opened abruptly. Bull strode into the room, his face flushed and stern. Taran and his friends regarded him in silence, Rienne's wide eyes betraying anxiety.

Bull didn't say anything, just crossed the room, grabbed the bottle of firewater—which Cal had decided not to touch—and ignoring the glasses, poured a generous measure straight down his throat. He closed his eyes, his mouth a grim line, and coughed.

Taran glanced at the others. "I take it that didn't go very well?" he said, keeping his voice level. Bull was obviously feeling tetchy, the last thing Taran wanted was to antagonize him.

The big man went to put the bottle down, then waved it inquiringly at his guests. Cal and Taran nodded, but Rienne declined. Silently, Bull poured three glasses of spirit and served them, keeping one for himself.

"He got snippy with her," he sighed. "I told him not to get snippy with her."

Taran raised his brows and Bull dropped into the nearest vacant chair.

"He's such a silly sod. He never learns. Why he's still here is a mystery to me."

"Isn't he a very good captain?" Rienne asked shyly.

Bull smiled ruefully. "He's a bloody brilliant captain, dear heart, that's his one saving grace. It's not his military skills that let him down."

He saw the confusion on their faces and took another swig of firewater. "Look, I'm not going to go into detail, it'd take too long. I have to go down to the cells in a bit anyway and get the idiot released. Suffice it to say that Robin's not good at obeying orders. He's also hopeless at the political stuff. He has a huge burr under his saddle where Blaine's concerned and he can't understand why Sullyan puts up with the situation."

"You mean considering her Artesan rank?" said Taran. "Robin told us Blaine's only a Master and the Major is Master-elite. I can see his point."

"Beg your pardon my friend, but you don't understand either. This is a military garrison, and we're answerable to the King. We're fortunate that Elias tolerates Artesans, but many of his nobles don't. Hate 'em, in fact. It would only take one slip, one tiny hint of misconduct from any of us, and Elias' councilors would force him to denounce us."

"Force him? But he's the High King."

"Yes, Journeyman, but he can't run the realm on his own. General Blaine is in a unique and privileged position because it was his expertise, and his private troops, that enabled Elias to win the civil war. That's the only reason Elias' nobles tolerate him as General-in-Command. Any flaunting of his Artesan powers could jeopardize his standing, and that could jeopardize the King's safety."

Taran frowned and Bull gave him a direct stare.

"Don't think for one minute that every noble in Albia supports Elias, my friend. Not every rebel was killed in the war, you know. If Elias lost the protection Blaine has provided, his life could well be in danger."

Taran's eyes widened; he hadn't realized the High King's position was so tenuous.

"So why did Robin end up in the cells?" asked Rienne. "Parren provoked him, after all. Didn't you tell the Major that?"

"She doesn't need telling where Parren's concerned," said Bull, smiling tightly. "But it takes two to duel. She could hardly punish one without the other. If word got out that Robin was let off, you can bet someone would report it. In Blaine's eyes, favoritism is as severe a crime as dueling. No, Robin got what he deserved, in fact, he got off lightly. I had to do some fast talking to persuade Sully not to transfer him.

"Now I'd better go get him out. His pride has taken quite a knock today, it'll be a while before he cheers up. And we still have to meet in Sully's rooms tonight."

Chapter Thirteen

Taran was pleased though surprised when his offer to accompany Bull to the cells was accepted. The big man regarded him for a moment, clearly in two minds, before nodding.

"Come on," he said, "I might need you if I can't talk some sense into him."

Taran followed him through the Manor's maze of corridors, down two sets of marble stairs and into the basement. This, Taran presumed, was where the servants lived before the place became a garrison. It was even plainer than the rest of the house, which had already been stripped of every luxury.

The rooms had solid wooden doors fastened with stout bolts. When the guardsman on duty opened one, Taran saw Robin sitting in a cell bare but for a wooden bench. He had his head in his hands.

Disinterestedly, the Captain glanced up. The guardsman rolled his eyes at Bull, muttered, "Good luck, mate," and left them alone. Taran waited by the door as Bull went in to sit beside Robin.

"So," said the Captain morosely, "when am I being transferred?"

"Don't be such an ass," snapped Bull. "I talked her out of it. Again. Don't hold the wake before the bloody funeral, lad. She won't lose you that easily."

Robin shook his head. "No, Bull, I've really done it this time.

Why couldn't I have kept my mouth shut and followed my own advice? Why did I have to backtalk her?"

"Why indeed? You're such a lackwit, Robin. How many times have we told you there are powerful people at court just waiting for an Artesan to make a mistake like that? Some of Elias' counselors would just love to pin a charge of serious misconduct on one of us."

"But what about Parren's misconduct? What about his foul mouth? Why is everyone so keen to protect him?"

Bull puffed his cheeks. "Why do you think Sully's been at such pains to prevent you from doing exactly what you did today? Not from any love of Parren, believe me. Gods, Robin, your hot-headedness rules your better sense sometimes and now you've forced her to take action just to maintain her own position. It takes two to fight a duel, you know. Why on earth didn't you wait until you were off duty? Why fight him on Manor land? And why, for the gods' sake, did you allow yourself, after all this time, to be goaded into dueling him anyway?"

"Why don't I just go and fall on my own sword and remove the problem for her?" snapped Robin.

Bull glanced at Taran with a long-suffering look.

"If you're going to go all maudlin on me, I'll leave you here all night. Snap out of it, Robin. She's going to need you in the next few days if this situation in the south gets any worse."

Robin shook his head. "I don't think so. I'm finished here, Bull. So much for being made Master, eh?"

Dispiritedly, he left the cell, brushing past Taran as if he hadn't even seen him. Bull pursed his lips and followed, the three of them walking silently back to their quarters. Word of his misdemeanor had obviously spread and the few men they passed glanced at the Captain sympathetically, or touched him on the shoulder. The support of his peers however, did nothing to lighten Robin's mood and Taran felt guilty relief when they left him at his door.

"Don't forget we're due at Sullyan's tonight," warned Bull.

"Try and snap out of it by then, won't you?"

"She won't want me there," said Robin, disappearing into his room.

Grunting in exasperation, Bull led Taran into his own suite. As they entered, Cal and Rienne glanced up.

"How is he?" asked the healer.

"Depressed," said Bull. "This isn't the first bollo ... pardon me, dressing-down he's received, but I've never seen him take one so badly. Mind you, Sully was furious and I've rarely seen her so angry. Never with Robin."

"Poor Robin," said Rienne. "Will she forgive him?"

"Almost certainly, provided word doesn't spread farther than the Manor. She always has before. But will the General? And will Robin forgive himself, or is his self-confidence too badly damaged? At the moment, I really don't know."

✦ ✦ ✦ ✦ ✦

It was past the hour of the evening meal, which Taran and his companions took in Bull's rooms. They had no stomach for the commons that night, although Bull went for a while. When he returned, he reported, "Most people are supporting Robin. Glinn Parren is not widely liked, he's too snide and self-serving for popularity and his few friends didn't put in an appearance. The consensus is that Robin would have won eventually had Parren not cheated. We soldiers are a simple lot and we don't like to see comrades taken advantage of. Parren will likely have some trouble from his own men over the next few days, provided he retains his rank."

"Is there a chance he might lose it?" asked Cal. "He deserves to, in my opinion."

"Yours and everyone else's," laughed Bull, his mood much improved by a full belly. "But that'll be up to his commanding officer."

"Not Major Sullyan?"

"No, luckily for him. Parren reports to Colonel Vassa, who looks very harshly on breaches of discipline. He's in for a rough ride, though I doubt Vassa will strip him of rank. That would necessitate a report to the King and none of us wants that."

He looked them over, visibly taking a steadying breath. "Are you ready? I don't want to keep the Major waiting, not after the day she's had. I warned you earlier to mind your manners and I'd encourage you to be especially careful now. Her temper might still be fragile, although she's usually too controlled to let it show. Cal, my boy, bring that bottle, will you? Sullyan doesn't drink but I fear we might need a drop later on. This could be a difficult meeting."

Cal picked up the bottle of firewater and Bull grinned at Rienne's wary expression.

"Medicinal purposes only, dear heart."

They came out into the corridor and Bull rapped sharply on Robin's door. There was no response.

"Oh, where did he go now?"

As Bull pushed the door open, Taran could see the Captain slouched in an easy chair, one leg hooked over its arm and a glass of something dark-brown in his hand. He looked up listlessly.

"Go away, Bull."

Swearing, Bull crossed the room and took the glass out of the Captain's hand. He sniffed its contents, his nose wrinkling.

"Give that back."

Bull ignored him and went into a side room. Taran heard him pouring the liquor away. "How many of those have you had?" called Bull.

"Only one," was the sullen reply.

"Good." Bull came up behind the Captain and pushed at his shoulder. "Come on, get up or we'll be late."

"I already told you, she won't want me there."

"Oh yes? Did she say you were excused?" The younger man

didn't reply and avoided Bull's eyes. "Well, did she?"

"No," mumbled Robin.

"Then you have no choice. Let's go."

Bull pulled him up by the arm and marched him outside. Taran smiled and Rienne walked beside him, her hand on his forearm. "It'll be alright, you'll see," she said.

All she received was a lukewarm glance.

When they reached the door to Sullyan's office, Bull pushed it open without knocking. The room was devoid of life and no sound could be heard from the apartment beyond. Robin hung back, the last to enter. Bull looked pointedly at him, obviously expecting him to open the inner door, but he didn't move. Instead, he stood with his eyes downcast, hearing, Taran supposed, echoes of his earlier dressing-down.

"Oh, bugger," said Bull. Softly, he knocked on the door.

Sullyan's lilting voice summoned them in. Bull ushered them inside and Taran looked around, interested despite his nervousness, fascinated as always by someone else's personal space.

He saw a very comfortable living room, furnished with deeply upholstered chairs and a low couch. A fire burned cheerily in the hearth and the cream-colored walls were bright with tapestries. On one wall hung a fine-looking sword, its point wickedly sharp, its guard engraved with a crest. He thought it was the sun-circled crown emblem of the Rovannons, the ruling House of Albia. He couldn't tell if it was the same weapon Sullyan had used that afternoon.

Low tables rested against two of the walls and two other doors led off into what he surmised were cooking and sleeping areas. Lamps glowed with amber radiance around the room, there was a faint fragrance to the air and the effect was welcoming and warm.

Sullyan emerged from another room and Taran stared in wonder.

She was dressed in a green silk shirt, open at the neck to show a fiery stone glinting at her throat. The shirt was loosely tucked into figure-hugging breeches of soft black linen. Her wondrous mane of hair was brushed and burnished, falling loose about her face. It flowed over her shoulders and back in rich tawny waves. Two more tiny fire stones gleamed in her ears, matching the one sparking from the gold ring on the middle finger of her right hand. She was stunning, Taran thought, quite unlike the fragile wraith she had seemed when he'd first seen her.

Her skin caught the amber firelight and her striking eyes were as gold as honey. She saw him staring and smiled, holding out her hand. Gallantly, Taran kissed it, bringing a faint flush to her cheeks that made her look very young.

"Welcome," she said in her musical voice, "make yourselves comfortable. Can I offer anyone fellan?"

Robin moved toward one of the doors and Taran guessed that as her captain, this was his duty. However, she waved him away. "No, Robin, you sit with the others. I can do for myself for once." She disappeared into the second room; they could hear the sound of cups being readied.

Robin looked at Bull, a stricken expression in his eyes. "You see? I told you she wouldn't want me."

"Shut up, you young fool. Can't you see she's trying to make amends?"

Morosely, Robin flopped onto the couch and Bull threw up his hands in despair.

Feeling awkward in the light of Robin's mood, Taran also sat down. To take his mind off his own nervousness, he glanced around the room, hoping to gain an insight into Sullyan's nature from her personal things. Only two objects seemed to convey any sense of her. One was the slender steel blade resting in its straps on the wall. The other was a beautifully tooled and inlaid lap harp sitting on one of the low tables, well away from the fire. He nudged Rienne, who was a musician, and drew her attention to it. Her eyes widened as she took in its craftsmanship and beauty.

Turning to Bull, Taran asked, "Does the Major play that?"

Bull glanced at the harp. "She does indeed and if you're very lucky, you might hear her tonight. It's one of her few pleasures."

Sullyan returned carrying steaming, aromatic cups. "This will not be as good as Bulldog's, I fear," she apologized, "but it should suffice."

She served them herself, which, judging by Bull's expression, was rare. Coming to Robin, she didn't immediately release his cup when he reached for it, forcing a startled glance from him. The color rose in the Captain's face.

Settling herself in a chair across from Taran, Sullyan cradled her cup. "Now," she said, "Bull and Robin have told me a little of your story. Would you care to tell me the rest?"

Taran drew a deep breath. "Yes, Major."

She forestalled him before he could continue. "Did Bull not explain?"

Taran frowned and looked at Bull, but the big man smiled unhelpfully.

Sullyan sighed. "Then he was remiss. Journeyman, these are my private rooms and tonight I am off duty. In here, I am not Major Sullyan but merely Sullyan, or even Sully, if you prefer. This is a sanctuary from my many responsibilities and it is precious to me. So, Taran Elijah, I would hear your story and I ask you to be plain and open. You have nothing to fear, it is not my intention to judge you, but I need to hear exactly what occurred if I am to determine what response, if any, may be necessary."

"Very well … Sullyan," he said, searching for the right way to start. He cast his eyes down, unequal yet to the task of holding her strangely powerful gaze.

He took a steadying breath. "As an Artesan, you can appreciate how desperate I became after the death of my father." He risked a brief glance, seeing her sitting with her legs curled beneath her, cup in her hands. She smiled gently, her astonishing eyes holding only calm interest. Suddenly, he realized he was more afraid of her censure and desiring of her good opinion, than he had previously thought. The approval of a Master-elite would mean more to him than he could express.

He took another breath.

"My father always led me to believe there were virtually no other Artesans left in Albia, and certainly none in Loxton Province. So I had no one to turn to for guidance when he died. I struggled alone, trying to build on what I had leaned, becoming more and more disheartened and increasingly desperate. So desperate, in the end, that I conceived the idea of trying to find an Andaryan Artesan of sufficient skill to teach me. I knew something of Andaryan customs from my father's notes, for he'd written that if an Andaryan was formally challenged to a duel and defeated—or at least held to a draw—then the challenger could name his prize, even to the extent of asking for knowledge."

"Sure," interrupted Bull sourly, "if you place the right restraints on them."

"Peace, Bull," said Sullyan softly. "Have you never made a mistake?"

Her reluctance to judge bolstered Taran's confidence.

"I constructed a portway and left Cal in charge of it. I didn't want to close it off behind me in case I needed to return in a hurry. I entered Andaryon in the late afternoon and spent the rest of the day searching for someone suitable to challenge. By nightfall I'd seen no one and was forced to camp at the edge of some hills. There was a forest not far away and I was going to try there the next morning before returning home. I'd told Cal I'd only be gone one day."

His eyes lost focus and his face reddened with shame as he recounted the following morning's terrible experience. He glanced up once to see how the Major was reacting, but she merely waved him on. His memory replayed it just as it had while he lay unconscious, his body exhausted, his mind damaged. His voice took on a hypnotic quality, as holding to a certain detachment was the only way he could deal with the humiliation and self-contempt he felt.

Swallowing, he went cold at the memory of the duel and recounted it dispassionately. Sullyan's eyes narrowed when he mentioned the noble's treacherous use of Artesan skills in a duel where the strict Codes of Combat forbade it. However, she remained silent until Taran came to his desperate use of the Staff.

This seemed to arouse her interest and she asked many complicated questions about how the Staff worked. Taran answered as best he could but it was evident that his replies didn't satisfy her. Finally, she released him to finish the tale.

Silence filled the room when he was done. He was almost panting with the remembered strain of effort and he felt drained. It cost him much to look into her golden gaze, dreading the rebuke he knew he deserved. But there was no reproach in her eyes, only thoughtful concern.

"So you killed an Andaryan noble. Who was he?"

Taran sighed. "Bull asked me that. I don't know, we never exchanged names. Is it so important?"

"It could be. Describe him to me."

Taran complied as best he could but when he had finished, she wanted something more. "What were his family colors, Taran?"

"His what?"

"There would have been a colored edge to his garments. What was it?"

Taran had to think hard before recalling this trivial-seeming detail. He tried to visualize the huntsmen who had surrounded him; the unpleasantly grinning young noble and the barely seen older man, who had kept out of sight to the rear. Then he remembered.

"Oh. Green, I think. Yes, pale green. The background was black."

She gave a sharp intake of breath.

"You surely don't recognize him?" Taran was amazed. There must be hundreds of nobles in each overlord's demesne, he'd never even dreamed someone might know the one he'd killed.

"In fact I do," she said. "I am familiar with the colors of all the noble Houses of Andaryon. Robin should recognize it too."

The Captain made no response. His hands were clasped about his cup, his eyes fixed unblinkingly on its contents.

Sullyan pursed her lips but didn't pursue the matter. Turning back to Taran she said, "Those colors and that description belong to a young noble called Jaskin. He was an arrogant young man, and responsible for many raids into Albia. The black is Lord Rykan's color and Jaskin is—or was—one of his lesser courtiers.

"Rykan, Duke of Kymer, is a hugely powerful man, second in wealth and lands only to Tikhal, the Lord of the North, and the Hierarch, supreme ruler of Andaryon. But any overlord of standing would want revenge for the murder of one of his nobles, even one as minor as Jaskin. And yes, Taran, he would see it as murder. You can plead self-defense if you choose but you were on Andaryan soil, an outlander who was trespassing. And besides, in Andaryon not even noble can kill noble with impunity. There are strict codes governing conflict between the nobility."

Taran flushed with renewed shame.

"Rykan will be furious over Jaskin's death. He will see it as a personal insult and will be avid for revenge. Your unfortunate failure to provide a witness to your contract with Jaskin and to place the customary restraints on Jaskin's retinue at the outcome of the duel has left Rykan free to demand the right of redress from the Hierarch. He has been awaiting such an opportunity for years, although I am surprised he has been allowed to break the Pact so thoroughly."

Taran sat in silence, his guilt and fear building.

"As for the weapon you brought through the portway with you," she said, "here I have to confess I am at a loss. I have no personal experience of such a thing and cannot say why you were unable to return it. However, from your description of the pain it caused you when you used it, and also its reaction when you tried to touch it again, I would guess that it has somehow been imbued with the power of its owner. Since it is an Andaryan artifact, such alien forces would react adversely with yours. This would explain why the portway, which contained your own metaforce, reacted so violently when the Staff was inside it. It also explains the temporary damage to your mind and I suspect you were inadequately shielded when you returned after killing the tangwyr. You were fortunate indeed to escape permanent damage, my friend, or even worse."

Taran shuddered.

"But I have no idea why, or how, such a terrible thing was created. It would need further study but that is something we will not have time for until this current crisis is resolved. At least we now have a clearer understanding of why the invasion has occurred.

"And I have to tell you that it is very bad news, Taran Elijah. Very bad indeed."

Chapter Fourteen

Thoroughly shamed, Taran lowered his eyes.

"Can anything be done?" he asked. "Can I do anything? I've been terrified that the Andaryans can somehow sense the thing and I know they would inflict dreadful suffering on my village if they came looking for it."

Sullyan regarded him. "If the artifact is buried deeply enough to need more than one day to dig out, as you have said, then I doubt even its creator could sense it. Certainly not from beyond the Veils. Besides, you killed its owner and there were no other Artesans in the party. So in that respect, I think you can be easy.

"As to what can be done, well, that is another matter. Somehow, the Pact has to be restored and that could prove tricky, maybe even costly. I am not prepared to make any decisions until my scouts return from the south, but that will not be until tomorrow evening at the earliest. Probably even the day after."

Her gaze was stern. "You would have done better, Journeyman, to have told Robin everything when first he asked. It was what you came to do, was it not?"

Deeply embarrassed, Taran hung his head.

He heard her sigh. "Ah well, done is done and cannot be undone. I see no advantage in discussing it any further at the moment, not until I have evaluated what the scouts have to say.

"Bulldog, why not distribute some of that evil liquor you insist on poisoning yourself with? We may as well enjoy the rest of the evening."

Glasses were produced for the men. Rienne declined the liquor, joining Sullyan in another cup of fellan. With the exception of Robin, who stayed resolutely silent, they sipped their drinks and indulged in conversation.

Slowly, the atmosphere relaxed. It turned out that Bull was an unexpectedly good storyteller and he regaled them with some tales of the Major's military exploits. Judging by the frequency with which she corrected him, they were not always accurate tales, but it soon became apparent that she was a gifted and respected commander.

After a while, Taran sensed Rienne gathering her courage. He knew how shy she could be, especially in the company of someone as poised and confident as Sullyan. So he was surprised when she asked the Major about the lap harp they had noticed earlier.

Sullyan eyed her with interest as she rose to fetch the instrument from the table. "Do you play?"

"Not the harp," admitted Rienne, adding timidly, "I'd love to hear it though. I'm sure it has a beautiful tone."

As she returned to her chair, Taran noticed Sullyan's eyes rest briefly on Robin, who had not glanced at her the entire evening. She sat, cradling the harp on her lap.

Bull winked at him. "We're in for a treat," he whispered.

Sullyan ran her fingers over the strings and liquid silver notes rippled around the room. Taran was no musician and could detect no fault in the tuning, but Sullyan used a harp-key on a couple of the ivory tuning pins. The next glissando was undeniably richer in tone. Laying her cheek against the warm satin wood, she closed her eyes and began to play.

They were all transfixed by the music. The airs were unknown to Taran but Bull obviously recognized them. After a while, she switched from the gently lilting sounds and the room was filled with the melody of a familiar folk tune. Taran smiled; it was one of his favorites.

Another sound insinuated itself within the music and he glanced around to see who else was playing. Bull saw him, grinned and indicated the oblivious Sullyan. With a start of delight, Taran realized that what he could hear was Sullyan humming the melody line. Because her cheek rested so intimately upon the wood of the harp, her voice had taken on the instrument's thrumming quality. He was captivated.

And then she began to sing.

She pitched her voice low so it fit perfectly with the harp. Running through the folk tune she then played several others, some known to Taran, some not. Then, glancing at Bull, who nodded, she switched to a martial air. She and Bull sang a marching song; the big man's deep bass voice a pleasant counterpoint to Sullyan's lighter lilt. Taran would have thought the harp ill-suited to a military air but surprisingly, it didn't sound out of place.

All through the song, he saw Sullyan watching Robin, obviously hoping he would join in. He didn't. The song came to a close and Bull grimaced. He traded another glance with Sullyan and she switched tempo once more.

This time the air was a sweet lament, a simple song of love found and love lost. Her voice thrummed with the sound of the harp, as if the instrument itself was singing. Taran noticed that Robin's eyes had filled with tears, although he still stared stubbornly into his glass. He thought Sullyan had seen it, too, for the tune of the lament changed again and became, if possible, sweeter and even more poignant.

She began to sing the words.

When Springtime's freshness found you,

tiny blossoms made you fair.

The young sun shone, the warm winds blew

so gently through your hair.
Come eventide the shadows grew,
we watched them cast their shade.
Farewell, my heart, in dreaming dwell;
so must all beauty fade.

Robin stirred and when he spoke, his voice was full of anguish. "Don't, Sullyan. Please."

But she would not stop. "Hush, Robin. It will be good for us both."

Then Summer came, its golden days
our growing love revealed.
Upon your face that early trace
your youthful joy concealed.
But noontide passed and all too soon
the twilit evening fell,
its purple gloaming dimmed your sight.
Farewell, my heart. Farewell.

With Autumn's gold and slanting sun
your smile lit waning days.
On gentle spirit, bravely borne,
the shadow cast its haze.
And then we knew, with heavy heart,
your path would turn away

from ours, and we must part,
as night-time follows day.

Now Winter's icy tempests blow
across an empty space,
but Springtime's warmth awaits its chance
to take white Winter's place.
And though fond hearts are filled with pain
our grieving cannot last,
for soon the Wheel will turn again
and Love unite the past.

When the song ended, tears poured unchecked down Robin's face. The last heart-rending chord rippling around the room slowly died, but no one moved or spoke. Taran saw that Sullyan's eyes were filled with tears also and looked away, feeling like an intruder.

Robin bowed his face to his hands and Sullyan rose from the couch, gently laying down the harp. She kneeled before him and held his trembling body, rocking him like a child. She whispered into his ear.

Taran saw Bull jerk his head toward the door. He stood, catching Cal and Rienne's attention. Quietly, and with relief, they left, leaving the pair by the fire to mend their fences.

In the corridor, Bull closed the office door. "Thank the gods for that," he said. "I thought the little fool was never going to break."

Taran thought that a bit heartless. "He seemed in genuine pain."

Bull nodded. "That lament always gets to him. Sully composed it when his sister died two years ago. He loved her very much and it always has the power to move him."

"Not a nice trick to play on him, though," said Rienne, her gray eyes narrowed in disapproval.

"Well, the lackwit had it coming," snorted Bull. "He may be hot-headed and stubborn but he ought to know by now that he'll never get the better of her. The sooner he realizes it, the less pain he'll suffer ... Oh, bugger!"

They all started at the expletive and he had the grace to look sheepish. "Sorry, but I've left my bottle of firewater in there."

He contemplated the door but Taran wasn't surprised when he shook his head. Certainly, he could conceive of no reason that could induce him to go back in.

"Come on," said Bull, "I've another in my rooms. Let's polish off the evening in style."

He turned, jumping half out of his skin as he came face to face with General Blaine. Coming to attention, he saluted smartly.

Once again, the General ignored Taran and his friends, and fixed Bull with a gimlet stare.

"So, he's back in her favor, is he?"

Bull gave a small smile. "I expect so, General, by now."

The imposing man stared at Bull and folded his arms implacably across his muscular chest. "And does he know how fortunate he is? It took all her powers of persuasion to convince me not to transfer him, and that was the least I wanted to do. Fortunately for him, she can be very persuasive."

Bull's cheery manner faded.

"You warn him, Bull," growled the General, "he's had his final chance. I've had enough of his childish ways. One more slip and he'll be turned out of this garrison, no matter what she says. If I have my way, he'll be out of the King's forces altogether. So you can tell him I suggest he reviews his behavior to date and makes some changes, fast. Is that clear?"

Bull frowned. "I'll tell him, sir."

"See that you do."

The General stalked away and Bull led his guests back to his rooms in silence. The mood had radically changed and no one felt like drinking. Bidding Bull goodnight, Taran and his friends retired.

✣ ✣ ✣ ✣ ✣

It was quiet in the commons the next morning. In fact, the place was deserted except for the cook and his serving lads. According to Bull, most of the men had risen much earlier and were already drilling under their sergeants. In the wake of the news of the invasion, they were waiting to take the field.

They had settled at a table by the time Robin appeared. He gave Bull a brief wave but didn't come over. Instead, he approached the cook and Taran saw him ask the man some questions. The cook then disappeared into his kitchen and returned with one of his serving lads—the youngest, by the look of him.

The boy was trembling, and Taran saw him flinch when Robin came closer. The Journeyman glanced at Bull, wondering what was going on, but the big man was also intent on the tableau. When he looked back, Robin had one hand on the boy's thin shoulder and was talking to him. He clasped one of the lad's hands and shook it, a very adult gesture. The boy stared up at the handsome Captain and the fear on his face was suddenly replaced by wonder. He straightened, visibly puffing out his chest, and as Robin turned to make his way to their table, Taran saw what could only be hero worship shining in the young boy's eyes.

Robin reached the table and sat down.

"Saved by a kitchen boy, eh?" said Bull.

"Poor lad was terrified," replied Robin, glancing over to where the boy was struggling to carry a tray laden with five plates of food. "He overheard Parren planning that little trick during the duel and didn't know whether to keep quiet or tell someone. He thought Parren might kill him for betraying him. Lucky he decided to take his chances with the Major."

"Lucky's one word for it," said Bull, turning to smile at the overburdened lad who had arrived without dropping anything. "What's your name, boy?"

The lad put the tray on the table, his eyes still shining.

"Tad, sir. Tad Graylin."

"Well, young Tad, in recognition of your attentive service this morning, tell Goran that we commend you and suggest he gives you extra rations tonight."

"Oh … thank you, sir," stammered the boy and, stepping back, he gave them a fair approximation of a military salute.

To his evident joy, both Bull and Robin came to their feet and returned his salute. Eyes brimming and cheeks burning, the boy dashed off. The two men sat down again, laughing.

"Well, that's one fan you've made today," grinned Taran, glancing over to where the boy was being feted by his envious peers.

"You certainly know how to turn on the charm," said Rienne.

Robin turned playful eyes on her. "Have I charmed you, fair lady?"

"Why yes, gallant sir," she simpered, her eyes sparkling. "How could I fail to be charmed by your stimulating company last night?"

"Ouch!" said Robin, clamping his right hand over his heart. "You have wounded me, fair maiden, and I might never recover."

"Not as deeply as you'd have been wounded if young Tad there hadn't had his ears open," she retorted. "And I'm not a maiden."

"And she's also attached," said Cal firmly. Taran could see he was uncomfortable with Rienne's flirting with the handsome young Captain.

"Never fear, my friend," said Robin, "my heart is committed elsewhere. And speaking of the Major, I have to tell you the General has ordered her to take a rest day today. She left instructions for the rest of us, though."

"Isn't that a bit unexpected?" said Taran, trying to hide his disappointment. Robin's earlier comments about training had led him to hope for something in the way of instruction today.

The Captain smiled. "I may not always admire the General but he does have his uses. Don't worry, you and your friends need not be idle today. Bull and I have some duties to attend to this morning but you will have our attention this afternoon. Might I suggest that you and Cal here spend some time practicing your link? You might also want to review your psyche's structure, see if you can spot the weak areas. Don't attempt to strengthen them until I can give you some guidance, though; you might do more harm than good."

Taran looked at him, feeling deflated.

Robin must have sensed this for he said, "Cheer up, Journeyman. I have a feeling that once your psyche's as strong as it should be, your elevation to Adept won't be long in coming. In some other areas, you're very advanced. Now, I'm afraid you'll have to excuse us. Duty calls."

He and Bull pushed back their chairs. They strode together out of the room, Bull murmuring to Robin as he went. Taran heard the name "Blaine" and saw Robin's back stiffen. His attention was distracted by Cal slapping him on the shoulder.

"How about that? Didn't expect that when we were pouring out our tale of woe to Paulus, did we?"

"Definitely not," replied Taran, smiling at Cal's delight. "When we get back we'll have to remember to thank him. I also want to ask him if he knows why my father never mentioned knowing someone here. Especially an Artesan of such elevated rank."

Ever since the Major's astonishing revelation, Taran had been feeling puzzled and more than a little hurt by his father's failure to mention their acquaintance, however brief it might have been. To allow his son to believe—no, to tell him—that there were no other Artesans in the province smacked painfully of mistrust and evasion. The Journeyman fully intended to ask Paulus about it when he got the chance.

"We're not going back just yet, are we?" asked Cal. "I got the impression we might be able to stay here and study. There are no opportunities like this at home."

Despite sharing Cal's sentiment, Taran was doubtful. "This is a military garrison, remember? No matter how unconventional they are, they're hardly going to let us stay and study. We're lucky they've been as good to us as they have considering the mess we've caused." He caught Rienne's sharp look. "Alright, the mess I caused. I imagine that once they decide what to do—how to put this right—we'll be sent packing."

Cal shrugged.

"So, let's take advantage of what's on offer while we're still here," said Taran. "What about you, Rienne, what are you going to do? Are you in a hurry to go home?"

Rienne's expression, which had shown alarm at Cal's suggestion they stay, softened. "No, not really. I suppose I could spend some time going through my medicinal supplies. I'm still short of a few items, despite our trip into Shenton. They must have an infirmary here. I wonder if I could buy fresh stock from their stores?"

"We'll ask Bull later," promised Taran. "Let's go back to his rooms, it'll be quiet there."

They spent the morning in Bull's suite. Cal and Taran sat quietly in a corner, generally with their eyes shut, working on their linking technique. Taran had been envying Robin's casual control since the Captain had checked on Sullyan the day before and was keen to see if he could emulate it. It called for total concentration and after a couple of hours, he felt he was making some progress. He and Cal began moving about the suite to test the link, going into separate rooms to stretch themselves further.

Rienne spent her time sorting the contents of her medicine bag, which never left her side. She had been light on a few remedies before leaving home and the herb sellers in Shenton hadn't been able to supply everything she needed. She made a list of the most important items and resolved to ask Bull if he knew where she might purchase them.

Once Taran was happy with the progress he and Cal had made, he spent a frustrating hour identifying half-a-dozen weak spots in the pattern of his psyche. He had never noticed them before and fervently hoped he had seen them all. The last thing he wanted was the embarrassment of having Robin point them out to him. He was preparing to go over the whole thing once again when Bull and Robin returned, both looking like they had had an energetic morning.

"Just general training, weapons practice and drill," said Bull when Cal inquired. "Even old soldiers need to train."

"You're not that old, you great ox," said Robin. "Give us leave to change, gentlemen. I hope you've been working hard, Journeyman. I have some more tests for you." He left for his own rooms.

When Bull emerged from his sleeping quarters in clean clothes, Rienne approached him, shyly holding out a fresh cup of fellan. "I hope you don't mind," she said.

He smiled. "Of course not, dear heart. Listen, if your young man ever strays or you get tired of him, you're welcome to come back here and look after me."

"Oh, thanks. Listen Bull, can I ask you something?"

"Certainly," he said, sitting down and sipping his fellan. "Mmm, this is almost as good as mine."

Once she had put her request to him, he told her that not only did the Manor have a dedicated infirmary, but it also boasted a well stocked pharmacy that was regularly supplied from the capital, Port Loxton. She was welcome, he said, to ask for whatever she wanted and he wouldn't hear of her offer to pay. Instead, he gave her a requisition note to show the Chief Healer, with careful instructions on how to reach the pharmacy, which was on the ground floor of the Manor, in one of the wings.

Robin re-appeared in time to hear the end of this conversation.

"We'll be out in the arena when you're done, or you can return here and wait for us. I'm going to have your young man put through his paces today, so if you don't want to see a man in pain, stay away."

The men left, all chuckling except for Cal.

✤ ✤ ✤ ✤ ✤

Left alone, Rienne gathered her bag and Bull's requisition note. She stepped into the echoing hallway. It felt odd to be wandering around on her own, especially when the place seemed deserted. She passed a couple of rooms where briefing sessions were obviously being held, and crossed the junction of two corridors, where she could vaguely hear a heated argument between two or more men. Before continuing on, she thought she recognized Captain Parren's voice. She shivered.

Eventually she found the pharmacy and there met the only other woman besides Major Sullyan she'd seen. Having a common interest, the two soon fell to talking as the Chief Healer, an auburn-haired older woman named Hanan, helped Rienne restock her supplies. Hanan, as she told Rienne, had spent her whole adult life at the Manor, having gone there as a young girl before the civil war to train with Lord Blaine's physician. When the older healer died, Hanan took over.

Proudly, she showed Rienne her domain. Rienne was fascinated by the infirmary, envious of the Manor's facilities. Initially, she was surprised at how sophisticated they were, but it made sense when she thought about it—a garrison would need the very best care for its soldiers.

She and Hanan chatted about medicines and the latest techniques in surgery far longer than Rienne had intended. Reluctantly, she excused herself to her newfound friend, thanking her for her help and promising to return before she left, if she could. She came out of the infirmary deep in thought and not paying attention to where she was going.

By the time she noticed she was lost, it was too late.

Chapter Fifteen

Irritated with herself for wool-gathering, Rienne tried to get her bearings. The trouble with the Manor, she thought, was that all the corridors looked the same. She tried retracing her steps but as she had no idea when she had first gone wrong, it was hopeless. She was forced to admit she was lost.

Having no other choice, Rienne continued on, hoping that sooner or later she would either recognize where she was or find someone to put her right. Eventually, she saw someone coming toward her and smiled in relief. Then her heart jumped into her throat and she stopped. It was Parren's loutish sergeant.

He was the last person she had expected to see, having heard Sullyan order him and the corporal confined to the cells. It was definitely him and she didn't know what to do. If she turned and walked away, she might provoke him into following her. Having seen the leers and obscene gestures he'd cast her way before the duel, the last thing she wanted was to meet him alone.

There was nowhere she could go. As he drew nearer she felt sick, for he was smiling slyly. A cold hand of fear gripped her belly but she forced herself to walk on and ignore him.

He wasn't having it though, and stepped in front of her before she could pass. Gathering her nerve, she stared him out.

"Let me by, please."

He grinned, showing two broken teeth. "Well now, my pretty one, what are you doing down here alone? Lost your friends?"

He stood with his hands on his hips. His weasely face with its weathered skin never lost that cruel smile. Rienne looked past him, desperately hoping someone else would come along, but the hallway was deserted.

"I'm on my way back from the infirmary. They're expecting me." She tried to sound convincing but her voice betrayed a tremor.

"Oh, I don't think they are." He was grinning lewdly. "They've all been seen out in the arena, so they're not missing you. Anyway, you're in the wrong place to be on your way back, my pretty. Perhaps you were looking for someone?"

He stretched out his hand to touch her cheek but she flinched and tried to dodge him. It was a mistake. He was too quick for her and grabbed her arm painfully.

She gasped in shock, really alarmed now. "Let go of me, please. If you were any sort of soldier you'd direct me back to the proper corridor."

"Would I? It's a pity I'm not a soldier anymore then, isn't it?" He glanced around, still holding her arm. "Let's see. Ah, yes. We won't be disturbed in here."

Brutally, before she could utter a sound, he twisted her around so her back was to his chest. He clamped his other hand over her mouth and pushed her into a vacant room. Kicking the door shut, he held her, breathing heavily. She could feel the thump of his heart and smell his none-too-savory breath. She frantically tried to think of an escape plan.

He forced her away from the door toward the opposite wall. She tried to struggle but he was far too strong. To her horror, she could feel that he was aroused. He spun her around and shoved her against the wall, pinning her with his body. Pressing tightly against her, he managed to secure both her wrists with one hand. The other still covered her mouth. She stared into his lustful eyes, trying not to panic.

He was starting to sweat as he brought his face close to hers.

She felt the rasp of stubble on her cheek. His licked his lips and removed his hand from her mouth. Rienne attempted to scream, but he clamped his lips over hers and forced his tongue between her teeth.

She almost gagged at his rancid taste and her heart hammered. She whimpered, but that only seemed to inflame him further. The hand that had covered her mouth now began exploring her body, and she tried her best to squirm away from his insistent groping. He grunted, ceased his mauling and brought his hand up to her face. In it he held a large, sharp knife. She stared in terror as he pressed it to her neck, beneath her ear.

His voice was husky. "Now, my pretty, we're not going to make trouble, are we? We're not going to scream or do anything stupid? I won't cut you if you do as you're told."

He slid the knife down her throat, following the line of her jugular. He ran it around to the hollow, where her pulse was jumping erratically. Then he slid it farther down, below the neck of her shirt and past the division of her breasts. He rested it there and pressed gently. She gasped in pain as a tiny bead of blood was drawn.

"You see?" he rasped. "My weapons are very sharp indeed, and one of them is fully cocked."

Releasing her wrists, he fumbled at her skirts, pulling them up. Really panicking now and not allowing herself to think what might happen if she failed, Rienne took advantage of her free hands. Lacing her fingers together, she jerked them up under his knife hand, at the same time jabbing her knee sharply into his bulging groin. She only had one chance, so she put all her adrenaline-fueled strength into the move.

The knife flew out of his hand, nicking her skin deeply, before flying across the room, where it landed with a clank on the floor. His face went beetroot-red and he collapsed with a strangled gasp. Moaning, he clutched at his groin.

Rienne fled, not knowing whether he was capable of following her. She was sobbing in terror, bag bumping her thigh, breath heaving through burning lungs. Blind panic lent her speed and she bolted up the nearest stairway, taking no note of where she ran.

She pelted down the corridors, taking random turns. Eventually, her body ran out of energy and she was forced to stop. Sinking to the floor, she huddled against the wall, desperately trying to listen over the sound of her own breathing, terrified of hearing following footsteps. As she gradually calmed and quieted, she realized there was nothing to hear.

Slowly, still trembling, she regained her feet. Looking around, she realized she thought she knew where she was. Although she had approached it from the other direction, she was sure that the door up ahead was the one to Sullyan's office. And while not exactly familiar, it was a sanctuary of sorts.

Without a second thought, she opened the door and slipped inside. The office was deserted. She closed the door with infinite relief and leaned back against it, trying to calm her thudding heart. He would never look for her here.

The trembling grew worse and her legs refused to hold her up. She slid to the floor, her mind replaying the frightening ordeal. She began to shake uncontrollably. Bringing her hands to her face, she let the tears come. Once she had opened the floodgates, there was no going back. Her body was wracked by huge sobs and she had to gulp in air. She bowed her head to her knees and cried out her heart.

After a few minutes, just when she was beginning to regain control, she heard a sound. Irrationally thinking that the sergeant had managed to find her after all, she looked up in alarm. Much to her embarrassment, she saw that the door to the Major's private rooms had opened and Sullyan was standing in the doorway.

She had obviously been bathing as her only garment was a voluminous green shirt, probably a man's, and she was toweling her wet mane of tawny hair. When she saw who was on her office floor, she dropped the towel and crossed swiftly to Rienne's side.

Kneeling down beside her she asked, "Rienne, whatever is the matter?" Her golden eyes narrowed as they fastened on the front of Rienne's shirt. "You are hurt."

Struggling to control her breathing, Rienne shook her head. "I'm fine."

"Then why is there blood?"

The Major reached out and moved aside the collar of Rienne's shirt. She stared at Rienne. "This is a knife wound."

Rienne had completely forgotten the nick in her skin but now that she noticed, it began to sting. She managed to say, "It's not too bad, it's just a scratch. I'm sorry, I didn't mean to disturb you. I just got lost and this was the only place I recognized. I'll go now."

Sullyan frowned slightly. "You have not disturbed me and you can go nowhere in that state. Come inside. I have some fellan brewing and you need to sit down." She rose, waiting for Rienne to come into her rooms.

"I don't want to put you to any trouble," protested Rienne. "It's your day off. I'm alright now, really. I'd better get back before Cal misses me."

The Major sighed. "You need not fret about your young man. He and Bulldog are sharing a bottle of firewater after a hard session in the arena. And I think it might be better if you washed and changed your shirt. He might panic if he sees that blood."

"Oh." Rienne looked down, surprised at how much the cut had bled. The younger woman was right, she could do with a hot drink and a rest before facing Cal and telling him what had happened. "Alright then. If you're sure … ?"

The Major simply turned and led the way back into her rooms. Once inside, Rienne looked about as the room was quite different with the late afternoon sun slanting through the windows. Not quite as cozy as the previous night, but still pleasant.

Sullyan went into the cooking room and shortly returned with two cups of steaming fellan. She waved Rienne to a seat and passed her a cup. Then she sat down opposite on the couch, curling up with her slim legs beneath her. Looking tiny in the oversized shirt, with her damp hair curling around her face, Rienne thought she looked about ten years old. Quite unlike a major in the High King's forces.

Rienne sipped her fellan. Its hot sweetness began to revive her but she still felt shaky. Delayed shock, said the healer in her.

"Can you tell me what happened?" asked Sullyan gently. "I trust it was not an argument with Cal?" She smiled, knowing it was no such thing.

"Oh no," said Rienne. "He'd never do anything so … "

She broke off and took another sip. The memory of her narrow escape brought the shakes back and tears of shock welled once more. She couldn't speak of it yet, it was too fresh.

The Major watched her. Laying aside her own cup, she uncoiled from the couch and crossed to the low table by one wall. She picked up the bottle there and brought it over to Rienne.

"Here," she said, pouring a good measure into Rienne's cup, "Bull left this behind last night. He is always telling me it is for medicinal purposes, so perhaps it will help. I can see it is too soon for you to talk about what happened, so we will not. There, is that better?"

The healer sampled the laced fellan and managed a shaky smile. "I can't comment on its medicinal properties, but it certainly tastes good."

Sullyan set down the bottle, picked up her cup and folded herself back onto the couch. In doing so, the oversized shirt rode up, revealing her left leg to the hip. Rienne gasped: there was a long, ugly scar running down the leg from the point of the hip to just inside Sullyan's knee.

"That was a nasty injury," she said, her professional interest piqued. "I'd say you were lucky it wasn't fatal."

"Very lucky," murmured Sullyan.

"How did it happen—that is, if I'm permitted to ask?" Suddenly, Rienne was overcome by shyness.

The Major smiled. "Of course you are permitted, it is hardly a secret." She put down her cup. "My company and I were in the field, tracking one of the raiding parties. We pinned them down and I managed to block their escape through the Veils. Lower-ranking Andaryans are not usually so tenacious and often surrender once trapped. This band, however, was very determined. They succeeded in killing a number of my men before a small group of them broke away."

Rienne's imagination, quite without her volition, showed her vivid images of what the Major was describing.

Sullyan's soft voice continued. "We pursued them and brought them to bay, but their commander refused to surrender. He came at me with almost desperate ferocity and a lucky thrust got past my guard. But the stroke unbalanced him and I repaid him for the wound."

Rienne frowned. "How long ago was this?"

"A week."

"What? That can't be right. You must be mistaken. That scar's much older than a week."

"I am not mistaken, Rienne. It was exactly seven days ago."

Rienne re-examined the scar. "How is that possible? It's healed so well. After such a serious wound most people would still be bed-ridden."

Sullyan smiled slightly. "Ah, but most people are not Artesans, Rienne. You are a healer, so I understand your confusion. But I assure you, it was last week." Seeing Rienne's lack of comprehension she added, "Those of us who can control our metaforce can use the power to influence healing. You live with two men learning the craft, surely you know this?"

Rienne thought for a moment, choosing her words so as not to sound disloyal. "Taran and Cal haven't had the benefit of much training, as you've heard. I don't think they're fully aware of what's possible. But I do remember Taran saying that his father used to do some healing."

"Much is possible when one has the right guidance," said Sullyan, "but even with trained power such as mine, these things have their price."

She watched Rienne's face as her meaning became clear.

"Oh. Is that why you looked so ill when we first met you?"

"That was the first day I was able to stay on my feet. I had expended so much strength in healing that I had precious little left." The Major smiled, as if at a private memory. "The infirmary was very happy to see the back of me, despite the Chief Healer advising against it. Even Bulldog thought I had left too soon, hence his concern for me that day."

"You didn't seem too pleased by his concern." The words slipped out before Rienne could stop them and she bit her lip in embarrassment.

Fortunately, Sullyan only grinned. "Bulldog and I have been together thirteen years. He has seen me take such injuries before and ought to trust me to know my own strength. A gentle reminder like that is good for him now and then."

Rienne tried to imagine what Sullyan considered a reprimand if her flash of temper that day was a "gentle reminder." Shaking her head, she changed the subject.

"Why do you call him Bulldog? That surely can't be his name."

Sullyan regarded her over her cup. "It suits him though, does it not? His real name is Hal Bullen and he was originally Mathias Blaine's sergeant-at-arms. After Blaine's appointment to General-in-Command, Bull became the Manor's sergeant-major. He was responsible for recruiting and training the extra men required by the King to make this a fully operational garrison. Throughout his military career, he was known as Bull because of his size. When I arrived, he and I became friends right away. I was very young and he looked out for me. He was so tenacious and loyal that the last bit came quite naturally."

"So is he still a sergeant-major?"

"Under certain circumstances," said Sullyan. "Officially, he has retired, but Bull is not the sort of man to thrive on retirement. I fear boredom would lead him to drink himself to death and I still find him useful. Now he is a permanent member of my personal staff. He accompanies me on diplomatic missions and helps me whip the Captain into shape."

Rienne frowned.

"When I said he used to look out for me," the Major said, "I meant he stood for me. You understand what that means?"

"Bull explained it to Taran that first day," said Rienne, smiling at the memory. "He was absolutely disgusted that Taran didn't know."

Sullyan snorted. "Yes, he would be. But despite Bull's fitness and size, he has a weakened heart. I feared that neither his physical nor his metaphysical strength would be able to cope with the demands I might make on them, so we decided to look for a replacement. Bull eventually found Captain Tamsen in Lychdale, a remote and poorly run garrison in the far west of Garon Province. Robin has great potential and could attain a much higher rank than Bulldog. He will only do so, though, if he can learn the proper discipline and control."

Without thinking Rienne said, "He tries very hard to please you."

Sullyan shot her a glance. "So he should."

Rienne thought that a little hard. "It's obvious he's very much in love with you."

She blushed, realizing the liquor in her finished fellan had made her bolder than usual.

The Major rose, plainly unwilling to continue this line of conversation. "I am well aware of his feelings, Rienne, thank you. More fellan?"

She gathered the cups without waiting for an answer.

This sudden change roused Rienne's curiosity. She was feeling quite comfortable and relaxed, the terror of her earlier ordeal having faded in a haze of liquor-laced fellan. Even her natural timidity was easing. She was warming to Sullyan and it felt good to have another woman to talk to, especially one who understood Taran and Cal so well.

The Major returned with refilled cups and offered Rienne the liquor bottle once more. Rienne nodded. She smiled as the Major poured a measure into the steaming brew. "Aren't you joining me? I happen to know that Bull has another bottle, so he won't miss this one."

"I am sure he has, Rienne, but I do not drink."

"Not ever?" Rienne was amazed.

Sullyan shook her head, her now-dry hair rippling like dark waves of amber in the fading light. "I am a senior officer in the High King's forces, Rienne, as well as a Master-elite Artesan. I have mastery over Earth, Water and Fire, and I can also influence Air. With that amount of power at my disposal, I can never risk losing control."

"Well, that must get very boring." Rienne was feeling more confident by the second. "Surely you can let your hair down now and then? Come on, you've had a day off and the evening is in front of you. Aren't you entitled to a little enjoyment? Here, just a tiny bit won't hurt you."

Before the Major could stop her, she reached over and poured a very small measure into Sullyan's cup.

The wary look in the Major's eyes made Rienne break into giggles. "Go on," she dared, "live dangerously. Stop being a major and just be a woman. That's allowed, surely, when you're off duty?"

The younger woman gazed at her in wonder; clearly no one had ever spoken to her like that before. She gave a tentative smile. "Do I have your permission in a medical capacity, Healer Arlen?"

"Absolutely," laughed Rienne, raising her cup. "To living dangerously!"

Their cups chinked together and Sullyan sipped cautiously at the unfamiliar taste. A delighted expression came over her face. "This is delicious."

Rienne found this inordinately funny and collapsed into breathless laughter. Sullyan watched her, smiling, while Rienne got herself back under control.

"Can I ask you a personal question?" said Rienne suddenly.

Sullyan sipped her fellan, savoring the heady flavor. "Yes, if you like."

"How old are you? And don't you have a first name? Maybe it's a Manor tradition, but calling you Sullyan seems so formal."

"Does it?" Rienne heard a rueful note in her voice. "Anyway, that is two questions."

"Are you saying I'm being nosy? You don't have to tell me."

Sullyan dropped her gaze. "I have no reason not to answer you." Diffidently, she said, "I am twenty-three. And it has nothing to do with the Manor, Sullyan is the only name I have."

"Really?" Rienne was taken aback. There was an undercurrent to the Major's tone that suggested she hold her tongue, but Rienne was more than slightly tipsy. "Surely everyone has a given name? And how on earth do you get to be a major at only twenty-three?"

"You are very good at asking two questions at once," sighed Sullyan, "and the answers are not necessarily straightforward. Perhaps I can best explain by telling you something of my life."

Rienne leaned forward eagerly.

"But I would appreciate it if you do not repeat what you hear. A garrison is unlike any other community and it is not advisable to let everyone know your private business. As the only woman in the King's forces, there are enough stories circulating about me. I do not want to add to them."

"I won't say anything," said Rienne, suddenly contrite. "I

didn't mean to badger you, I'm only interested. Please don't feel obliged to tell me."

The Major waved off her apology. "I have no authority over you, Rienne. You are free to ask any question you choose. But where to begin? There are still a few people here who remember the events surrounding my arrival. General Blaine and Bull, of course, and one or two others. Robin has heard the story but I have never sat down with anyone else to talk about it. I have never had the opportunity before."

She sounded wistful and Rienne suddenly pitied her. Life must be strange for such a young woman surrounded by only military men and duty. She picked up the liquor bottle and added a little more to their cups. Sullyan didn't seem to notice.

Rienne asked, "Don't you have any non-military friends?"

"The Manor is my home and its routine my life," said Sullyan. "My company is my family and we rely on each other. Some of the men have wives and partners in the nearby villages but most of us do not have friends in the way that you mean. I suppose Robin and Bull are the nearest I have to friends, but Bull has served under me and is now a member of my staff. As for Robin, well, things are … complicated."

"I'll say," said Rienne, a gleam in her eye. "If I had someone like him head over heels in love with me but under my command, I'd feel life was complicated, too."

Sullyan flushed. "Yes, but it is complicated even further by the depth of my feelings for him." She took another swallow of fellan, as if for comfort.

"I knew it!" crowed Rienne. "But how could you not want him? He's so extremely handsome."

"You think so, too?" Sullyan leaned forward, lowering her voice. "Sometimes, it is as much as I can do to keep my hands off him."

Rienne's eyes widened. "Off him? Are you telling me that you don't … that you aren't …?"

"No, Rienne." Evidently embarrassed, Sullyan's flush deepened. "How can we? I am his commanding officer, our relationship would never be the same again. I could never let personal feelings interfere with my duty."

"Piffle," said Rienne scornfully. "You can't throw away what might be your only chance of happiness because of duty."

She was shocked when tears appeared in Sullyan's eyes. Immediately, she was sorry for goading the younger woman, for presuming to tell her how to run her life.

"Don't listen to me," she said. "My tongue isn't usually this unruly. Your life is your own. I don't understand the situation here so I'm not qualified to comment." She glanced at Sullyan sidelong. "It is a pity, though, because he really is incredibly gorgeous."

Sullyan sighed. "If I was going to lie with anyone," she admitted, "I would lie with him."

This insight into the Major's personal life left Rienne feeling it would be better if she changed the subject. She returned to a previous question, sensing she would be on slightly safer ground.

Chapter Sixteen

"You were going to tell me how you got to be a major at only twenty-three."

Smiling faintly over her cup Sullyan said, "I became a major at twenty."

Rienne's eyes popped. "Twenty? Good grief, did you do something seriously heroic?" Snagging the half-empty bottle of firewater, she splashed more liquor into their cups, not noticing the fellan was gone.

Sullyan laughed a bit breathlessly. "Maybe I should start at the beginning."

Rienne cradled her cup in both hands and tucked her legs comfortably beneath her. The Major sipped unthinkingly from her own cup and spoke.

"I spent my early childhood in a village on the Downs, a few miles west of here. I was not born there. I was a foundling, left on some village woman's doorstep. I was so young that I remember nothing of my origins, nothing of my parents. Were they too poor to keep me, or was I simply the result of a casual tumble in the hay? Are they even still alive? I have no way of knowing. The only things I have connecting me to my birth are these gems."

She briefly touched the glinting stone around her neck, identical to the ones in her ears and on her finger.

"They are fire opals and extremely rare, they are not mined in Albia. But they gave me my name, for they were found around my neck in a small leather pouch with the word "Sullyan" stitched onto it. This was assumed to be my family name and is the only identity I have."

She fell silent, her glorious eyes clouding. Before Rienne could speak, however, she continued, and her voice was a shade harder than before.

"My life on the Downs was not happy. I had no roots, no ties to its people. They were plain and simple folk with no wealth, so I was a burden to them. I cannot claim I was neglected or ill-treated, but there was never any love. I was always the stranger who did not belong."

Rienne looked scandalized and Sullyan smiled gently.

"You must understand how they saw me, Rienne. Everything about me was different. The color of my hair, the color of my eyes, the way I spoke. These things set me apart and I cannot blame them for not being able to accept me."

"But you were a child," protested Rienne. "A baby."

"And they raised me as best they could. It is long in the past now, Rienne. Long forgotten."

Rienne said no more but she heard the regret. Heard, too, what could never be forgotten, despite the Major's assurance—the echoes of an abandoned child's unabating loneliness.

Sullyan continued to speak, sometimes swirling the contents of her cup, sometimes sipping from it, despite the fact that she didn't drink alcohol. Rienne sat mesmerized, lulled by the lilting voice and the mellow glow of firelight in the comfortable room.

"As my Artesan powers began to emerge, I learned to use them first by trial and error. When the Downlanders learned what I was, I did not understand their mistrust, but I did learn to conceal what I could do. Then one day, quite by accident, I discovered how to cross the Veils, and soon I was spending more and more time away, exploring the other realms."

She raised her eyes, allowing Rienne to see her candor.

"This is why I understand how bereft Taran was at the death of his father and the desperation that drove him to such extremes. I had no mentor at first and was fortunate to escape unscathed. Now I know the value of caution, but I am in no position to criticize Taran's actions or vilify his mistakes."

She dropped her eyes to her cup again, resuming the thread of her tale.

"When I was about ten years old, news of unrest reached the Downs. It was the beginning of the civil war and it sowed chaos among the lords. Each had to decide which faction to support, each sent men to uphold his chosen cause. This left large tracts of land, as well as villages and towns, undefended. The Andaryans had largely ceased their raiding by this time but the Relkorians, always quick to seize an opportunity, took advantage of the lords' distraction and their forays into Albia increased. A band of them began plaguing the Downlands and the elders were forced to beg the Lord of the Downs for help.

"Relkorians are a cruel, fierce people, Rienne. Many of them are slavers who raid the other realms for captives, whom they sell to the owners of Relkor's numerous quarries. I learned much about them from my travels through the Veils and even at that young age knew more about them than most Albians did.

"Eventually, the elders' pleas were heard and a company of swordsmen was sent to deal with the raiders. I had seen Lordsmen before, of course, but never such a well-drilled, cohesive unit. They were different from the usual loose-knit band of young nobles. They were confident, obedient, ordered. I was fascinated, drawn by their aura of camaraderie and belonging, and by their synchronicity of purpose. These were things lacking in my own life and they appealed to me.

"Once they had scouted the area and discovered the raiders' location, I followed them. I concealed myself as they made camp and watched as they began their preparations. I wanted to see how they dealt with the Relkorians' ferocity.

"I soon discovered that although their commander was a competent leader who was well respected by his men, he was totally lacking in detailed knowledge of his opponent. I thought this was a fundamental mistake, for how can you fight what you do not understand? Even I knew the Relkorian scouts were aware of him, and I knew they would lay up their numbers in ambush.

"He did not know, so I decided to warn him. When it was dark, I slipped past the guards. I found the commander in his tent preparing his attack, and told him he would be leading his men into a trap."

Rienne gasped. In her mind was a vivid picture of a slight, tawny-haired, ten-year-old girl effortlessly slipping past the sentries of a crack fighting company. She giggled at the audacity of it.

Sullyan continued quietly.

"He did not believe me, of course, and became quite unreasonable. He told one of his junior officers to confine me in a field tent and then led his men out. I could not let him walk into the trap without trying again, so I managed to convince my jailer I had fallen asleep. As soon as he took his eyes off me, I left the camp.

"I tracked the men easily, but I was too late. I was forced to hide and could only watch as all those brave young men were massacred in the ambush."

Her eyes, which had been glowing warmly in the firelight, were now fully dilated, huge and black. She had taken hold of Rienne's imagination and the healer could now see, hear and smell the ensuing battle. She heard the screams of the dying, smelled the acrid reek of spilled blood, and tasted the rank sweat of fear on her lips. Thoroughly caught up, she gave a great gasp as the little girl of her vision ran out in front of the badly wounded commander—the last man alive—and spread her small arms against the invading forces.

She stared in amazement as the hazy lines of an Earth barrier appeared around the stricken man, repelling the raiders' attempts to reach him. She watched as they tried, one by one, to break through the barrier before finally giving up and riding off, leaving Sullyan alone with the dying man.

"When they were gone," the hypnotic voice continued, "I turned my attention to the commander. He was barely alive. I knew little enough but I sensed that if I left him to go for help, he would die. He was the last of that brave fighting company, all the rest had perished." She shook her head sadly.

"I kneeled down beside him, trying to decide which of his wounds needed immediate attention and which I could safely leave. I had no medical training, only intuition to guide me. It was lucky for me—and more than fortunate for him—that he was an Artesan, although I did not know it at the time. But when I touched him, he must have sensed it in me, for his psyche accepted my aid. I managed to stem the flow of his blood and reach inside to strengthen his heart. I could feel the effects of blood loss and shock creeping up on him, so when I had done what I could, I covered him with the coats of his dead men, caught a loose horse and rode as fast as I could to the village."

She paused, gazing at Rienne's rapt expression.

"His life was saved by the village healer but it was only later that I learned his name. He was Lord Mathias Blaine."

"Blaine?" pounced Rienne, Sullyan's spell abruptly broken. "As in General Blaine? Oh, my. What happened next?"

Sullyan took another sip of liquor. "There is not much more to tell. Once he recovered enough to understand what had happened, he sent for me. We talked and he found out about my powers. The village elders told him I had no place in their community so he decided I might be useful to him. And here I am."

"But what about your military rank?" asked Rienne, her shyness receding with every sip from her cup. "Don't I remember Robin saying that your other talents outrank the General's?"

"As to military rank, Rienne, you only need to show aptitude and confidence to achieve promotion. Once the civil war was over and Mathias Blaine had settled into his new duties, I managed to convince him to let me train. After two years, I graduated as a captain and was given my own company.

"Three years later, we were part of a major offensive against Relkorian slavers. The General never forgot the massacre of his men and he harried them constantly. Finally, he gained the King's permission to concentrate on dissuading them from raiding us. It was a decisive move. I played a pivotal role in his strategy because of my knowledge of their customs, and our success gained us notoriety throughout the Third Realm. But then came the final battle, the Relkorians' last and most desperate counterattack.

"They killed my commanding officer, Major Anton. He was a man I liked and respected and his death angered me greatly. Without thinking, I assumed overall command and beat the Relkorians back. We defeated them so thoroughly, they have not invaded in any great numbers since.

"For this and for bringing Anton's body home, I was promoted to major."

She broke off and gestured around, her golden eyes faintly sad.

"I still miss Beris Anton. These were his rooms and most of the things you see here were his, including the harp. Anton gave it to me before he died. He was the one who encouraged me to play, although he did not teach me. But he was a very gifted musician and we spent some wonderful evenings here."

After a short silence that Rienne didn't want to break, Sullyan sighed.

"The main reason for the General's interest in me—apart from gratitude—was my Artesan power. He, at the time, was an Adept-elite and he recognized my potential. However, when he began my training he was amazed—and rather dismayed, I think—to discover that I was his equal, despite being untutored. Anton, who was a distant cousin to Mathias and also an Artesan, was a Master, so he confirmed me in the rank."

Seeing Rienne's incomprehension, she stopped.

"Artesans only progress to the next level when someone of higher rank confirms them," she explained. "The exception is the highest rank of Senior Master, where the confirmation of another Senior Master is all that is required. That and the testing, of course."

She grinned when the bemused expression stayed on Rienne's face.

"Have I lost you? Well, maybe it will not be long before Taran has sufficient knowledge and control to support being raised to Adept. Then you will see. We make quite a ceremony of promotion here, whether military or metaphysical.

"But to finish the story—and I will be brief—six years after joining the Manor, I became a Master Artesan. That was also the year I finished my military training. Despite personally nurturing my talents, the General was displeased to have a captain with a higher metaphysical rank than his, so he managed to attain Master status himself. That was as far as his talents could take him. He was content for a while, but it was soon obvious that my own powers were not so limited.

"A couple of years later, I achieved Master-elite. After Anton's death, the General had no choice but to recommend me for promotion, but he was far from pleased with the situation. There are many powerful nobles at court who are less than comfortable having so many Artesans in the King's forces, despite our usefulness. King Elias may be sympathetic toward us, but we still have to be careful.

"Hence my anger over that ridiculous duel. Aside from my personal fear for Robin, it could have had very serious consequences. Any hint of scandal or misconduct would cause much trouble for General Blaine and, by association, the King.

"However, that is not your concern. Despite the disparity of our status, the General and I get along well. I do not challenge his military judgments—although I do advise him on matters relating to the other realms—and he usually defers to me in metaphysical matters. At least, behind closed doors. It makes no difference where the idea originated, provided the orders come from his office."

Without thinking, Rienne said, "So that's why Robin doesn't like him. He thinks you don't get the recognition you deserve."

Sullyan's eyes narrowed. "He had no right to speak of such things. He must learn to conceal his feelings."

Alarmed that she had spoken out of turn, Rienne said, "Oh, please don't say anything to him. He didn't mean to let it out. Now I've broken a confidence and I will feel terrible if you say something to him."

"He should not have mentioned it in the first place," grumbled Sullyan, but she let it go.

Suddenly, she reached for Bull's bottle, emptying it into both cups. She gazed speculatively at the amber liquor. "Am I going to regret this very badly in the morning?"

"Probably," chuckled Rienne, feeling very mellow. Another feeling stole over her and she wobbled to her feet. "Could I use your … ?"

"Of course. Through the sleeping room." The Major gestured vaguely.

Rienne tottered across the room, glancing about with fuzzy interest as she entered Sullyan's sleeping chamber. There wasn't much to see, it was almost as impersonal as the living space. A large bed stood in the middle of the floor, its plain blue coverlet neatly straightened. Brushed and oiled combat leathers hung on one wall, next to a russet dress uniform. Boots sat below, gleaming softly in the dim light. On a low chest at the foot of the bed lay a couple of books, rare though they were in Albia. There was nothing else in the room.

Rienne stumbled through to the privy and while she was there, a foggy thought occurred to her. Fumbling in her pocket, she placed a small item on the night-stand. Then she spent a few moments checking and cleaning the cut on her chest. It wasn't serious, just a deep scrape, but her shirt was a mess and the blood had dried beyond any hope of rinsing it out.

She called, "I don't suppose I could borrow a spare shirt? Mine's ruined and I don't want Cal to see it."

"In the chest," came a sleepy reply. "Leave the stained one there. My valet will see to it in the morning."

Rienne found the selection of everyday shirts, cream or white, cotton or linen, and exchanged her soiled one for a clean one. Feeling much better, she was about to return to the living area when she spotted something she hadn't previously seen.

Hanging on the wall by the door was a beautifully crafted small guitar. Made of dark varnished wood, it had exquisite tooling around the sound-hole and tuning heads. She reached out and gently brushed her fingers over the strings. They were in perfect tune; their tones warm and mellow.

"Take it down."

Rienne jumped; she hadn't heard the Major approach.

"Are you sure?"

Sullyan, though, was already returning to the couch, leaving Rienne to carefully lift the little instrument from its pegs and carry it into the room.

She sat down with it and began to strum. Not having played for a while, her fingers took some time to remember their skill. Sullyan listened in silence, her eyes closed.

Her confidence returning, Rienne played a simple folk tune she learned as a child. Her alto voice was pleasant but had no great range, so she was pleased when the Major joined in the chorus, adding her rich tones to Rienne's. Emboldened, she began a more difficult piece and this time the Major sang the descant. Rienne was amazed by her range; the night before she had sung in a throbbing contralto.

Once the song was finished, Sullyan reached for the instrument and deftly de-tuned it. She played a complicated melody.

"Do you know this one?"

After a few bars, Rienne recognized a sweet lament. She nodded.

"You take the female part," said Sullyan, and together they sang the sorrowful tale of two parted lovers.

When that song was over, Sullyan re-tuned and played a livelier air. Rienne recognized "The Drunken Maidens" and laughed. She laughed even harder when Sullyan changed the words to "The Drunken Major" and then "The Drunken Healer." The two of them giggled like little girls.

Having refreshed herself from a rapidly emptying cup, Sullyan glanced slyly at Rienne. She then sang a lewd and hilarious variant of "Fly up, my Cock." It was one Rienne hadn't heard before and she collapsed in scandalized laughter. Not to be outdone, she took the guitar back and countered with "The Ups and Downs," also changing some of the words and incorporating the names of their male counterparts.

The two women had trouble finishing the song due to uncontrollable laughter. They ended up in a heap on the floor, exhausted by laughter and liquor.

The guitar lay forgotten as they sprawled together, Sullyan propped against the couch with Rienne's dark head in her lap. Their cups sat empty beside them as they drifted quietly to sleep.

✢ ✢ ✢ ✢ ✢

It wasn't the Count's man but one of the Duke's retainers who tapped on Sonten's door that evening to summon him to Rykan's presence. Sonten nodded and heaved himself to his feet, placing the crystal goblet of barely tolerable wine on the stained table.

Muttering, he rubbed his sore back. The badly upholstered chair had seen better days, as had most of the furniture in this damnably shabby place. The Count's mansion was barely fit for peasants, in Sonten's opinion, not at all suitable for entertaining the second most powerful man in the realm. He knew the Duke thought so, too, but for once, he was keeping his feelings to himself.

They had only been here a day and a half and Sonten already had had enough.

He considered the servant as he followed him down the poorly lit hallway. His Grace was obviously taking no chances with the execution of his plan; he didn't even trust the Count's servants to carry a simple message, let alone accomplish the vitally important but relatively uncomplicated main task. It was essential that Count Marik remain ignorant of the real reason behind the Duke's unexpected visit; they couldn't take the chance that one of his chattels might drop some damning piece of gossip.

Sonten grinned. From what he'd seen of the lean Count so far, he shared the Duke's mistrust. The man's melancholy nature bordered on suicidal; Sonten would gladly have helped him on his way. But trustworthy or not, he was useful, and his men—such as they were—would swell his Grace's forces, willingly or not. The General supposed they might be useful in the front lines, if only to shield the Duke's warriors from the initial attack.

Dismissing the gloomy Count from his mind, Sonten concentrated on appearing supportive. He still had grave misgivings about the part the Albian Baron, Rykan's secretive ally, was playing in all this, but the truth was that the Staff would never have existed without the Baron's gold.

Sonten had never discovered how the Baron had obtained such colossal wealth and truth be told, he didn't care. For although the Staff was lost, its creation had re-awoken the General's long-abandoned dreams of power. Soon, he would have more important things on his mind than their outlander ally. That would be his Grace's problem and Sonten would be free to explore his slowly emerging plans for Heron.

He grinned unpleasantly. The power-stealing capabilities of the Staff, useful though they had been, were not the only options open to an ambitious, unscrupulous man …

They reached the ill-fitting wooden door that led to the ducal chambers. His Grace had been given the Count's own suite, but he was scarcely more comfortable than anyone else in this impoverished place.

Sonten snorted as he remembered the Duke's expression on being shown these rooms. Never a patient or tolerant man, his Grace had stopped short of venting his outrage only by exerting considerable effort. Not through any desire to spare the Count's feelings, but simply so as not to terrify him into a gibbering wreck. They needed the Count in as normal a mood as possible until the plan was executed.

The servant tapped on the door and opened it without a reply. He ushered Sonten inside where warmth and light from the twin hearths gave an air of comfort to the shabby room. Here, the wall and floor coverings were the best Sonten had yet seen, but that was all that could be said in their favor. They were obviously old—a generous soul might have said antique—but any value was overridden by their dilapidated state. In the Duke's palace, they would be considered too threadbare even for dogs.

Pushing the mansion's dilapidated state from his mind, Sonten bowed as the Duke stalked toward him from the sleeping room. Clad in his customary black and silver, his Grace the Lord Rykan was an undeniably impressive figure. Powerful and muscular yet agile and slim, he carried his forty-five years lightly.

Once again Sonten felt envy strike his heart but he ignored it, concentrating on the matter in hand. If his Grace should sense even a hint of his true feelings, Sonten would survive no longer than the duration of the Duke's brutal pleasure.

He tried to gauge his overlord's mood; except when his temper was roused, Rykan rarely displayed his emotions.

"Is there any news, your Grace?"

As Sonten had expected, the Duke's voice remained level.

"Nothing definite, though I'm loath to place much faith in the Count's scouts. I've decided to send out two units of our own men to watch for an approaching party and to keep an eye on that rabble he calls a fighting force. Hand-pick the men, Sonten.

I want them to attack the party if possible to lend credence to the tale of unrest. Target the men only, of course, and no fatalities. Our foresight in panicking the peasants has brought admirable results, but we must keep up the pretense for another few days at least. The Count thinks it won't be long now, although he'll say anything to save his worthless skin."

"And what of the Albian offensive, my Lord?"

"I agree with your assessment, Sonten, keep up the pressure. Our losses to date have been pleasingly light and you may convey my approval to Verris and Heron. I'm sending them fresh troops, and I want the action escalated once we return to Kymer. It shouldn't be for long but we have to occupy the Albian forces and prevent them from interfering in my plan. The Baron thinks they could well mount a retaliatory assault unless their attention is fully engaged."

Sonten sniffed. "Well, I can't see it, myself."

"I have no interest in what you 'see,' Sonten," growled the Duke. "Just carry out my instructions. Until the challenge is formalized, I'm taking no chances. Anything that gets in my way—or anyone, General—will be dealt with. Do I make myself clear?"

"Yes, your Grace."

Sonten lowered his eyes. He could not allow his half-formed plans to shadow his tone or his gaze. Utter obedience and unswerving loyalty would ensure he stayed close to the Duke. And it suited Sonten to be very close to the Duke.

Bowing stiffly to hide his smile, he left.

Chapter Seventeen

Cal was panicking and Taran wasn't having much success calming him down. Rienne hadn't been seen since leaving Chief Healer Hanan—Bull had checked with her when Rienne didn't return—and Cal was desperate to scour the Manor for her. Although Taran didn't think Cal taking off on his own was a good idea, he understood how he felt. He was anxious for Rienne, too.

Suddenly Cal broke free of Taran's grasp and bolted for the door. Just as he reached it, someone knocked brusquely. Cal yanked it open, obviously hoping to see Rienne. Instead, a man in dress uniform stood there.

"Colonel Vassa," said Bull, pushing past Cal and flipping a quick salute. "What can we do for you?"

Vassa came into the room, glancing at Cal and Taran. He was slightly younger than General Blaine but no less imposing. Taran felt his heart clench because Vassa didn't look like a man bearing good news.

"A short while ago I found Sergeant Morin collapsed on the floor of one of the lecture rooms." Vassa's voice was sharp with dislike. "He had injuries to his balls. I marched him down to the duty sergeant, who forced him to confess what had happened." He glanced again at Cal and Taran saw his friend's dark face go quite pale. "It seems he tried to rape your young lady."

Taran felt the fear and anger that raced through Cal's veins. He put a hand on his Apprentice's arm.

"He swears he didn't hurt her. Apparently, she disabled him before he could do anything, but I found his knife on the floor. The blade had blood on it that certainly wasn't Morin's."

Cal made a strangled sound and Taran barely heard Bull thanking the Colonel. When he left, Bull turned to them.

"Cal, you come with me, we'll search the east side of the Manor nearest the pharmacy. Taran, go rouse Robin and ask him to help you search the west side. Tell him we'll keep in touch. If neither of us finds her, we'll meet in the commons."

Taran nodded and went to thump on Robin's door. The Captain answered immediately and when Taran told him what Vassa had said, he led Taran off at a run.

They did a thorough search of the rooms on the Manor's west side with no success. Everyone they met was asked if they had seen Rienne, everyone they met shook their heads. After an hour of fruitless searching, Robin led Taran back to the commons.

Bull and Cal got there first but as Robin had linked with Bull beforehand, Taran already knew they had no luck either.

Cal looked sick and Taran had a hard knot of fear in his guts.

"Perhaps she went outside to look for us and got lost," said Robin. "She'd have been pretty distressed, perhaps she couldn't remember the way back. Do you think that's possible, Cal?"

"How should I know?" retorted Cal. He was wringing his hands in panic. "She'd be in shock. She could have gone anywhere."

"Calm down, Cal, we'll find her," said Taran, hoping Cal couldn't sense his own anxiety. "We know he didn't manage to … hurt her."

But Cal refused to be calmed. "Do we? Do you trust what that bastard says? I don't. He obviously did something to her, Vassa found that bloody knife, remember? A man who could try something like that might say anything. Just let me get my hands on him, I'll break his bloody neck!"

"Alright, Cal," said Robin, and Taran saw him trade a swift glance with Bull. The older man nodded. "There's one avenue of inquiry left," he continued. Cal swung around and he held up a hand. "I didn't want to do this as the Major doesn't get much free time, but it's very possible that she could find Rienne."

"Well, what are we waiting for?" said Cal, swinging toward the door.

Bull grabbed his arm. "Whoa, lad. Don't go off like a broken bow. The Major might be sleeping, she might not even be in the Manor. Robin will go ask her if she can help. The rest of us"—he fixed Cal with a firm eye—"will wait here."

Robin left and Cal reluctantly stayed where he was. They all waited anxiously, Cal's eyes never leaving the door. Taran's heart began thumping painfully as, after an interminable wait, he heard Robin returning.

The Captain was running and he skidded to a stop at the door, amazement on his face. "You've got to come see this."

"Have you found her?" snapped Cal. "Is she alright?"

"Just come. And keep quiet."

They followed Robin to the Major's office and filed through the room.

"Quiet," he warned, before pushing open the inner door.

They all stared in astonishment at the two women lying on the floor.

"Rienne!" said Cal, starting forward.

Robin hissed at him but Bull was grinning. It seemed he had spotted something.

"It's alright, Robin," he said, picking up the empty bottle of firewater and inspecting it wryly. "They're not going to hear you."

"Sullyan won't be drunk," interjected Robin. "She doesn't drink alcohol."

"I think you'll find she is." Bull was smiling broadly.

Robin clearly didn't believe him and went closer, raising his brows when he smelled her breath. "But she never drinks."

The women slumbered on, oblivious.

Bull chuckled. "Well, she did tonight."

Taran felt a whisper touch his psyche and realized it was Bull, accessing his metaforce. He wondered why.

Suddenly, the big man snorted. "Robin. Read the room."

"Bull," said Robin indignantly, "that's a gross invasion of privacy. I'm surprised at you."

"Just shut up and do it. You'll get a surprise."

Despite his reluctance, Robin did as Bull suggested. His control was so fine, Taran could only just feel him sampling the top layer of the room's metaphysical atmosphere. After a few seconds, he flushed red with embarrassment.

"Oh, Robin," laughed Bull, "I never knew you were such a prude."

Robin smiled wryly. "I'm not, I just never realized she wasn't." He eyed Cal. "It must be Rienne's influence."

Cal looked up. "What must?"

"Share it with them," said Bull. "The Major won't mind."

By now, Taran's curiosity was climbing the wall. He was pleased when Robin said, "I suppose you're right. Taran, Cal, remember what we were working on today? Just relax your thoughts and I'll show you what I picked up from the substrate."

They did so and Taran felt the Captain's metaforce merging with his own. Soon, he heard snatches of saucy folk tunes and caught some of the women's frankly admiring comments. Cal's dark face flushed even darker and Taran could see why Robin was so embarrassed. Personally, he found the whole thing extremely funny, but then most of the rude compliments hadn't referred to him.

Clearly, Cal's feelings were similar to Robin's for Taran saw him regarding his slumbering partner suspiciously. He nudged him. "'The Ups and Downs,' eh? I wonder where she learned that one."

Cal frowned. "It wasn't from me."

Robin moved forward and kneeled to look closer at Rienne.

"I can't see any signs of injury on her and if she had been hurt, the Major would have taken care of it. She wouldn't have kept Rienne here if there had been anything seriously wrong. Seems that brute of a sergeant was telling the truth."

Cal appeared relieved but Taran could still feel his anger.

"We'd better make them more comfortable," continued Robin. "Cal, can you carry Rienne back to Bull's and put her to bed?"

Cal nodded and carefully lifted Rienne into his arms. Neither woman stirred. Shaking his head, he carried her out. Taran went to follow, but stopped just by the door. He watched as Bull and Robin stood looking fondly at Sullyan.

He heard Bull murmur, "So she's finally found a friend. I'm glad for her. It's about time, and she could have done a lot worse than Rienne."

"Maybe, Bull, but how long can it last? They're not going to be here forever."

Taran's heart fell at Robin's words, even though he knew they were true.

"And what about tomorrow?" the Captain continued. "The scouts are due back by morning and she's going to have one hell of a sick headache when she wakes. Can you imagine what Blaine will say if she reports to him like that? He's hardly in the best of moods at the moment."

"And whose fault is that? Alright, lad, don't bristle at me. Maybe you had better stay here tonight and get ready to be nursemaid in the morning. It's not going to be a pretty sight. I'll leave you to it."

"Thanks," muttered Robin.

Taran turned away before Bull could see he'd been listening.

The big man ushered him into the corridor, leaving Robin to deal with the slumbering Sullyan. He pulled the door closed behind him and led Taran back to his rooms.

✤ ✤ ✤ ✤ ✤

Blaring trumpets outside roused Taran from a vaguely disturbing dream. The sensation of having just accessed his metaforce was uppermost in his mind but the picture in his memory was of Sullyan's golden eyes. As he tried to remember the dream, the sound of movement coming from the living room distracted him. Dissolving like mist, the image slipped from his grasp.

He dressed hurriedly and left his sleeping chamber, coming face to face with Bull. The big man was obviously about to knock on his door and the appearance of Cal's sleepy face from the opposite door showed he had knocked there first.

"Come on," he said, "the scouts have returned. We ought to get to the commons, that's where we'll hear what they've learned."

When they arrived, the commons was packed and Taran was surprised there were so many men at the Manor. It was the most they had seen gathered in one place. He took a chair at the table Bull managed to commandeer and Cal, followed by a pale-faced Rienne, did the same. Taran glanced at the healer with sympathy. Despite having taken a strong infusion of willow, she looked truly awful.

The young serving lad Tad suddenly appeared with a tray of food. As he placed it on their table, he didn't try to hide his hopes of seeing Robin. The Captain wasn't there however, and crestfallen, Tad left.

The commons door opened and the hubbub of voices stilled expectantly. Every eye turned toward it but it was only Robin, and the conversations resumed.

He strode to their table and sat down, shaking his head briefly at Bull's inquiring look. Taran saw the big man frown.

"How's the Major?" asked Rienne, glancing up at Robin from

red-rimmed, bleary eyes. "If she feels as bad as I do, she'll still be in bed."

Robin gave her a quick smile. "She probably ought to be, but she's not. I don't know where she is." Taran heard the concern in his voice and raised his brows. "She wasn't there when I woke this morning. I even asked Emos—that's her valet—if he'd seen her, but all he said was that she must be with the General. I'm a bit worried about her. I was going to check with Hanan at the infirmary when the reveille sounded."

Rienne was about to reply when the commons door opened again. The atmosphere was suddenly charged with expectation and the room filled with the sound of scraped-back chairs. Every man came to attention and saluted.

General Blaine strode into the room, followed by Colonel Vassa. Both senior officers acknowledged the massed salute. Taran noticed that Robin was slow to lower his arm and was standing rigid, his jaw hanging open.

When he took a quick glance at the door, Taran immediately understood why.

Entering behind the General, neatly dressed in spotless combat leathers, eyes bright, hair braided and sword at her right hip, was Major Sullyan.

Taran could see Robin staring at her, clearly stunned. She didn't glance their way and her expression remained serene. He saw the Captain shake his head and even Bull looked surprised. The alcohol she had drunk the night before, thought Taran, obviously hadn't affected her.

The "at ease" order was given while Taran continued to gaze at Sullyan. She stood at the General's left shoulder, legs slightly apart, hands clasped behind her back, her stance one of relaxed readiness. He thought he caught a glimpse of amusement in her eyes.

His musings were interrupted by the General clearing his throat.

"Gentlemen, one hour before dawn this morning, the scouts

of Major Sullyan's company returned from the south. The news they brought is not good. It seems that a large force of Andaryans has invaded our realm, targeting southern Loxton as well as the provinces of Arnor and Rethrick. They are showing no mercy and laying waste to all in their path."

There were angry mutterings from the assembled men.

His voice gruff, the General continued. "Colonel Vassa will coordinate our opposition and he will take the bulk of our strength to the south. He will draw reinforcements from the local garrisons, as I will not strip Loxton of its defenses. In the meantime, Major Sullyan has been assigned the post of Acting King's Envoy and she will mount an ambassadorial mission to Count Marik, our ally in the Fifth Realm. He may know the reason behind this invasion, and perhaps diplomacy can solve the problem before too many more lives are lost. Rest assured, we will cover all options."

Turning to Vassa, he said, "You have your orders. Instruct your commanders and report back to me in an hour. You too, Major."

Both saluted promptly, as did the assembled men. The General returned the homage and left the room. Colonel Vassa then began detailing his men. From what Bull had told him, Taran knew that Vassa commanded several companies of swordsmen and bowmen, as opposed to the mainly mounted men of Sullyan's own command.

The Major stood lightly at ease beside him until he was done.

"That's all, men," he finished. "Go about your duties and I will join you at midday. Over to you, Major."

He turned and left, his men filing out behind him.

Moving gracefully, Sullyan approached Bull's table and leaned her back against the wall, hooking her hands through her sword belt. She regarded them with a level gaze and Taran couldn't see a single sign of last night's excesses. He noticed that Robin and Bull were studying her, too. From their expressions, they had found nothing amiss, either.

"Well, gentlemen," she said softly, "we have a real problem

on our hands. The Pact has been well and truly broken. It seems something has given the Andaryans the idea that the time is ripe for invasion. We must do everything in our power to convince them otherwise."

Taran felt himself flush with shame. "Is it because of what I did?"

She turned her glorious eyes on him and he felt the weight of her gaze. He feared her censure but she replied mildly, "That, my friend, remains to be seen."

Her gaze remained on him and he knew she was aware of the other question hovering on his lips. Clearly, she wasn't prepared to help him with it.

He forced himself to speak. "Is it possible ... would it help ... I mean, would I be permitted to go with you? Maybe I could do something to repair the damage ... to make amends?"

He heard Robin draw breath and expected a flat denial. Instead, Sullyan astounded him.

"General Blaine has already granted permission for you to accompany us."

She turned to Robin, who looked shocked. "Captain, take Taran Elijah to the Quartermaster and have him issued combat leathers and arms. He will become one of us for the duration of this mission. Bulldog, go to the horse lines and have our mounts saddled. Tell Solet I will ride Mandias. Taran, I assume your horse has never been through the Veils before?"

Caught off balance by the suddenness of events, Taran stumbled over his words. "No, I ... how would you get a horse through a portway?"

She didn't reply. "Bulldog, select a mount for Taran."

She turned to Cal. "How strong is your link with Taran, Cal?"

Taran started to reply but she waved him silent, her eyes holding Cal's. The Apprentice shrugged and said, "Fairly strong, I think, after our practice session yesterday."

"Then I would like you to stay here as contact, in case of an emergency."

Cal nodded, frowning over the word "emergency."

Sullyan turned her attention to Rienne and her businesslike manner softened.

"Healer Arlen, while you are here, would you be willing to be attached to our infirmary? I have a feeling we will need every experienced hand in the weeks to come. General Blaine has approved it and if you agree, I am authorized to offer you the post of Acting Captain for the duration of this crisis."

Taran could see that Rienne was totally taken aback. Cal too, was astonished. The Major however, hadn't finished.

"Of course, you will also draw a captain's pay. I understand you are already acquainted with Chief Healer Hanan?" At Rienne's slightly bemused nod, she continued. "Then if you would report to her, she will show you to the Paymaster's office. He has been informed of your status."

She hesitated before adding, "Rienne, I would take it as a personal favor if you would consider yourself attached to my company. I like to ensure the best possible medical care for my command."

Rienne nodded again and Sullyan turned back to Robin. "Captain, when you see the Quartermaster, arrange billeting for Rienne and Cal. Make sure they get quarters large enough to accommodate Taran when we return. I think Bull has already been more than generous with his space. Now, if you will all excuse me, I must report back to the General. Meet me at the horse lines in two hours."

Bull and Robin snapped a salute and Cal followed them out. As Taran turned to go with them, he saw Sullyan place a hand on Rienne's arm. The healer hesitated and Taran would have waited, but Robin called him and reluctantly, he left.

✦ ✦ ✦ ✦ ✦

Bemused by what had just happened and still more than a little hung-over, Rienne gazed inquiringly at the Major. She wasn't sure whether she had imagined it last night, but now, despite her pounding head, it was undeniable. There was definitely a connection between them. She smiled; it was a good feeling.

Sullyan smiled too. "Thank you so much for last night, Rienne, and for the little gift you left on my nightstand. Without it, I doubt I would have woken had the bugler stood by my ear. Willow, was it?" Rienne nodded. "Well, you have done wonders for my reputation. Did you see the look on Robin's face when I came in? I am in your debt and I do not forget my friends."

She dropped her eyes, appearing, thought Rienne, uncertain.

"Rienne, I have heard what happened to you yesterday before you came to my room. I want to assure you that the matter has been dealt with. Morin is in the cells and Corporal Rusch has joined him for good measure. I have let it be known that you are under my personal protection, so there will be no more trouble of that nature. You should have no worries about your safety while you remain among us."

Rienne didn't know what to say, her thumping head had prevented her from thinking about her ordeal the day before. Yet the fear would have returned, she knew, and she appreciated the trouble the Major had taken.

"Thank you," she said, "that makes me feel much better."

Sullyan smiled warmly and departed, leaving Rienne struggling with what she had heard. She was more than a little surprised.

Rienne hurried to catch up with the others, excitement making her forget the ache in her head. She couldn't deny it, she'd been missing her patients in Hyecombe and they would certainly be missing her, but this opportunity seemed to offer much in the way of compensation.

Since enjoying Hanan's tour of the Manor's sophisticated facilities, Rienne had been feeling quite envious. Now she would get to use them herself, maybe even learn new skills and techniques. And she would be paid, to boot. She smiled. All of this had come about because she had blindly stumbled into Sullyan's office looking for sanctuary. Instead, she had found a friend. That was well worth a pounding head and queasy stomach.

When she finally caught up with them, Robin and Bull were discussing their amazement over the Major's swift recovery from alcohol poisoning. Rienne hid a smile and swore a silent oath never to tell a soul her secret.

They also discussed Taran's astonishing inclusion in their mission. Taran, she could see, looked concerned and she wondered if he was worried they might resent his presence. However, they merely seemed surprised and she saw him visibly relax when Robin admitted this would be his first diplomatic assignment.

"You've been on a few, though, Bull," said the Captain. "What can we expect?"

Bull shrugged. "Almost anything. Marik's alright in a gloomy kind of way but he's a reluctant ally and I don't altogether trust him. Just keep your eyes open and be careful not to give offense."

"Why?" asked Taran.

"Because the Andaryan social structure is different than ours, and it's easy to make a wrong step. The other thing you have to remember is their attitude toward women. In their eyes, females are only there to propagate the species. They hold no lands or wealth, or power of any kind. Including ours."

Rienne frowned. "No power at all? There aren't any women in the nobility?"

Bull shook his head. "Andaryans place great store in physical and metaphysical prowess. Generally nobles rise no higher than count unless their power is strong. The metaphysical kind is prized above all, and since the Artesan gift only passes through the male line in the Fifth Realm, it effectively precludes all women."

"So why is the Major accepted as the King's ambassador?" asked Taran.

Bull grinned wickedly. "Count Marik has had, er, personal experience of her skill at arms. She's proved herself equal to him or any of his swordsmen. She's widely respected in the province of Cardon and I would bet there are plenty of other commanders who are aware of her reputation."

He sobered. "But still, even she has to abide by Andaryan customs. My advice is to take your cues from her. Just hope and pray that Marik doesn't have any balls or banquets planned—they can be murder.

"Now, I'd better go. I've got to pack and get down to the horse lines. I'll see you later."

Robin guided the others to the Quartermaster's office. Rienne felt a bit embarrassed that they were getting their own rooms, but it seemed to be easily arranged. There was a small vacant suite of rooms fairly close to Bull and Robin's, and it even had an extra room that Taran could use.

"It'll feel strange not staying with Bull," she said. "What can we do to thank him for his hospitality, Robin?"

The Captain laughed. "Oh, that's easy. Get him another bottle of liquid poison. I'll send a runner to Milo's, if you like."

Taran was issued combat leathers by Quartermaster Adyn and Rienne was happy to accept the light blue clothing worn by the healers. Taran was also allocated a russet dress uniform for formal occasions and Rienne shared his astonishment when he, too, was assigned a temporary captain's rank. They stepped into a curtained-off area to try on their new clothes.

"Not bad for civilians," said Robin when they re-emerged, "but I know which of you looks best."

Rienne blushed under the handsome Captain's gaze. She felt very smart in the trim blue uniform and luckily Cal thought so, too.

Robin obviously caught his admiring look because he said, "If I were you, I'd keep an eye on some of the junior officers, Cal, my lad." Cal looked startled and Rienne blushed even deeper. "Just remember, both of you," continued Robin, "you hold rank now, however temporary. Don't do anything to bring it into ill repute."

Rienne and Taran assured him they would be careful. The Quartermaster then presented Taran with a light sword, which the Journeyman buckled onto his sword belt. Rienne was surprised to see Robin take a small and sturdy crossbow, the sort that could be used on horseback. From the way he handled it, she could see he was very familiar with it.

"We'd better go pack," Robin said.

He glanced at Rienne, giving her a special smile. "Will you two be alright while we're gone?"

She nodded. "We'll be fine, Robin. I'm almost looking forward to it. Have you any idea how long you'll be?"

"Could be anything from a couple of days to a week, I imagine, depending on what Marik can tell us. But we'll keep in touch and Taran can practice his link with Cal so you'll know what's going on. If you have any problems while we're away, go to Hanan. She'll know how to sort it out.

"Come on, Taran, we'd better pack. Sullyan hates to be kept waiting."

Chapter Eighteen

Taran packed quickly and helped his friends move what little gear they had into their new quarters. The rooms were bare but clean and he watched Rienne bustle happily about, planning how to make the place more homely.

Soon, Robin appeared at the door to collect him. Taran took an apprehensive leave of Cal and Rienne but he knew they would be fine until he returned. He was less confident about his own safety.

His pack over his shoulder, he fell into step beside Robin. They made their way to the commons, where Robin collected a pack of supplies, probably ordered by the Major. Young Tad fetched it for them and saluted proudly as he handed it over. Both men returned his salute and Taran made a fair job of it, which drew a smile from Robin.

"Good luck, sirs," called Tad as they waved a farewell.

On reaching the main outer doors, they stepped out into an autumnal day bathed in pale sunshine. There was a definite chill in the air and Taran thought he'd be glad of the warm cloak in his pack.

When they arrived at the horse lines, Bull was already there. His pack lay on the ground next to a large military-style saddle and he was engaged in an animated conversation with a tall, thin, middle-aged man who sported sandy hair and a sullen expression.

Bull stood next to a stocky bay stallion that was half-dozing, one hind leg propped. There were only two other stallions beside it, a darker bay and a chestnut with a white face. All three looked powerfully strong.

As he and Robin came closer, Taran realized the conversation was actually a heated argument.

"She specifically requested Mandias, Solet, those were her orders," Bull was saying loudly. "If you want to tell her to take a different horse, then be my guest, but I wouldn't bet on you still having your post tomorrow."

Clearly unimpressed by the threat, the thin man thrust the halter he was holding toward Bull. "Well, you go catch him, then. I'm not risking it, I tell you, not with a mare in season out there."

"It's not my job to catch your horses for you," snapped Bull. "If you can't manage the mares, perhaps you deserve to be relieved of your post."

The stablemaster was about to reply when Taran and Robin caught up.

"What's going on?" demanded Robin, dropping his pack beside Bull's. "Why isn't Mandias ready? You know the Major doesn't like to be kept waiting."

Solet turned to him, appeal in his eyes. "You know the horse well, sir, would you care to catch him? He's not taking any notice of me."

Robin frowned. "I'm not surprised, man, if there's a mare in season out there. Why isn't she with the brood stock?"

Unseen by Solet, Bull winked at Taran and leaned back against his stallion's rump, clearly content to let Robin continue the argument.

"Took us by surprise," Solet was grumbling. "Wasn't supposed to come into season for another month."

Irritably, Robin said, "Very well, I'll give it a try, but don't think I'm doing you a favor. It's only because the Major can do without the aggravation. But I'm warning you, Solet, if he kicks me anywhere painful, you'll have me to deal with as well as her."

He snatched the halter out of Solet's hands and approached the field where twenty or so horses were grazing. Dumping his pack on the ground, Taran went to watch. His own horse was a gelding, he had no experience with stallions.

Robin stopped by the fence and gave a peculiar, chirruping whistle. A horse in the middle of the field flung up its head, whickering in response. It was a handsome beast and Taran admired the small, neat ears, strongly muscled neck, clean legs covered with delicate but profuse feathering, and powerful hindquarters. Mandias was huge—Taran thought he must be at least eighteen hands at the withers—and coal-black but for a white star in the center of his forehead.

The horse watched Robin, ears flicking backward and forward. He took a step toward him, then stopped. The Captain whistled again and the stallion swished his long tail, as if at a fly. He raised his muzzle, snuffling the wind, then dropped his head and took another mouthful of grass.

The Captain vaulted the fence into the field. Concealing the halter behind his back, he walked nonchalantly toward the horse. Taran could see the big beast watching him as it continued to graze. Almost casually, each mouthful took it a step farther from the approaching man.

Robin continued to advance, now and then giving that strange whistle. Eventually, he managed to come up to the stallion's shoulder. The horse ignored him. Robin gently put out his hand and stroked the beast's hide. The horse continued to crop grass. Slowly, Robin eased the halter out and slipped the end of the lead rope into his other hand. He laid it across the stallion's neck and left it there while he stroked the gleaming shoulder. Then he slid his hand under the powerful neck, grasped the end of the rope and drew it around to secure the horse.

Just then, the neat little roan mare grazing nearby gave a whicker and flashed her light-colored tail. The stallion's head flew up, knocking the rope from Robin's hand. The end slapped onto the ebony neck, causing the great beast to shy off. As it turned, it barged into Robin, who yelled a profanity. Helplessly, he stood in the middle of the field, watching as the stallion herded the mare away.

Taran heard footsteps and glanced over his shoulder. Major Sullyan appeared, carrying a pack that she deposited beside a small light saddle on the ground. She was frowning.

She turned to Solet. "Well?"

The stablemaster gestured in frustration. "He won't leave that mare. Why don't you take Drum?"

Taran heard Bull snatch a breath.

Sullyan glared. "I may need Drum for combat, Solet, if my reasons are any of your business. It looks like I shall have to do your job for you yet again, and I am tiring of it."

Solet's face paled and Taran rather pitied the man, but blame could hardly be apportioned anywhere else.

Robin had vaulted back over the fence and Sullyan took the halter from him. She stared at the stallion grazing peacefully with his mare safely away from the other horses.

She cast Solet a withering glance over her shoulder. "Prepare a stall."

Then she strode across the field, haltered the mare and led her back, the stallion following docilely like an immense black dog. Robin held the gate open, a wry smile on his lips, and Sullyan led both horses into the stall. Solet closed the door behind her. Imperiously, she held out her hand for the bridle, which he supplied, and then she led the stallion out, leaving the flirty roan inside.

Shaking his head, his mouth a hard line, Solet swiftly curried the restless black down.

Sullyan stood at its head for a moment, stroking its nose. Then she picked up her saddle and soon the horse was ready. The others were attaching their packs, Taran having been assigned the dark bay stallion named Thunder. It was much larger and stronger than his own riding horse and was fitted with a curb bridle. Taran was a fair rider but he hoped this was not an indication of its temperament.

Following Robin's instructions, he fitted his pack to the harness rings. He noted that Robin's saddle bore both his own pack and the Major's, as her light saddle was much smaller than the others and bore no rings. It didn't have the high pommel and cantle characteristic of the military combat saddle either and looked, to Taran, to be far less comfortable.

She saw him studying it.

"Mandias will not bear the combat saddle, Taran. Normally I ride him with no saddle at all, but he will tolerate this light one when necessary."

Taran regarded the great black beast warily. It was mouthing the bit and drops of foam fell from its lips as it restlessly tossed its head. The tiny ears were laid flat and a hind hoof was raised threateningly when Taran's mount moved a little too close.

Sullyan slapped its neck sharply. "Mandias, enough." The horse snorted and sidestepped.

"Gentlemen," she sighed, "it looks like I shall have to run this out of him or he will be impossible all day. Finish your preparations and meet me on the other side of the ridge. You know where."

Turning, she regarded the stablemaster with cold golden eyes. "I thank you, Solet, for your help today. I will not forget it." The tall man paled again. "Remove the rest of the mares from the field, lest the roan infect all the others. I suggest you separate them earlier in future and maybe there will be no more accidents."

Solet swung away and called for his stable hands, gathering up halters as he went.

The Major leaped easily into the curvetting black's saddle. Taran was intrigued to see that she had arranged her sword belt crosswise over her breasts so that her sword reared up behind her head, where it could be drawn with either hand. Bull and Robin were more conventionally armed, having theirs slung at the left hip.

The stallion's muscles were quivering as Sullyan backed him out of the lines. Chin pressed tightly to his chest, his powerful neck arched, he pranced on the spot, his lips still foaming. The Major sat him quietly, not curbing him, just running a hand lightly down his sweaty neck.

Mindful of the other stallions they had to pass, she guided Mandias out of the yard. Once safely in the lane, she gave him his head. He squealed and bunched his powerful hindquarters. Forestalling the intended buck, Sullyan pressed him into a standing-start, flat-out gallop, and laid herself low over his neck as he churned the ground. They soon disappeared in a splatter of mud, the stallion's ebony mane flying in the wind and his full tail streaming behind him.

Uneasily, Taran turned to Robin. "Are the others going to be like that?"

The Captain grinned. "Don't worry, you'll be alright with Thunder. He's probably the best behaved of the lot. Mandias is herd leader and has a reputation to maintain, but he's getting on a bit now, which is why the Major uses him for noncombat missions. She has his younger brother, Drum, for the more energetic duties."

Taran raised his brows. "I don't think I'd care to sit on anything more energetic than that."

Robin laughed in agreement. "I'm hoping his son will be a bit more biddable. I'm training him as a replacement for Torka here in a few years' time." Affectionately, he slapped his chestnut's rump. The horse laid back its ears and rolled an eye.

Packs secured and halter ropes stowed, the three men mounted up. Jogging slowly out of the yard, they followed the gouges left in the earth by Mandias. Taran was relieved to find his stallion had very comfortable paces and a light mouth. Whatever the Major's opinions of Solet's horse-management he thought, the man obviously trained the animals well.

As he followed Bull and Robin along the track in the strengthening sun, Taran tried to get his bearings. They were passing through the Manor's extensive estate and he saw both pasture and woodland. Gradually, the terrain inclined and soon the ridge Sullyan had mentioned came into view. They had quickly lost the stallion's trail, having passed where the Major must have jumped him over a huge fallen tree by the edge of the track.

Topping the ridge, they rode along it for a short distance before descending the other side, and now Taran could see the Major riding toward them. She was going at a hand canter, the horse loping easily with none of his former tension. As she rode up to them, she drew in alongside Robin. Her face was glowing with the speed of her ride but otherwise she might have been for a gentle meander in the woods.

Easing the reins, she patted the stallion's neck. "That seems to have done the trick, he should be more biddable now. Curse that fool of a stablemaster; I swear he does it deliberately."

Robin snorted. "He wouldn't dare."

She grinned. "Maybe not. Ah well, no harm done. Now then, gentlemen, a word about our mission." She smiled across at Taran. "Journeyman, this will be a first for both you and Robin and I want you to remain alert at all times. Count Marik is an old friend"—she smiled at a private memory—"and Bull and I have partaken of his hospitality many times. These things are never without risk, though, especially in the light of the current situation. Take your cues from me, but otherwise be polite, be unobtrusive, and be aware. Keep your ears open, all of you, and remember what you hear. Even the slightest rumor could be of importance, so take note of what the servants say. No one can gossip like a servant, so discount nothing. I want to hear every comment, however trivial."

They nodded.

"Taran, we will include you in all our metaphysical dealings on this trip. This is an opportunity for you to practice and learn as much as possible. This is not solely for your benefit; our lives may depend on it. Robin, Bull and I know each other very well and mesh instinctively together, so we will try to remember to include you. But you must not hang back and wait to be offered your place. You must reach out and take it, do you understand? I cannot afford the time to nursemaid you, although I have briefed Bull to look after you if necessary. It will be up to you to make yourself a part of our team, but I will not pretend it will be easy. Do you have any questions?"

Taran thought for a moment. He had not expected inclusion and was taken aback.

"Well, I'll try and do as you say," he said, "but I'm not familiar with your personal patterns. I'd need to memorize them and then see them all overlaid."

Sullyan nodded approval. "Very good, Taran, that is the proper place to start. I believe Robin gave you some guidance yesterday in the strengthening of your psyche?"

"He didn't need much guidance," put in Robin, "and he'd already identified the problem areas. Once he's thoroughly familiar with its new configuration, he'll be much stronger."

Taran smiled gratefully.

"Very well," said the Major. "You have the ideal opportunity to join our overlay, Taran, because we are about to open the Veils."

"I still don't understand how you're going to fit the horses through a portway," he said. "I didn't think it was possible to make one that large."

"We use a completely different and more versatile construct, one which affords access to many men and horses at the same time," she said. "How do you think Relkorians bring their raiding parties through? And Roamerlings their wagons? They use a tunnel, Taran. How strong is your influence over Water?"

He frowned and she smiled. "Come, let me show you."

They had reached the bottom of the slope on the far side of the ridge, where a pleasant valley with a flat, grassy floor spread out before them. A small meandering stream cut through the meadow, glinting in the sun.

Approaching the stream, they halted on its near bank. It wasn't very deep and was crystal clear down to its pebbly bed. The water gurgled gently as it flowed and tiny brown fish flashed suddenly silver along the edge. A tall, stately heron paced the far bank way off to their left, unconcerned by their presence. Dippers bobbed in and out of the water, searching for food.

Sullyan dismounted and the others followed suit.

"Loop the reins around your arm or you'll go through without your horse," cautioned Robin. They lined up on the bank of the river, Sullyan in the middle of Bull and Robin, and Taran to Robin's right.

"Now Taran," said Sullyan softly, "we will construct our tunnel here because the river makes a natural boundary and we are well away from any populated areas. We could do it anywhere we chose but as this is your first experience, we will make it as simple as possible. Once you know the technique, you will be able to construct your own.

"As I am sure you know, Artesans of Master level and above can direct such crossings to open in a specific area, provided they are familiar with the region they wish to travel. But I want to ride through Marik's province before we arrive at his mansion, so we will not direct this structure.

"This is how we proceed. Using the element of Water, Bulldog and Robin will form a portway, anchoring each edge of the construct to the river bank. Their strength in the structure will minimize any leakage of power that could occur before it is fully contained. Once they are done, I want you to cap the power. Then I will push the force out into the substrate and this will form the tunnel. Do you see?"

"I think so," said Taran, nervous and excited. The last thing he wanted was to embarrass himself in front of the Major.

He could feel both Bull and Robin accessing their metaforce

and watched carefully as two columns of power appeared in the air directly over the stream bed. Each bore the unique impression of its creator's psyche, and twined within was the unmistakable signature of Water. Smoothly, the walls of energy grew taller until two pillars stood about ten feet apart, holding between them the characteristic gray shimmer of a portway.

Sullyan's voice came dreamily to Taran. "Now, Journeyman, fit your psyche to the edges of the others' and cap the power."

Hesitantly, Taran reached out and overlaid his glowing pattern across the two pillars, being careful to incorporate the element of Water within his working. He had never used the slippery element like this before but the mesh of psyche was remarkably easy, and he felt a thrill as he capped off the structure.

"Very good," murmured Sullyan, "you should have more confidence in your abilities. Now, I will add my power to yours."

He saw another, incredibly complex pattern superimpose itself across the entire structure. All four blended seamlessly together. Taran felt a tremendous shock of power and realized that if he was the one controlling such forces, he could do almost anything. He felt momentarily giddy, and swayed on his feet.

"Steady," Sullyan warned and he shook his head, taking himself in hand. "Better," she said. "Now follow me as I push the power back, forcing it through the substrate."

He did so, amazed by how easy it was. Very quickly, the energy thinned at the retreating end and he could see it passing through the Veils. Soon, it opened out like a flower, and there was their entrance to the Fifth Realm.

"Now anchor the power at the Andaryan end, and when we return through the tunnel, it will stand alone."

Carefully, Taran did so and when he was done, he saw a tunnel of pearly light standing firm, contained and shimmering in the sunlight.

"Did I really help construct that?"

Sullyan laughed with the simple pleasure of helping the

development of powers long denied the guidance of an experienced hand.

"Well done," admired Robin. "My own first effort wasn't nearly that strong."

Sullyan smiled at her captain. "You should watch out, my friend. You may have competition here one day."

Touched by their approval, Taran experienced a rush of pride that he had not felt since becoming a Journeyman.

One by one, they led their horses through the tunnel, all four beasts giving it a wary eye. Taran knew his own gelding would never have gone through and was glad of the trained stallion.

Sullyan asked him to come through last and told him how to dismantle the structure as he did so. He kept the pattern-meld together as she had told him, and under her guidance disassembled it into its four component parts, learning each psyche intimately. He felt drained, but his hard work earned him a congratulatory slap on the back from Bull.

Remounting, they rode on. The land around them was scrubby, the dry earth turning under the horses' hooves. There were low, dark hills to the north before them and a nondescript forest of fir behind. The Major told him its name was Tarla Brake. Apart from this, the land was barren and colorless, and uninhabited as far as Taran could tell.

Riding in silence, all four used their metasenses to search the surrounding land. Sullyan wore a slight frown; both Bull and Robin looked uneasy. Eventually, the Major drew rein and sat quietly, staring around her. The others waited patiently. Taran threw out his own senses again but could detect nothing.

"Nothing indeed, Taran, and that is very wrong." Sullyan spoke softly, catching Taran off guard. He was amazed she could sense his working. "I can detect no signs of life at all. The Count's mansion is among those hills to the north and there are settlements scattered throughout his lands. As you have sensed, they are empty. But why?"

Chapter Nineteen

They didn't see a single soul all morning. The three villages they passed through were abandoned and silent. At midday they made a short stop to rest the horses and eat a light meal. The eerie silence continued throughout the day. As the light began to fade, they came upon a small pond sheltered by a copse of scrubby trees.

Sullyan halted Mandias and allowed him to drop his muzzle to the water. She glanced at her companions.

"We will camp here, I think. Once we are settled I will make a thorough sweep of the area."

They dismounted and saw to their horses' comforts. Taran was unsurprised when Sullyan took her share of the camp duties. He helped her and Robin organize the camp and site the latrine, while Bull set up the fire. The welcome aroma of fellan soon pervaded the evening air.

Breaking out their trail rations, they gathered around the cheerful blaze. Despite the warmth of the Andaryan day, the evening quickly grew chilly. They padded the ground with their thick cloaks and rested their backs against their saddles. Bull's rich fellan washed down a meal of meat, bread and cheese, while the untethered horses chewed contentedly on a ration of grain, the rhythmic sound of their jaws comforting their riders in the dusk.

Once the meal was over, Sullyan sent out her senses to search the area for its inhabitants. Taran could see that she was puzzled when she found no signs of life nearer than the Count's mansion. Despite the area's apparent desertion, she allocated watches throughout the night. Taran hesitantly offered to take first watch and was gratified when Sullyan accepted.

He settled himself on a large rock from where he could see the campsite as well as the surrounding land and rested his sword across his knees. Bull and Robin saw to the fire, checked the horses, and then rolled themselves in their cloaks. Using saddles as pillows, they fell asleep with the ease of men long used to life on the trail. Sullyan, however, seemed unwilling to rest yet.

She left the glow of the banked fire and came to sit beside Taran. She was so close that he could just feel her arm touching his. Strangely, this barest of contacts sent a shiver through his body that he was hard-pressed to explain.

She loosened her tawny hair and it rippled over her shoulders and back like a river. As she stared out over the twilit land, Taran covertly studied her face. She must have sensed his scrutiny, for she glanced at him before looking down at her hands, which were clasped about her knee. She seemed uncomfortable and this disturbed him; he had grown used to her confident ways. He began to worry, fearing she had some bad news for him. Perhaps something to do with his talents that meant he wouldn't be able to progress as far as he hoped.

He was so engrossed by this thought that when she did finally speak, she caught him off-balance.

"Taran, I have been waiting for a chance to speak with you alone. I fear I must make you an apology."

He stared in surprise. "An apology? Whatever for?"

She took a small breath. "Do you recall me saying, when first we met, that I knew who your father was?"

Taran nodded. He wasn't likely to forget it.

She hesitated, as if unsure how to proceed.

"I knew him because he once came to the Manor with a request. Well, a favor. It must have been … oh, three years ago now."

Taran's eyes widened, he hadn't expected this. "My father came to ask you a favor?"

"Oh, not me personally. But he had heard there were Artesans at the Manor, and he thought there might be training and guidance available. He wanted to know if he could share it."

"What? My father came asking for tutoring?"

Taran couldn't believe it. It was hard and hurtful enough to learn that his father had known about the Artesans at the Manor— including this beautiful and powerful young woman—yet had denied his son the knowledge. But to be told that Amanus, his overbearing and disdainful sire, had actually gone cap-in-hand to strangers to request tutoring stretched Taran's credulity to its limits. His father had never asked for anything in his life.

Sullyan looked up at him and he was arrested by something in her eyes. "He was not asking for himself," she murmured.

His whole body went cold. He just couldn't take this in. It was inconceivable that his supremely self-confident father, who had always considered himself the ultimate authority, would have asked a stranger to train his son. Yet slowly, a glimmer of understanding dawned and he shivered. He thought he knew where this was heading.

He made himself say, "So what happened? I presume he was refused."

The Major looked away, out into the night, her fingers twisting at the ring on her right hand. "Amanus was an arrogant man. He was … vainly proud of his rank and achievements, and not at all pleased to be in a situation where he was forced to ask for help."

Although the words made sense to Taran, her meaning was unclear. "Why was he forced to ask for help?"

Sullyan turned her gaze on him. Once again he felt a chill shock at the touch of those glorious eyes. She lowered them, as if aware of their effect. Taran could feel her whole body trembling.

She whispered, "He did it, Taran, because he knew he was dying."

He sucked in a breath. "He knew?"

This was too much. He stood and turned away. Her revelation, coupled with her closeness, was just too much. He hadn't wanted to admit the irresistible effect she was having on him, but to feel her so near and see her so vulnerable was more than he could take. Why she was quite so disturbed by what she was telling him he didn't know, unless she could guess how deeply it would touch him.

"You loved him very much," she said.

"I owe him everything I am." He didn't turn around. "But I was never good enough for him. I worked hard and studied harder, but he was always telling me I should be doing better, progressing farther, learning faster. Whatever I did, it was never enough. And now I know that what I did learn was flawed. When I think of the years I spent struggling to improve on my own, desperate to seek out those who could help me, and never finding them. All that striving for knowledge and risking my neck looking for it. Even planning to challenge a demon, damn it, because I thought that was the only way I stood any chance of advancement. And all that time, help was nearby. I could have been spared all of that if he had just told me about you."

Frustration and resentment colored Taran's voice. He suddenly swung back on her, seeing concern reflected plainly in the dark pools of her eyes. "And now you tell me he came to you because he knew he was dying?" He shook his head. "I want to know exactly what happened."

Sullyan sighed and her eyes lost focus, remembering that time three years ago.

"It was unfortunate, Taran, that when your father arrived, his arrogance led him to insist on an interview with General Blaine. This did not help his cause. Major Anton, in whose company I served at the time, was also a Master Artesan and a gentler soul than Mathias. He may well have given your father's request a more sympathetic hearing. However, Amanus would speak with no one but the General. Mathias Blaine is a blunt man and uncompromising, he would have spared no thought for your father's problems. So I am sorry to say that Amanus received the treatment his pride deserved. Mathias sent him packing."

She paused, glancing at Taran. He stood a little apart from her, his arms crossed over his chest, his face set. He didn't speak and she looked down at her hands again.

"I came by Amanus as he was leaving, and I could see his pain and anger. I asked him what the problem was and he told me all about you. He told me how proud he was of you and how hard you worked. He said he knew he only had a short time left to live, and spoke of his anguish at not being able to bring out your full potential." Her golden eyes held Taran's once more as she said, "He told me how much he loved you."

Taran felt his eyes sting. His legs suddenly refused to hold him and he sat heavily on a rock across from her, burying his face in his hands.

After a few moments he said huskily, "He never told me. He never once said he was proud—or even pleased, damn it. He certainly never, ever, said that he loved me."

"Well he did, Taran, very much. I could see it in his heart. But I could also see the pain it cost him to tell me, for he was not comfortable with strong emotions. He knew he had not taught you well. He wanted you to continue learning after he was gone because there were gaps in your knowledge and he knew you needed guidance. He made me promise to try to change the General's mind about accepting you at the Manor. If I could not, then he asked me to help you myself."

Taran's head came up like a hound scenting prey. "Are you saying he wanted me to enter the military?"

She smiled sadly. "No, my friend, and that was the heart of the problem. He wanted the training but not the commitment, which is why General Blaine would have none of it. I did keep my word to your father. I tried hard to persuade Mathias, but he became angry. He forbade me to speak to your father again or have anything more to do with him. In my position at that time, I had no choice but to obey. I am sorry for it."

He shook his head, how could he blame her?

"I understand. You have nothing to apologize for."

She leaned forward. "But I do, Taran, because I too know how hard it is to have no mentor. Like you, I spent my early years struggling alone with my power. Once I knew about you, I wanted to help you, but I could not disobey the General. I heard nothing more from your father and as time went by, I confess my promise slipped to the back of my mind. But I never forgot it entirely. Forbidden to go myself, I eventually sent Robin to your village, although this was long after Amanus' visit. I feared he had died and you had moved away. I could not risk Robin asking for you by name so I instructed him to speak to one of the elders, plant the suggestion that if ever you were in serious trouble, there was someone you could turn to. It was all I could do without angering the General."

Taran's mouth was a hard line and he sat with his head bowed, thinking of what might have been.

"Do not think too badly of Mathias, Taran. Our position in the King's forces is tenuous and he rightly fears the malcontents at court. Any hint of disobedience on my part would have elicited a swift reprisal, and I valued my position far too much to risk it. But perhaps I could have tried harder, found a way around the General's veto. If I had, perhaps you would never have been forced to fight and kill Jaskin."

Taran's tone was bitter. "And we wouldn't be in the middle of a demon invasion?"

She shrugged, spreading her hands against his pain. "We do not know for certain that the invasion is the result of your actions. Do not blame yourself until we know the facts."

He remained unconvinced. "Is that why you brought me with you, why you've been so good to me? Because you feel guilty about your promise to my father?"

"Partly. And partly because Amanus was right. You have great potential and I do not like to see such talent go to waste."

He colored at this praise even as a sudden thought struck him. "Does the General know who I am?"

She smiled. "He has not said so. And I have not told him."

She rose and came to him, laying her hand on his arm. "Try not to worry, Taran. I am sure we will get to the bottom of this once we have spoken with Marik. He will know who is behind the invasion and the reasons for it. But you must not forget that Jaskin and his retinue were also at fault for breaking the codes and ignoring the contract, so we would have some bargaining power, at least.

"Now, I am going to rest. Contact Cal before you finish your watch and make sure you rouse Robin at the appointed time. Despite his training, my captain could sleep for his country, given half a chance."

Nodding distractedly, Taran watched her cross to her cloak by the fire. She cast him one last thoughtful glance before wrapping herself in its heavy folds and lying down to sleep.

He turned back to staring out at the night and his thoughts were disturbed and chaotic.

✤ ✤ ✤ ✤ ✤

In the wintry pre-dawn gloom, Commander Heron surveyed his men. He was pleased with them so far; they had obeyed his orders to the letter, ignoring the obvious temptations of the sacked towns. They knew they would get their due reward—Heron was known for his fairness and generosity in the face of a job well done.

Heron was an Adept-elite Artesan. He understood the value of discipline to the military and the metaphysical realm. He also knew the value of reward and although he was no soft touch—any man under his command who thought otherwise soon learned his mistake—he only used harsh methods when they were warranted. His men respected and understood him.

His eyes slanted sideways, fixing on his fellow commander who was poring over a pile of booty on the ground. Heron's lip curled and he allowed himself a brief snort of disgust.

He knew Verris thought himself safe in his position as the Duke's man, for he never failed to remind Heron of it. As if that counted for anything in a situation such as this, thought Heron sourly. Their forces were equal here in Albia, both dependent on each other for their safety and success.

Verris, however, was a greedy man, concerned only for his own welfare. He ruled his men harshly, permitting them no independent thought. Heron considered this a mistake. Men who were not afraid to think for themselves were often more successful in unexpected situations. Those who were loyal to their commander were much more likely to work together and help each other. Verris' men, though, whenever they broke free of his draconian grip, could be trusted only to act in their own interests and leave their commander to suffer the consequences. Heron was very sure Verris would come unglued before much longer.

He was aware they were nearing the end of this campaign. Fresh troops were due that morning—hence his early rise—and the push they had begun four days ago would be consolidated over the next few days. He hoped it would not be much longer before they could go home. However, that was when the real conflict would begin and Heron was less than comfortable about his lord's plans for the future. Not that Sonten had told Heron the details, of course. The commander knew how ambitious Sonten was—every bit as ambitious as the Duke—and he was sure Sonten had some self-advancing scheme that would involve him. He had hinted as much a few days ago when he gave Heron the order to intensify their campaign.

Knowing Sonten well, Heron was aware that something had

happened recently to upset the General, but he had no idea what it was. All he knew was that after the incident in Durkos—Jaskin's unfortunate murder—Sonten had been beside himself. Something had happened to make him afraid, even terrified. Something more serious than his nephew's death.

Heron could only assume that what Sonten had so obviously dreaded had not come to pass. Yet he had still worn the air of a man under sentence of death. His mood was uncertain and his unstable temper shorter than usual. That however, was all in the past. Now, he was positively bullish. Now, he was back to his old scheming self. And now he had let Heron know that once this Albian invasion was over, he had plans that closely concerned his commander.

Heron was not pleased to hear it. He was loyal to Sonten but fearful of what those plans might be.

Sighing, he turned from his thoughts. Verris had straightened and was striding toward him.

"Got a good haul from that last town yesterday." The man was gloating, clearly trying to irritate Heron.

"Good for you," said Heron tonelessly.

His look of disgust made Verris' grin widen. "How've you done?"

"I've had more important things on my mind," snapped Heron, tired of the baiting.

"Oh, more important things, Heron, eh?" Verris imitated Heron's voice with snide accuracy. "What's more important than being rich, I'd like to know? Don't you like gold? Or are you too good for wealth? I forget, you're relying on your precious lord to see you alright, aren't you? Well, I've got news for you. Your fat and ugly general doesn't care a pig's fart about you. I've heard him talking to his Grace. All he's worried about is his own advancement. You make one mistake, Heron, one tiny little slip, and you'll see that your flabby general is the same as the rest of us. Look after yourself, because no one else will."

Heron stared into Verris' pale, slitted eyes, knowing the insufferable man was right. He, Heron, was only valuable to Sonten as long as he obtained the results the General required. If he failed in his duties, he would be replaced. But that was only natural; a commander was only as good as his last successful campaign. If he couldn't fulfil his orders, he deserved to lose his post.

However, he was spared the task of replying; the blank look on Verris' face told him that his fellow commander was in communication with the Duke, no doubt getting ready to receive the fresh troops. Verris turned his gaze back to him with a predatory gleam.

"Here we go, Heron. Mark my words, I'm only a few days away from promotion into his Grace's personal bodyguard. So you enjoy the war, my loyal friend, but don't forget what I said.

"You'd better rouse your men. We have to make sure these Albian bastards don't know what's hit them. By the time our boys have finished, they won't know which way to run. With any luck we'll keep them guessing and stop them from hitting us all at once. And this time, Heron, I'm doing things my way. There's no fun in running away all the time. My lads want a bit of action, not all this peasant-baiting."

Heron stared in alarm. "Remember your orders, Verris, or you could jeopardize the entire campaign. Don't forget, every available man is needed for the war. If you get your command embroiled in a pitched battle, you'll run the risk of serious wounds. You know what that means."

"Don't be such an old woman, Heron, I know my duty. I just want some fun. Don't worry, I won't involve your lads, even though I've heard some of them moaning about all this soft stuff."

Heron doubted that. His men understood why they weren't supposed to engage the Albians. He gritted his teeth to stop Verris seeing his frustration. It never did to let the man know he'd riled you.

Just then, he felt the tingle that heralded the opening of the substrate. His argument with Verris was forgotten as both commanders concentrated on the fresh troops emerging into the Albian dawn.

Chapter Twenty

The morning was gray and overcast with a wintry chill. Taran roused slowly, unsure of where he was. He was unaccustomed to sleeping in the open and his back ached fiercely from the hard ground. He looked around at the sleeping Bull and Robin before noticing the empty place beside Sullyan's tiny saddle.

He sat up carefully, as much in deference to his tender back as to the others' slumber. He saw Sullyan standing by the rock where he had kept watch the night before. She was braiding her glorious hair with quick, deft fingers. As she was turned away from him, looking out over the land, she didn't see him watching.

He rose quietly and walked over to stand beside her. She turned her head and smiled, raising her brows in query.

During the night, he had come to terms with what she had told him, although he was still hurt that his father had hid the Artesans at the Manor from him. However, he had pushed it to the back of his mind. Now, he wanted to discuss his conversation with Cal from the previous evening.

"Have you spoken with the General since last evening?" he asked.

If she'd been expecting him to refer to last night's conversation, she showed no surprise. "I spoke with him at first light. Why do you ask?"

He was relieved. "Then you've heard about the invasion."

Cal had told him what he'd heard about the Andaryan forces pushing farther north. Taran hadn't wanted to be the first to tell Sullyan.

She finished her hair and pulled on her jacket. "Yes, the situation is growing worse. But if it comforts you, Taran, I believe there is more to this than a desire for revenge, even for the death of a noble. The sooner we obtain more information, the better. Are the others awake yet?"

She turned without waiting for a response; Bull and Robin were already rolling to their feet and the aroma of fresh fellan soon filled the damp air.

They ate a quick breakfast of bread and cheese. Nothing unusual had occurred during the night and both Bull and Robin were dismayed to hear about the advancing outlander forces.

"Things are getting serious, Sully," said Bull, shaking his head. "This isn't some outraged lord looking for revenge over the death of a courtier. An invasion on this scale points to someone with real power. Who would risk such an aggressive act, what could they hope to gain? Who else commands that many troops, apart from the Hierarch?"

Taran watched as Sullyan considered the question. "To my knowledge there are only two lords powerful enough to mount such an invasion, but I cannot see the Hierarch granting either one permission to do so. What reason could he possibly have for upsetting the balance we have achieved over the last twenty-odd years?"

"Would they need the Hierarch's permission?" asked Taran. "Perhaps one of them fancies gaining some glory and status for himself by proving his forces against ours."

Sullyan shook her head. "That is not how their society works, Taran. Minor raiding by hot-headed heirs or young bloods is one thing and the Hierarch might turn a blind eye to the occasional sortie, despite the Pact. But this is a full-scale invasion, guaranteed to incur retaliation. As the Hierarch outwardly supports the Pact, I can see no reason why he would agree to any action provoking such hostilities."

Taran frowned.

"The Hierarch is Andaryon's supreme ruler," she explained. "The Fifth Realm's ruling structure is power-based, so he is always the most powerful Artesan. This means he can also raise the largest war-host.

"When a new Hierarch takes the throne, all the other lords pledge to obey him. In return, he is honor-bound to support them and would be forced to use his own troops in their defense should their lands suffer attack. Any noble who acts without the Hierarch's approval would have his overlord's support withdrawn. No high-ranking lord would risk that unless he intended to challenge for the throne.

"To my knowledge, there are no other Senior Master Artesans in Andaryon, so there is no impending challenge to the Hierarch's power. And neither of his highest-ranking nobles—Tikhal, Lord of the North, and Rykan, Duke of Kymer—could raise sufficient men to challenge his massed forces. It remains a mystery and we will have to wait and see what light Marik can shed on the situation."

Abruptly, she changed tack. "Now, gentlemen, before we start our preparations for the day, there is something I want us to practice. Journeyman—have you ever participated in a Powersink?"

Taran was intrigued. "No, not really, although I understand the principles. I've used Cal's power to augment my own, but it's not the same thing, is it?"

She smiled. "Not at all. In order to create a Powersink, each Artesan must enter a collective psyche. One by one—starting with the lowest rank—we overlay our patterns until they form a meld. The power builds as each new pattern is absorbed. Then, once we are all linked, any one of us can use the accumulated power with no restrictions. There is no overriding control. For you—and I mean no offense—it will be a heady experience as between the three of us, we wield tremendous strength. You will have felt nothing like it before and I want us to attempt it now so that if we need it in an emergency, you will know what to expect. But heed this warning, Taran. It could overwhelm you."

"I'm ready," said Taran. He saw Bull and Robin grin and knew they could sense his eagerness.

Judging by Sullyan's cautionary tone, she could, too. "Just be sure you have yourself well under control," she warned.

He nodded but was almost trembling with anticipation. He saw her eye him thoughtfully before she said, "This is how we proceed. Taran, you will lay out your pattern first. Bulldog will be next, followed by Robin, then me. We will go slowly so you have time to assimilate the buildup of power. Then, when you feel you are ready, I want you to throw a shield of Earth force over us—over the entire camp—as if we were under attack. Do you understand?"

He nodded again, wanting to get on with it, desperate for this new experience.

They faced each other over the fire. Closing his eyes, Taran surrounded himself with his psyche before laying it out in the substrate in the center of the group. Bull overlaid with his and the two patterns melded strongly. There was no guiding hand on the resulting force and Taran felt a thrill deep within his soul as the power levels rose significantly. Then Robin came into the structure and Taran saw why he was potentially much stronger than Bull. Despite being the same rank, the Captain's pattern was far more subtle and complex than the big man's, capable of channeling huge amounts of metaforce.

Taran felt himself swelling with the depth of power being raised; his whole body tingled with potential. And then Sullyan's psyche was added to the glowing structure.

As her pattern merged flawlessly with the others, a vast Powersink appeared. A seemingly inexhaustible supply of energy was waiting to be tapped, controlled and directed. Taran thought his skin would burst. He would be invincible with such power at his command. He could lay waste to a thousand cities—an entire realm—and never notice what he'd done. Transported, he began to call on the power to see how it would feel.

A shock slapped him. He felt like he'd been slammed against an invisible wall and his head snapped around in surprise.

Sullyan was staring at him with huge black eyes, her iris obscured. He felt her rebuke and recalled her instructions.

"Shield," she snapped and he immediately obeyed, throwing a dome of Earth force over them all, including the horses. He hadn't even had to think about raising earth, the dome had formed the moment he'd shaped it in his mind. He had never felt so full of potential.

Sullyan's pupils contracted as she inspected the shield. "Very good," she approved. "Now release it."

He found that harder, letting go of the energy, the seductive call of power. His instincts fought against it, he didn't want to give it up. Eventually though, he realized he must and it slipped from his mind, returning to the Powersink. His soul protested the loss.

As the others disentangled their patterns, the energy field dissipated. Taran gave a deep sigh and returned to himself. When he raised his head, Bull and Robin were laughing at him. Even Sullyan was smiling.

"What?" he demanded.

"Good thing the Major didn't give you the whole lot," chuckled Robin.

Taran swung around on Sullyan. "What does he mean?"

She threw up her hands, as if to ward him off. "I only released half my force. You were not stable."

"I was," he said, lying outright. There were more grins. "Oh, alright." He smiled reluctantly. "But I didn't know how glorious it would be."

"Hence the need for caution."

The Major's tone took the sting from her words. It was an intimate tone and the look in her eyes—mingled pride and approval—gave Taran the impression he had just passed some kind of test. He blushed. The moment of intimacy was broken as Bull and Robin began to break camp.

Once they were mounted, Sullyan said, "We should arrive at the Count's mansion before darkness. As we ride, I suggest we practice the shield technique until we are sure we can all mesh perfectly. In view of our situation, I feel it would be prudent."

They moved into the gray morning. As they rode, they practiced with the Powersink, giving Taran time to prove he could handle the temptation. After a while, Sullyan, clearly satisfied with his progress, instructed them all to call out "Shield," at random moments, as if they were under attack.

This ploy worked so well and they were all so proficient at an instantaneous and perfect structure that when the crossbow bolt thumped sickeningly into Bull's left shoulder, pitching him forward onto his stallion's neck, the shield came into being simultaneously with Sullyan's barked command.

Robin swore and grabbed Bull's reins, using his free hand to steady the big man. Sullyan wheeled Mandias, seeking the source of attack.

"There," cried Taran, pointing to a band of riders galloping toward them out of some trees to the west.

"Ride," yelled Sullyan. "Taran, hold the shield. Robin, support Bulldog. We must try and outrun them."

As they spurred their mounts to a flat-out gallop, the Major pointed ahead. "Make for that range of hills. We can lose them there."

They fled their attackers, Robin using some of the Powersink's vast resources to flood strength toward Bull. The big man had recovered enough to stay on his horse and keep up with the others, but his face was ashen, drawn in pain. There was an ominously spreading stain around his left shoulder where the end of the bolt could clearly be seen.

"Taran," snapped the Major, "take the shield. I will try to turn them back."

Taran took full control of the shield, expecting it to be tricky as they were moving so fast. However, the vast store of power flooded out on his command and he found deflecting the murderous bolts being shot at them no great effort.

He watched as Sullyan, throwing glances back over her shoulder, began placing obstacles in the riders' path. There were ten of them, mounted on sturdy, speedy horses. The riders' clothing was dark and unmarked.

She managed to bring down the two leading attackers with her first Earth barrier, riders and horses sprawling together in the dirt. The band, surprisingly, seemed unprepared for offensive moves but soon got smart. They spread out, making less obvious targets.

Sullyan then began lobbing balls of force at the horses' feet. They exploded on impact and she managed to eliminate two more. This brought the odds down to six to four and even with one of the four wounded, their pursuers obviously didn't rate their chances. Suddenly they wheeled their mounts, leaving their quarry to ride on alone.

Sullyan let the horses run a little longer before giving the order to rein back. The powerful stallions were hardly blowing as they slowed to a walk. She brought Mandias alongside Bull, studying his sweating face with concern.

"How is it, my friend?"

"I'll live," he rasped.

She patted his leg. "Be sure you do."

They entered a small range of hills, losing themselves among the baked-dry mounds. Sullyan and Taran held the shield intact while Robin used the energy to support Bull and numb some of his pain. Finally, they found an area Sullyan considered defensible while she dealt with Bull's shoulder, and she directed them toward some fallen boulders at the foot of a slope. The space behind them was just wide enough to camp. They halted the horses and dismounted, Robin helping Bull off his mount. The big man grimaced despite Robin's soothing flow of metaforce.

Gratefully, he sank to the ground and Robin stripped off his blood-soaked shirt. His hugely muscled torso was sheened in sweat, the ugly metal bolt sticking obscenely out of the flesh. Sullyan inspected it gravely. It had sunk to its metal fletching in the muscle at the top of the shoulder, nicking the collar-bone. Its tip was barbed and whichever way it was drawn, it would leave an ugly wound. Bull sat quietly, breathing heavily, waiting for the pain.

"Bulldog," said Sullyan softly, "do you have any firewater with you?" He nodded carefully. "Good." She turned to Robin and Taran. "Robin, increase the flow of metaforce until he sleeps. Just remember to keep an eye on his heart. Once he is unconscious, I will draw out the bolt. Taran, have you ever seen Rienne cauterize a wound?"

Taran grimaced, the memory of burned flesh in his nostrils. "Once or twice."

"As I draw out the bolt, follow through the wound with metaforce. It will have the same cauterizing effect as fire. We can afford no possibility of infection—it could be fatal in this realm."

She stepped to Bull's horse and rummaged in the saddlebag, returning with a small brown bottle. She offered it wordlessly to Bull. He took a long pull before giving it back. She settled in behind him, supporting his body with hers.

"Go ahead, Robin."

Taran could feel the Captain gradually increasing the flow of metaforce. Eventually, it put the big man to sleep. "Keep him out, but not too deep," the Major warned.

She raised the liquor bottle and poured a generous stream of firewater over the wound. Then she glanced up at Taran. "Ready?"

He nodded, concentrating his mind on the end of the bolt.

Using exquisitely fine control, Sullyan used her power to push the embedded metal rod. As it moved slowly, she was able to grasp it in her fingers and help the process along. Bull moaned faintly as the bolt moved and she stopped, looking over at Robin. After a few seconds, he nodded and she continued. This time, the big man was silent and she was able to remove the bolt. Taran carefully guided power through the hole, disgusted by the sound and smell of searing flesh. No more blood was lost, however, so it seemed his work was effective.

Sullyan looked satisfied as she inspected the wound. She cleaned the blood with a cloth soaked in firewater. Finally, she made a bandage and sling from the cloth and bound the shoulder. Then she eased from behind Bull and laid him down gently, placing her hand on his brow to check his temperature.

"Let him sleep," she said, and they stepped away to leave him in peace.

The Major set about making a fire so they could have fellan while they rested. They kept up the shield while waiting for Bull to rouse, taking turns to hold it in place. Taran was amazed when he felt no strain from the effort—having so much power to call on, even without Bull's contribution, made all the difference.

Sullyan scanned the area more than once, finding no trace of their attackers. She found it strange. "Things are not as they should be in this realm, either," she said, sipping her fellan. "The raiders must be the reason for the land being abandoned. I expect we will find large numbers of refugees have gone to the mansion. Although I cannot imagine why Marik has sent no troops to drive off the raiders."

Soon, Bull began to stir. Sullyan kneeled beside him. Taran saw him open his eyes and Sullyan smiled at him.

"How is it now?"

He grimaced. "Could be worse."

"You are very lucky, my friend. Can you sit up?"

Gently, she helped him sit, studying his still-gray face. "You need more help," she decided.

He frowned. "I'll be alright, Major."

She wagged a finger at him. "No heroics. I will use the Powersink."

He acquiesced and she laid her hand lightly on his wounded shoulder. Her pupils expanded, turning her golden eyes black. Taran was fascinated by this physical sign of her power; he had never seen anything like it and there was no mention of such things in his father's notes.

He could feel her drawing power from their pooled source and watched as she channeled it around Bull's wound. Some color returned to his pale face and the tiny lines of pain faded. Sullyan removed her hand and stood, helping Bull rise. She steadied him a moment, watching his eyes. After a few seconds, he nodded and she released his arm. He walked slowly to his horse and drew a fresh shirt from his pack. Robin helped him into it and resettled the sling.

"We are only a couple of hours from the mansion," said the Major, "so I suggest we change into dress uniform here. I can detect no raiders nearby but we will keep the shield intact. Bull, take what you need when you need it, I want you as fit as possible."

He nodded.

They changed into dress uniform, the Major completely unselfconscious beside the men. Bull and Robin took no notice, well used to Sullyan's ways, but as she stripped off her leathers, Taran had to turn away to hide his flaming face. Robin helped Bull finish his dressing and then boosted him into the saddle.

They emerged cautiously from their campsite and encountered no one. The Major rode in the lead, her russet-brown uniform lending her an even greater air of authority. Her double-thunderflash rank insignia and battle honors glinted gold on her breast in the sun.

After a couple of hours, during which Taran felt Bull draw healing power more than once, they came to the last hill. The horses cantered easily up it. From its crest, they looked over a large stretch of rolling grassland.

Perched on a small mound rising out of the terrain a few miles away was a building. Taran could see it wasn't large, but it was surrounded by a sea of temporary huts, tents and shanties, all manner of crude dwellings, hastily erected and looking ill cared for. This was what Sullyan had expected to see, he thought, this was where the land's inhabitants had run to, and it confirmed her suspicion of widespread unrest.

Sitting motionlessly, she stared down at this motley sea of life. Even from this distance, Taran could hear and smell the effects of so many people camped so close together.

"What has made them gather so tightly?" she mused, almost too low for him to hear. "These lands have been ruled by Marik's family for generations. His standard still flies above the mansion, so why are his people so fearful?"

None of them had answers. They nudged their mounts down the slope.

As they neared the mansion, their senses were assailed by all manner of sights, sounds and smells. Taran had to block some of the worst and was aware of the others doing the same. They entered the outskirts of the shanty town, following the path that led inexorably to the mansion gates. The horses stepped fastidiously over piles of dung and refuse, avoiding certain puddles of liquid that, by their color, were not water.

Some of the peasants gave the four riders furtive glances. Many hid from sight. Still others emerged from their huts to see who was riding so boldly through their midst. Some wore hostile, hate-filled expressions.

Sullyan rode calmly, with no outward expression, but Taran could see her keeping a wary eye on her surroundings. It would not do, he thought, to be caught unawares here.

They safely reached the entrance to the mansion courtyard, where the huge wooden gates were firmly closed. There was a small sally port to the right of the gates behind two guards holding crossed halberds.

Sullyan drew rein beside them and saluted from Mandias' back.

"I send greetings to Count Marik," she said formally. "Please inform him that Ambassador Sullyan has arrived, as arranged, to see him."

Chapter Twenty-one

The guards did not respond and Taran thought there would be trouble. However, before anyone could speak again, the sally port opened and a man in elaborate court dress emerged. His maroon-edged black mantle flared around him as he strode over to Sullyan's horse, and she dismounted, stretching out her hand.

He took it, raising it to his lips. "Welcome, Ambassador, it is a pleasure as always. We've been expecting you. Will you come inside?"

Taran studied the Andaryan with interest, wondering if this was the Count. He was certainly a minor noble, judging by the quality of his attire. Typical of the race, his eyes were slit-pupiled like a cat's, and they were pale gray. Taran knew that Andaryans generally had very pale irises and had heard that even an all-white eye was not unusual. It made their faces strange and their expressions hard to read, he thought, remembering the noble he'd killed. He certainly wouldn't care to play cards with one.

The Andaryan had swarthy skin, dark and neat hair, and an ingratiating smile. Taran instinctively distrusted him but Sullyan greeted him cordially.

"Well met, Lord Nazir. There have been some changes since last I was here." She indicated the dirty cluster of huts with a wave of her hand.

He sniffed, glancing disdainfully at the hovels huddling around the mansion like beggars around a fire. "There have been raiders abroad, Lady, and commoners are easily frightened. Pay them no mind. I bid you and your friends welcome to Count Marik's home. Please enter and allow us to offer you accommodation and refreshment."

He saw Bull and his pale eyes widened. "Your companion is wounded. Did you encounter the raiders? Does he need medical attention?"

"I thank you for your concern, my Lord," said Sullyan, as the great gates creaked open and they passed inside. "He will be well with a little rest. Is Count Marik not here to greet us?"

Taran saw irritation cross Nazir's face but his reply was calm.

"The Count is detained at present, Lady, and sends his sincere apologies. He is looking forward to speaking with you at the feast tonight."

Taran heard Bull's low groan and remembered what he'd said about Marik's interminable feasts.

"What is the occasion, my Lord?" asked Sullyan as the noble snapped his fingers to summon grooms. Mandias laid back his ears at the man who took his bridle and Sullyan spent a few minutes reassuring the horse. The groom eyed him warily as he led Mandias away.

"The Count needs no excuse to hold a feast, Lady," said Nazir, his smile not touching his pale eyes. "But I believe it is mainly in your honor."

He led them across a large cobbled courtyard and into the mansion proper. Taran gazed at the cold and drafty entrance hall with interest.

"The Count is too gracious," said Sullyan, and Taran was sure he caught a hint of sarcasm in her voice.

The noble didn't seem to notice, however, and continued through the hall. It was poorly lit by huge, guttering tallow candles.

They cast a greasy yellow light, causing shadows to sway over the faded tapestries covering the gray stone walls.

As they followed Nazir, their footfalls rang on the flag-stones. They passed several rooms in which Taran saw flickers of firelight and heard the muted hum of conversation. He also smelled the pleasant aroma of food and drink. A few of the mansion's other occupants passed them, all glancing curiously at the Albians' eyes and unfamiliar dress.

Nazir led the way up a narrow flight of twisting stairs and eventually halted in front of a door at the end of a short passageway. He flung it open and ushered them into a large and reasonably comfortable-looking room.

The candles here were brighter and there was a roaring fire in the grate, dispelling the season's damp chill. Dark and heavy drapes of what had once been good quality cloth obscured what Taran assumed were tall windows, and worn but serviceable carpeting covered the floor. The room contained an enormous bed, two low couches, and several well-used easy chairs. Another door in the far wall led to what Taran thought would be a washroom.

"I hope this is satisfactory, Ambassador," said Nazir, bowing low. "I believe you have occupied this suite before?"

"Indeed we have, my Lord. We will be very comfortable, I thank you."

He inclined his head, saying, "I will send a servant with refreshment and water for washing. The feast starts in two hours. I look forward to seeing you there." With a smile that showed his teeth, he departed.

Bull dumped his pack on the floor and sank gratefully into one of the chairs. Sullyan helped remove his jacket and shirt so she could inspect his wound. She undid the bandage and gently probed the outraged flesh. Bull winced but made no sound.

She frowned at him. "What did I say to you about drawing power, man? You have not taken nearly enough. I need you fitter than this. Taran, Robin, meld with me, please."

They did so and Sullyan again laid her hand on Bull's shoulder. A deep amber glow suffused the air around him and he sighed with relief. She withdrew from the power source and removed her hand.

"Better," she said. "It will not be fully fit for a few days, but at least it will not incapacitate you." She replaced the bandage and sling.

A tentative knock sounded at the door and Robin went to answer it. Their visitor was a stooped and wrinkled woman, so shrunken that her head barely reached the tall Captain's chest. As she peered around Robin into the room, Taran saw she was holding a tray of steaming cups.

"Harva," exclaimed Sullyan, as she waved the woman inside. "I had not thought to see you here. Do you still serve the Count? I thought you would be peacefully tending your garden by now."

The elderly servant crossed the room carefully and deposited her tray on the low table. She embraced Sullyan with genuine affection.

"Bless you, Lady," she said. "I've served here since I was a little girl. I wouldn't know how to do anything else. Now, I know you prefer fellan but we're running low so I've brought you spice tea. The maids will be here soon with hot water for washing."

A change came over her; she seemed afraid. Sullyan raised her brows.

"Lady," said Harva, lowering her voice and glancing at the door. "Beware while you're here. These are troubled times and not safe for you. Don't stay longer than you need."

She gave Sullyan a quick smile before scuttling from the room.

Robin frowned as he closed the door. "What on earth was that about, Major? Does she have her wits?"

Sullyan flashed him a look. "Just because she has reached a venerable age, Captain, does not mean her senses are failing. Harva was nurse to Marik's father, and also to Marik when he was young. She has served this family faithfully and knows more than her appearance suggests. You would do well not to underestimate her. I will heed her warning but I wish she had told me more."

Taran passed out the mugs of spice tea and before they were finished, the maids arrived with hot water. Four perspiring girls staggered in, carrying a huge steaming copper pot that they emptied into a chipped stone bath in the washing room. Sullyan retired happily to bathe. Taran could hear her splashing and humming to herself.

While they waited for her, Bull, revived by the hot drink and Sullyan's ministrations, regaled Robin and Taran with tales of the banquets he had attended in the past. They were humorous accounts but they made both men more nervous than they had been before.

The Major eventually emerged from the washroom, toweling her mass of wet hair. She was wearing one of the robes provided, but it was so short that it left very little to Taran's imagination. Robin saw his embarrassed flush and said, "Sullyan," in a reproving tone.

Clearly startled, she stared at them until she realized what the problem was. Then she laughed at Taran's discomfort.

"I beg your pardon, Taran. I am so used to the company of these two that I forget others are not used to me. I will try to behave more decorously."

Taran reddened more. "Please don't trouble yourself on my account."

"Gallantly said, Journeyman." She laughed again. "We will make a courtier of you yet."

Crossing the room, she sat before the fire to dry her hair.

Taran joined Bull and Robin in using the hot water to freshen up. When he returned to the main room and saw Sullyan standing by the window, he simply couldn't suppress a gasp of admiration.

The full-length, green satin gown she was wearing flowed over her slim figure like liquid beryl. She had braided part of her hair into a coronet around her head; the rest rippled down her back like tawny fire. Her fire opals spat sparks from her throat and ears, and her golden eyes were huge and lustrous. She was wearing a subtle perfume that just caught at the senses, and Taran knew he had never seen anyone so poised and beautiful in his entire life. His heart pounded at the sight of her.

She caught him staring and smiled. He blushed furiously.

"Why, thank you, Taran," she said softly. "You look very handsome."

That brought the color even higher in his face. To his relief, Bull saved him from replying by giving a loud snort.

"Enough, Major. If I didn't know you better, I'd say the atmosphere was getting to you already. These two lads are going to have enough to cope with tonight without you making matters worse."

Taran frowned and Robin, who had also been staring at the Major, turned on him. "What do you mean?"

Sullyan shifted, clearly about to speak, but Bull waved her to silence. "Let me, Sully, you'll only confuse them."

Taran raised his brows, expecting the Major to take offense at his tone. Surprisingly, she only smiled and turned away.

Bull sighed. "Andaryans are a very sensual people," he said, "the nobility more than the rest. The stronger Artesans among them often use their talents to flood the atmosphere with … er, shall we say 'erotic thoughts' … on occasions like this, to make the game more enjoyable. Their object is to find a partner for the night, regardless of whether they're wed or not.

"Young and handsome specimens such as you two are going to be the target of every lady's desire tonight. They have little else to do with their time other than indulge their petty pleasures and they will be falling over themselves to see who can provoke the greatest … er, reaction … in you. Do you understand what I'm saying? It's tiresome but it's almost impossible to resist them, so don't be too embarrassed if you find yourselves responding to them.

"But whatever you do, don't make any promises to them. Especially don't, under any circumstances, leave the hall with anyone. Sully and I will try and keep an eye on you but we'll both be affected too—especially with her looking like that—so you'll need your wits about you."

Taran stared at him, apprehension flooding his heart.

"One other thing, gentlemen," said Sullyan. "Do not touch or eat with any of the silverware. Some of it is likely to be spellsilver and if it touches your skin, it will cut you off from your power."

"Spellsilver?" asked Taran nervously. "What's that?"

"Spellsilver is an ore that occurs naturally in Andaryon. It looks the same as ordinary silver and can be worked in the same fashion. However, it has strange properties where metaforce is concerned, properties that make you feel nauseous, drain your strength and prevent you from using your powers. It works through contact with skin or blood and shuts down all metaphysical processes. Touching it is very unpleasant, although the effects only last as long as the contact continues. Being forced into contact with it—or worse, having it enter your bloodstream by, let's say being stabbed with a spellsilver knife—is a dreadful and terrifying experience. I would not recommend it."

Taran's heart fell even farther. The feast sounded like an ordeal.

"Fortunately," she continued, "it has never, to my knowledge, been discovered in Albia, so we have little cause to fear it. Here, however, where the acquisition of power is paramount and all means used to obtain it are considered justified, it is widely employed. Including it among the silverware of a feast is just another part of the power game.

"So, gentlemen, keep yourselves tightly shielded and do not attempt to contact one another through the substrate. It is too dangerous."

Taran returned to his dressing, feeling more nervous than ever and reflecting that his father had left much that was important out of his son's education. The only comfort the Journeyman could draw came from the equally uneasy look on Robin's face. The Captain's lack of experience in such matters made Taran feel marginally better.

They had just finished their preparations when they heard the second hour strike.

"Ready, gentlemen?" asked Sullyan. "Remember, shields up, be unfailingly polite even to the most persistent and obnoxious admirers, make no promises, and do not touch the silver."

She took a deep breath, the first sign of nervousness Taran had seen. "Shall we go?"

They left the suite and descended the long, twisting stairs. Sullyan led the way, her long gown flowing around her legs as she walked, surrounding her with an air of grace and stature. She paused at the bottom of the stairs to let the others flank her. Taran could hear music coming from the main hall along with the muted murmur of many voices. He walked beside Robin toward the brightly lit hall which, when he reached it, was packed with more people than he had expected to see.

The hall was decorated with colorful tapestries and banners, and was bright with the warm glow of countless lamps and candles. Here, Taran saw nothing of the shabby air pervading the rest of the mansion; the hall was a study in wealth and opulence. The mellow sound of minstrels blended with the noise of servants bustling among the tables.

Sullyan stopped at the doors and Taran saw her searching the throng, presumably looking for the Count. However, the Master of Ceremonies spotted them before she saw their host and struck the huge brass gong for silence. Every eye in the room turned toward them. Taran felt apprehensive as he suddenly became the object of many ladies' scrutiny. Robin shifted beside him, clearly sharing his unease.

Sullyan appeared serene, outwardly unruffled by the attention her appearance was earning. When he risked a quick glance, though, Taran noticed the gem at her throat pulsing with the rapid beat of her heart.

The Master of Ceremonies announced them, giving their rank and Sullyan's title, and as they followed her into the room, they were approached by a tall, thin man whom Taran thought was in his early thirties. He was dressed in maroon velvet trimmed with black and silver fur and he had very pale gray eyes with the characteristic slit pupils. Pupils that were, Taran saw, rather dilated, giving the man a febrile look. His face was pleasant in a lean, melancholy kind of way, and he was richly adorned with gold. It glinted from his ears, throat, wrists and fingers. On the middle finger of his right hand gleamed a huge ruby cabochon.

The man stepped up to Sullyan, smiling nervously.

"Lady Sullyan, my dear," he said, as he took her right hand and raised it to his lips. "How good to see you again. Your companions are welcome in my hall." He swept a dismissive look over the men and Taran felt Robin tense. Bull touched the Captain's arm and the younger man relaxed.

Sullyan frowned at the Andaryan but made a small and graceful curtsey as she replied to his greeting.

"Count Marik. I am pleased to be here, my friend, despite the circumstances behind our visit. I look forward to discussing matters with you in tomorrow's council."

The Count appeared none too pleased to be reminded of the council meeting. Ignoring Taran, Bull and Robin, he took Sullyan by the arm and ushered her through the throng of people. "There will be time for business tomorrow. Come, my dear, there is someone who desires to meet you tonight."

Sullyan suffered herself to be led, although she glanced in puzzlement at the Count's eager face.

Taran, watching the noble's back as he escorted Sullyan, could sense the air of nervous apprehension swathing the man. It was, he thought, totally out of place for a noble in his own mansion surrounded by his own people. His preoccupation with the Count's strange demeanor consumed him and he hardly registered the faces of the other guests.

The Count led Sullyan to the far end of the hall, where a tight knot of people surrounded a tall, regal-looking man dressed in black trimmed with red and silver. A fluttering group of young ladies appeared to be hanging on his every word and they parted reluctantly as Count Marik led Sullyan through.

The man in black turned to see who was approaching.

Taran felt the shock that ran through Sullyan when she saw his face. He sensed, rather than heard, her tightly hissed whisper in his mind—*Beware!*—before her mental shield snapped down. With amazement, he saw the very deep obeisance she accorded this arrogant-looking lord, and watched as he took her hand with a predatory smile. A strange light glowed in his pale yellow eyes.

The Count licked his lips and cleared his throat before announcing, "Most noble and gracious Lord, may I present the Lady Ambassador Sullyan, of whom you have heard me speak many times. Lady Sullyan, it is my privilege to present to you his Grace Lord Rykan, Duke of Kymer."

The saturnine lord gazed intensely into Sullyan's face. She had frozen her expression in a smile but Taran could feel tension radiating from her.

"My dear Lady Ambassador." The Duke's voice was deep, rich and silky-smooth, and his eyes looked as sharp as an eagle sighting prey. His darkly handsome face was perfectly complemented by an aquiline nose and the very pale gold of his slit-pupiled eyes. Despite his clear middle age, his slim and powerful body positively radiated strength and virility.

He smiled, showing white, even teeth, and held fast to Sullyan's hand as his raptor's eyes traveled her body, drinking in her curves.

"The Count has told me of your beauty, Lady," he murmured, "but at his most effusive he did not do you justice. You are a flawless gem among women. No one here could outshine you."

"Your Grace is too kind," responded Sullyan, casting down her eyes. She tried to reclaim her hand but the Duke was having none of it.

He turned, obliging her to fall into step beside him, and moved toward the highborns' feast table at the far end of the hall.

"Marik."

The Count scuttled nervously after him.

"Your Grace?"

"It is my pleasure to be the lady's escort tonight. Make other arrangements for her … companions."

"Yes, your Grace."

With much flapping of his long hands, the Count ushered Bull, Robin and Taran to tables at the long side of the hall. Bull and Robin went reluctantly, the Captain clearly unhappy at being separated from the Major. Sullyan, when Taran glanced back at her, seemed to be coping with her shock, for she sat and talked with the dark lord while the other guests found their seats.

"The Duke of Kymer?" hissed Robin. "What the hell's he doing here?"

Bull shook his head.

"I've no idea. All I know is that we've been warned about him before. Leaving aside our suspicions as to who's behind the invasion, Rykan's probably the most influential and dangerous person in the entire Fifth Realm. He has a reputation for ruthlessness and cruelty and I've heard he has an insatiable appetite for women.

"Coincidence it may be, and nothing to do with the raids, but his presence here means there's something afoot. He's got under Marik's skin too, by the looks of things. The Count may be gloomy by nature but he's not normally so nervy, although I'd expect him to be on edge with Rykan here. The Duke's a harsh overlord and Marik's not wealthy.

"Keep your wits about you, lads. Sullyan's in no danger

at present but if Rykan takes a fancy to her, she'll need all her diplomatic skills to wriggle out of it without giving offense."

✣ ✣ ✣ ✣ ✣

There was one guest in the hall whose thoughts were not occupied by the Duke's sudden interest in the Lady Ambassador. This man stood glaring at the floor, his unwieldy bulk quivering with anger. Lord Sonten's fleshy face had turned purple and the bustle of the guests as they competed for seats gave him the space he needed to calm himself. The unexpected and totally shocking appearance of the Albian Journeyman—Jaskin's murderer, the man responsible for all of Sonten's troubles—sent conflicting emotions surging through him. He was finding it hard to breathe.

He couldn't believe it. After days of panic and terror, and the rage of seeing his ambitions die with his nephew, Sonten had finally regained some composure. He had even resurrected his plans, altering them most cunningly to compensate for Jaskin's death. Accepting that he would never be able to avenge the murder, he had recalled the huntsmen set to watch for the Journeyman's return. Yet here he was, the murdering bastard, cocky as a cat. Strolling about right under Sonten's nose, threatening to wreck his ambitions all over again! Sonten's face flushed with outrage, for under these very public circumstances, there was nothing he could do. He couldn't afford to draw the Duke's attention to this man and certainly couldn't do anything that might jeopardize his Grace's plans. He glowered at the Duke, sitting so smugly at the highborns' table, drooling with disgusting eagerness over the young human witch.

Sonten felt sick. If the Duke's plans should succeed –and there was no reason to believe they wouldn't—there was a high risk of the Journeyman revealing his fatal meeting with Jaskin; even worse, Jaskin's use of the Staff. If that happened, then Sonten's life would be forfeit and the General knew his overlord well enough to realize that his execution for treachery would be neither swift nor painless.

He fumed. It was imperative that Rykan didn't get his hands on the murdering outlander. If Sonten could only spirit the man away, he could ensure his eternal silence. And maybe, he suddenly realized with a jolt, just maybe he could also learn what had become of the precious Staff.

The thought sent his pulse racing and he wracked his brain for a plan. There had to be something he could do; some way of quietly removing the Albian while also avenging his nephew's death and recovering that damned Staff before the Duke discovered it was missing!

Sweat prickled his skin; time was running out. He was sure the Journeyman wouldn't recognize him; he had been very careful to stay concealed during the duel. Jaskin had been right to insist on that. He simply couldn't stand here, powerless, doing nothing. It ate at his soul and he quivered with rage. Surely he could think of something? He couldn't let the man fall into Rykan's clutches; the risk would be too great. No matter how much Sonten might enjoy watching Rykan torture the man.

Yet those risks were not the only consideration, he realized abruptly. If he could recover the Staff, he could also revive his original plans, if not improve on them now that he had Heron to work with instead of his independent nephew.

His eyes narrowed. What if he could recover the Staff but keep it for himself? What if he didn't return it to his Grace? Why should the Duke suspect his general even if he did discover the priceless artifact was missing? Maybe Sonten had been worrying unnecessarily. If that was so, then what advantage was there in returning the Staff to his Grace? Its possession would guarantee the success of Sonten's plans, for no matter what Heron's Artesan rank, even the vastly more experienced Rykan would be powerless before the mighty weapon.

These thoughts and emotions caused Sonten's heart to contract painfully. He struggled to breathe and stared maliciously at the Albian Journeyman. He just had to get him away from his two companions.

As he fought for composure, he glanced down at the table beside him. The glitter of a silver knife caught his attention and he frowned. Then a smile twisted his thick lips as, unobserved by his fellow guests, he palmed the knife, concealing it within the folds of his cloak. If the Journeyman could somehow be maneuvered away from the throng, one stab of this knife would render him weak and powerless...

Darting around the room, Sonten's gaze rested on a young, attractive courtesan from his Grace's retinue. When she looked his way, he beckoned her to him. Whispering urgently in her ear, he passed her the silver knife. She slid it out of sight, her nod and silent smile accepting his commands.

As if she had any choice, he thought, his hooded gaze sliding back to the unsuspecting Albian Journeyman. Satisfied, he sat; the servants were beginning to serve the food.

Chapter Twenty-Two

Taran was distracted from his worries about Sullyan and the Duke by the arrival of the food. Suddenly, he, Bull and Robin found they had more than enough to cope with as a bevy of Andaryan ladies fluttered about them, each determined to win their attention.

Bull's injured shoulder brought him more admiring sympathy than he could take, especially as he only had one good arm with which to fend off prying hands. Robin was trying to hold three conversations at once. Taran was turning to help the Captain when an eyeful of creamy bosom appeared before his face. Startled, he looked up at the young woman who stood smiling down at him. He smiled tentatively back and when she slid onto his lap, he realized his mistake. The soft and yielding flesh, barely covered by her low-cut gown, was now even closer, and he could smell her alluring perfume. Embarrassed, he averted his gaze and she took full advantage by trailing her hands over his body.

He found her appealing in a puppy-dog kind of way and didn't want to offend her by pushing her away. Her caresses, though, were too intimate and her smile too lustful. She was hard to resist and, to his horror, he felt his body responding. Her delighted grin told him she could feel it, too, and his face burned with shame. He tried to gently push her off but she clung to him. Unwilling to cause a scene, he fixed his gaze on Sullyan, using the concern he could sense from Robin to distract his unruly body.

He, Bull and Robin traded frequent despairing glances. Between trying to do justice to the truly fine meal, avoiding the silverware—of which there was far too much for Taran to even try judging which was spelled, so he used his own eating knife—and trying to dislodge his admirer, the meal passed in a blur.

Of all of them, it seemed Sullyan was having the easiest time. She had only one admirer to entertain and, judging by the way the Duke held fast to her hand throughout the entire meal, he was not about to let her escape. The other ladies who had managed to secure places at his table were being well and truly ignored and if their venomous looks were anything to go by, vengeance would be sought.

Endless though it seemed, the meal was eventually over and the servants cleared the tables. Taran sighed with relief, hoping to lose his determined little temptress in the crowds. But then the musicians struck up and her adoring eyes glowed. "Oh, good! Dancing," she gushed, and grabbed him by the hand before anyone could take him from her.

Taran's heart fell; he was not a natural dancer and the thought of close physical contact with that shamelessly heaving flesh was almost too much. Bull and Robin had also been claimed for the first dance, both looking as desperate as Taran felt.

He had a moment's respite when the Master of Ceremonies announced the dancing would be led by Lord Rykan and the beautiful Lady Ambassador. They took the floor and Taran thought the Major looked a little strained around her eyes. As the Duke turned to her, though, she curtseyed, displaying an easy grace that drew glares from several ladies.

He realized his simpering young escort had ceased caressing his thigh. Instead, she was watching him archly.

"You're in love with her, aren't you?" she accused.

Startled, he glanced at her. "No, not really." He indicated Robin, standing nearby with a voluptuous lady on either arm. "Besides, she's already spoken for."

The woman followed his gaze, appraising the Captain, running her eyes appreciatively over his powerfully lithe body. She snorted and turned back to Taran.

"Him? He's handsome enough, I'll grant you, but he'll be no match for milord the Duke should he decide to have her. You'd better warn him to stay clear if he values his health, or there will be trouble. His Grace doesn't take kindly to interference."

He heard her gasp and shot her a look. She was staring across the room but he couldn't see the reason for such a reaction. "Come on," she said, tugging at Taran's arm. Resigned, he joined her on the dance floor.

✤ ✤ ✤ ✤ ✤

The evening faded into a haze of female faces, a tangle of women's bodies. Their perfume, their greedy clutches, their aggressively amorous looks, Taran found them nearly impossible to resist. More than once he had to steer himself and his partner away from the doors leading out to the darkened balconies as all of them, and especially his increasingly desperate little temptress, seemed determined to drag him out there. If any of them had succeeded in getting him alone, he only had his imagination to tell him what trouble there would have been.

Only a handful of times did he get a glimpse of the Major, monopolized as she was by Rykan. Not even the Count, it seemed, was allowed a dance with her and no one was foolish enough to try. Eventually, and to Taran's immense relief, the musicians finished their sets. During the polite applause that followed, servants brought seats and arranged them in a ring around the room. He, Robin and Bull secured seats near the head of the ring where they could see Lord Rykan and the Major clearly.

Taran thought Sullyan looked tired, but she still spoke with and smiled at the Duke and laughed gently at some of his comments.

He still held her fast by the hand and she no longer tried to extricate herself.

Once all the guests were seated—Taran experiencing a moment of triumph when the rush to secure the best seats denied the now-frantic courtesan a spot by his side—there was movement by the doors. Three servants carried in a huge floor-harp and set it before the Duke.

Taran had never seen a harp so large and wondered how one person could possibly play it. He soon had his answer when two minstrels moved forward and stationed themselves one on either side of the magnificent instrument. They played a set of songs that were alien to Taran's ears, although the guests appreciated them loudly. Then, as a final piece, and after Rykan had sent a servant to speak with them, they played a love song that Taran recognized. He was disquieted by the look the Duke was giving Sullyan as the song was played, although she betrayed no emotion. He was also feeling rather proud of Robin, who was restraining himself admirably in the face of the Duke's interest in his love.

Once the song was over and Sullyan had shown her appreciation, Rykan at last released her hand. He stood, the room instantly going silent.

"My dear Count Marik," he began, his voice ringing deeply, "nobles and ladies all. It is late and we have been most royally entertained tonight."

The guests applauded loudly.

"But before the evening draws to a close, I have a request to make of the lovely Lady Ambassador, who so graciously consented to be my consort tonight."

Taran saw the momentary start Sullyan gave at the word "consort" and the wariness that crossed her face. Beside him, Robin raised his head like a hound sensing danger.

The Duke turned to Sullyan. "My vassal, Count Marik, tells me you have some skill with the harp, Lady. Would you do us the very great honor of playing the final piece tonight?"

A murmur ran around the assembled guests. Taran heard astonishment, delight, and even pique from some of the other ladies. He saw the Major close her eyes momentarily as if overcome by weariness, but she stood with liquid grace and gave a small nod of acceptance.

"The honor is mine," she said and moved toward the harp.

She positioned herself to one side of the vast instrument and spread her hands on the strings. Soft, liquid notes rippled around the room and the crowd fell expectantly still. There was a pause while she stood with her head bowed, her eyes closed. Then her hands moved on the strings and the first sweet notes of a melody filled the air.

Taran recognized the tune—it was one of those timeless airs, ancient beyond knowledge of its origins—but when the Major began to sing, he could make no sense of the words. They had a profound effect on Lord Rykan, though. He seemed mesmerized by Sullyan's skill, her mastery of the huge instrument a wonder to them all.

As the last throbbing notes of the song faded, silence descended. Taran looked around at the rapt expressions on the guests' faces, none of whom wanted to break the spell. Just when it seemed they would sit that way forever, Lord Rykan stood, leading an applause that swept the room and rang to the rafters, the entire audience surging to its feet.

The Duke stepped forward and took both the Major's hands in his. "I had no idea you knew the old high language, Lady. You have done us great honor tonight, for which we can only thank you."

Sullyan bowed her head and returned his smile. "It is I who must thank you, my Lord, for giving me an evening I shall never forget when I return to Albia."

Taran didn't miss the double meaning of her words. The Duke however, was concerned by her mention of leaving and his predatory eyes narrowed. "Lady, it would please me greatly if you would accept an invitation to be my guest at Kymer. The comforts of my palace are surely far more conducive to diplomatic discussions than this poor place."

"You are too kind, your Grace," replied the Major smoothly. "Under happier circumstances I would be honored to accept your invitation. However, at this time, I fear I must decline, as after the council meeting tomorrow I am constrained to return to my duties. I do trust I have given no offense?" She executed a deep obeisance.

The Duke looked offended, but could say nothing in the face of her courtesy. His yellow eyes flashed in annoyance as he said, "Very well. I will excuse you this time, my Lady Ambassador, provided you do me the honor of promising to return soon to accept my hospitality."

There was steel in his gaze and hunger on his face. Taran shuddered.

"If my General so wishes it, your Grace, I will indeed return," replied the Major, keeping her head bowed demurely to avoid his furious eyes.

She curtseyed again as Rykan stamped away, followed by his retinue.

The rest of the guests drifted off to their rooms. Taran sighed with relief as the courtesan who had been vying for his attention all night left as well, not daring to come near while Sullyan was with them.

The Major was the subject of many envenomed glances as she left the hall. She was obviously exhausted and remained silent as they climbed the stairs to their suite. Once the door shut, she collapsed onto the bed.

Robin sat beside her and gathered her into his arms, stroking her hair. Taran watched in quiet concern. After a while she revived a little and, pushing herself away from the Captain, sat up.

"Oh, gods," she said wearily, "I never would have come if I had known he would be here. No wonder Harva told me to beware. Curse Marik. What was he thinking of, why didn't he warn me?"

"What's Rykan doing here, Sully? Did you get any idea what he's up to?" asked Bull. The big man was occupying an overstuffed chair, trying to ease his shoulder.

Sullyan's eyes narrowed at this display of pain and she moved toward him. "I have a nasty suspicion that he intends to go against the Hierarch."

"Bloody hell," said Bull. "Civil war? Is he strong enough to risk such upheaval?"

She placed her hand over the wound in his shoulder, clicking her tongue at the heat in it.

"Ordinarily I would say no." Closing her eyes, she gave Bull more healing. "For all his wealth and standing, I think he has neither the power nor the might to challenge the Hierarch openly. However, something is happening here that I do not like. For all his faults and reluctance, Marik and I are friends. He would not normally allow me to walk into such a trap. The fact that he said nothing tells me something is badly amiss.

"But although I dislike the coincidence of finding Rykan here while an invasion force attacks our lands, I cannot, at present, see a connection. The Duke is a skilled tactician, well known for taking personal command of his troops. I would not expect to find him attending the banquet of such a minor vassal as Count Marik while his warriors were laying waste to our realm. Even if the Count is known to be our friend."

Bull's face was losing its pained expression under Sullyan's touch. Taran saw him begin to relax.

"It is not as if the Duke would fear Marik coming to our assistance," she continued. "The Count cannot afford to maintain a force of trained fighters and the levies he could raise would pay for land laborers, at best. Neither does he hold knowledge that might be of use to the Duke. He was never a prolific or a successful raider, and I would wager that Rykan has a far greater knowledge of Albian defenses than Marik does. It is a puzzle I do not yet understand. All I can do is try to find out more tomorrow."

She nodded at Bull and removed her hand. Taran felt envious fascination; he had never seen anyone capable of using power for one thing while talking about another.

"Will Rykan be at the meeting tomorrow?" asked Robin, his tone a touch too casual.

Sullyan smiled. "No, Robin. He intends to leave for Kymer before first light. I am relieved, I do not think I would have the strength to resist him again." She headed for the washroom. "Come, gentlemen, we are all tired and I know you had your hands full of your own problems tonight. You did very well, by the way. I was proud of the way you resisted such temptation." She grinned at their sudden embarrassment.

"Tomorrow will be a busy day and in the light of the evening's events, I feel we should be on our guard tonight. Taran, will you take first watch again? Robin and Bull will take the later, and I the dawn watch. Let us see what tomorrow's meeting brings."

✣ ✣ ✣ ✣ ✣

Most of the day was spent carrying out lightning raids. Heron's company—like Verris', augmented by the extra men he'd received—pushed relentlessly northward, firing villages throughout the provinces of Arnor and Rethrick, reaching the southern borders of Loxton.

Heron kept in touch with Verris through the substrate, coordinating their companies' efforts while keeping the forces sent to oppose them from organizing an effective defense. He knew the Albian swordsmen had caught only rare glimpses of them; their orders to inflict damage and flee meant they posed a frustratingly elusive target. By the time news of their presence in a particular area reached the local defenders, they had vanished, only to resurface somewhere else.

He and Verris had roused their men just before dawn as usual. By midday, they were drawing closer together. Their routes brought them on converging lines and by the time Heron's scouts caught sight of Verris', they were well into the remoter districts of Loxton Province, territory controlled by the personal forces of Elias Rovannon, High King of Albia.

Heron knew Loxton was an open province, consisting mainly of grasslands and rolling hills. The vast forest surrounding Port Loxton, Albia's capital city, was far to the north and the few wooded areas of the south offered little cover for raiders who wished to remain hidden. However, he was anticipating changes to their orders very soon and open countryside would better serve their needs.

Shortly after noon, he and Verris had finally met and they were allowing their men a breather under the scant protection of the only tree cover for miles. Abruptly, with no warning, Verris received the message they had both been waiting for.

He dropped the chunk of cheese he was eating and his eyes lost their focus. Heron stopped chewing his strip of meat and watched his rival. The huge grin that appeared on Verris' face told Heron that all was going to plan. He was both relieved that their initial task had been successfully completed and anxious about the next stage.

He knew there would be major casualties this time, it was inevitable. The Albian forces were every bit as well trained as his and they would be fighting for the protection of their people. They would be intent on inflicting serious injury, while his and Verris' orders were to preserve their men and keep as many fit for action as possible. Knowing how skilled Albian swordsmen were, Heron was fearful this instruction was going to prove impossible to obey. He could only do his best.

"Well, that's it, Heron," said Verris suddenly, smug satisfaction coloring his tone. "Now the real work starts. I'm going to enjoy this. No more running away like frightened sheep, now we get to show these peasants just how well we can fight."

"Just remember the reason we're doing this, Verris," cautioned Heron, disliking the gleam of menace in his eyes. "Lose too many of your lads and you'll be called to account. That won't advance your career or endear you to the Duke."

"Do you think I don't know that?" Verris sneered. "Think I'd jeopardize my position? I'm not going to throw my lads away on the real fighters, I'm not stupid. No, I'm going to target the ones who can't fight back. I'm fed up with burning houses and cow byres, it's time to show these Albians what we can really do. And what better way to lure out the human forces? How much quicker do you suppose they will respond when they see their precious peasants dying?"

"Yes, but that's my point, Verris. You get them really angry and you'll have to stand and fight them. That's what we've been instructed to do. Keep up the pressure, intensify the action. If we're to convince them we mean business, we can't turn away when they send out their strength. That's when our lads will begin to pay."

Verris scowled. Heron knew that caution was not in his nature. Verris knew their orders as well as Heron did and he was not under Heron's command. If anything, he probably thought Heron should be answering to him; he was part of the Duke's forces after all, while Heron merely served under Sonten. And everyone knew Verris had no respect for Sonten. In his eyes, the General was nothing but a lump of lard with no expertise. Verris thought Sonten held his rank through political skill, not tactical. He had said on many occasions that he could do a better job on both counts. The coming conflict, thought Heron, would give him the opportunity to prove it to the Duke. The rank of general, he knew, would suit Verris fine.

"You do what you feel comfortable with, Heron," said Verris. "You carry on as you always do, stay within your boundaries and take no risks. That way you'll keep your rank. Just don't get in my way and don't countermand my orders. You may be happy to remain a commander but I have higher goals. I suggest you rouse your men because we have a war to wage and I, for one, intend to enjoy it."

He took to his feet, scattering the remains of their makeshift meal, and strode toward his men. Heron watched him go before gaining his own feet, frustrated and angry. Verris was a good leader, no matter Heron's reservations. He could wish the man was less abrasive, but that was just his nature. Irritatingly, he was as likely to succeed in his ambitions as anyone Heron knew. Sometimes, Heron wished the man would fall over his huge ego and suffer the same humiliations everyone did. The day he did would be the day Heron began to like him.

Sourly thinking that the day would never come—some men seemed immune to paying for mistakes, no matter how obnoxious they were—Heron dismissed the man from his mind and began planning his forces' deployment. The rest of the day and night would be exhausting enough without concerning himself over Verris.

Chapter Twenty-Three

Dawn was chasing away the shadows as Taran woke from a vague and disturbing dream. He moved his head to ease the kink in his neck and as his eyes opened, he saw the Major sitting cross-legged on the bed. Her eyes were open, huge and black but unseeing, and Taran guessed she was communing with General Blaine. He wondered how the General would take the news about Rykan's presence and Sullyan's suspicions.

The Major had obviously been awake for some time; she was fully dressed in her combat leathers and her hair was partially braided. The rest of her things were neatly folded on the bed, her sword lying beside them. As Taran watched, her eyes returned to normal and she shook her head. She noticed him and smiled. "Wake Bull for me, Taran," she asked softly.

He rose and shook Bull's good arm. Sullyan leaned over Robin and gently touched his shoulder. Both men woke easily, the result of their training and instincts. Taran envied their lack of yawning and eye-rubbing that accompanied his own return to wakefulness.

As they dressed, Robin asked casually, "Any news from the Manor?" Sullyan closed her eyes and the Captain caught her expression. "What?"

Bull looked sharply over. The Major regarded them all before she spoke.

"The news is not good, gentlemen. The invasion has intensified and the fighting has crossed the borders into Loxton Province. It seems the Andaryans have changed their tactics. They are no longer content with burning and destroying buildings, now they are taking a heavy toll on the people. This is an act of outright war."

Taran went cold and the two military men stared in horror.

Sullyan continued. "Vassa and his men are doing their best and the Colonel has mobilized all the local garrisons, but it is not enough. He has requested support from the Manor. The General wishes to deploy my company, gentlemen, and so you are recalled."

"We are?" said Robin sharply. "Not you?"

She shook her head. "I cannot leave yet. I must stay for the council meeting and maybe a day or two longer to do what I can to alleviate this situation. I must find out the reason behind the invasion and see what diplomacy can do to rectify it before I return. You must lead the men for me, Captain. You are ready for command and they will follow you. Use your judgment and training to deploy them. General Blaine ordered it and I told him I have every confidence in you."

Robin was clearly not impressed by this show of trust; his concerns were more immediate than the prospect of assuming his first solo command.

"I can't leave you here alone," he said. "Especially not with that predator Rykan."

Sullyan glared at him. "You have no choice, Captain. The orders are given and we must obey." Seeing his anguished look, she softened. "Besides, Lord Rykan has already left. I watched his train move out at first light. You need have no worries on that score. I am well on my guard now, he would not trap me like that again. Gentlemen, I suggest you pack and be ready to leave as soon as possible. I will send for the horses. The sooner you return, the sooner my company will be in the field."

They finished their preparations and a light breakfast that was brought by a maid. Sullyan had hoped to see Harva again, but the elderly woman was nowhere to be found. A servant tapped at the open door and announced the horses were ready. Taran trailed the others as they filed down the stairs. None of the ladies or nobles from last night's festivities seemed to be up and about yet, much to his relief.

They emerged into drizzly gray daylight and began shrugging into their riding cloaks. The air was much colder and the heavy clouds threatened serious rain. The horses were waiting by the gates, held by grooms. Before he mounted up, Robin turned to Sullyan.

"I really don't like this, Major. Will you be alright here on your own? It goes against all our training to leave you like this. At least one of us should stay with you."

She smiled, the gentle expression warming Taran's heart even though it wasn't directed at him.

"I know, Robin, but we have no choice. The General needs you to command my company. Bulldog is wounded and I will not risk his weak heart by keeping him here. And Taran is not one of us, for all that he is an Artesan. I will be well enough here. I will stay only today and perhaps tomorrow, but no longer than is necessary. When I return, I will join you and the men in the field. Meanwhile, I will be reporting to the General, and Bulldog can pass the information on to you."

Taran could see Robin wasn't convinced.

"I will be as concerned for you as you are for me," she continued. "I know you will not let me down. Remember your training and everything I have taught you. Keep shielded when you can. Be sure to send any wounded soldiers back to Rienne."

She gave Taran a quick look and his heart flipped. "Taran, please give Rienne and Cal my regards."

He nodded and her smile encompassed them all. "Gentlemen, I strongly suggest you return through the Veils as soon as you can. It will mean a longer ride through our own lands, but I will be happier knowing that you are safe on our own soil. And keep an eye out for raiders before you pass through, I want no more injuries before you reach the Manor. Robin, remember to shield Bulldog when you cross the Veils to be sure he takes no more harm from that shoulder."

She gave Bull's good arm a squeeze and he grinned. Then she cast Taran a look he couldn't interpret but before he could speak, she had turned back to the Captain.

"Robin, a private word, if you please."

She moved away and after passing his reins to Bull, Robin followed.

Taran watched them with interest as they talked. He saw Sullyan gesture, whether toward him or Bull, he wasn't sure, and Robin's nod. When they returned, the Captain was wearing a small smile. He didn't speak, he merely took back his reins from Bull and mounted.

Taran mounted his own stallion, making sure his sword was in hand. Bull did likewise and Robin rested his crossbow across his saddle. With a wooden groan, the great mansion gates wound open and they rode slowly through. Sullyan followed them to the gate and watched them ride down the shanty town's refuse-strewn track.

When he reached the last hut, Robin reined in and turned. Sullyan still stood in the gateway and she raised her hand in farewell. Robin returned her salute, Bull and Taran doing likewise, and she disappeared back through the portal. The huge gates thudded securely shut. Robin sighed, a worried look on his face, before resolutely turning away.

"Come, on," he said, "let's give the horses a run before we cross the Veils." He put Torka into a gallop that Taran and Bull leaped to match.

They ran the horses until they reached the top of the ridge from which they had first seen the mansion the day before. There, Robin drew rein and Bull and Taran joined him, allowing their mounts to breathe. Robin sat Torka and looked back down the valley, staring solemnly at the dark building with its dirty skirt of huts.

Bull reined over beside him. "Are you alright, lad?"

"I don't like it, Bull. I don't like it one bit."

The big man reached out with his good hand and gripped Robin's shoulder. "No more do I. But you must remember that she's been crossing the Veils on and off for more years than you've had your powers. She knows what she's doing. She knows these people and their ways better than anyone else alive."

"Yes, and look what happened last night. Don't tell me she wasn't afraid of the Duke, Bull. I saw the look in her eyes."

Bull gazed back at the mansion. "No, you're right, that's the first time I've seen her betray fear of any of them. But Rykan's an extremely powerful and influential lord and if he has decided to challenge the Hierarch, things could get very serious here. Rykan is Master-elite and as far as I'm aware, Sully is the only individual besides the Hierarch with enough power to rival him. But we don't meddle in Andaryan affairs, why should we? We don't care who rules the Fifth Realm and if the Hierarch can't hang on to his crown, he deserves to be ousted. That's the natural way of things. There's no reason for Rykan to feel threatened by the Major. She's not here to interfere in his plans."

Taran dared to speak up. "Maybe Rykan doesn't see it that way." The others turned in their saddles to look at him and he flushed slightly. "I mean, if he intends to start a civil war here, the last thing he'd want is outside interference. An invasion is a very good way of keeping another realm's forces fully occupied."

Robin and Bull looked thoughtful. Encouraged by their lack of criticism, Taran carried on. "Maybe the Hierarch doesn't know about Rykan's plans, maybe the Duke's hoping to catch him unaware. If the Major chose to warn him, Rykan would find himself challenged."

"Good point," said Robin, giving Taran a look of respect,

"although if the invading troops are Rykan's, then he's playing a risky game. Committing that many men through the Veils is a huge gamble for a man who plans to start a war in his own realm. I can't believe he commands so many that the loss of his invasion force wouldn't hurt him."

He glanced at Bull, who gave a lop-sided shrug. Robin turned his eyes back to the mansion. "Well, if he thinks he can raid our lands with impunity, keep his forces intact and pull them back when he pleases, we'll have to make him think again. The sooner we oppose him, the sooner he'll leave us in peace."

He wheeled Torka around. "Come on, we need to get back. I think I remember a spot not far from here that should serve as a crossing. I hope you're feeling strong, Taran."

Before Taran could ask what he meant, he was leading the way off the ridge. Soon, though, Robin halted by a small stream they had crossed the day before. He nudged Torka to its edge and had Bull scout for raiders.

"No one around," said the big man.

Robin nodded and turned to Taran. "Journeyman, can you recall the method for constructing a Water-based tunnel?"

Taran nodded, then stared hard at him. "Do you mean for me to make the whole structure by myself?"

"Only if you feel up to it," said Robin.

Remembering Sullyan's private talk with Robin earlier, Taran narrowed his eyes. "This was the Major's idea, wasn't it?"

The Captain merely smiled.

Taran suppressed his reluctance, taking a moment to compose himself. He remembered what Sullyan had shown him, but his many failures and embarrassments were too recent and painful to be ignored. However, he was certain he could do this and he owed himself the chance.

Closing his eyes, he took a deep breath and reached for his psyche. Strengthened by Robin's coaching, it glowed with untapped potential. Taran let it surround and suffuse his soul before building the portal.

The elemental force of Water answered his call and rose shimmering with power on two sides. Smoothly, he completed the arch. Bull and Robin were radiating approval as Taran gently pushed back on the power, forcing it through the substrate until it opened into the familiar landscape of their realm. Carefully, he anchored the structure at each point as he returned, then stood back with the others to inspect his work.

"Very good," approved Bull. Taran grinned. He felt Robin shielding Bull as he rode his stallion confidently into the structure. Robin followed on Torka, and Taran came last, freeing the anchorage points and gathering the fabric of the tunnel as he did so.

When they were all standing on Albian soil, he collapsed the portal. He was about to ride on when he realized the other two men were watching him with huge grins.

"What?" he said, feeling his face redden. They didn't reply and he frowned, his heart sinking. He must have forgotten something obvious. A quick glance round, however, revealed nothing out of place.

Bull and Robin were now openly laughing.

"What is it?" Taran said again, becoming irritated.

"You have no idea what you've just done, have you?" chuckled Robin.

"Come on, Captain, put him out of his misery," said Bull. "Look at his face, he thinks he's done something wrong."

"Will you either tell me what it is, or shut up?"

Robin rode close and placed a hand on Taran's shoulder. "Major Sullyan will confirm you herself as soon as she can," he said, "but in the meantime she has authorized me to tell you this.

"Taran, that was your test of mastery over Water. You have achieved the rank of Adept."

✤ ✤ ✤ ✤ ✤

Morose and silent, Sonten rode hard by his overlord's shoulder. He was in a contradictory mood.

On the one hand he was fearful and furious—once more in terror of his life, once more seething with impotent rage. The brutal way he had used the young courtesan who had failed him the night before had merely slaked the lust such fury often aroused in him; it had done nothing to relieve his anger. There had been no sign of her that morning, she might have died or crawled away somewhere to lick her well-deserved wounds. Sonten didn't miss her and certainly didn't care.

Yet on the other hand, he felt strangely relieved, as if a burden had somehow been lifted. It took him some time to realize why.

It was obvious, really. If the girl had succeeded in luring the Journeyman into an ambush, his disappearance would have been noticed. His friends had been too watchful to have missed him for long. The resulting confusion as they searched for him would have infuriated the Duke, and would probably have ruined his careful plan. If so, he would certainly have taken out his rage on Sonten. The General knew that Rykan was already enraged by the witch's resistance to his charms, despite knowing that she probably would refuse his invitation to the palace. It was the reason the Duke had brought his own retainers, men and women who even now were about their master's business.

Sonten sighed heavily. If he had succeeded in taking the Journeyman prisoner, he'd have been hard pressed to hide the man. And if he'd been discovered while in Sonten's possession– dead or alive—then Sonten couldn't have justified his actions without divulging his reasons. He couldn't think of an excuse that would have satisfied Rykan.

No, thought Sonten, it was just as well his hasty plan had failed. Bitterly, he snatched a glance at Rykan's face.

The Duke rode at the head of their column. Dewed as he was by the morning drizzle, Rykan's slim black-and-silver figure was impressive and commanding, as always. He rode his high-mettled bay stallion with instinctive ease, his expression habitually arrogant, his darkly handsome face and the carriage of his powerful body proclaiming both confidence and pride.

This morning, his predatory gaze was tinged with excitement and menacing anticipation glowed behind his eyes. Sonten scowled and turned away, envy flooding his heart. Rykan had every right to his smug expectancy, for little went wrong for the influential lord. His brutal reputation and high standing meant that few dared disobey him. Fewer still failed in their duties once his wishes were known. Sonten knew that Rykan's scheme would succeed, and the overlord would have his way.

Well, let him, he thought venomously, careful to hide the hatred in his eyes. Let him enjoy the witch's surrender; let him take his pleasures while he could. After all, there were other, and less risky methods by which Sonten could ensure the Journeyman didn't give him away. Sonten had taken the time to think things through more calmly and had firmed up his own plans, which he was certain would see him through to success. He was content now to wait until they all returned to Kymer. Then let Rykan see who had the upper hand! There would be many opportunities in the confusion of the coming civil war; many chances there for the taking for one prepared to watch and wait in silence.

Sonten could bide his time. Hadn't he already done so these many frustrating years? He hadn't risen to the post of general under the most powerful noble in the realm by mere chance. And, he reflected, it was no bad thing to be backing the next Hierarch, to be the one responsible for gaining him the Crown. He even thought it might suit him very well to enjoy the fruits of such a powerful victory until he was ready to make his move. It might behoove him to wait a little longer; to build up a good, strong power base and consolidate his plans.

He allowed himself a bitter smile, comforting his ambitious soul by imagining the support he would receive from the new Hierarch, unwitting though it might be. The Duke rewarded those he trusted. Brutal and cruel he might be, and swift with vengeance, but he also valued faithful service and repaid his supporters well.

Except that damnable Albian Baron, thought Sonten. That one would reap not gratitude but a swift sword in the guts, if Sonten knew his overlord. And it couldn't come too soon. Their last meeting had made Sonten's teeth itch, such was the Baron's arrogance. How he dared believe himself on a par with the Duke of Kymer, Sonten could not fathom. Once Rykan decided he'd outlived his usefulness, the Baron would find that nothing could protect him from cold, sharp steel.

A sharp pain in the ribs jolted Sonten out of his reverie. He gasped, glancing down at the dagger that was pricking his skin. The Duke was glaring angrily, the hand holding the dagger poised to ram the blade home.

"Your Grace?" quavered Sonten, fearing Rykan had somehow divined his treacherous thoughts. The knife was slowly withdrawn, leaving a neat but sizeable slit in Sonten's expensive robes.

"I don't like being ignored, Sonten," growled the Duke. He fingered the dagger before ramming it irritably back into its sheath. "When I speak, I expect you to listen, not continue your irrelevant woolgathering."

"My apologies, your Grace." Sonten struggled to calm his racing pulse.

Rykan held his gaze just a fraction too long for the General's liking. Then, dismissively, he turned away. "It's time."

With a jerk of the reins, he turned his stallion's head. The fine beast, blood spotting the foam at its mouth, tossed its head in discomfort. The Duke curbed it harshly. Sonten gazed at the terrain in surprise, he hadn't realized they had come so far. His plotting had occupied him a while.

They were on the west side of Haligan Forest, its fringes just visible on the horizon. When Sonten nudged his stocky horse level with Rykan's slimmer beast, he could just make out the standard flying from the highest point of the Count's dilapidated mansion.

Its ragged huddle of peasant huts was invisible, hidden by the rise of the land.

Rykan bore a sensual and considering smile. "Yes, more than enough time, I think, Sonten, if my instructions have been obeyed."

As if there's a chance they won't be, thought Sonten. "Whatever you command, your Grace," he said, trying to conceal a worm of fear. He might have dealt with last night's panic and made plans to eliminate the Journeyman's threat, but there was still an element of risk. He was very far from safe.

With a thump of his heels, he sent his ungainly mount plodding after Rykan's pureblood bay. The rest of their column re-formed around them, ever watchful, ever alert.

Enjoy your successes, my proud Duke, thought Sonten. Enjoy your diversions while you may. I have plans and information that will bring you to your knees, and the day you take the crown will be one day closer to your untimely death. His eyes bored into Rykan's back as he followed the Duke, his heart full of bile.

Chapter Twenty-Four

The rest of the ride passed in a haze for Taran, who couldn't quite believe he had attained the next level after only a few days of instruction. After his many failures since his father's death, he hadn't realized how close he'd been. It had only taken improving his psyche and a few lessons in merging techniques to give him the strength to master Water.

He couldn't wait to tell Cal; as soon as he, Bull and Robin had settled for the night in a wooded valley, he reached out to his Apprentice. Cal didn't immediately recognize his master's touch and Taran sensed Cal's pleasure and pride when he shared his good news.

However, Cal sobered when Taran asked what was happening at the Manor. Taran melded with Bull and Robin so they could hear Cal's report.

It's organized chaos here, said Cal in his head. *Every company except the Major's has left for the front lines. They're only waiting for Captain Tamsen so they can go, too.*

Taran inquired about Rienne and could picture Cal's rueful smile.

Oh, she's in her element. I've resorted to helping her in the infirmary, it's the only way I get to see her. I've never seen her so happy.

Robin and Bull laughed.

It was a shrewd move of the Major's to get Rienne involved in the infirmary, said Robin. *She always recognizes a person's potential. She must consider Rienne a very gifted healer, especially since she attached her to our command.*

Would Rienne be permitted to stay if she wanted to? Once this is all over, I mean, said Taran. In reality, he was thinking more of himself and Cal and the possibility of more training.

Oh, yes, said Robin. *Even if the General objected, though I don't suppose he would, Sullyan would simply attach Rienne to her personal staff as she did with Bull. But what about you and Cal? You wouldn't want to enter the military, would you?*

I don't know. I've never really thought about it.

Robin grinned but did not reply.

He'd been instructed by General Blaine to return swiftly. Bull's wound, aided by metaphysical healing, was mending and no longer gave him pain. The following morning they rose just before dawn and rode at a hand canter all day.

Taran realized they were approaching the Manor from the northeast. They arrived in the mid-afternoon and Robin had time to rest and change before leaving.

Cal was waiting for them and there was much greeting and back-slapping—and concern for Bull—before Robin left to repack. Bull reported to the General before heading for the infirmary and Cal took Taran to see their new quarters, which Rienne had made more comfortable.

"We want to hear all the details," Cal told him, "not just the little bits you were able to pass through the link."

Taran wasn't really listening. He'd been full of thought since his elevation to Adept and had formed a loyalty to Sullyan completely separate from the strong physical attraction he felt. She was a Master-elite—the highest-ranking Artesan he was ever likely to meet—and she'd recognized and encouraged his talents. She'd given up some of her Captain's time to help him and, despite the obvious inadequacy of his training, had treated him as an equal, something his father had never done.

Yet what he felt wasn't simple gratitude. In spite of her assurances and reluctance to judge—and their suspicions concerning Rykan—Taran felt more responsible than ever for what was happening in Albia. Without his interference, the Andaryans might never have invaded and Taran wanted to do whatever he could to atone for his mistake. Robin's reference the previous evening to joining the military had him thinking.

Ignoring Cal's request, he said, "Cal, how would you feel about going out with the Major's company?"

Cal was startled. "Fight the invasion, you mean? Do you think they would let us?"

That reply told Taran all he needed to know. "I'm not sure, but I intend to ask. Cal, the Major's been left behind in a potentially dangerous situation, and she's on her own. It is partially my fault, no matter what anyone says. Now, you and I can both handle weapons and take orders, and we have our other talents. I want help. Are you with me?"

"Of course," said Cal. "Though I don't know what Rienne will say."

They found out at some length what Rienne had to say after Taran had offered their services to General Blaine. They had been accepted on a temporary basis.

Robin was delighted to have them. Rienne, however, was not happy. She'd been dealing with some of the wounded from the front lines and knew what Andaryan weapons could do. Taran's assurances about their shielding skills and swordsmanship didn't comfort her one bit.

"You didn't see the horrendous scar Sullyan sustained in that last battle," she snapped. "And what about poor Bull's shoulder? They're trained and experienced fighters. If they can be hurt that badly, what chance have you two got?"

"Thanks Rienne," said Cal. "It's nice to know you're confident in me."

She burst into tears. "Don't be such a fool," she cried. "The last thing I want is to see your bodies brought in here for me to sew up."

"Look, Rienne, I promise we'll stay out of the worst of the fighting," said Taran. "We're novices and we know it. Robin won't want us getting in the way. We'll be pushed to the back, likely as not, so we don't cause him any problems. All we'll be doing is mopping up the stragglers."

"Just see that you are," she sniffed.

She made Taran promise to talk to Bull each day. The big man was acting as contact and coordinator as he usually did; his shoulder, although healing, precluded him from anything else. She returned to the infirmary, unable to watch them leave.

Robin made sure they had all the field equipment and weapons they needed, then led the way to where the rest of the company was waiting. There were at least four hundred mounted men drawn into formation behind their sergeants and every one of them cheered as Robin took the saddle. Taran and Cal accepted their horses from the stable lads, Cal suspiciously eyeing his fiery little chestnut.

Robin addressed the men, his voice betraying none of the apprehension Taran guessed he was feeling at assuming his first solo command.

"You all know Major Sullyan is unable to lead us this time," he called, his voice ringing clearly, "so it's up to us to make her proud. We'll turn the invasion back, drive the demons south, back to the rat holes they crawled from. Show them they have no hope of victory here. Sullyan's waging her own diplomatic battle beyond the Veils and she's relying on us to buy her the time she needs.

"What do you say, lads?"

The cheers crescendoed as Robin took the head of the column and moved them out. Taran and Cal fell in behind.

✢ ✢ ✢ ✢ ✢

The company moved fast through the chilly autumn evening, not halting until several hours had passed. It was dark by the time they were settled and Taran was glad for the campfire he'd made. Robin had offered to share his tent as it was easier than them taking one of their own. He showed Taran and Cal the routines of field camp: caring for the horses, laying out and inspecting all their gear and cooking an evening meal. They accompanied him while he made his tour of the men, introducing them to the members of the company. Taran was pleasantly surprised to find how easily they were accepted.

Once the tour was complete, he and Cal followed Robin back to the tent, which was little more than an oiled leather sheet stretched over a pole. They drank a last cup of fellan before turning in. Robin contacted Bull to get an update on how Sullyan was faring and Taran noticed his worried expression as he broke the link.

"What is it?" he asked.

The younger man answered slowly, concern plain in his eyes.

"No report from the Major."

"Maybe there's nothing to report?" said Cal.

Robin shook his head. "We always report. It's one of our firmest rules. Like the one about never leaving each other alone beyond the Veils." He stared moodily into his fellan. "I knew I should never have left her."

Taran slept poorly, wrapped in blankets on the ground, and woke to Robin shaking his shoulder. Stiffly, he climbed to his feet, immediately inquiring after Sullyan. The Captain shook his head, his face haggard as he supervised the breaking of their camp.

There followed another hard day of riding before they received any news of the fighting. One of Robin's scouting parties encountered some wounded swordsmen making their way back to the Manor and brought one of them to speak with Robin. The man, his right arm crudely wrapped in a blood-stained bandage, slid awkwardly from the scout's horse and steadied himself against the beast's shoulder.

"Get this man some water," called Robin, dismounting. Once the swordsman had taken a few swallows from the water, Robin asked, "What news of the invasion?"

"No good news, Captain." The swordsman was hoarse. "They crossed Loxton's border to the east of the Downs and are still pushing hard northward. We'd manage to hold them for a bit but then they'd come back at us stronger than ever and sometimes broke through our lines. They're losing fighters all the time but they don't seem to care. It's strange. I've never known demons fight so hard."

The news was sobering and once Robin got the enemy's last known location from the wounded man, he urged his company onward. Knowing the Andaryans were being unusually dogged caused him to call battle formations well in advance of where he expected to find them. He also doubled the number of outriders.

This foresight likely saved many casualties when they startled an Andaryan scouting party well forward of its lines. Taran and Cal watched in admiration as Robin's swordsmen made brief work of the small band.

The Captain ordered a halt to allow his men to deal with some minor injuries. Then he led them forward, soon making contact with Vassa's defending forces. They were already camped and Robin sent his company to settle among them. Once he'd made a tour of his men, he went to speak with Colonel Vassa and the captains of the other three companies that made up this fighting force. Taran offered to set up the tent and see to Robin's gear and horse. The Captain gratefully accepted.

Taran also contacted Bull to save Robin the trouble, but there was no good news. The General had not heard from Major Sullyan. When Robin returned to the tent to take some fellan before getting some sleep, he was devastated to receive this information. Taran tried to reassure him but failed. All they could do was press on, do their job and hope for the best.

✠ ✠ ✠ ✠ ✠

It had been a week since Heron and Verris received the change to their orders and now they were holding yet another hurried command conference in the field. This was taking longer than either of them had expected, but when Heron asked his fellow officer if he knew the reason behind the delay, Verris replied scathingly.

"The Duke doesn't tell me his reasons, Heron, any more than your fat general tells you. He just gives orders and expects me to obey. I'll tell you this, though, he's in a ranting powerful rage. I don't know what caused it but I wouldn't want to be on the receiving end. He's been known to do murder when something angers him like that. We're better off where we are, Heron. I hope your lord knows how to keep his head down."

Heron and Verris had come to an uneasy arrangement over the deployment of their joint forces. They had agreed to put aside their rivalry to concentrate on presenting a united front once the true skill and experience of the Albian forces became apparent. Although fully expecting a strong response once Verris' brutal tactics began to bite, neither of them had anticipated the strength of the companies sent against them, nor their coordinated skill.

Since the Hierarch's edict against wholesale raiding into Albia, the Andaryan nobility had had no opportunity to test Albia's defenses. The elusive nature of Heron's and Verris' initial attacks hadn't increased their knowledge. Although neither had expected an easy ride, the effectiveness and determination of the Albian swordsmen was a nasty shock.

However, the Andaryan companies were also strong and had swelled over the past week with fresh troops. They had continued to push the Albians hard, forging their way northward. They had no definite goal other than the emphatic order to keep the Albians occupied, and this did not help morale. Heron and Verris, however, gave their men no time to ponder the whys and wherefores of their duty. They had been instructed to engage and harass the enemy at every opportunity and they did.

Once they had decided the day's strategy, Heron and Verris parted, each with their own section of the countryside. They had agreed to split up, but not so far apart that they couldn't come to each others' aid. Heron strode back to his assembled men and gave the order to mount.

In keeping with the week, it was another exhausting day of harry, engage, retreat and regroup. Heron kept in touch with Verris through the substrate and they managed to push the enemy forces farther north. Late in the day, Heron felt a familiar touch on his mind as Verris passed him the long-awaited command: they were at last to begin falling back.

He was relieved. He was finding it hard to obey his orders while keeping his men alive and free from serious wounds. Those who suffered incapacitating injuries were sent back through the substrate immediately, before the wounds could become infected. The severely injured were killed. This did not sit well with Heron but he recognized the need. He signaled his men and they began a slow, organized retreat.

He rode behind his men, leading them through what cover they could find. Suddenly, a dreadful pang shot through his brain, nearly knocking him from his horse. The shocking death cry—Verris'—reverberated in his mind, blinding him, making him gasp with agonizing pain. It was swift, it was violent, and there was nothing he could do. The cry was automatic, subconscious, and it only reached him because of the intimacy he'd shared with Verris during the campaign.

Fearful, his brain aching fiercely, Heron shook his head to clear his mind. He yelled his men onward, heading for the designated campsite where the remnants of Verris' command would meet him.

Once the last straggler had ridden in to the camp in the frosty darkness, Heron called one of Verris' men over. "What the hell happened?"

The swordsman responded sullenly. "He took a crossbow bolt right between the eyes, Commander. Right between the eyes! Bloody lucky shot if ever I saw one."

"What in the Void was he doing to leave himself open to crossbows?" Heron was furious, only too sure he knew the answer.

There were smaller crossbows that could be shot from horseback but mainly the weapon was used by foot troops. This meant that either Verris had ridden into an ambush, which wasn't likely as the humans couldn't possibly have known where they would be, or Verris had taken advantage of the order to fall back and had stopped to do some looting. That would have left him and his men vulnerable.

The swordsman's shifty demeanor confirmed Heron's suspicions. "What the hell did he think he was doing? How many survived?"

"A handful," the man said, drawing another curse from Heron.

"Get them over here. You're all under my command now and there are going to be some changes. If you and your comrades want to make it back alive, you're going to have to learn to obey new orders. Jump to it."

The man hastened to do Heron's bidding and the Commander watched him go. So, Verris had finally reaped the rewards of his greedy nature and vastly inflated ego. Heron couldn't say he was surprised—or particularly sorry—but he was furious. Any failure of this magnitude would reflect badly on him and he still had Lord Sonten's as-yet-undisclosed plans to worry about, not to mention the forthcoming conflict in his own realm.

Assimilating Verris' disaffected men was not something he wanted to deal with right now, but he'd have to do it. Every available man was needed for the war and Heron could not afford to lose any more. Cursing under his breath, he swung away to instruct his own company leaders.

✢ ✢ ✢ ✢ ✢

The week passed incredibly quickly for Taran, caught up as he was in fighting the invasion. Each day blurred into the next, each consisted of scouting, fighting, sleeping and eating. The weather was cold, gray and damp. He never seemed to be able to get warm unless he was fighting and then he was too warm.

At least he seemed to be acquitting himself well with his comrades. Some of his broadsword maneuvers were even being copied as they proved most effective against the raiders. He and Cal were also increasingly respectful of Robin's leadership and they had learned that Robin was an ace shot with both longbow and crossbow. Taran had heard some of the men boasting about it earlier in the week but had treated the stories with skepticism. Until now. That very afternoon they had come across a group of raiders looting an abandoned village. Robin immediately took advantage of their greed, he and his men taking a heavy toll. Taran himself had witnessed Robin killing their leader, an unerring shot that took the demon squarely between the eyes.

This feat seemed to ease Robin's soul, for which Taran was grateful. During the week, Robin had grown increasingly distraught at Sullyan's silence. Bull's obvious fretting, which the big man couldn't hide when any of them communed with him, didn't help.

The young Captain was desperate to return through the Veils to the Count's mansion, to demand answers, but he was tied to his command, responsible for his men, and couldn't abandon the fighting. Each night he'd railed against the General's refusal to send someone to relieve him.

He tried again that evening, once the men were settled. It had been a fairly light day for once—the outlanders finally seemed to be falling back. From his seat opposite, Taran watched as Robin's eyes cleared from contact with the General.

"Bloody bastard cares nothing for her," snarled Robin, startling both Taran and Cal. "You'd never believe he owed her his life, would you? He doesn't know the meaning of the word 'gratitude.'"

"He owes her his life?" said Taran. He hadn't heard the story Sullyan had told Rienne.

Robin spat. "Oh, yes. A command of his was overrun by Relkorians. He'd have died had she not staunched his wounds and run for help. She even warned him before he engaged them, but he wouldn't listen. Typical of his bloody arrogance."

"When was this?" asked Taran.

"Oh, years ago, before she came to the Manor. That's what started it all. She saved his neck and beat off a raiding party all by herself, and she was only ten years old."

"Ten?" said Cal, looking up from oiling his sword. "That's incredible."

Robin's voice was suddenly tinged with exhaustion. "Yes. She's an incredible person."

He flung himself onto an old log that was doing duty as a stool, his anger abruptly draining away. He dropped his head into his hands.

"Oh, gods, I can't lose her. I really couldn't stand it. She's all I've ever lived for. She's taught me everything I know, from soldiering to using my powers. She's made me what I am. If something really bad has happened to her, I just don't think I could go on."

This speech frightened Taran. Robin had never let himself go quite so thoroughly before. They were all tired and worn down by the constant fighting and they all had minor wounds and aching muscles. The last thing they needed was for Robin to lose control. Yet Taran couldn't think of a way to comfort the young man. He appreciated how the Captain felt, being more than half in love with Sullyan himself.

Handing Robin a mug of fellan fresh from the pot, he patted his shoulder. "Perhaps we'll be free to go search soon," he said.

"The Andaryans were definitely falling back today. The worst is over and once we drive them back, we'll be recalled. Then we can cross the Veils again and go and see what's happened. You never know, there might be a simple explanation. Communication through the substrate is never constant, something might be blocking her link."

Robin shook his head. "I appreciate what you're trying to do, Taran, but I know for sure something's wrong. She'd never be gone this long, no matter what the reason for the invasion. No, she's either hurt, or prisoner, or both. I pray to the gods it's not worse."

Taran could only drink his fellan in silence.

✣ ✣ ✣ ✣ ✣

That night, in the dark and weary early hours, Taran woke. He thought he'd heard a cry and sat up, his heart beating painfully in his throat. Vaguely, he was aware of having been in an unpleasant dream. It seemed that Cal had also been disturbed because he, too, was sitting up, already reaching for his sword.

A noise across the tent drew Taran's attention. Robin had thrown back his blankets and was looking wildly around. "Did you hear that?" he asked.

Taran shook his head. "I was having a nightmare, I think. What did you hear?"

The camp was silent; there was no outcry from the sentries, no warning of raiders. Robin stood and Taran could see him trembling.

"It was Sullyan," he whispered. Taran stared at him. "She was calling out to me, screaming. I know it was her." He hugged his chest. "She's in great danger and pain, Taran. We've got to find her."

"Can you sense her now?" Taran asked.

Robin drew a shaky breath, sat on a log and closed his eyes. Taran waited. Cal climbed from his bedroll and came to sit beside him.

The Captain eventually opened his eyes, punching the log in frustration. "Nothing!"

"Let's try a Powersink," suggested Taran.

Robin grabbed the idea. "Yes, that might work. Cal, you'll have to be passive in this, we just need your strength. Taran, will you let me have control?"

"Of course."

They showed Cal what to do and the three patterns flowed effortlessly into one. Taran felt Robin take hold of the power and cast it beyond the Veils. He sent it arrowing across the alien terrain in the direction of Marik's mansion. Taran felt as if he were flowing over the land on a wave of power, seeing but not quite seeing the familiar outlines of the mansion's structure. Yet it was only an impression of the stones and mortar; only an imprint of its substance in the substrate.

They searched for signs of life and one psyche in particular. After a thorough but fruitless search, Robin pulled them back.

"Where are they?" Taran asked.

Robin shook his head. "Either there's a powerful and impenetrable shield over the entire building, or there are only a few servants left. Even the shanty town's deserted. I don't understand it. I felt no evidence of disaster, only abandonment. Sullyan definitely isn't there. What do I do now?"

"Why don't we widen the search a little and look in the surrounding countryside?" said Taran. "If there was a fight or a raid, she might have fought her way free. Maybe she's lying injured somewhere."

They meshed again and returned to the mansion's vicinity, gradually widening the area of search. Again, they drew a blank. They couldn't find even the merest hint of her passing in the substrate.

Robin swore. "I really don't understand this. There ought to be some trace of her somewhere. It's as if she's completely vanished. Just ceased to exist."

They puzzled over their lack of success, Taran and Cal throwing out ideas that really only served to pass the time. Suddenly, they heard a commotion on the outer edges of the camp. Robin left the tent and Taran followed, amazed to find that dawn was breaking. He hadn't realized they had spent so much time searching through the Veils.

The unrest turned out to be a bunch of outriders returning from night-scout duty. One of them, seeing Robin, cantered over his lathered horse. He called the Captain's name.

"What is it, Dexter?" said Robin, striding forward.

The Sergeant pulled up in front of his senior officer. "It's the invasion, Captain," he said, short of breath. "It's over."

Chapter Twenty-Five

"The invasion's over?" repeated Robin. "What do you mean? Details, man."

Dexter took a deep breath, sweat sheening his ruddy face. "They've withdrawn, Captain. Just before dawn."

"What, all of them? Completely?" Robin clearly couldn't believe it.

"The entire invasion force, yes sir. A few raiding parties remain but they're well scattered. The scouts all report the main body of warriors seemed to get some sort of signal at the same time and began an immediate retreat through the Veils. They've killed the severely wounded but taken the rest. You know what that means, sir."

"Yes I do," said Robin. He sounded both amazed and puzzled.

Taran didn't understand, so Robin explained. An Andaryan badly wounded on this side of the Veils, he said, would be unable to travel back through them without risking serious damage to both body and mind. If the wound was infected, they were unable to return at all, they would die in screaming agony if forced into the Veils. And they would only be able to survive a few months if trapped permanently in an alien realm. The same principle applied to Albians, which was why Sullyan had been so careful with Bull's shoulder wound. Whoever had sent this invasion force was clearly willing to risk the probable damage to recover the troops, which meant numbers must be vitally important.

Taran realized how little he really knew about the life he'd chosen to lead. Clearly, he'd been lucky to escape serious injury in the past. He'd known that the inhabitants of each realm couldn't exist long in another but hadn't appreciated the significance of an outland infection. The thought of what could have happened because of his ignorance turned his blood to ice.

Robin and the Sergeant were discussing the arrangements for returning to the Manor. The Captain ordered Dexter to take about a hundred of the fittest men and remain in the area to keep an eye on the situation in case the Andaryan withdrawal was a feint. The taking of their wounded, however, had convinced him it wasn't. Whoever was behind the uprising needed every available warrior, damaged or not.

When he was done, he turned back to Taran and Cal. "From what Dex has told me, the mysterious signal that caused the Andaryan withdrawal occurred at almost the exact moment I heard the Major call me." His voice was tight with strain. "That's too much of a coincidence. Come on, we're breaking camp. The sooner I get the men back, the sooner I can search for her."

"Will the General allow that?" asked Taran.

Robin's expression was grim. "He won't be able to stop me."

✤ ✤ ✤ ✤ ✤

The company, tired and grimy, followed Robin back to the Manor. They met and merged with some of Vassa's men, each captain leaving a small detail of scouts behind to mop up any straggling raiders. The Colonel himself had ridden on ahead.

Robin had them ride on full alert, weapons ready, in case the withdrawal should turn into an ambush. All the reports, however, both from scouts left behind and those in front confirmed the original report. The invasion forces had departed. The only outlanders left were those who had taken advantage of the situation to do a little looting.

Their camp that night was only a few hours' ride from the Manor. The men were tired and in all conscience, Robin couldn't hurry them. He chafed at the delay but wouldn't leave them to ride on alone. Sullyan had given him this command and if he couldn't immediately go searching for her, he wasn't about to let her down by abandoning his responsibility.

Taran cooked a meager supper, although none of them had any appetite, while Robin spoke to Bull back at the Manor. The big man, he reported, was as worried as they were, and if not for the stricture of not braving the Veils alone, he'd have gone to search for Sullyan. Apparently his shoulder wound was fully healed, so it wouldn't stop him from traveling. He had nothing encouraging to tell them, but he had one unusual piece of news.

They linked together so they could all hear him. He told them that for the last three or four nights, Rienne, who had worked tirelessly in the infirmary, earning admiration and gratitude from swordsmen and healers alike, had suffered a recurring nightmare. She could make no real sense of it except to say that it definitely concerned the Major.

She'd had visions of strange faces looming above her; feelings of great pain and pressure, of terror, torment and chains. Startling awake with sweat pouring off her and her heart aching in her chest, she would be left with nothing but a sense of holding on, of not giving up, which for some reason was vitally important.

After suffering this nightmare two nights running, Rienne went to Bull. He'd tried his best to catch a glimpse of her visions, but he simply didn't have the skill. He'd reassured her as best he could, but told them she'd be infinitely relieved when they were back.

Why didn't you tell me this sooner? demanded Cal.

What would that have achieved except to worry you even more? said Bull. *Besides, she asked me not to until you were nearly home. She didn't want you worrying. She thought you might lose concentration and take an arrow in the back.*

Cal grimaced but remained silent.

But why should Rienne be able to pick anything up from Sullyan? said Robin. *She's not an Artesan. And I've been open for days to anything the Major might send.*

All I can think, lad, replied Bull, *is that Rienne's an empath. I know a lot of healers are, it's what makes them so good at what they do. And she and Sullyan did spend that evening getting drunk together, remember? From what I recall of some of the things they discussed, I reckon they got pretty close that night. Although empaths are not Artesans, they are far more sensitive than ordinary folk. Rienne might well have formed a strong bond to Sully that night, enough to enable her to 'hear' the major.*

An empath? asked Cal. *Wouldn't one of us have picked that up before?*

You'd have thought so. Bull's voice carried a touch of sarcasm. *I imagine you and Taran were too wrapped up in your own business to wonder about Rienne. Especially if she's showed no overt signs until now.*

Tell her we'll be back tomorrow morning, said Robin. *If she gets anything else, we'll need to know. I'm planning to set out through the Veils just as soon as I've reported to Blaine. If you're coming, Bull, you'd better be ready. Oh, and I'll need a remount. Tell Solet to make sure it's Torka.*

He broke the link.

"We're coming, too," said Taran, his assertion drawing a startled glance from Robin. "Well, you didn't think we'd stay behind, did you?"

Robin smiled and gripped his arm. "Thanks, you don't know how much that means to me. I've a feeling we're going to need all the power we can get."

They collapsed into their bedrolls early that night, anxiety and weariness taking their toll. Taran half expected to be woken by a nightmare, but his exhausted sleep was undisturbed. He didn't know whether to be alarmed or relieved.

✣ ✣ ✣ ✣ ✣

Robin roused everyone early and the company moved off in the pre-dawn light. The weather had taken a turn for the worse and it was raining. Eager to reach the Manor, they kept the fastest pace they could sustain.

The sentries saw them coming and opened the gates. They rode in to the cheers of their comrades who had made it back before them. Taran saw Cal looking for Rienne, but she wasn't there. He guessed she was already in the infirmary.

They dismounted at the horse lines, giving charge of their mounts to the stable lads who came pouring out of their barracks to help. Hearing a youthful, high-pitched voice frantically calling for Robin, Taran looked around and caught sight of the kitchen lad, Tad. The young boy seemed desperate to reach Robin as he rushed headlong into his arms.

"Whoa, young man," said Robin, steadying the boy. "Whatever is it?"

Tad caught his breath, his chest heaving with the effort of his run. "Healer Arlen sent me to tell you immediately, sir. She said you'd want to know. The Major's horse is back, sir."

Robin stared. "Are you saying the Major's returned, lad?"

"No, sir, just the horse. And he's in a bad way."

Keeping a grip on Tad's skinny arm, Robin spun round. "Solet!" He spied the tall man attending to a lame beast over by the isolation stables and strode over. Taran and Cal followed.

Solet looked up as Robin rounded on him. "I'm told Mandias is here. Where have you put him?"

Solet pointed to a line of loose boxes. "He's down there at the end, Captain. Don't disturb him. He's had a rough time and I've given him something for the pain."

Robin ran to the box indicated. Ignoring Solet's instructions, he flung open the door. He stopped, brought up short by the sight of the beast. Taran and the others caught up with him and also stopped, gazing in sympathy at the injured horse.

Mandias was lying on a thick bed of fresh, yellow straw. His head was down, his chin resting on the straw, his eyes half-closed. There was mucus running from his nose and eyes and his breathing was husky. He had numerous whip cuts and what looked like bites on his body. He was very thin. Taran couldn't believe it was the same beast that had gone snorting and bolting out of the yard nearly two weeks before.

He saw tears in Robin's eyes. Approaching the horse quietly, the young man kneeled down beside it. He put out his hand and softly stroked the once-velvety neck. Mandias managed to raise his head a little and whickered wetly down his nose.

"What on earth happened to you, old boy?" murmured Robin. "You've really been in the wars, haven't you?"

He stayed a moment longer, pulling gently on the stallion's ear, before abruptly standing up. Solet appeared in the doorway. "How long has he been back?" demanded Robin.

"One of the night lads found him staggering around outside about four hours ago," the stablemaster replied. "He was trembling all over and barely on his legs. Been traveling a while, I reckon, by the state of him."

"Will he recover?" asked Robin.

"Possibly. Maybe not completely, though. That's a nasty wound on his right fore and he is getting on a bit now."

Robin's face was pale. "Do your best," he said. "You know how the Major loves that horse."

As they left the horse lines and walked up toward the main building, Cal asked, "How did the horse get back without the Major?"

"Mandias is very special, one of only a few horses that can cross the Veils by himself," said Robin. "It's why he's so prized as a stud. His full brother, Drum, can do it too, and I'm hoping my own colt, which was sired by Mandias, will show the same talent when he's grown. But this has got me even more worried now.

Sullyan wouldn't have parted with him willingly, nor sent him back alone unless she had no other choice."

Taran could feel the implications quivering in the air as he and Cal followed Robin in silence.

Once they entered the main building, they were met by Bull. He slapped Robin on the back and shook both Cal's and Taran's hands.

"You've done very well by all accounts," he said as he accompanied them toward the General's office. "I wouldn't be surprised if there's promotion in this for you, lad."

Robin didn't even smile. "There's only one thing on my mind right now, Bull, and it isn't promotion. If I can't get Sullyan back, my career will mean less than nothing."

Bull shook his head and left them at the General's door. Robin knocked and, beckoning to Taran and Cal, entered when he heard the gruff reply.

The meeting, thought Taran, was stormy. Robin went into it with a huge burr under his saddle over Blaine's refusal to free him to search for Sullyan. It seemed he wasn't about to back down from his determination to leave as soon as the session was over.

It was clear to Taran that the General had guessed Robin's intention. He was obviously expecting the Captain to be prickly. He didn't, however, seem prepared for the depth of resentment the Captain expressed. Robin's abrupt attitude, terse replies, and plain impatience with the procedure soon irritated the short-tempered General. Once the debriefing was over, he deliberately kept the young man at attention until Robin was forced to look him in the eyes.

His voice deceptively mild, Blaine said, "Do you have something else to say, Captain?"

Taran was pleased to note that Robin took a moment to think before replying. The responsibility of solo command must have matured him a little; the Robin they had known on arrival wouldn't have hesitated to leap in with both feet.

"I believe there's a more important task awaiting me than giving you details of the past campaign, sir," he said, as respectfully as his resentment would allow. "Others could do that as well as I, and I can't think why you'd want to delay me. The Major's been officially missing for more than a week, sir, and we have reason to believe she's in danger."

Blaine's face flushed and he rose from his chair. "Oh you do, do you? What reasons would they be, Captain? Dreams, vague feelings of disquiet? A horse returning alone? Hardly good military reasons for you to go haring off on some foolhardy rescue mission. Especially as we're still on full alert following a major invasion."

Color rose in Robin's face, too, but he kept his temper in check.

"Aren't you concerned by her lack of contact, sir? She's never failed to report before. And yes, I do think that the abandonment of the invasion and the vague nature of the few contacts we've had from her are connected. When you consider the state of her horse and the fact that three of us in metaconcert could find no traces of her, I think it's grave cause for concern. And that's putting aside the debt you owe her for saving your life, sir."

Taran thought this was going a little too far and it seemed the General thought so, too. His face flushed even deeper and he loomed over Robin.

"Beware, Captain. You're walking a knife-edge with me after that duel. Not to mention all your other indiscretions over the past two years. I've already told you you've had your last chance. Left up to me, you'd have been transferred long ago. Any more of your insulting and insubordinate behavior and you'll be up before a martial court."

Taran could see that Robin had pushed the General about as far as he would go, yet the young man appeared unmoved. Taran got the impression he had prepared a strategy for this situation. He was proved right as Robin backed up a pace, executing a smart salute.

"Permission to lead a search party to the Fifth Realm, sir."

Blaine's eyes bulged. "Permission denied, Captain. Dismissed!"

Promptly, Robin produced a parchment from inside his jacket and held it out to Blaine. "Very well, General," he said, "I have a letter resigning my position."

Taran gasped; he hadn't expected this. He watched Blaine closely to see what he would do.

The General stared at the letter but didn't take it. Then he looked into Robin's eyes and the color faded from his face. He folded his arms.

"Oh, for pity's sake. Alright, Captain, you win. I don't stand a chance, do I, when she commands such loyalty?"

Robin smiled as he tucked the letter back inside his jacket. "My primary loyalty might lie with the Major, sir, but I know for a fact that hers lies very firmly with you and the King."

Blaine frowned. "I do know that, Captain. But it's not quite the same thing, is it?"

He was silent for a while, regarding each of them in turn. His gaze settled on Taran. "I suppose your presence here means the two of you intend to go with this love-struck idiot?"

Relieved, Taran grinned. "Someone's got to keep an eye on him, sir."

"I wish you luck." Blaine stared back at Robin. "Very well, Captain, you're released from duty to search for the Major. But," he added, as Robin made to leave, "I can't send anyone with you and I'll be expecting regular reports. Until I decide otherwise, you're still under my command."

Robin snapped a salute that Taran and Cal echoed. They left the General's office and made for their own rooms.

Cal gave Taran a wide-eyed look before turning to Robin. "Were you trying to get thrown out? That was a huge risk you took."

"Not really." Smiling, Robin extracted his letter and handed it to Cal.

Taran looked over as Cal unfolded the parchment. It was blank.

✤ ✤ ✤ ✤ ✤

Bull and Rienne were waiting for them in their suite. The healer and Cal shared an emotional embrace; they had neither seen nor spoken to each other for more than a week. When they finally parted, Taran caught Rienne's eye and pointed to the pack resting on the floor by her feet.

"Have you packed us some extra supplies?"

"I'll give you supplies," said Rienne. Cal frowned at her and she placed her hands on her hips. "You didn't think you were going off again without me, did you?"

Cal stared. "But you can't come." He turned to the others for support. "Can she?"

No one spoke.

"And just how are you going to stop me? I'm just as concerned as you are. Don't forget, I've been receiving messages from the Major for a few days now, even if they did seem like dreams. And when she asked me if I'd work in the infirmary, she also asked me to consider myself attached to her command. That means I have to go with you, if there's even the slightest chance she's been hurt."

"It's more than a chance, I'm afraid," murmured Robin, his face betraying his worry. "I can't think of any other possibility for her silence. Rienne, I'd be very happy to have you along."

Cal glared at him but knew he was out-maneuvered. Robin asked Bull to see to their horses, agreeing to meet him at the horse lines, while Taran led Cal into their quarters to pack.

An hour later they were riding along the same track they had followed the Major's horse two weeks before. To Taran, it seemed like years ago. Robin was obviously remembering the day, too, as he was introspective and silent. Bull, clearly recognizing Robin's pain and not wanting to intrude upon it, told Taran and Cal what would happen.

"We'll start by heading for the mansion," he said. "Maybe, once we're physically through the Veils, Robin will be able to sense the Major. If so, we'll follow his lead. If not, the mansion's our only hope of picking up the trail. It'll be interesting to see if Marik can throw any light on what's happened. I thought it was odd at the time, but looking back, his behavior at that damned banquet seems even stranger now. He was definitely jittery about something."

"Do you suspect him of harming the Major?" Taran was surprised. "He's supposed to be an ally."

Bull huffed. "He is supposed to be an ally, although it wasn't his personal choice. I'll tell you the tale one day. But I've said it before and I'll say it again—demons are devious. Marik's never really been useful except as a host, and you've seen how interminable his banquets can be. Sully always said he'd show his worth one day but I've never held my breath."

Taran shrugged. "Well, if he had anything to do with this, he's hidden himself away. Robin and I could only find traces of a couple of people at the mansion. It was virtually deserted."

Bull glanced at the silent Captain. "If that's the case, we should still be able to read the substrate, pick up a clue. Failing that, we'll just have to scout the countryside to see if we can sense where they went." He turned to Cal, who was riding protectively close to Rienne. "Cal, my lad, you're going to have to be very alert on this trip. What are the chances of you learning how to shield Rienne? You're likely to be quickest in her defense if there's any trouble. What do you think, Taran?"

"I'll learn it," said Cal before Taran could reply. Rienne smiled.

"You can leave group shielding to us," continued Bull. "We'll call on you if we need you. Fair enough?"

"Fine by me," said Cal. "Rienne's never been through the Veils before. She's a bit nervous."

Rienne chuckled. "I'm sure the four of you will be able to protect me."

"Seriously, though," said Robin, coming suddenly out of his preoccupation, "we'll all have to shield Rienne when we pass through the Veils. If Bull's right and she is an empath, it might affect her. Especially as she has no idea how to shield."

Rienne frowned. "Empath? What's that?"

Bull tried to explain and as he did so, the healer's face cleared.

"I think I know what you mean," she said. "When Sullyan and I were talking about her past, I could see in my mind some of the things she was telling me. At the time I thought it was because I'd had too much to drink, or that Sullyan was a very good storyteller. But I seemed to be able to feel what she was feeling, almost taste and smell what was going on around her, if you understand me. And I really did 'see' her run out in front of Blaine to fend off the attackers. Does that sound right?"

"It does," agreed Robin. "Empaths are often receptive to an Artesan's mind, especially a powerful one like the Major's. They're also often highly attuned to the emotions and feelings of ungifted people, picking up on the slightest change of mood."

He turned to Taran and Cal. "That would explain why Rienne got those nightmares instead of me. They've already been linked and if she's injured, Sullyan would find it much easier to reach Rienne in her sleep than to communicate with me while awake." He sobered. "So at least we now know one thing. The Major was definitely alive a couple of days ago. Rienne, please let us know immediately if you feel any more contact with her, or if you get any sudden, unexplained hunches as to where she might be. Even the vaguest sensation might be important."

Rienne nodded, a worried look in her soft gray eyes.

Chapter Twenty-Six

Robin led them to the stream where they had crossed through the Veils before. The day was chilly and overcast, there were no wading birds or bright fish flashing through the steely water. They reined in along the bank and dismounted, pulling their cloaks tightly around them. Robin glanced at Bull, who said mildly, "This is your show, lad. Do it your way."

The Captain nodded gratefully and turned to Taran. "Will you form the structure for us again? I'll go through first and scout the area, Bull will follow me, then Rienne and Cal can come through together. You can collapse the structure behind you. Everyone agree?"

They nodded and Taran went to work, feeling Rienne's eyes on him as he formed the tunnel. She had never been allowed to watch anything like this before; Taran had always been careful of her safety. He doubted she could see the structure as clearly as the others, but he thought it likely she would sense it on her skin. As if confirming this, she gave a gasp as the tunnel blossomed beyond the Veils.

Robin led his horse through, naked sword in hand. He seemed to dwindle and fade as he progressed, but once he emerged from the other end, his substance returned. The same thing happened to Bull and then it was Rienne's turn.

Cal took her by the arm and led her through the clinging fog of the Veils. Taran could see her staring in awe but the shield they were holding around her protected her from harm. The sensation must be odd, he thought, disorienting, and he could see she was relieved when it was over. She and Cal emerged beside Robin and Bull, and Taran led his horse out to join them.

They rode on, Rienne taking in the terrain with interest. It wasn't so different from Albia's, although Taran did hear her asking Robin if he knew what medicinal herbs grew here. He smiled to himself; she would be wondering whether any of them could be useful. The terrain might not be so different, he thought, but the weather certainly was, it was colder with a hint of frost. They would all be glad of their heavy woollen cloaks.

Robin led them at a hand canter for most of that gray day with only a brief stop for food, bodily needs, and to rest the horses. None of them saw any sign of the land's inhabitants; it was all as it had been the first time they had come. Occasionally, Robin would ask Bull and Taran to take care of the shielding while he closed his eyes, trying to pick up even the faintest trace of Sullyan. He always met with failure, becoming more depressed with each attempt. Taran knew Rienne longed to comfort him.

Camp that night was made in a stand of trees that sheltered a soft carpet of old leaves on the ground among their peeling trunks. Once the horses had been seen to and a hot meal eaten, Bull proposed they try a Powersink. He asked Rienne to take a turn on watch while they were occupied and she agreed, although Taran could see she didn't feel confident.

Bull reassured her. "Just let yourself be open to any feelings of danger," he said. "Keep your eyes peeled and if there's anything you don't like the look of, don't hesitate to rouse us. This shouldn't take long. It'll either work or it won't."

As Rienne walked to the edge of the trees, Taran guided Cal through the principle of the Powersink . He was quick to pick it up and Taran praised him. "I wouldn't be at all surprised if you came out of this an Apprentice-elite," he said. Cal smiled with pride, he'd been working all afternoon on the shielding technique and was learning fast.

This Powersink was vastly different to the first one Taran had participated in. The absence of a Master-elite's strength—even if only half of it had been available to him—made this one a much less powerful and heady experience. However, two Adepts-elite, one Adept and an experienced Apprentice could wield considerable strength. Robin was confident as the power was surrendered to his control and he used it to fling a wide net of awareness toward the mansion.

After only a few minutes, he turned away in disgust. The place was as deserted as the last time they had looked. Only two or three people—probably guards—remained within; everyone else was gone.

Puzzled, he widened the field of search, but as he had no specific direction to work with, he was questing in the dark. Deflated, dispirited and depressed, he eventually relinquished the Powersink.

Taran watched in sympathy as the young Captain lowered his face to his hands. Bull stood and leaned over, patting Robin's shoulder. "Come on, lad," he encouraged, "let's not have the wake before the bloody funeral. We've only just started looking. There's plenty we can do yet."

Robin nodded, only marginally cheered. Bull then walked through the trees to relieve Rienne, who made her way back to the campfire. She crossed immediately to the despondent Captain, accepting a mug of fellan from Cal as she passed.

Sitting down by Robin, she murmured, "I'm sure she's still alive."

Robin raised a haggard face, his eyes red. "I wish I could believe that."

"But you're so close to her, don't you think you'd have felt it if she had ... died?" Rienne was plainly reluctant to say or even think the word.

Robin's hands twisted together in pain. "Yes, I'm sure I would. So if she's alive, why can't I sense her presence?"

Rienne had no answer and could only offer her hand on his arm for comfort.

"Could she have crossed to another realm?" asked Cal.

Robin shook his head. "Why would she? And I'd still be able to link with her. I'd still be able to pick up her trail, especially with all of us in concert. No, there's some other explanation, though I dread to think what it is."

Bull came back through the trees. "The mansion's still our best bet," he said. "With the speed we've made today, we should be able to reach it by midday tomorrow. We'll gain entry—by whatever means necessary—and do a thorough search. If we read the substrate from inside, either in the rooms we used or maybe the council chamber, I'm sure we'll pick up some clues. Meanwhile, we need to set watches. There's nothing moving around right now but I'd feel safer if we did. Cal, will you take first watch?" The young man nodded. "Then you, Taran, then me. Robin, will you take the early turn?"

The Captain nodded and Taran realized that Bull had assigned him the watch usually taken by Sullyan. He doubted Robin took any comfort from it, though.

✣ ✣ ✣ ✣ ✣

Morning dawned bright, the previous day's cloud cover having been blown away by a breeze. As he struggled from his blankets, Taran thought it would get colder as the day progressed. He was thankful for the hot breakfast Rienne made; it would help warm bodies not used to sleeping on the ground. He did his share of the camp duties and they were cantering on their way again only one hour after dawn.

Soon, he spotted the small range of hills that had sheltered them after Bull had been shot. Now they were in sight of their first goal. Robin led them on warily, aware that despite what they had seen on their search, there might still be raiders or members of Marik's court in the hills. Cautiously, they approached the rise before the mansion plain. Once they crested it, nearly an hour later, they could look down on the building.

Even from this distance, it was clear to Taran that all was not well. The shanty town that had clung to the mansion's walls like fungus on a dead tree was completely deserted. Half-demolished, there was evidence of fire and hasty evacuation. Robin pointed out that Marik's standard was missing from the flagpole on the topmost turret. It had been flying when they left; now, it was empty. He glanced at Bull.

"At least the lack of people should make getting in easier," he said. "What do you think? The frontal approach or sneak in around the back?"

Bull thought for a minute. "It can't be a trap," he said, "we know there are few guards. There are enough of us to provide a solid shield if anyone decides to try a shot, so I'm inclined to use the front door. Much quicker. We could spend hours finding the back way. Any other suggestions?"

"As long as we keep Rienne out of the way until it's safe," said Cal.

"Of course. She can wait in the trees over there where she can see the gate, and we can signal when we're in."

Rienne wasn't happy about being left on her own, but she knew her skills were no use in this situation. She knew nothing about fighting; only the damage weapons could cause. She agreed to the plan.

Robin led them on a circular route as they descended the ridge, coming at the mansion through the trees where they left Rienne. As they rode through the wreckage of the shanty town, Taran sensed no hostile eyes.

The mansion's massive gates and the postern gate at the side were shut.

"Let's try the polite approach," said Robin. Bull gestured for him to go ahead.

Up to the huge gates he rode and with the pommel of his sword thumped loudly on the wood. "Open up, messenger for Count Marik."

Taran didn't expect a response and for a moment there was none, but then he heard the bolts of the postern being drawn. Robin leaped from his horse and Bull did likewise. As the door was pushed ajar from within, the big man grasped it in powerful hands, heaving it fully open. Robin had his sword to the guard's throat before the startled man had time to react.

Yelling for Taran and Cal to follow, Bull slipped past the gate. They dismounted and drew their weapons, edging through behind him. Two more guards dashed out of a small guard house to help their comrade.

"Taran, Cal and I will take care of these two, you go and see if there are any more," shouted Bull.

Sprinting toward the guard house, Taran ignored the sounds of combat behind him and slipped quietly through the door. The building was deserted. Re-emerging, he saw that Robin had tied his man securely and was helping Cal and Bull, neither of whom seemed under pressure. Swiftly, he looked around, identifying the mansion's entrance as the only other possible source of danger. He ran around the courtyard, keeping out of the direct line of sight of the open doorway, and sidled along the wall until he could see into the passage beyond. It was clear.

He jumped through the doorway and listened intently in the pale light of a few tallow torches. There was nothing to hear or sense. When he turned back to the others, two of the guards lay bleeding their last on the slick cobbles and Robin was menacing his prisoner, trying to make the demon tell him if there was anyone else inside.

The guard stayed defiantly silent, staring at Robin through pale, slitted eyes, until Bull came up behind him and casually sliced off an ear lobe. The demon's agonized shriek echoed around the courtyard.

"Where's the Count?" repeated Robin.

"Gone," rasped the demon, blood streaming down his neck.

"Gone where?" yelled Robin.

Bull laid his dagger beneath the guard's other ear and the demon flinched, sweat beading his face. "They've gone to Kymer," he spat. "They left two weeks ago."

Robin and Bull stared at each other.

"Kymer?" said the Captain. "That's Rykan's province." He turned back to the guard and shook him roughly. "Are you telling me Rykan came back for the council meeting?"

Despite his pain, the guard smiled wolfishly. "He never really left. There was a tasty morsel here he fancied."

Robin stamped furiously on his arm and the demon grunted in pain.

"I knew we shouldn't have left her here," raged Robin. "If Marik's betrayed her, I'll slice out his heart. The gods know what's become of her now. Curse Blaine for recalling us too soon."

Bull frowned. "Calm down, Robin, getting angry won't help us. We don't know this is Marik's doing. And if Rykan's that enamored of her, he's not going to do her any harm."

They became aware of a rasping sound. It was the demon guard laughing at them as he bled. "No lasting harm?" he wheezed. "She'll be dead by now if I know Lord Rykan. He'll have had what he wanted of her ten times over. There will be no stopping him now."

Taran gasped and Bull wasn't quick enough to prevent the enraged Robin from running the guard through the throat with his sword, grounding the weapon on the cobbles. He leaned on it, panting as the demon's life bubbled out. Finally, he jerked it out of the bloody flesh and wiped it clean on the body. Bull stared in disapproval, hands planted on his hips.

"What?" said Robin.

"What the hell did you kill him for? How are we going to find her now? Do you know where Rykan's palace is? We can't search the whole of Andaryon for her."

"He deserved it. I wasn't going to listen to any more of that."

"You should have walked away! We'll have to waste more time now."

Robin spun on him. "You heard what he said. He'll have killed her."

"Shut up, you idiot, and think for a minute. We know she was alive the day before yesterday, don't we? Why should that suddenly change? What did he mean by Rykan being unstoppable now? Doesn't that imply he wants her for a reason? Something to do with his plans to challenge the Hierarch, if Sully was right. And you know she wouldn't surrender without a fight. Come on Robin, don't write her off so easily."

Voices by the gate tore Taran's attention away. Rienne had arrived, presumably following Cal's all-clear signal. She was none too pleased to find three dead bodies in the courtyard and stared hard at Robin and Bull.

"Couldn't you have restrained them? Locked them up or something?"

"They weren't too keen on the idea," said Taran.

"It's done now," said Robin. "We need to search the mansion, see if there are any clues as to where Rykan's taken her."

As they entered the mansion, Taran told Rienne what the guard had said. She pursed her lips, her face pale. She followed him, Cal behind her, as they made their way up to the suite Lord Nazir had shown them. The room looked the same as Taran remembered; Sullyan's clothes and sword were still lying on the bed where she had left them the morning after the banquet.

Robin and Bull traded grim glances, disturbed that she was unarmed.

Taran helped them read the substrate in the room but none of them found traces later than the morning they had left. The traces were extremely faint and it was only because the mansion was abandoned that they had been retained at all.

Silently, Robin put Sullyan's things into her discarded pack and picked up her sword. He turned to leave when a faint noise in the corridor caused them all to whirl around in alarm, swords drawn. The wizened old woman who appeared in the doorway gave a terrified squeak as she found herself facing four blades, each one aimed at her heart. Hands clutched to her mouth, she stood in frozen fear.

Bull recovered first, recognizing the elderly servant who'd waited on them before. "Harva? What are you doing here?"

The others sheathed their weapons and the old lady breathed again.

"Oh, masters," she panted, "I hoped you'd return. I hid when the others were driven off and I've been waiting ever since, hoping you'd be back."

Robin strode over and took her roughly by the arm. "Can you tell us what happened to Sullyan?"

Harva shrank back, cringing away from his urgency. "Gently, Robin," said Bull. "She wants to help us, remember?"

Robin colored, seeing the old lady's fear. "I'm sorry, Harva." He released her arm and stepped back. "I didn't mean to startle you. It's just that I'm so worried and I'm not thinking straight. Please, tell us what you can. We're frantic to find her."

"I don't know very much, master," she said, her voice wavering.

Bull approached her and led her farther into the room. Guiding her to a chair, he helped her sit. "You tried to warn Sullyan before the feast, didn't you, Harva? What worried you? Was it Rykan?"

At the mention of Rykan's name, Harva paled and her rheumy eyes flicked around the room. "I heard them talking in the corridor, the day before you came."

"Who did you hear?"

"His Grace and the Count. They didn't see me, master, the

lords never do. Anyway, I heard his Grace telling the Count that
he didn't want the Lady Ambassador knowing he was here until
the Count introduced them at the banquet. The Count wasn't
happy—I could see his face—but the Duke's his overlord, he
hadn't any choice."

"So Rykan knew Sullyan was coming?" Robin shot a swift
glance at Bull. "How did he know that?"

"Well I don't know, master, I expect the Count told him." The
old woman's voice carried a touch of asperity. "The Duke came
four days before you did, he'd come to speak with the Count. I
think he stayed because of your visit."

Bull's eyes widened. "He was waiting for us? So there's more
to this than just a passing fancy for a pretty girl?"

Harva sniffed. "His Grace never does anything for a passing
fancy. He covets the throne, we all know that. I might be only a
servant but even I know he's been plotting for years to challenge
the Hierarch."

She glanced up at Bull, suddenly timid. "I don't know this for
fact, master, but his interest in the Lady might be something to do
with that."

Robin frowned. "He'd never get Sullyan to help him defeat the
Hierarch. She'd never get involved. It's none of our business who
rules here."

"But could he force her to help him?" the old woman said.

Robin stared at her. "I don't see how. They're metaphysical
equals, so he can't compel her, and I can't see how holding her
against her will would help him. As a hostage, she means nothing
to the Hierarch, so it can't be bargaining power he's after. And
if he hopes to ransom her to us, he'll be disappointed there, too.
Blaine would never make a deal with him, no matter what he
owes her."

Bull asked, "When did he take her, Harva?"

She rubbed her rheumy eyes with a large-knuckled hand. Taran
watched her with admiration, thinking it couldn't have been easy

for her hiding here, just waiting on the off chance they would return. Her regard for Sullyan must run deep, he thought.

"He came back during the council session," she said, "just before noon. But he didn't go in. He didn't have to." Her wrinkled mouth thinned in disapproval. "He'd left his own servants and guards to do his work for him. Once you left, they herded us together in one of the halls. We were held there, not allowed to do our duties. The kitchen servants were there too so the meal must've been prepared by his own people. I think the food was drugged because everyone was carried out unconscious, including the Count and the Lady Ambassador. His Grace had them put into carriages and driven away. He even took all the horses."

"So that's how he did it." Robin jumped up, startling Harva. "She'd never suspect the food if they were all eating it. That must be why we can't contact her, Bull. He's keeping her drugged."

"I'm not so sure," said Bull slowly. "You'd still be able to sense her psyche even if she was insensible. Drugs don't stop the mind from working, they only put part of it to sleep. There's more to it than that, I'm sure. I just can't think what. Go on Harva, what happened after that?"

The old lady sighed, folding stiff hands in her lap. "His Grace's personal guards ordered the rest of the court—those who hadn't been drugged—to follow the Duke to Kymer. A few were stupid enough to resist and they were killed. The servants—we were all terrified—were run off, including the peasants and laborers who'd come to the mansion for protection. There's been talk of war all summer, everyone's been nervous. The Duke's men threatened us with death if we came back and then set fire to the settlement to show they meant business. No one stayed after that, they all bolted for the hills."

"Except you," said Bull.

She gave him a shy smile. "The Lady Ambassador was always kind to me, she didn't treat me like a servant. I was fond of her."

"Why did the Duke's men want the Count's to follow him to Kymer?" asked Cal.

Harva said, "The Duke needs as many men as he can get for his war."

"So why run off the servants?"

Her look was withering. "Most of us have been with the Count all our lives. We might only be servants, but we're loyal. The Duke knows that. He has his own servants who know better than to cross him, and none of us were trained to bear arms. We're no use to him."

Cal flushed and Taran smiled to see him so thoroughly put in his place.

"Well, at least we know the how, if not the why," said Bull. "Harva, what are our chances of getting into Rykan's palace unobserved? Would we be able to get her out of there?"

The old woman looked sad. "I really couldn't say, master. I did go there once with the Count but that was years ago. I only saw the Count's rooms, I don't know what the rest of the palace is like. But I do know the Duke keeps a full complement of guards. And if he's planning a revolt, he'll have called out his levies. The province will be full of his troops. How would you get past them without being seen?"

She began to weep and buried her head in her hands. Her voice was muffled. "Oh, I wish I'd known what he was planning, I could've warned you properly when you were all here."

Rienne moved over and sat on the arm of her chair. She patted Harva on the back and spoke soothingly to her. Bull drew the others to the far end of the room.

"Sounds pretty bad," he admitted. "What do you think, Robin?"

The Captain's face was a study in anguish, his dark blue eyes almost black with grief. "We can't just leave her there, Bull, who knows what torments she's enduring? No matter how many troops there are or how secure the palace is, there has to be a way in. No place is impregnable. We'll just have to scout around and try to find a back way. Perhaps we can pass ourselves off as servants, or stable hands, or even mercenary forces." Struck by this idea, he stared at the big man. "Bull, you know how chaotic it'll be with all those unfamiliar companies camped around. We could blend in with Rykan's levies, no one would know the difference."

Suddenly seeing Bull's expression, he stopped. "What?"

"We're not Andaryans. Our eyes will give us away."

Robin's face fell.

Taran thought they were missing something. "Not necessarily. Isn't there something we could do about that?"

Robin's expression cleared and he perked up. "Try illusion, you mean? It might work, Bull. There are enough of us to form a respectable Powersink. As long as we stay together, it could work."

Bull looked unconvinced, but didn't say so. In the absence of any other plan, thought Taran, it had to be worth a try. They could experiment on the way to the palace.

Bull turned back to the old woman, whom Rienne had soothed. "Harva, could you tell us how to find the palace without showing ourselves too early?" She nodded, wiping a shaky hand across her eyes. "How far is it?" he asked.

She sniffed. "Only a day's ride away, on good horses."

"So close?" said Robin.

The look she gave him was reproachful. "We're right on the borders of Kymer, master. Right on the edge of the Duke's province. Why else do you think the Count's supported him? He'd rather fight for the Hierarch but he's not powerful or wealthy enough to oppose his Grace. You could say he's been held to ransom all these years."

Taran thought Robin looked less than convinced by Harva's interpretation of the Count's loyalties.

"But if you're set on going," she continued, turning back to Bull, "then you'd do best to cross the River Yrrin and approach the palace from the south. Kymer's mainly rolling hills but from what I remember, the palace is in a valley surrounded by the southern end of Haligan Forest. Unless they've cleared it since I was there, there's tree cover right up to the walls. His Grace will have patrols there but most of his vassals live to the east, so that's probably where his forces will be."

Taran was impressed by Harva's thinking and remembered Sullyan telling Robin not to underestimate her. She might be a servant but she was obviously capable of using her wits.

"You leave worrying about them to us," Bull said. "Is there any food left in the kitchens? We'll need extra supplies now, this could take some time."

They left the suite, taking Sullyan's things with them, and followed the old woman to the kitchens. She told them to help themselves to whatever they wanted. "Half of it's spoiling anyway," she sniffed, plainly disapproving of the waste.

Harva tried to get them to stay and rest until morning as it was growing late and the wind, which had been gusty all day, was cold with the promise of frost. Taran wasn't surprised when Robin hustled them away, he was clearly fretting to be gone.

As they took their leave of Harva at the gates, she caught Robin's stirrup. "Master," she said, her wrinkled face full of care, "when you've released the Lady, come back to me. I know a little house where no one would think to look. I could take care of you all until you're ready to go."

Taran could see Robin was touched by her offer despite his urgent need to leave. He supposed the Captain was remembering Sullyan's genuine affection for the old crone. If not for her determination to wait and warn them, he realized, they would still be riding the open countryside, desperately searching. They owed her thanks for that, at least.

The Captain thought so, too. He reached down and patted her aging hand. "Thank you, Harva. We won't forget your help today."

He led them out of the huge wooden gates. Without another word, they galloped off in the direction Harva had given them, wind tearing icily at their cloaks.

Chapter Twenty-Seven

Bull's knowledge of the area was sketchy, so he recommended they make a large eastward sweep to come at Rykan's palace from the south. They made good time through Marik's province as the horses were rested and strong and had no difficulty finding a good place to cross the wide but shallow River Yrrin. But evening was coming fast and Robin decided they should camp; it would be too easy to stumble into a patrol in the darkness. Besides, they had their strategy to plan and a disguise to attempt. If Taran's idea didn't work, they only had hours to come up with another.

They found a suitable spot to camp and quickly took care of camp duties. Bull lit a tiny, well shielded fire and once they had eaten some of Harva's food, they discussed their plans.

The idea of a disguise appealed to Robin because it would allow them free movement and the chance to gain information. None of them knew if it would work, though. Their first task was to see if they could create and maintain the illusion of the slit-pupiled Andaryan eye.

They sat in a circle, Rienne off to one side, and formed a Powersink. Robin took control and Taran sensed him concentrating on the color of his eyes. First, he attempted to fade his dark blue irises and Taran watched in amazement as they slowly bleached to a lighter hue. Robin's handsome face looked very strange in the firelight; the frost-pale color made his eyes seem larger.

"That's enough," said Bull, "or your eyes'll end up white."

"Some of them do have white eyes, so I've heard, so it wouldn't look that odd." Robin was clearly pleased with his efforts.

The pupils, thought Taran, would be trickier as they had to react to light the same way as round pupils. Narrowing the pupils would be easiest; learning to expand them would take some practice. Robin mastered it after about fifteen minutes and Taran thought it looked very convincing.

Under Robin's guidance, everyone tried the disguise. Cal was the only one who had any real trouble, and he had to draw heavily on the Powersink. Not surprising, Taran told him, given his limited experience. He eventually got the hang of it after an hour of intense practice.

Rienne sat quietly throughout this process, faint worry on her face. At first, Taran thought she was simply concerned about Cal's ability to hold the disguise, but then, with a leap of intuition, he realized she was unsure of their plans for her. Obviously, she couldn't alter her own appearance and he guessed she was worried they might leave her behind. He was uneasy about taking her into Rykan's stronghold, he knew it would be extremely dangerous. One tiny mistake and they could all be killed.

He did know, however, that she would be happier if they stayed together. She had no expertise in concealment and didn't have the skills necessary to avoid Rykan's patrols. She wouldn't even be able to defend herself were she unfortunate enough to be found. If the worst should happen and they were all killed inside Rykan's palace, Rienne would never see Albia again. She had no means of crossing the Veils and would be an obvious and vulnerable intruder wherever she went. She might, he supposed, manage to return to Harva, but she must surely be aware she wouldn't survive long away from home.

He was distracted from his thoughts by Bull, who got to his feet to replenish the fellan pot. The big man turned to Rienne, passed her a cup and said, "Come on, my little lovely, your turn now."

Helping her up, he drew her into the circle. "Right, lads. Let's see what we can do to improve our healer's looks, eh?"

Taran could see Cal about to defend Rienne and nudged his elbow. "Ease up, Cal," he murmured, "Bull's only joking. We're all in this together."

Rienne sat in the center of their circle and Taran could feel relief and apprehension radiating from her. "Will I feel different?" she asked.

"Shouldn't think so," said Robin. "You might feel a sensation on your skin as the power touches you, but no more than when we shield you. Your eyes won't feel any different and it would be better if you try to ignore what we're doing so your reactions will be normal."

She sat stiffly, clearly trying not to think about what was happening, and Robin began to work. Taran, Cal and Bull all stared critically at her, making comments while Robin altered her appearance. The Journeyman shuddered when he finished; he'd never imagined that the color and shape of someone's eyes could make such a difference. All their faces had taken on a feral appearance and it was no longer easy to read what they were thinking.

They let the disguise settle before feeling confident it was as natural as it was going to get. Robin suggested they maintain it even when they were alone. If they should come across one of Rykan's patrols unexpectedly, the disguises would already be in place.

"Will it last overnight?" asked Rienne.

Robin shook his head. "We need the Powersink to maintain the disguise and that would be an unnecessary drain. It's going to tire us enough as it is. I suggest that whoever's on watch keeps up their own disguise, it'll be good practice. Who knows what might happen if we manage to join Rykan's forces? It's likely we'll have to do some quick thinking if we're not to get separated."

He flicked both Taran and Cal a grim glance. "I'm not going to pretend this will be easy. Far from it. It'll be risky and dangerous and we'll be lucky to get out alive. The only way it'll work is if we're tight, sharp and swift. Ideally, I want to be able to ride in there tomorrow, use our cover as mercenaries to do a bit of reconnaissance—which shouldn't be too difficult as the place will be in chaos—find out where he's keeping her, and effect our rescue during the night."

Noting Taran's raised brows, his mouth tightened. "Yes, I know it won't be as simple as that, but I have nothing else to offer until I know what we're up against. One thing I can tell you. The longer we're there, the greater the chance of discovery. Our only advantage lies in surprise, but it's no guarantee of success. If anyone wants to back out, now's the time to say. Bull and I won't think any less of you."

Taran traded glances with Cal and Rienne and then shook his head. Robin's relief was plain.

"We need to be up early in the morning, so unless there are any questions, I suggest we grab some sleep."

⁜ ⁜ ⁜ ⁜ ⁜

It was damp and misty when they woke, but not as cold. Breakfast was a hurried affair, taken while breaking camp. They spent some time re-establishing the illusion and Taran was relieved to find that it was significantly easier than the night before. Robin organized them into something resembling a militia unit come to join the Duke's forces, although his plan was to locate a patrol, sneak up on them and try to gain some intelligence before they rode in and announced themselves.

Since Rienne couldn't pass for a warrior even if Andaryan women were allowed to bear arms, Robin decided she would be a healer attached to their party. Hopefully, a skilled healer would be acceptable to anyone's war effort, whatever their gender. He asked her to ride in the middle, the place of greatest safety. This had the added advantage of placing her at the focus of the illusion.

They traveled warily for most of the day, the tree cover

increasing the farther east they went. The hills were getting steeper and they soon realized they were climbing a substantial ridge. Harva had told them the palace was in a valley, and Taran guessed they were riding up its southernmost slope.

So far they had seen no patrols, but Bull had spotted signs of old campfires and the tracks of horses. Most of the tracks were heading toward the palace, but some seemed to be circling the area in a logical pattern. As they finally began descending the ridge, they entered the forest Harva had mentioned. It wasn't far off midday and Robin called a halt.

He gathered them around. "I think the time has come to find out exactly what we're walking into. There's a thick stand of trees over there, large enough to hide in. I suggest Rienne, Cal and Bull wait here with the horses while Taran and I go forward on foot. I want to locate a patrol, see if I can do a spot of eavesdropping. There must be one around here somewhere, their tracks are everywhere. We'll try not to be too long and I'll report back to Bull now and then, but I don't want to use too much power in case I'm overheard."

Once they had dismounted, Bull, Cal and Rienne led the horses deep into the thicket. Robin checked that Bull and Cal could maintain three disguises, and that Bull knew to get the others away if Robin and Taran got into trouble. Then he led Taran away in search of a patrol.

They crept through the silent woods, the continuing absence of bird-song ahead a sure sign they were not alone. It wasn't long before Taran saw Robin give a quick gesture and he followed the Captain as he worked his cautious way toward a clearing in the trees. Taran couldn't see the signs Robin had spotted but once he was lying on his stomach near the edge of the clearing, concealed among bracken, he cautiously raised his head and saw the four-man patrol.

They must've halted for a breather because they hadn't set a watch. All wore the black and silver of Rykan's forces but none bore the scarlet flashing of an officer. Taran assumed they were guardsmen scouting the forest for stragglers and he soon realized their hearts weren't in the task.

"Damn stupid peasants," one of the swordsmen was saying. "You'd think they would be capable of understanding a simple command. What's so hard about 'make your way immediately to his Grace's palace?'"

"Can't think why his Grace wants such sheep shite anyway," said one of his comrades, passing around a water bottle. "Half of them don't even know their own names, let alone which end of a sword's sharp."

The others laughed.

"They're arrow fodder, nothing more," said another, wiping his mouth on the back of his hand. "They will be shoved to the front, to take the first wave of arrows. That's all they're good for—shielding proper swordsmen."

"And the second wave will be for Marik's rabble, if we're lucky," said the first one. "Bloody mercenaries. Think they know it all. I tell you, that lackwit Nazir's going to feel my sword in his back just as soon as I can get behind him. Can you believe he had the bloody nerve to tell me my swing was unbalanced? I'll give him unbalanced. Let's see how balanced he is with his guts around his feet."

"Still, at least he's here," said the last man. "I've just about had enough of raking this damned forest for bloody stragglers. Marik's useless peasants can't even walk a straight line, let alone obey a call to arms."

Taran risked exchanging a look with Robin, knowing the Captain was thinking the same thing. If they could pass themselves off as stragglers from Marik's province, their appearance at Rykan's gates would be credible. They were already acquainted with Marik and had some knowledge of his lands, so their chances of being caught out were greatly diminished. He grinned at the Captain and was about to suggest they retreat when Robin put a finger to his lips. Taran turned back to the patrol.

"When's his Grace expected back?"

Taran and Robin stared at each other; they had never even considered that Rykan might not be at the palace.

"Word is he's due back sometime late tonight. Quartermaster says that now his Grace has issued his formal challenge, he just has to finish what he started with the human witch before giving the order to move out. Said he'd spoken to the jailer and that he reckoned she's more'n half dead anyway, so one more session ought to do it."

The men laughed, a deeply unpleasant sound.

"I reckon his Grace will enjoy that!"

They made lewd comments about Rykan's "pet chained witch" and Robin went pale. He started sweating and might have drawn his sword had Taran not placed a hand on his shoulder. He could feel the young Captain shaking with rage and drew him away as carefully as he could. The patrolmen weren't being particularly watchful but they still had ears.

They returned to the others as quickly as they could. Robin was still shaking, so Taran reported what they had heard. When Bull realized the reason for Robin's anger, he took him by the arms. Taran really hoped he could calm down the Captain because he was worried by the dangerous glint in Robin's eyes.

"You're going to have to control your emotions better than this," Bull told him sternly. "It's highly likely we'll hear more of that kind of talk inside the palace and if you react like that, you'll give us away."

"I know. I'm sorry," said Robin. "It's just … it's so hard, you know?"

"Of course I know. Don't you think I feel it, too? I'm as frightened for her as you are. You've got to remember your training, lad, it's more vital now than it's ever been. Remember what she's tried to drum into you these last two years. What's she always telling you?"

"Humility, discipline, control," Robin growled. "I've never been very good at any of them."

"Then I suggest you get good real quick. Maybe luck's with us at the moment but it's still going to be bloody dangerous. All our lives are at stake, not just hers. You and I know what we're doing, we can take care of ourselves, but Taran and Cal aren't trained for this. And there's Rienne to think of, too." He shook his head. "I hate to think what Sully would say if she knew we were bringing Rienne in with us."

He held Robin's alien gaze. "You're in command here, Captain. The responsibility's yours. Think like Sullyan. You've seen her lead often enough and she's taught you well. You showed that when you led the lads against the invasion. Do it like she would. This is your chance to repay her for all her hard work, your chance to prove her right and Blaine wrong. Make us proud of you, Captain. Make her proud!"

"Let's go. We've got to get in there, do what we have to do, and get out safely before Rykan returns. We won't get a second chance."

Robin gripped Bull's shoulder and turned to the others. His stern expression softened when he saw Rienne's pale face. The patrol's comments concerning Sullyan's state of health had frightened her and her gray eyes glittered with tears. "I hope we're not too late," she said.

"We won't be," said Robin. "Everyone, form up as we agreed. Let's not run into any patrols if we can help it, I don't want any delays. Rienne, pull up the hood of your cloak and keep it there. I want you concealed as much as possible.

"Ready? Let's go."

They made good time in the failing light, managing to avoid two more patrols. Convenient as it was, Robin was disgusted at the ease of it; his opinion of Rykan's regulars went down considerably.

"No one would be able to approach the Manor like this if we

were on a war footing," he said. "Our patrols are much more alert."

"Well, good for us that Rykan's aren't," said Bull. "Look, that's the main gate ahead. We'd better ride up in full view as we're supposed to be joining up. Keep alert, everyone, and remember, you're demons now. Rienne, a word of caution. Women are much more subservient here so keep your head down. Don't say anything if you're addressed, let us do the talking. You might not like it, but men are the masters here."

"Yes, you love that, don't you?" muttered Rienne from under her hood. Taran knew the sarcasm was to mask her fear. "Don't worry," she added, "I can do subservient when I want to."

Cal snorted but didn't comment.

They rode openly to the gates and two guards holding loaded crossbows stepped smartly in front of them. Robin held up his hand to halt his party. Dismounting, he flung his reins to Taran, who fortunately was alert enough to catch them. Dismissive of the crossbows, Robin stalked toward the two guards.

"Is this the welcome we get after riding for days to join his Grace's assault force?" he sneered. "We left our homes and livelihoods to come here. It had better be worth it."

His high-handed tone seemed to distract the guards, who lowered their crossbows. "Whose men are you?" one of them said.

Robin looked down his nose. "Our lord is Count Marik."

"Oh, priceless! More crack troops." The demon rolled his eyes and spat at Robin's feet. "Much good you'll be."

"Who commands the patrols in the forest?" asked Robin, giving him a venomous look.

"They're Lord Rykan's personally trained troops," snapped the demon.

"Well if they're so good and we're so useless, how come we've just evaded three patrols? I could have marched a whole company through that forest without being seen. They were more concerned with getting back in time for dinner than they were about security. They wouldn't last a day under my command."

"You can tell his Grace that when you see him. Perhaps he'll put you in charge of the van if you're so bloody good," the guard sneered.

Irritably, he scanned the rest of Robin's group, his pale brown eyes widening as he spotted Rienne. The healer had lowered her cowled head and was staring at her horse's mane but her hands, visible on the reins, were unmistakably a woman's.

The guard turned to stare at Robin, a sly grin on his face. "I know you was told to bring your own supplies, but I don't think that's what his Grace had in mind. The other lads will be grateful, I'm sure."

He shoved past Cal's horse and strode up to Rienne. Taran could see her trembling. The guard laid his hand on her thigh and Taran tensed, ready to defend her. He needn't have worried. Before anyone could speak or react, Robin's sword was out of its sheath, the point resting solidly between the guard's shoulder blades. The demon stiffened, his slit-eyes narrowing.

"Take your hand off her, friend," said Robin, his tone softly menacing. "She's our healer and a damned good one. I'm not giving her up to the likes of you. We might need her skills before too long and I want her left undamaged. Now, are you going to tell us where we can put our gear? We've come a long way for this, but we can just as easily ride away if our swords aren't welcome."

The demon's eyes held a promise of retribution but Robin's sword dissuaded him from action. He stepped slowly away from Rienne, glaring at them in dislike.

"Get inside the compound. We've just about had enough of waiting for you lot. We're likely moving out tomorrow, so you'd better look lively. The count's rabble are billeted over by the dung pile where they belong. I'm sure you'll find some old friends over there, if they haven't already deserted."

Turning, he flung open the main gate and the other guard did the same. Taran could feel their venomous gazes boring into his back as he followed the others into the compound. He heard Bull whisper, "Well done, lass," and saw Rienne flash him a wan smile. The gates slammed shut behind them.

They were inside the enemy's lair now and needed all their wits.

The vast area was seething with men, horses, gear and weapons. Momentarily overawed by the sheer numbers around them, they came to a halt to get their bearings.

"Get out of the way, you idiots," yelled someone behind them. "Get those horses to the stables and sort yourselves out. You part-timers are more trouble than you're worth."

To avoid further confrontation, they quickly found a space by the wall of the stables. Most of the men around them seemed to be from Marik's province, judging by the lack of black-and-silver uniforms. Marik's people wore ordinary combat leathers if they were trained fighters, or an assortment of whatever they had on hand if they were of peasant origin. Being only a count, Marik didn't have the funds to outfit a dedicated fighting force and clearly relied on mercenaries and a few of his landholders to supply men when he needed them. This was very convenient, thought Taran, as it wouldn't seem odd if no one knew them.

As Robin had predicted, the atmosphere in the compound was one of seething chaos and no one gave the newcomers a second glance. Their disguises were holding, so Robin accosted a passing swordsman and asked for the Quartermaster. Beckoning to Taran, he followed the directions he was given and they eventually located the man. There were many others clamoring for the Quartermaster's attention but Robin pushed through them, rudely demanding stabling for their horses.

He asked where the training ground was and who was in charge of supplies and feeding. His overbearing manner seemed to be having the desired effect as the Quartermaster, an older, harassed-looking man with an irritable air, eyed them distastefully.

"No one's in charge of much here, mate," he said. "Welcome to the arse-end of warfare. No one's going to bother with you 'til the Duke's generals form the regulars up tomorrow. Then you'll be divided up among the existing companies. You're arrow-fodder and nothing more. You ought to be grateful his Grace is giving you the opportunity to prove yourselves. If I had my way, you'd all be lined up and shot. So if you didn't bring your own supplies like you were told, you'll have to go without."

Taran heard Robin chuckle under his breath as they returned to the others. "It couldn't be better, so far," the Captain said. "No one knows anyone else, no one's in charge, and no routine's been set up. They're all too busy with the regulars to worry about a worthless bunch of peasants, which is why we've all been penned up in here. This could work in our favor, Bull. If we go for a stroll now and then, no one will notice. We only need to make sure our horses and gear are safe and that we can get out when we need to."

"And how are we going to do that with guards on the gates?" asked Cal. "Aren't we trapped in here? Someone will definitely notice if we go thundering out in the night, especially if we've got the Major with us."

"We'll think of something," stated Robin. "At least we're in. Rykan's not here and we've a few hours, by the sounds of it, before he returns. Bull, are you alright with the disguises?" The big man nodded. "Good, I think it's best if you wait here with Cal and Rienne in case there's trouble. Taran and I will take a look round. Rienne, keep out of sight as much as possible, pretend to be asleep or something. We'll be as quick as we can."

Taran followed him into the throng of men, trying to look as if he had every right to be there. Robin was a veteran of many campaigns and knew the workings of military camps. The grumbles and grudges of soldiers, he told Taran, were much the same wherever you went. By a judicious remark here, and keeping their ears open there, they learned much about the situation and what might happen tomorrow. No one, though, could tell them much about the Major, why she was so necessary to Rykan's plans, or where she might be held. Like the patrol in the forest, though, they were happy to make bawdy comments, most of which were highly unpleasant. Robin's face grew tighter and tighter as he held himself in and his lips were gray by the time he and Taran made their way back to the others.

Bull and Cal had made their little corner as comfortable as possible and had lit a campfire, like many others had done. It was fully dark now and the seethe in the compound had settled. Bull broke open their supplies and they made a quick supper while Robin told them what he and Taran had heard.

"What do we do now?" Bull asked when Robin had finished.

"We'll have to do some exploring. The servants' quarters are over there and I'm sure we could get into the palace that way and have a look around. By the smell of things, there's a kitchen in there, too, and soldiers are always hungry. It'll look natural for us to be sniffing around the kitchens, especially with food in short supply. Taran and I will go, the rest of you wait here. Bull, I'll contact you if we find anything useful."

He watched the compound a while longer, noting the movements of the servants by the kitchens. They were coming and going fairly frequently and Robin wondered whether there was a feast of some sort going on inside. "If I'm right," he said, "it'll mean less chance of encountering nobles strolling through the palace."

"I wouldn't mind betting it's in anticipation of the Duke's return from his challenge to the Hierarch," said Bull. "With any luck, they will be so far in their cups and so preoccupied with back slapping, they won't have time for anything else."

Robin agreed. "Let's not forget what that patrol said, though. Rykan's got unfinished business and it's likely he'll pay Sullyan a visit when he returns. We have to get her out before then."

"Better get on with it, lad. You won't learn anything sitting here."

Leaving Bull, Cal and Rienne huddled by the fire, Robin and

Taran rose, making their way around to the servants' quarters. As Robin had thought, there were plenty of swordsmen hanging around, hoping for scraps from the kitchen. He and Taran moved among them with familiar camaraderie, joking about being starved.

Slowly, they edged farther in, past the great, steaming ovens and roaring spit-fires with their carcasses of cows, sheep and swine turning and crackling over the heat. Pot boys in greasy aprons, cooks in striped livery, all manner of serving men thronged the place, carrying food, wine, ale, empty plates and silverware. In the general melee, it was easy for Taran and Robin to slip out into the corridor.

They turned away from the route taken by the serving men; there was nothing to be gained by heading toward the banquet. The hallways leading away were deserted and they prowled along, senses alert, ready to leap into one of the unoccupied rooms if necessary.

Listening at various doors and opening them once convinced of their vacancy, they found themselves among the nobles' private suites. Desperate to hear something that might direct his search for the Major, Robin hunted for signs of life. The halls were only faintly lit by torches which cast long and useful shadows around door lintels and statue niches. It was cold; no heat from the kitchen fires reached this far and the individual suites had their own fireplaces to warm them. The floor was flagged, giving ample warning of approaching feet, so when they finally did hear someone coming their way, it was simple to slip into a deep doorway and become lost in the velvety shadows.

There were two people approaching, thought Taran, judging by the voices. The stone floor and plaster walls made sound echo and jump; there were no hangings to soften it. Despite this distortion, both he and Robin stiffened.

One of the voices was familiar.

Chapter Twenty-Eight

From where he was concealed, Taran couldn't yet see the two men. Nevertheless, he could tell they were walking slowly, ambling almost, and they were talking quietly about the forthcoming war. The owner of the unfamiliar voice, his tone oily but reasonable, was saying, "I understand your concern, but if your men make a good showing, you stand a better chance of reinstating yourself with the Duke. I know your people aren't regulars but that doesn't mean they can't fight. All you need to do is be a good general, direct them well and be seen doing so. His Grace always rewards good service. Who knows? You might even win your manor back."

"Do you really think so, my Lord?"

Taran and Robin exchanged a look. The familiar, weary voice belonged to Count Marik. Taran thought he sounded gloomy and dispirited.

"After my last interview with his Grace I got the distinct impression he's hoping I'll lose my life in this campaign. It would save him the trouble of taking it later."

Carefully cocking his head around the lintel, Taran watched the two men around a curve of the hallway. Head lowered, Count Marik studied the floor as he walked, his dark mantle of maroon velvet dragging at his long legs. His companion, a much shorter and fatter man, was watching him narrowly. The faint torchlight flickered over the heavy gold chain circling his neck. His black robe with silver and pale-blue trim proclaimed him one of Rykan's higher-ranking nobles.

Taran saw him smile at Marik's morose tone, although his pale-green eyes held no warmth.

"My dear Count," he said smoothly, "you only need make yourself useful and his Grace will be generous. He doesn't throw away the lives of loyal subjects. He is unsure of you and your men, that's all. Just prove yourself in the coming weeks, aid him in his bid for the Hierarchy, and your future will be guaranteed. No one who serves him well goes unrewarded, I assure you."

"Well, you've done alright for yourself, Sonten," said Marik.

Taran and Robin drew back as the men came abreast of their hiding place but neither glanced toward the doorway's shadowy depths. They continued on and Robin indicated that Taran move to the other side of the door to remain out of sight in case either man turned around.

Marik's steps were faltering. "Do you know," came his depressed tone, "I really don't feel like feasting tonight. You go on, Sonten. I think I'll go check on my men and maybe change some of my strategies. I want to be sure they're well-prepared for tomorrow."

Sonten's chuckle sounded nasty. "You do that, Count. Make sure your men are first in the battle lines. Impress my Lord the Duke. But if I were you," his lowered voice was malevolent, "I'd not be absent from the Hall when he returns tonight. He just might misconstrue your absence."

Taran heard him saunter off, still chuckling under his breath.

Marik clearly didn't move for a moment but then the sound of his footsteps grew louder. Taran risked a swift glance. The Count was totally preoccupied, twisting his long-fingered hands together, muttering to himself. Striding back up the corridor, he glanced nervously behind him every few seconds and soon passed the Albians' hiding place. He didn't see Robin, or his dagger, until it was too late, until the Captain's strong arm was about his chest, the sharp blade pressed high under his ear.

Marik gave a startled squeak and Robin hissed for silence. Taran opened the door behind them and Robin shoved his captive into the empty suite.

The Count's face was a picture of terror, which told Taran just how safe he felt here in Rykan's palace. Robin spun him to face them.

"What's the meaning of this? How dare you!"

The Count's indignation trailed away as Robin's knife pricked his throat. His gaze flicked between his captors, a wary look coming into his pale gray eyes. "Do I know you?"

"We have met," said Robin, momentarily letting the disguise drop.

Relief flooded Marik's lean face. "Captain Tamsen. And ... and ... ?"

"Taran Elijah," said Taran.

Robin, the knife still held tightly against Marik's corded throat, growled, "You're not going to do anything we'll regret if I remove my knife, are you?"

"Gods, it's far too late for that," hissed the Count. "I've already done too many things I regret. But if you mean am I going to give you away, then of course I'm bloody not! Where have you been? We've been waiting days for you to get here. What the hell took you so long?"

Plainly taken aback, Robin said, "We?"

"Sullyan and me," snapped the Count. "Tonight's her last chance. If we don't get her away in the next couple of hours, it'll be too late. Rykan's issued his formal challenge and time's running out. He'll kill her for sure if he doesn't get what he wants, but I think he probably will. She can't possibly resist him any longer. Either way she'll die, if she isn't dead already. Are you alone?"

The frantic jumble of words and sudden change of tack put Robin off balance. The Count's urgency was infectious but Robin retained control.

"No, there are three more of us here. We joined your forces, Count."

"You entered the compound?" The Count was dismayed. "What the hell did you do that for?"

Robin bridled. "It was the only way we could get close. Do you have a better idea?"

Marik glared at him. "Yes, but you have to be outside and free to move if it's going to work."

Robin was about to argue when Taran touched his arm. "Do you have some kind of plan?" he asked.

The thin man nodded. "I know where she is. I've been secretly visiting her when I can, taking her food and water. Rykan hasn't bothered with either since he's had her and she's very weak. She'd have died of thirst by now if I hadn't been able to get water to her. Luckily, one of the jailers is sympathetic and turned a blind eye whenever I could get down there. The last couple of days though, I couldn't get near. Rykan's given her no rest, he's been with her the whole time. Since he's been gone, I've been watched. I'm sure he suspects something."

Marik paused, giving them a strange look. "I fear what he's done to her, gentlemen. Rykan's neither a patient nor a gentle man and what he can't get by persuasion, he gets by violence and abuse. He had her flogged, she was in a bad way and … well, I fear for her life."

Taran felt sick and Robin was bone-white. "We can't just whisk her away through the Veils?" The Captain's voice was hoarse and Taran realized that their most favored course of action was lost.

The Count reacted violently, surprising them both. "Hell, no!" Hastily, he modulated his tone. "No, she's too injured for that. I have something else in mind but we have to hurry. We've wasted too much time already."

Robin stared at him. "We'd better get on with it. What do you suggest?"

"First, we need to get you outside, with your horses and gear. I'll come down with you, I've already told Sonten I was going to check on my men. The patrols will be in now except for the honor guard on the main gate. They're waiting to welcome his Grace home. I'll order the guards to let you out—I'll say you've brought word that some of my men are injured and are waiting for you in the forest. They wouldn't let me out but there's no reason why they should stop you. Make your way westward around the perimeter wall. That'll keep you in the trees and bring you around to the back gates from the dungeons. You'll find them easily enough. It's where they haul the bodies when Rykan's torturers are done with them."

"Won't they be guarded?" asked Robin. Taran could sense he felt his authority was being leeched away. Clearly, he was unwilling to place his trust in a man who had already betrayed Sullyan once.

"Of course they will be guarded," snarled the Count. "I trust you can use that sword?"

Robin nodded and rolled his eyes, gesturing for the man to continue.

"Maybe one of you should come with me. If my friendly jailer isn't on duty, we'll have to kill whoever is. I doubt anyone would go down to the cells before Rykan comes, but you never know. The jailer will have the keys to the chains on him, at any rate."

"Chains?" said Robin.

The Count seemed about to snap again when he saw Robin's stricken look. "Yes," he said tersely. "He has her in spellsilver, too."

Robin gasped in sudden understanding. "That's why I couldn't sense her. Was it on her all this time?"

"Yes, of course, he wouldn't risk her power without it. She's his equal, a Master-elite. Why do you think he wanted her in the first place? If he can force her to surrender her power to him, he'll be bloody unstoppable."

Robin's face suddenly flooded with understanding and the Count snapped again, his pale eyes sparking with fury. "For the Void's sake, didn't you know? Hadn't you worked it out? Rykan had the whole thing set up. The invasion into Albia was purely to force your general into sending her here as ambassador. Rykan was counting on it. For four days he crouched in my house, him and that fat pig, Sonten. Forced me to wait on them hand and bloody foot. Crouched like a bloody great spider, just waiting for her. He's planning civil war, gentlemen. He's going to challenge and depose the Hierarch. If he can force Sullyan to surrender her powers, he'll be the Hierarch's metaphysical bloody equal!"

He paused, his voice losing some of its strength. "If he wins the throne, he'll kill the Hierarch, as well as Prince Aron, his Heir and only son. None of the other nobles are strong enough to stop him. Once in power, he'll rescind the Pact and recommence raiding Albia, targeting any Artesans who oppose him. There's a rumor he's got an influential ally, someone who's been supplying him with funds, although I don't know the truth of that. I'm not in his inner circle like Sonten, privy to his personal dealings."

Robin glanced at Taran; this was a serious piece of information that could have far-reaching consequences. His startled expression angered the Count even more.

"If Rykan becomes Hierarch, none of the realms will be safe," he hissed. "He's ruthless, ambitious and kills without pity. And for the past two weeks, he's been stymied by a little chit of a human woman who's been locked away from her powers. Can you imagine how furious that's made him? She's resisted his every move, no matter how violent. If he can't overcome her bloody-minded stubbornness tonight, he'll kill her. And if he finally succeeds in ripping her powers from her, she'll still die."

He thrust his face close to Robin's. "Now do you see? Now can we stop wasting time? We have to get her away from here!"

Robin took a deep breath and laid his hand on the Count's arm. "Alright. I'll go with you to the cells. The others will go and wait by the dungeon gates and deal with whoever's guarding them. What then?"

"Then we ride as fast as we can for as long as we can," snapped Marik. "When Rykan discovers she's gone, this whole place will be in uproar but he won't be able to turn out more than a few patrols because of the arrangements for tomorrow. At least that's one thing in our favor. Now that he's issued his challenge, he can't back out. That should make our escape easier."

"Our?" Robin was plainly still unwilling to trust the Count. "Are you planning on coming with us?"

"Of course I bloody am! Do you think I'm here for my health? Do you think my life would be worth the effort of taking it once Rykan realizes what's happened? The best I could hope for would be a sword in the guts, but it's more likely he'd brick me up behind a wall and leave me to rot."

"Wouldn't your men defend you?" asked Taran.

The Count shook his head. "If I had men capable of defending me against Rykan I wouldn't be here now. Even the Duke's personal bodyguards are greater in number than the few trained swordsmen who are loyal to me. They would make pig-slop of us. Now for pity's sake come on, we're wasting what little time we have."

He strode to the door, opened it and glanced out. With a nod to Taran and Robin, he stepped into the hall. They followed, Robin making sure their disguise was firmly in place.

"Walk behind me," Marik hissed. "Don't speak unless you have to."

He led the way toward the kitchens but turned into another hallway before he got there. There was no one around except a few servants who Marik ignored. As they approached a door at the end of the hall, he said, "I don't suppose you have any medical knowledge? The last time I saw Sullyan, she was in a very bad way. After two more days of Rykan's abuse, who knows what state she'll be in, if she's still alive."

Robin went white but replied levelly. "One of our group's a healer. Shall we take her with us?"

"Wouldn't do any harm. A woman, though? You Albians are strange. Is she combat trained?"

"No," said Robin. "She has no weapons skills."

The Count sighed. "We'd better keep her out of the way when we reach the cells. We'll be incredibly lucky if my friendly jailer's on duty tonight."

He reached the door at the end of the hall and flung it open. It led to the compound directly opposite their campsite. Taran could see that Bull had noticed them immediately for he nudged Cal with his foot. Rienne had her head down as Robin had advised; she seemed to be feigning sleep.

Directed by Robin, Marik strode toward their camp. As he came nearer, he started yelling orders. "On your feet. I need a patrol to collect some injured men. Saddle your horses, you need to leave at once. Take remounts for the wounded."

As Bull and Cal scrambled to their feet, Robin reached them. In a few terse words, he told them what was happening.

"You," barked Marik, pointing to Rienne. Startled, she looked up. Taran saw Robin make a covert signal and was relieved when Rienne seemed to understand. "Come with us," snapped the Count. Robin pointed to Rienne's medicine bag and she grabbed it as she rose to meet them.

She looked pale and Taran didn't like the idea of leaving her inside the compound. He had no choice though, and took his horse's reins from Cal. They led their mounts, as well as Robin's and Rienne's, into the center of the compound. Quickly, they mounted.

"Guards, open the gates," yelled Marik. The gate guards had changed, the ones Robin had insulted were nowhere in sight. Still, they hesitated. Marik, clearly nervous, used his fear to good

effect, threatening them with dire consequences should his Grace
the Duke learn they had delayed the arrival of more troops. They
finally did as Marik bid, although Taran saw suspicion in their
eyes.

He, Bull and Cal cantered through the gates, swiftly moving up
the road toward the trees.

✠ ✠ ✠ ✠ ✠

Rienne stood at Robin's side, apprehension flooding through her.
She trusted the Captain, but the sight of Taran, and especially Cal,
disappearing out of sight as if they had abandoned her made her
heart hammer with fear. She had no idea where they were going
or who the man with Robin was. All she could do was follow his
lead, she had no other choice.

"Don't just stand there man, shut those gates." The barked
order made Rienne jump. The lean man whirled on her, snapping,
"Come."

She felt Robin's hand on her shoulder and the touch reassured
her. Allowing him to urge her, she followed the other man as he
led them back to the door he'd come through. Once inside the
palace, he shut the door firmly. Then he gave a great shuddering
sigh and leaned against the wall. His long face was pale, his eyes
closed.

Roughly, Robin grasped his arm. "Good grief man, don't give
way now. We've only just started." The thin man pushed away
from the wall and ran a trembling hand over his sweaty face.

Swiftly, Robin introduced him and told Rienne what was going
to happen. She blanched on hearing their fears for Sullyan but
remained silent, trusting Robin. The Captain shoved Marik to
start him moving again, and they followed him down the hallway.

Marik led them to another doorway that opened to reveal a dark
stairwell. There were no torches along its length but they could
dimly see the bottom step by a light somewhere below. Marik
shut the door behind them and they stood still, waiting for their
eyes to adjust.

"This is where it gets tricky," said the Count. "I have no good reason to be here, this stair leads only to the dungeons. If we see anyone, I'll be hard pressed to explain myself. I don't think there will be anyone here except the guard, but it wouldn't hurt to be prepared." He turned to Rienne. "Do you have a dagger or something on you?"

"No, I don't," said Rienne. "I save lives, I don't take them."

The Count flapped his hand. "A fine sentiment in peacetime, my dear, but hardly appropriate now. If we're to help Sullyan, you should at least be prepared to defend yourself."

"Here, Rienne, take my knife," said Robin, slipping the foot-long blade out of its sheath. "The Count's right, it's a last resort."

She took the weapon, holding it awkwardly away from her. The Count sighed and began descending the steps.

When they reached the bottom, he looked cautiously down the hallway that stretched for perhaps a hundred yards before it turned. It was lit only at the far end and it was deserted. Glancing at Robin, Marik soundlessly drew his sword and held it before him. After a moment's hesitation, Robin did the same. Motioning for silence, the Count led them toward the torchlight. Rienne was last, casting nervous glances over her shoulder.

They reached a right-angled bend in the hall and the Count risked a look around it. With a sour expression, he turned to Robin. "No luck. It's not Calder on duty."

"How far away is he?" whispered Robin.

"About twenty yards. He's sitting at a table in front of the gate leading to the cells. We need to get the keys, both to enter the gate itself and also to unlock the cell. The door through the palace wall is at the far end of the cells, through another locked gate."

"What does Rykan do with soldiers who disobey orders?" asked Robin.

The Count looked startled at this change of tack. "Has them flogged and thrown in the cells. Why?"

"Right," said the Captain, ignoring him. "Rienne, you wait here." He handed his sword to the Count and took back his dagger from Rienne. Holding it behind his back, wrists crossed as if they were bound, the dagger was hidden from view. Then he nudged the Count sharply with his foot. "Come on man, you're about to deliver a flogging."

Rienne saw comprehension in the thin man's eyes. Abruptly, he shoved Robin in the back, sending him stumbling into the corridor. Rienne stifled a gasp as she heard the jailer rush to his feet. She peeked around the wall, her heart jumping into her throat.

"Get along, you," snarled the Count, pricking Robin in the back with his sword. "Jailer, one more for the cells. This man's due a flogging for disobedience and I intend to administer the punishment myself. Perhaps a flayed back and a night down here will make him realize where his duty lies." He pushed Robin on with the flat of his blade.

The jailer barely looked at Robin. "Can't keep your men under control, can you, Count? That's the third one this week."

"And there will be more if they don't shape up," snapped Marik. "I've had to leave a perfectly good banquet to deal with this so I'd like to get on with it."

From around the wall, Rienne saw the jailer turn and approach the gate. It was a wrought iron affair of tall bars, criss-crossed with strengtheners and secured with a very substantial lock. She heard the jangle of keys and, while he was searching for the right one, Robin sprang on him. Wrenching back the jailer's chin, he rammed the dagger up through the back of his head and into the brain. With his other hand clamped firmly over the jailer's mouth, there was no sound.

The demon slumped in Robin's arms and he pulled out the dagger. There was surprisingly little blood, thought Rienne. She shivered. Until now, she hadn't thought of any of her new friends as killers but it suddenly dawned on her that Robin was exactly that; a trained and deadly killer. And by association, it followed that Sullyan, small and delicate though she seemed, was a killer too. Rienne felt sick.

Marik darted forward, grabbed the keys and after some hurried fumbling, unlocked the great gate. Robin dragged the jailer inside and flung the body into the nearest unoccupied cell. He slammed the door shut and stood, breathing heavily.

Rienne ran through at Marik's beckon and he closed the iron gate behind her. It wouldn't conceal what they had done, thought Rienne, but it would slow any pursuit.

"Which cell?" urged Robin, taking back his sword and sheathing the bloody dagger.

"The one with the silver lock," replied Marik, pointing to a door a few feet away.

"Spellsilver?" asked Robin. The Count nodded. "Not taking any chances, was he?"

Robin sprinted down the line of cells until he reached the one Marik had indicated. His hiss of pain and anger brought Rienne running. "Quickly man, the key," he snapped. "I can't touch this thing."

"Well, it won't be easy for me, you know," said the Count, fumbling with the keys. "I don't have much power, it's true, but what I have will react." His shaking fingers couldn't cope with the effects of the spellsilver key and he dropped it.

"Oh, for goodness sake," said Rienne. "Let me."

"Hurry!" urged Robin.

Rienne scrabbled for the tiny key on the floor but when she grasped it, she nearly dropped it again. Unaccountably, all her strength had suddenly ebbed away. Robin hissed in frustration. "Bull was right," he said, "you must be empathic or it wouldn't affect you. Can you open the lock?"

"I'll have to," she said, gritting her teeth. She kept her eyes on the lock, trying desperately not to look inside the cell. Her fingers were shaking but eventually, she got the key in the lock. To her horror she was unable to turn it. "I can't do it," she wailed.

Robin made a strangled noise. He was staring in at the cell and what he saw there had clearly distressed him. Tears filled his eyes.

"Use the end of your knife." Marik's voice cut through Rienne's stasis. She jumped and Robin handed her the dagger. As she slid its slim point through the small hole in the key's head, she tried to ignore the blood covering the blade. With the knife as a lever, she managed to turn the key and spring the lock.

Robin wrenched open the door and they rushed into the cell. What Rienne saw there brought her up short, her heart pounding at her ribs. Robin went down on one knee beside the figure on the floor, a sob on his lips. If not for the glorious tawny hair, matted and dirty, Rienne wouldn't have recognized the broken body.

Sullyan lay on her left side, her face half-buried in filthy straw. Her hands were cruelly drawn behind her back and fastened with silver manacles from which ran a chain attached to a ring in the wall. She was naked, her wretchedly thin body covered in contusions, scratches, wounds, old blood and gore. Rienne could also see horrible welts on her back where someone had wielded a whip with great force.

Her face, what could be seen of it, was bruised and scratched, and puffy under the eyes. There was a nasty-looking area just below her right breast where someone had delivered a good kick, driving in a few ribs. As Robin gently moved back her hair to see her face better, Rienne caught the gleam of a silver collar around her neck, and the raw skin beneath.

Robin's voice contained a note of panic. "Rienne, is she alive?"

Jolted out of her dismay, Rienne kneeled down. The flesh, where it was not black with bruise or brown with dried blood, looked gray. She pressed her trembling fingers to the jugular beneath the jaw and was relieved to feel, after a few agonized moments, a faint, thready pulse.

"Just," she said. "But only just."

"Marik, how are we going to get these off her?" Robin indicated the manacles.

"We're not." Marik's voice sounded odd and Robin stared at him. Rienne clearly felt his sudden suspicion but Marik waved it off. "Just break the chain," he snapped. "Even if you could get the spellsilver off her, it wouldn't be a good idea. Think what would happen if she woke up and started expending power. With the treatment she's had over the past couple of weeks, do you think she'd hold back from destroying whatever she could reach? And I wouldn't bet much on her sanity after being locked away like this, either. Spellsilver's funny stuff, it plays with your mind."

Rienne felt Robin's surge of anger. "Are you saying that if we get her out of here, if she survives what he's done to her, she might be insane?"

The Count hung his head. "She certainly wasn't sane the last time I spoke to her. She only had stubbornness, hope and faith. And two days ago, the hope and faith had gone. Stubbornness was all she had left."

"Faith?" whispered Robin.

"Yes," cried Marik suddenly. "Faith in you, you lackwit! She kept telling me over and over that you'd come for her. Especially once she got me to release that nasty black stallion."

"That was you?"

"Of course it bloody was! Gods but you're stupid, what does she see in you? Who else did she have to help her? You weren't here, were you?"

Rienne lost her temper. "Shut up, you two." The two men ceased their bickering and stared at her. "Let's worry about the details once we're out of here, alright? Count, how do we break this chain?"

Marik took a deep breath. "It's not very strong, it's only silver. Wedge a sword-point through the links, that should do it."

His face drawn and pale, Robin set his sword through one of the links as near to the manacles as he dared. With his foot on the longer section of chain, he levered away at the link until it finally broke.

CAS PEACE

"Marik, give me your cloak," he said. The Count rather reluctantly surrendered his thick velvet mantle and Robin wrapped it gently around the thin, limp body in the straw. "Will we do any damage if we move her?" he asked Rienne. "I can't use metaforce to support her while she's wearing spellsilver."

"Just be careful of those ribs, some are definitely broken."

"You have no choice, anyway," muttered Marik.

Robin glared at him and gathered Sullyan into his arms, wary of the spellsilver collar. "Let's go."

They left the awful cell and Marik kicked the door shut. It wouldn't fool anyone for long, thought Rienne, not without the guard there.

She followed the men down the line of cells, trying to ignore the few feeble cries she heard. Her instinct was to help, but there was nothing she could do. The dreadful smells of the place—human waste, old blood and the rank stench of fear—assailed her senses as she ran.

They reached the next gate and Marik seemed to take an age finding the right key. Rienne had to stop herself from screaming and Robin was breathing heavily behind her. Eventually the gate opened and they passed through. Marik locked it behind them; it might buy them some time.

A dark and slimy passageway, rank with damp and mold, led toward the final door in the palace's outer wall. It was bolted and locked from the inside. Halting just before it, the Count turned to Robin. "If your friends haven't dealt with the guards, we're all dead."

Robin glowered at him. "They did." Nevertheless, he stood listening at the door for a few moments. "No sound."

He closed his eyes and Rienne felt him questing outward for contact. Quickly, she glanced at the burden he carried. Sullyan hadn't shown a single sign of life since Robin had lifted her. Rienne thought she might very well have died in the Captain's arms and she could see no vital signs. The fur trim of Marik's cloak was unruffled by any breath. Rienne sighed; there was nothing she could do until they reached someplace safe.

Robin's eyes opened. "All clear, both guards were disposed of. But Bull thinks Rykan's already returned, there was a commotion near the main gate about ten minutes ago."

"Bloody hell," rasped the Count. "Quickly." He drew back the topmost bolt and Rienne grabbed the lower one, leaving the Count free to work the large key in the rather rusty lock. He had trouble with it so she lent her strength to his and together they got it to turn. The door squealed on its hinges alarmingly. A dark and bulky shadow suddenly loomed beside them, making Rienne jump, but it was only Bull bringing the horses over.

"Don't ask," snapped Robin as Bull glanced at Sullyan. "Let's get out of here as fast as we can."

He handed the unconscious woman to the big man and swung onto his horse. Bull passed her back to him and handed him the reins. He helped Rienne onto her own mount and looked inquiringly at Marik.

"He can share with me, I'm the lightest," hissed Rienne, clearing the stirrup for the Count, who vaulted up behind her. Bull leaped for his own horse and they kicked their mounts to a gallop, Robin leading the way into the trees.

Rienne was relieved to see Cal and Taran waiting for them. "A patrol's been sent from the compound," said Taran as soon as they reached him. "They're in black and silver, so they're Rykan's."

"Curse it," moaned Marik, "I knew the gate guards were suspicious. They must have tipped off the sergeant-at-arms when you didn't come back. Let's hope they think you're deserters because if they've missed me or looked in the cells, we're in real trouble. We'd better circle around to the southwest in case Rykan left scouts in the forest. We can head north again later."

"We'll follow your lead," said Robin, "you know the area better than we do. Just don't head straight back to Cardon. That's the first place they will look."

Marik gave him a withering stare before kicking Rienne's horse to a gallop. The others leaped to follow, senses strained to the limits.

As they fled deeper into the midnight woods, Rienne prayed their luck would hold. Against all odds, they had snatched Sullyan from right under Rykan's nose. The euphoria of that still flowed through her veins, adding to the adrenaline of their flight. But she knew it wouldn't last. Exhaustion would overtake them, if Rykan's swordsmen didn't get there first. And what of Sullyan herself? What injuries had she sustained? Rienne badly wanted to examine her, give her what treatment she could. Their efforts would count for nothing if this wild ride through the darkness killed her.

Unable to follow her instincts, Rienne clung to her horse's mane. She prayed, as hard as she knew how, that Sullyan would survive.

The End

Glossary

Albian Characters

Adyn. The Manor's quartermaster.

Amanus Elijah. Taran's deceased father, an Artesan Adept.

Baily. A captain at the Manor under Colonel Vassa.

Beris Anton (major—deceased). Sullyan's former commanding officer.

Bull, or Bulldog. Major Sullyan's aide.

Cal Tyler. Taran's Artesan Apprentice.

Dexter. A corporal at the Manor under Captain Tamsen.

Dyler. A farmer from Hyecombe, friend of Jaspen.

Elias Rovannon. Albia's High King.

Emos. Major Sullyan's valet.

Jaspen. A farmer from Hyecombe, friend of Dyler.

Jerrim Vassa. Colonel at the Manor, General Blaine's second in command.

Hanan. Chief Healer at the Manor.

Hyram. General Blaine's valet.

Kandaran (deceased). Albia's former High King; Elias's murdered father.

Mathias Blaine. The Manor's senior officer and General-in-Command to High King Elias.

Milo. Keeper of tavern on the way to the Manor.

Morin. A sergeant at the Manor under Captain Parren.

Parren. A captain at the Manor under Colonel Vassa.

Paulus. Hyecombe's innkeeper and village elder.

Rienne Arlen. A healer, and Cal's lover.

Robin Tamsen. A captain at the Manor under Major Sullyan.

Rusch. A sergeant at the Manor under Captain Parren.

Sofira. Elias's Queen.

Solet. The Manor's stablemaster.

Sullyan. A major at the Manor under General Blaine.

Tad Greylin. Young kitchen boy at the Manor.

Taran Elijah. An Artesan who is desperate to learn his craft.

The Baron. Mysterious ally of Rykan, Duke of Kymer.

Wil. A corporal at the Manor under Captain Tamsen.

Andaryan Characters

Galet. Successor to Perik as lead huntsman.

Harva. Marik's elderly former nursemaid.

Heron. Sonten's Artesan commander.

Hierarch (the). Andaryon's ultimate ruler.

Imris. Sonten's young Artesan messenger.

Jaskin. Sonten's nephew.

Marik. Count of Cardon province under Rykan.

Nazir. One of Marik's minor nobles.

Perik. Lead huntsman prior to Galet's appointment.

Rykan. Duke, Lord of Kymer province and aspirant to the Andaryan throne.

Sonten. Duke Rykan's ambitious general. Lord of Durkos province.

Verris. Rykan's greedy Artesan commander.

Realms of the World

First Realm—Endormir

Endormirians are sometimes known as 'Roamerlings' because of their itinerant habits. They are small and slim, dark skinned, with brown or black eyes showing hardly any whites. The Artesan gift runs only through the males, and gifted males always become clan-leaders. As Endomir suffers from severe winter conditions, its people cross the Veils into the other realms for the winter months, where they are well known as traders.

Second Realm—Sinnia

Sinnians are tall and milk-haired, with pale skin. They live in clans and were once nomadic but now live in settlements. All are born able to control their metaforce up to the rank of Adept and are thus considered 'sports'. Their race often produces highly gifted musicians and storytellers.

Third Realm—Relkor

Relkorians are small, fierce and stocky, notorious for raiding the other realms for slaves to work their mines and quarries. Their Artesans, both male and female, invariably become slave-lords.

Fourth Realm—Albia

Albia is the human realm. The Artesan gift runs through both male and female lines, each gender being equal in potential. The craft is currently out of favour due to raiding by both Relkorian and Andaryan Artesans. Albians widely believe that all Artesans use their powers only for gain and control.

Fifth Realm—Andaryon

A warlike race characterised by eyes with slit pupils. They fight constantly amongst themselves, vying for position within the Hierocracy. The Artesan gift passes only through the male line and females play a minor and downtrodden role. Only the most powerful Artesan can become and hold the rank of Hierarch. Their battles for supremacy are governed by strict, ritualistic laws.

Terms

Artesan. A person born with the ability to control metaforce and master the four primal elements.

Codes of Combat. Strict laws governing any conflict between Andaryan nobles.

Demons. Derogatory term used in Albia to describe those of the Andaryan race.

Earth ball. An explosive sphere of Earth element formed by an Artesan for use as a weapon.

Fellan. A dark, aromatic and bitter beverage brewed from the seeds of the fellan-plant.

Firefield. A barrier formed from the primal element of Fire, through which only Artesans can pass. Firefields formed by those of inferior Artesan rank can easily be destroyed by those of a higher rank.

Firewater. Incredibly strong liquor.

Kingsman. Term used to describe members of the High King's fighting forces.

Metaforce (also called life force). The force of existence pertaining to all things, both animate and inanimate.

Perdition. A state of non-being for the soul—a place where souls with no ultimate destination reside.

Primal elements. Earth, Water, Fire and Air.

Portway. Structure formed by an Artesan from a primal element— usually Earth or Water—which gives its creator access through the Veils.

Psyche. An Artesan's unique and personal pattern through which they can manipulate metaforce and channel the primal elements.

Roamerling. Slightly derogatory term for the nomads of Endormir.

Sally port. A small door within a larger fortified barrier, allowing only one person to pass through at a time.

Substrate. The medium in which the primal elements reside, and in which the world and all things have their being.

Tangwyr. Monstrous Andaryan raptor trained to hunt men.

The Pact. Widely believed to have been brokered in Andaryon by an Albian Master-elite, in order to reduce Andaryan raids on Albia. Apparently supported by the current Hierarch.

The Staff. Mysterious and terrible weapon capable of stealing and storing metaforce. Can only be used by Artesans.

The Veils. Misty barriers separating the five Realms of the World. Only Artesans have the power to move through the Veils.

The Void. Dark abyss at the end of life into which all souls pass before reaching their final destination.

The Wheel. Central principle of Albian faith.

Witch. Derogatory term for an Artesan.

Artesan ranks and their attributes

Level one: Apprentice. Person born with the Artesan gift and the ability to influence the first primal element of Earth. Able to hear other Artesans speaking telepathically but unable to initiate such speech.

Level two: Apprentice-elite. Has some skill in influencing their own metaforce. Has attained mastery over the element of Earth. Able to initiate telepathic speech but only with Artesans already known to them. Able to build substrate structures, identify a person by the pattern of their psyche, and counter metaphysical attack to some degree.

Level three: Journeyman. Has mastery over Earth and is able to influence Water. Able to build portways and travel through the Veils. Has some skill in using metaforce for offense. Also able to initiate psyche-overlay and converse telepathically with any other Artesan. Possesses some self-healing potential.

Level four: Adept. Has mastery over both Earth and Water. Able to build more complex substrate structures such as corridors. Able to influence where such structures emerge. Possesses stronger offensive and defensive capabilities. Able to merge psyche fully with other Artesans. Increased healing abilities.

Level five: Adept-elite. Has mastery over Earth and Water and is able to influence Fire. Possesses great healing powers which can even aid the ungifted (with their permission). Able to initiate powersinks and merges of psyche. Able to construct such structures as Firefields.

Level six: Master. Has mastery over Earth, Water and Fire. Able to control the power of an inferior Artesan against their will. Control over personal metaforce now almost total. Possesses incredible healing powers.

Level seven: Master-elite. Has mastery over Earth, Water and Fire and is able to influence Air, the most capricious primal element. Able to absorb a lesser or even equal-ranked Artesan's power and metaforce provided some link or permission (however tenuous) can be found.

Level eight: Senior Master. Has complete mastery over all four primal elements. Is able to absorb another Artesan's power by force, even sometimes without a link. Possesses a high degree of metaphysical (and usually spiritual) strength.

Level nine: Supreme Master. It has never been fully established whether this rank actually exists. Supreme Masters are supposedly able to influence Spirit - largely regarded as the mythical 'fifth element.' Ancient texts refer only to the possibility; no mention has ever been found of a being attaining Supreme Masterhood.

Sport or lay-Artesan. Freaks of nature, sports are thought to be able to control their own metaforce from birth, to whatever level of strength they inherently possess. As they receive no training their working is often undetectable. They are also believed to be able to 'hear' the thoughts of those around them; gifted or ungifted, and directly, not through the substrate.

Cas Peace

Cas Peace was born and brought up in the lovely county of Hampshire, in the UK, where she still lives. On leaving school, she trained for two years before qualifying as a teacher of equitation. During this time she also learned to carriage-drive. She spent thirteen years in the British Civil Service before moving to Rome, where she and her husband, Dave, lived for three years. They return whenever they can.

As well as her love of horses, Cas is mad about dogs, especially Lurchers. She enjoys dog agility training and currently owns two rescue Lurchers, Milly and Milo. Milly has already had some success in the agility ring, and Milo will begin competing in late 2011. Cas loves country walks, working in stained glass and folk singing. She has also written a nonfiction book, "For the Love of Daisy," which tells the life story of her beautiful Dalmatian. Details and other information can be found on her website, www.caspeace.com

Artesans of Albia

Book Two, *King's Champion* available August 2012

Book Three, *King's Artesan* available August 2013

Lightning Source UK Ltd.
Milton Keynes UK
UKOW051656181111

182291UK00001B/8/P